Eugene Kennedy

QUEEN BEE

QUEEN BEE

Eugene Kennedy

DOUBLEDAY & COMPANY, INC.

Garden City, New York

1982

For
my wife, Sara,
and
our sister-in-law,
Dorothy Bloodgood Kennedy

This is entirely a work of fiction. No resemblance to any persons, events, or places—except for the physical city of Chicago—is intended and none should be inferred.

Library of Congress Cataloging in Publication Data

Kennedy, Eugene C.
Queen bee.

I. Title.
PS3561.E4258Q4   1982   813'.54
ISBN: 0-385-17509-4
Library of Congress Catalog Card Number: 81–43918

I am grateful to James F. "Spike" Hennessey for his friendship and advice. And to Mary Louise Schniedwind, who is a wonderful secretary.

Much of fancy has been written about the queen bee. Her very name is misleading, for there is nothing to indicate that she has anything to do with the government of the colony. In fact, the very opposite is true, for the worker bees are very solicitous concerning her and often oppose her will and restrain her actions. While old-time writers saw in the queen "their lawful sovereign" and lauded the loyalty of the subjects which could not be tempted to any act of disloyalty, "nor is there to be found as much as a single rebel in the community," present-day beekeepers know such talk is nonsense . . . The queen enjoys less freedom than any other inmate, for the very life of the community depends upon her and she is cared for and protected accordingly.

Frank C. Pellet
*The Romance of the Hive**

* The Abingdon Press, New York, 1931.

PART ONE

Chicago, the Nineties . . .

1

*P*aul Michael Martin was, you might say, single-minded. He wondered about women's breasts all the time. He wondered about breasts, and the bellies falling beneath them like the biblical fields of wheat, even when he was covering a story that had nothing to do with the lines of a woman's body. He had a nightly television commentary and wrote a rag sheet column. P.M. might be at a legislative hearing on sanitary landfill, getting it all down in his pad while he let his imagination scale and explore the architecture of every female bosom in view. While the chairman banged his gavel, P.M. would be thinking of banging some secretary in the second row, or the court reporter, or the woman whose body, in whatever garb, seemed to give the best promise of meeting his anatomical ideal, which, simply put, required youth and firm breasts.

P.M. enjoyed his fixation and never questioned it. He lived it out with a certain amount of dash. He certainly looked dashing as he sat in the first row of the shifting British Square of newsmen who were waiting for old Mayor Tom Cullen to deliver his budget message in the Chicago City Council Chamber. P. M. Martin was thinking of other things, his big teeth sparkling through the half-open sensuous lips like ivory crammed in a chamois bag, his blue eyes shooting every woman who walked into the hall.

Not much else was happening while the Chamber filled up with members of the City Council, municipal department heads, committeemen, hangers-on of several varieties, assorted flunkies, girl friends, and publicists who showed up at the edge of every event held in the City of Chicago, especially where there were free eats. Some of them made a living at it. There was a larcenous humidity in the atmosphere of political Chicago, and if a man knew his territory, he could squeeze a pretty fair living right out of the air.

Nobody was surprised to see Richard Barone, the blue-chinned financier and real estate speculator, show up on occasions like the budget message. Lots of the union leaders and bankers dropped by, each of them keeping an eye on the side door through which Mayor Cullen would make his entrance, each one as eager as a plebe to be spotted at

roll call by the commanding officer, and everyone, even those as powerful as Richard Barone, anxious that old Cullen would notice if they
weren't there.

Thomas H. Cullen knew how to make an entrance, the first rule of
which was a variation on the dynamics of the burlesque house. He let
the expectations of the members of the crowd work up their enthusiasms
for his arrival while he glided down in an elevator, his eyes fixed on the
floor, toward the marble-clad hallway that led to the City Council
Chamber.

No entrails ever told witch doctors more than Cullen's guts told him
about what and how to do things. They gave off the infinitely subtle
messages—a slight tremor here, and an all but imperceptible quiver
there—by which Mayor Cullen judged men and events. He trusted his
stomach more than his assembled advisers. He almost felt his way toward grand entrances. Cullen's stomach purred; he was right on schedule.

Down in the well of the City Council Chamber the light, except for
that which shone on the Mayor's elevated marble slab of desk, was subdued. The half shadows imparted a certain softness to the faces which,
in their hardness and puffiness, in their traceries of lines and veins, in
their well-used-by-life quality, would have delighted a Renaissance portrait painter. The slight overcast also accented the reality of Chicago
government and politics. The Mayor, who was head of the Democratic
Party organization in Cook County, dwelt like God on an old tapestry in
a pinnacle of light. He was the supreme authority before whom the angels and elders of the City Council bowed or, in some cases, prostrated
themselves out of fear. Cullen ran the show, that was the main rule, and
all the other corollaries of political and municipal wisdom flowed from
that.

That was why he liked to gain as much attention as possible through
his entrances. There was something to carrying the Pope into St. Peter's
on that life raft, Cullen thought as he drew near to the City Council
Chamber; there was something in what his mother had taught him long
ago: "Always get the animals on their chairs before you close the cage
door. You'll have damned little time to teach them their manners afterwards."

The Council Chamber itself was a great show; P. M. Martin was
checking out the women, including Florence Mack, whose eyes of
different colors, unsettled their beholders. P.M. liked the way her
breasts, like tumbling melons escaping the grocer's hands, stressed the
filmy panes of her dress. She was the secretary of Larry Johnson, the
black preacher and politician, who was talking to Richard Barone. An
unlikely pairing, but politics is all about the birds that climb into the
same nest when the worm season is on.

Just below Cullen's desk stood Francis Rafferty, "The Rosary," as he was called because of his piety. Old Francis, who was seventy-one, was always going to Mass and visiting churches, talking about the lives of the saints and "Glory be to God, couldn't the world use a real saint now," all of which threw the casual observer off. "The Rosary" was answering questions put to him by Max Day, dean of the City Hall reporters, a gnarled sixty-year-old man who knew plenty, including how to read the annual budget.

Max studied Rafferty's marvelously seamed face, as cracked and as dry as an arroyo below his small, brown eyes. It was like looking at New Mexico. He wondered just what tricks Rafferty might have played in helping to write this new budget. He admired Rafferty as a cunning survivor and a man knowledgeable about government. Day also admired the fact that Rafferty had acquired a large fortune over the years through his ability to assemble small pieces of land and, like a magician making a cut-up newspaper whole, to turn them into valuable tracts on which important buildings were to be erected. Inside information might have helped and Day was sure that Rafferty had always had it, even though he was an impressively shrewd guesser, or maybe his prayers were answered.

A few desks away, short, swarthy Sam Noto, alderman for a near West Side ward, looked cautiously at a loose thread on the sleeve of his maroon suit. Sam had never emerged from the double knit era of clothing and he was always in danger of unraveling or setting himself on fire with the ashes from one of his cigars. He felt comfortable in artificial fibers and they matched his spirit and style very well.

"Hey, Rich," he called to Barone, "how ya' doing? Ya' doing okay? How's the family?"

"Fine, Sam," Barone replied easily. They were involved with each other on many levels and had overlapping interests. Sam was alderman for the syndicate which operated legitimate above-the-surface businesses, such as the provision of hotel linens and restaurant napery. Below the ground was something totally different. Noto and Barone used to say they were cousins. Although they weren't sure exactly how they were related, but, if Sam's sister's son-in-law had a cousin who married Barone's wife's second cousin, and they both went to the wedding and danced with each other's wives and gave each other a public embrace, they felt related in a way that gave them an edge together on the other paisanos.

Barone clapped his relative on the shoulder, a habitual gesture that combined aggression and affection.

"Hey, Rich," Noto said laughingly, "watch the suit."

Not two yards away from Noto and Barone, just behind the next sweep of desks that arched in a slow breaking curve across the hall, stood another cluster of aldermen who were often seen together at public events like politicians' wakes and championship fights. Alex Wendel, from a big undertaking family on the South Side, represented a tough new generation of Chicago politicians. As pushy and nervy as a B-movie gangster, Wendel made no bones about the fact that he was looking beyond the Cullen years. Just thirty-nine, broken nose handsome, Wendel liked expensive suits that set off his year-round suntan. He was talking to Felix Ramirez, a fellow who had come a long way since his parents climbed out of the Rio Grande. He was bouncy, and he sounded a little like Desi Arnaz, mostly when he wanted people to think he wasn't as smart as he really was. Ramirez felt that his people were the natural descendants of the Irish politicians. The Irish, however, didn't like to remember how their great-grandfathers had been looked down on as dirty foreigners just a hundred years before and didn't see any resemblance at all. Ramirez and Wendel were close only because they shared a conviction that they could get a bigger piece of the action after Mayor Cullen left the Windy City and entered the heavenly Jerusalem with no return ticket. That did not mean that they trusted each other.

"Good morning, gentlemen." The voice belonged to Alderman Raymond Carney, a tall, sweet-smiling fellow of flawed innocence. He chaired the committee on police.

"Hello, Ray," Wendel replied offhandedly. "Find any crooked cops lately?"

Carney shook his head as Ramirez grinned at both of them. "I didn't think you two would show up today. What do you want—to make sure the old man sees you?"

"No," Wendel answered, his eyes twinkling, "I like to check the old man's color. Undertakers develop a keen eye for early signs; helps you know when to hand out your business card."

"Forget it," Carney said as he waved a greeting to a friend. "Cullen's old man lived to be eighty-eight."

Across the hall Martin nudged Max Day. "There's an unholy threesome." Martin turned away from the aldermen.

"And who is this?" Martin asked as two women, escorted by Monsignor Morgan Fitzmaurice, the sleek and knowing Vicar General of the Archdiocese of Chicago, entered the Chamber. "Very nice," Martin said half-aloud, "very nice." Martin was studying a pug-nosed redhead of about thirty-five, a woman who appealed immediately to him. He quickly appraised the possibilities of the body beneath the tailored black suit; he expected it to be firm, well molded, with no stretch marks.

The other woman, wearing a gray suit and a frilly blouse, was in her fifties, too thin to stir even mild interest on Martin's part. She wore no makeup and projected an air of distractedness.

"Who the hell is the redhead, Max?"

"Her name's O'Brien. She's here with her cousin, old Fitzie. The other dame is Mother Francis. She's president of that college out in Plainfield, Our Lady of Peace, you know, where the rich micks send their daughters. Virgin Acres, they call it."

"This gal has gone on to graduate work," Martin said as he watched the women take their seats in the V.I.P. guest section behind the groups of standing aldermen. He turned directly toward Max Day who, along with everybody else in the Chamber, had caught sight of the Mayor's entry door as it opened a crack. Quiet fell like an executioner's blade on the crowd. The door opened and Mark Richler, Cullen's closest adviser, slipped into the Chamber. The crowd let out its breath and the buzz of time-killing conversation picked up again.

Max Day touched Martin on the arm. "She's named O'Brien, like I said, and she's head of some group of wives whose husbands are still missing in action from the war. The Council's voting them a citation for their work and she's going to accept it. That's the story as far as I know it."

"Missing in action?" Martin mused quizzically. "There's a girl shouldn't be missing the action at all." He flashed a nervy but charming smile right at her.

As Ann Marie O'Brien's cousin, Monsignor Fitzmaurice was all that was left of a once large Irish Catholic clan. At fifty he had become Vicar General of the Catholic Archdiocese after a great career in running the Catholic Cemeteries. He still ran them. He and Mother Francis were a couple of ecclesiastical professionals who went out each day and got the job done. Ann Marie looked pouty as she marched in between them. The Monsignor and the Mother President could have been strong-willed parents bringing their strong-willed daughter back to school, or home after a divorce. They arrived at their places like a team of horses, each pulling in a slightly different direction.

Ann Marie was aware that somebody was watching her as she entered, not that she disliked the idea. Dressed in black and riding point on Mother and Monsignor, she didn't really even see other women when she entered a room. Just the men, and she wanted them all to look her way. The invitation only went so far, of course, since she took her relationship to her missing husband, Charlie, very seriously and she pulled her conscience on like a hair shirt every morning. But she did like attention.

There was another false alarm about the imminence of Mayor Cullen's arrival and, after the crowd broke apart as some of the Council members took their seats, Ann Marie could see the man who was eyeing her steadily. She looked away. She didn't want a medical exam across a crowded room. Ann Marie turned to Mother Francis, who had removed her engagement book from her briefcase and was making some notations with a silver pencil.

"Mother, do you know any of the newspaper people?"

Mother Francis looked up, took off her reading glasses, and peered across the room to the table at which Paul Michael Martin sat.

"You mean the one who looks a little like Warren Beatty," Mother Francis asked dryly, "the one who's staring at you? I think he's that fellow who makes commentaries on NBC. Martin, yes, that's it, Martin."

"I thought he looked familiar." Ann Marie's tone seemed to dismiss Martin.

"It's the nature of the business he's in. That's Max Day next to him and Eleanor Hanford . . ." Ann Marie was no longer listening. She was now elaborately ignoring Paul Michael Martin, pulling out the notes, all in the finest Catholic schoolgirl's penmanship, from which she would later read brief remarks to acknowledge the citation for the MIA organization she headed.

Alderman Carney had settled into his chair and was talking to reform-minded Alderman Louis Schroeder when the blue-uniformed sergeant-at-arms tapped him on the shoulder.

"There's a call for you, Alderman. It's from Police Headquarters. They said it was important."

"Okay, Tony," Carney replied as he reached across and patted Schroeder on the arm. "Tell them I'll call as soon as the Mayor gets in and gets started."

The sergeant-at-arms nodded noncommittally and eased back to the side aisle.

O'Hare Field is only ten miles from downtown Chicago, 35,000 people work there and over 150 policemen function just like they do in any town. One of them, patrolman Victor Hackman, was walking through the third level of the parking garage, cold and dark as a back alley, a place in which people never spoke to you, they just hurried along, carrying their bags to or from their cars. Those going away looked relieved that they had found a parking place and those coming home looked relieved that their cars were still there. A place of relief, thought Hackman, who was a college graduate going to law school, a place of some relief but no lasting city.

"Officer," a man in a raincoat full of buckles called to him. He lifted a bag to point back down a row of dusty-looking cars. "Officer, I think there's something you ought to take a look at down there."

Hackman nodded and smiled. "Yes, sir, just what is it?"

"Well, I just parked. I'm running a little late. When I went around to get the bag out of the back of my car, I couldn't help but catch a slight odor, a smell I remember from the war."

Hackman became fully alert. "Yes, go on . . ."

"Well, I don't want to get involved, you understand, but I looked at the car just behind mine. It had been backed in so I was standing right next to its trunk. Then I saw this stuff leaking out of it. Just a minute ago. I was going to call and then I saw you . . ."

"Just where is this car?" Hackman asked. "You'd better show me exactly."

"Well, my plane . . ."

"I'm sure you'll catch it. Just show me where it is . . ."

The man in the raincoat sighed and, shifting the weight of his bag, began to lead the officer down the line of automobiles. The quiet closed in on them as they moved along. There were no echoes, just the sounds of distant traffic, then a snatch of conversation and laughter as an elevator door opened about fifty yards away and two businessmen emerged, each with a suitbag trailing over his right shoulder.

"Here, officer," the man said anxiously, dipping his bag toward a yellow Cadillac.

Hackman felt the top of the hood. It was cold. Letting the list of appropriate police procedures roll through his mind, he moved around the car, checking his two-way radio and touching his gun.

The odor was not strong but it cut through the fume-filled atmosphere. Hackman glanced down and saw an ooze of indeterminate color that had seeped out of the closed trunk and down the rear bumper. A drop bulged off the last curve of the chrome and plunged to the darkened floor below.

The patrolman looked up at his anxious informant on the far side of the car. "I'd like you to wait for a few minutes. I'll have the gate called to tell them you're coming." He braced himself and popped the trunk lid, which jolted open, bouncing with a squeak until it settled like an awning above the open space. The smell rose pungently and Hackman moved his head back slightly as he looked down at the bloody back end of a naked dead young man who had been jackknifed down so that his buttocks jutted upward. Long hair stiff with blood stuck out in spikes across the battered face. Caked blood and bruise marks covered the arched back. But it was the marker pen printing on the buttocks that held the patrolman's eyes. On one cheek in jagged letters was the word F-A-G. On the other, N-O-T-O. "Jesus," Hackman whispered as he peered around the sticky trunk, "Jesus Christ."

He stepped back and pulled his radio device up away from his belt. He gestured to the traveler to wait another moment as he began to speak, "Captain Vincent . . ."

Paul Michael Martin shifted in his chair to get a better look at Ann Marie O'Brien, who had put her notes away and was inspecting the glass-faced visitors' gallery that hung above the floor of the Chamber at mezzanine level. A group of Orientals and Latinos from a local civics class had come to witness municipal government in action, and to be part of what the pols called the "ruly" crowd, the artfully assembled mix of wide-eyed kids and obedient City Hall workers who filled the observers' seats at such sessions. Mayor Cullen liked applause more than placards waving about the heads of jeering demonstrators. "Keep the robbers out of your attic," his mother had told him many times, "if you want to sleep peacefully at night."

Monsignor Fitzmaurice had taken a seat near Alderman Rafferty just below the Mayor's desk. He was scheduled to give the invocation when the City Council meeting finally began but the paper he studied with such concentration did not contain a prayer; it was a memorandum on "Land Use and Cost Effectiveness in Above Ground Interment." A few chairs away Mark Richler, Cullen's adviser who had prepared the budget summary the Mayor was about to read, looked at his watch. It was three minutes past ten. Richler knew from so many years of close association with him that the old man should be there by five minutes after the hour.

The sergeant-at-arms had returned to whisper in Alderman Carney's ear. With one last hesitant glance toward the door through which Cullen would enter the Chamber, Carney rose and followed him up the aisle.

Mayor Cullen tugged at the edges of his suit coat and then smoothed his thatched roof of white hair as the elevator doors opened onto the corridor that led to the City Council Chamber. Four bulky bodyguards surrounded the Mayor as he double-timed it toward the entrance door. Alderman Carney and a man in civilian clothes who was Assistant Superintendent of the Police Department were standing in front of it. Cullen's insides roiled slightly. Without a word and without changing his expression, Cullen stopped and waited for whatever message these men wanted to give him. It had to be important to interrupt him on the way to a grand entrance.

"Mr. Mayor," Carney said quietly, "Superintendent Hanlon thought we ought to let you know about this right away." Cullen's face remained impassive.

"Sam Noto's nephew—we're sure that's who it is—was just found dead in the trunk of his car at O'Hare Field," Hanlon said flatly.

Cullen's eyes did not flicker; he did not even need to raise a questioning eyebrow to get the answer he wanted.

"Sam doesn't know yet," Carney said. "We thought we'd get the details from the M.E. first."

Cullen turned away and, as his guards shifted gears around him, stepped toward the door.

Max Day elbowed P. M. Martin and asked him a small talk question about his TV commentary. As P.M. turned toward him, Ann Marie, as if by unbidden instinct, moved her attention from the school children to Martin's profile. She studied his face and the shirt, tie, and what she could see of the suit below it. She was good at appraising sensual objects; she could feel men from fifty feet away. Ann Marie experienced a mixture of attraction and revulsion, a familiar reaction, one that had tracked her days almost as long as she could remember. Living uncomfortably on the sharp spine of a conflict between impulsive action and dutiful restraint, she lowered her eyes just before P.M. turned away from his fellow journalists to look back toward her.

The door that had received so much attention from the crowd cracked open and the first pair of bodyguards stepped swiftly through it, sending a signal for silence and attention across the crowd. A split second later Mayor Thomas H. Cullen broke through the open space and strode briskly through quickly swelling applause to his desk. He looked up at the school children and smiled at their waving hands. Cullen lowered his eyes and, without moving his head, checked the front row of applauding aldermen.

Below and to the left he could see Rafferty smiling above the flutter of his applauding hands. The bastard would clap more if I dropped dead right now, Cullen thought, as his eyes swept across the crowd. Sam Noto was whistling through his teeth to prove his loyalty. Cullen's face remained solemn as he looked beyond Sam and saw his old friend Mother Francis standing next to a handsome woman in black. He thought about Noto and the fact that he did not yet know of his nephew's death. Cullen's stomach roiled again. Too bad, but he wanted nothing to do with it. He raised his right hand and the applause diminished to rattles around the edges of the hall. Mark Richler looked at his watch. It was seven minutes after ten.

2

*C*ity budgets are written in a language all their own. Most people can read numbers but not many can really understand them. Fakers abound in the balance sheet reading business. The words are important too; they are what you must understand to comprehend the budget itself. Few can do that either. The old Mayor knew both the words and the numbers. The power of the purse was the essence of political power and control in Chicago and Cullen hadn't needed his mother to tell him that.

Mark Richler put the summary message in shape for Cullen after he got the final figures about a week before the mid-November date when, according to law, the document had to be presented to the City Council for final approval. That was always a scramble but Richler had grown accustomed to sixty- and seventy-hour weeks in his work with Cullen. He was an outsider in the mainly Irish Catholic government, a Jewish intellectual who always looked a little rumpled and bemused as he carried out his duties as a kind of utility infielder—he could play a lot of positions—and speechwriter to the Mayor.

Cullen had opened the cover on the budget message, but that was only one of the small signals he gave off when he wanted silence. He nodded toward the sergeant-at-arms, who introduced Monsignor Fitzmaurice, a clerical ballroom dancer who never made any unnecessary moves. Quick and to the point, Fitzmaurice beseeched the Almighty to grant light and wisdom to the legislators gathered so humbly below him and to bless the fair city of Chicago, blah, blah, blah, through God the Father, Amen.

The colors were presented, a number of resolutions honoring dead aldermen and other citizens were introduced and voted on affirmatively. The budget message still lay open on Cullen's desk as he introduced Ann Marie O'Brien as "the valiant wife of one of the greatest unsung heroes of the United States, a woman who now fights for the men who fought for all of us." Not only did Cullen get away with sentences like that, but he half-charmed the audience, even staying the harpoons of the cynical journalists, who looked on him as the Moby Dick of big city bosses.

Over the years scores of people had come up to receive citations from the Chicago City Council. They were not exactly Academy Awards and most of them get stuffed in drawers or propped up on mantels next to the bowling trophy. The crowd was accustomed to these preliminaries as they waited for the main event, the Mayor himself. But let a good-looking young woman come walking across the front of the Chamber and it's no surprise that she receives more attention than that grandmother of a secretary who's getting her scroll for thirty-five years in the typing pool. That's the way it was that morning.

Something about Ann Marie O'Brien, even when she was in a plain black suit, caught everyone's eye. In the dozen or so steps that Ann Marie took as she made her way from her chair to the Mayor's desk she didn't wiggle or shake but she looked like she might at any moment.

P. M. Martin watched her, noting a girlishness about her that again stirred his fantasies.

The Mayor handed her the citation and leaned forward, grandfather-style, and kissed her lightly on the cheek. Ann Marie took the award, her face hard and determined as she thanked the Mayor and the City Council members in tones strong enough to stand on. She looked up at the children from the civics class who were visiting in the closed-off balcony that hung above her, and after the expected applause died away, she spoke again.

"You children from school, remember this day. Some of you have lost brothers, some fathers. There are missing places and missing persons in your lives just as there are in ours. When I finish these remarks life will go on again as though I had never been here. But not for those of us who have loved ones still missing. Don't let older men send you off to battle for them. Make the future different so that never again will this City Council have to give an award for work on behalf of men missing in action." She chopped these sentences out angrily and the crowd stiffened, the way people do when somebody who is supposed to be playing knocks the breath out of them.

There was the slightest pause and then Mayor Cullen applauded and that, naturally, cued the crowd into a modest ovation. Ann Marie, looking neither to the left nor to the right, strode behind Monsignor Fitzmaurice, who raised his eyebrows as he turned his head to watch her move briskly away clutching her plaque as though it were a schoolbook. Mother Francis rose with an expression on her face designed to shield Ann Marie from the ripple of uneasiness that had lifted off the reacting crowd, a "That was just fine" look. Across the room at the journalists' table, Paul Martin whispered into Max Day's ear, "That's one angry pussy."

Mayor Cullen's face betrayed no reaction to the young woman whose intense and accusatory speech had surprised the aldermen and the onlookers. "Let the clerk call the roll," he said, invoking one of the rituals that induced glazed eyes more swiftly than Seconal. This move restored the dull rhythm that was essential to the transaction of business in any legislature. Cullen sat down and looked out at the crowd. Alderman Noto had been the first to yell "Present!" as the clerk reeled off the names of the council members. The sergeant-at-arms was whispering in Noto's ear as the alderman pushed back his chair and left the hall. He'll be finding out about his nephew, the poor bastard. The Mayor had no intention of displaying any interest in the affair; his stomach had given him a clear warning about that back in the hallway when he had seen the look on Assistant Superintendent Hanlon's face.

Out at O'Hare Field the Medical Examiner—they had called the publicity-loving chief, Maxwell Thorne, M.D., from downtown once they realized that Sam Noto's nephew was the victim—had just about concluded his examination in the now roped-off section of the parking garage where the yellow Cadillac had been discovered. A small crowd of police personnel clustered around the car, mostly men in plain clothes, their badges pinned to the lapels of their topcoats. Captain Vincent, the commander of the O'Hare detail, was talking to Walter Gleason, commander of the 16th Police District. Men from the crime lab were dusting the car for prints and other clues; a wagon from the 16th District had arrived and two uniformed officers sat inside waiting for the Medical Examiner to authorize the removal of the body to the nearest hospital. The few media people who had come out were being kept back almost half the length of the garage.

"Hell of a thing," Captain Vincent said to Commander Gleason, "this Noto kid getting it this way."

"*Especially* this way," Gleason answered. "You seen anything like this lately? I mean, in a syndicate killing?"

Captain Vincent rubbed his chin. There had not been much that he had not seen in his twenty years on the force.

"No, no, not since I worked the North Side. Plenty of gay murders there. But that's a different scene, altogether different. I never saw the mob do anything like this, never . . ."

"Well," Gleason sighed, "there is a first for everything. Maybe the fucking mob is coming out of the closet."

Doctor Thorne had just straightened up and, wrinkling his forehead, slipped back into his raincoat. He carefully lighted a cigarette before turning toward Captain Vincent and Commander Gleason.

"They can take him now, Commander," he said in world-weary tones. "Cause of death is strangulation. He was stabbed later. He has also been sexually assaulted. His sex organs have been mutilated and his anus has been lacerated." He paused and drew on his cigarette. "This is something different than you usually have here. Everything else is the same—

the use of the victim's car, the garage location. But this is homosexual rape and homicide combined. There is little question in my mind about it. Of course, we'll know more after the work at the hospital."

"Look, Doctor," Commander Gleason said, "we've got a problem with this. We had to notify the First Deputy Superintendent, because the victim was related to an alderman. And he passed it along to Hanlon, who'll tell the Superintendent. But they don't know any details, they don't know the gay part of this."

"What are you suggesting?" Thorne dropped his cigarette on the floor and looked down as he stepped on it.

"Alderman Noto and the family don't know anything about this. We don't think we need to give out any details. The kid is dead, his name is Noto. He died of strangulation. The reporters don't need to know any more than that, do they?"

Doctor Thorne frowned as he looked down the garage to the place where half a dozen people from the media were waiting for him to make a statement.

"No television," he said with a grunt. "These things are getting so routine, Commander, they hardly seem to cover them anymore." Thorne cleared his throat. "I shall say very little. They'll find out eventually, you know that, don't you?"

"Maybe, but not right now. And we don't tell them about the writing on his ass or any of that."

"No," Doctor Thorne said as he buttoned his raincoat, "but it was an interesting touch, wasn't it?"

Colorful as Tom Cullen was in other ways, a certain train-conductor-like tone crept into his voice when he read addresses in public. Nobody would know what he thought of the report; perhaps he wanted everyone to guess, since his defense against the press was a deadpan expression and a low throttled delivery. Paul Martin once did a television commentary on "The Mask of Power," in which he compared Cullen's dealing with reporters to Britain's condescending relationship with Ireland. Martin had a peculiar knack for grabbing the old man where it hurt. The fact that Cullen held all the power and kept everybody more or less under control was one of the most maddening aspects of life under him, for it did seem more like an imperial reign than a term of elected office.

Cullen slipped out of the Hall with the bodyguards fanned out around him. "The Rosary" Rafferty took over the chair after the Mayor left and a lot of the guests who had come to see and be seen by Cullen quickly filled the outside hallway with laughter and conversation. Ann Marie O'Brien, still giving off enough static electricity to make men's eyes cling to her, had made her way up the aisle. Mother Francis followed her, still looking distracted, one poking hand rearranging the contents of her large pocketbook. Paul Michael Martin's eyes followed Ann Marie.

"See you later, Max," Paul whispered without looking down at his journalistic companion. "There's a story I want to cover."

It did not take Martin long to get to the large crowded hallway where he could see Ann Marie and Mother Francis nearing the stairway.

"Say, Martin, what's the hurry?" Richard Barone, halfway into a blue topcoat, called to him. Paul kept moving, responding with a grin.

"Wait, Martin, I gotta ask you something. What do you know about Sam Noto? He left early and didn't come back before the old man was through. Is something up?" Barone shrugged the coat fully onto his shoulders and his large hairy hands popped out of the ends of the sleeves. His face was about the length of a cigar from that of Paul Martin, whose grin covered his preoccupation with the erotic promise that lifted off the just-vanishing backside of Ann Marie O'Brien.

"Dick, I don't know anything. I haven't heard anything. I'm interested in another story." He began to edge past Barone.

"You shitting me? You're supposed to know everything. I got a feeling that something's up."

"Dick," P.M. replied while he watched Ann Marie disappear around the corner, "Dick, swear to God, I haven't heard anything about Sam. On my mother's grave." He traced a cross on his heart. "On your mother's grave."

"Crissake, Martin," Barone snarled, "don't make fun like that. I wouldn't feel safe with you even near her grave. Never mind that redhead you been chasing. You wanna lay her before she gets out of the building?"

P.M. reluctantly relaxed. The redhead was lost in the crowd of the main floor of City Hall. He had missed this chance but he knew her name and he could find out her number. Still, a loss was a loss in such matters, and Martin hated to drop the first round of a promising match, but he could not ignore Barone. The reporter had taken what he liked to think of as "gifts" from him over the years.

"That's better," Barone said, shifting his stance like a gangleader showing off on a street corner. "Now, Martin, see what you can find out for me. You got a phone paid for by the city. Maybe somebody in the pressroom already knows why Sam left." He put his arm around Martin's neck.

"Jesus," Martin said, pulling away, "not in public, Dick. You'll be kissing me next and people will think I'm one of your family."

"Always the funny guy, right, Martin?" Barone nodded his head toward the entrance to the pressroom. "What's the matter, you don't want to do me a favor?"

Paul Michael Martin grinned uneasily and headed for the door.

Ann Marie and Mother Francis had crossed LaSalle Street to get the
nun's modest car from the clanging cage of the multilevel parking garage. As they waited Ann Marie glanced back across the street at the
door of City Hall. She wondered if Martin would come blinking out into
the pale November sunshine looking for her; she was sure that he had
started to follow her.

"Your talk went very well, Annie," the older woman said. She was accustomed to the silences that passed for replies from her former student.
Ann Marie had always had a quiet side, but since Charlie had been
missing there were times when she seemed closed down for good.
Mother Francis thought of Ann Marie as accidentally caught and without choice in a vocation like her own, as a celibate keeping faith for her
missing husband out of love. She also sensed Ann Marie's restlessness, so
she tolerated with romantic sympathy the younger woman's periodic ex-
cursions into some inner room of her personality.

Ann Marie didn't feel anything like a nun, even though people had
placed her in that category since Charlie led a night raiding party into
the bamboo thickets, not to return. But was it really his last mission, and
where the hell was he, and what the hell did he mean, doing this to her?
She shook her head but her yearning held. Would Paul Martin appear
suddenly? Ann Marie would have liked to tell Mother Francis what she
had been thinking, but the older woman would have smiled and quoted
Virginia Woolf, as if that made the world all right again. Ann Marie felt
like screaming. Instead, she asked brightly, "How about lunch? I'll buy."

3

*A*nn Marie refreshed her lipstick and studied the side door of City Hall as Mother Francis edged the car into the heavy traffic of LaSalle Street. It wasn't so much that she wanted Paul Michael Martin specifically, but she wanted somebody, anybody, to come through the door looking for her, wanting her, and decisively taking her. Settling at least something in her frozen and suspended life.

Like all the mannered graduates of Our Lady of Peace College, Ann Marie had learned how to keep public control of her private longings, but now she had trouble maintaining their trademark pure look. Except for the flashes of anger such as the one that had startled her City Hall listeners into attention, she kept her personality in neutral. She knew, as she made an entrance undulating just enough to give a signal, that she was coming on strong—that was the pattern, putting out and pulling back—and she felt the sour dissatisfaction with herself that well-bred Catholic women experienced when the animal in them coiled and snarled and would not be still.

"It's been hard for you, Annie," Mother Francis said softly. "These last four years have been very hard, haven't they?"

"Yes," Ann Marie answered, glad to have someone recognize the edge of her restlessness. "Sometimes I don't know what to do with myself."

As they waited for the traffic to move, she glanced at the glass doors of City Hall that had begun to swing open again. Paul Martin stepped through them and looked to left and right just as the policeman at the corner waved their car forward. Ann Marie resisted the physical pull within her to turn her head. What did it mean? Except that she was lonely, that she had had enough waiting, and, that she wanted something, some kind of close contact, even if it was with this journalistic hunter. Would she be less lonely afterward? She didn't know.

"Have you thought of doing something else besides this MIA work?" Mother Francis placed the question tentatively as a juggler might balance the last object on his pole.

"What do you mean, get a job?"

"Well, there might be another focus for you. Right now you spend most of your time with Matthew and the other women whose husbands are missing. Aside from your son, you don't have much but the sadness and the waiting."

Ann Marie looked at Mother Francis, whose carefully phrased insight —that's the approach that got her the college presidency—hit the mark. A.M. loved eight-year-old Matthew, but she had to pull back from him a little for his own good as well as hers. She didn't want to explore that feeling too much. She was weary of the other women in the MIA organization with whom she had done so much waiting and crusading. Not one of their men had come out of the jungle yet and Ann Marie had grown tired of some of her colleagues, who talked about the same things all the time—kids, and places to go on vacation, and pets—they bored her. Excitement filled their work at first, but then came the terrible ups and downs that had gradually flattened out after news had dissolved into rumor and then into silence. It was the waiting now, the goddamned waiting, during which the women did all the talking and their men on the other side of the earth kept their terrible silence.

"What were you thinking of, Mother? I know when you use that tone it's not the first time you've thought of a subject."

"Well, when I watched you speak this morning and saw the attention you got from that strange crowd . . ."

"Yes?" Ann Marie watched the older woman as she made an illegal turn.

"You know, Ann, they should never have banned left turns here," Mother Francis said, cutting in front of a taxicab coming from the opposite direction. "It makes getting around ever so much more difficult."

She ignored the cabdriver's anguished Middle Eastern curse and raised finger as she pulled into a parking lot next to a restaurant called Candles, which occupied a mansion that once belonged to a packing house tycoon.

"I wonder if you might think of public service, Ann. Something in government, maybe with the city or the county." Mother Francis accepted a ticket from the parking attendant and made some stage business of putting it into her pocketbook.

"Politics?" Ann Marie asked quizzically, intrigued by the gutty overtones of this invitation to a smoke-filled masculine world. Politics in Chicago was, as Mother Francis had said in class years ago, a game the devil took cards at. "Politics?" she asked again. "You always said that we Catholic women should keep politics at a distance."

"It's all a question of emphasis, isn't it?" Mother Francis answered, a diplomatic smile breaking on her face. "Let's talk about it at lunch."

Sam Noto arrived at the hospital near O'Hare Field shortly after his nephew's body did. Sam was accompanied by another nephew, from his sister's side of the family, Joey Rocco, a quiet, competent aide who had gone to law school and then to work in the alderman's office.

Police Commander Gleason and Captain Vincent met them at the emergency room—the reporters were camping in the main lobby—and escorted the men back to the holding room where their dead relative lay on a thick slab, his dark and swollen face thrusting out of the shroud of sheets. Noto moved hesitantly toward the table and made a clumsy sign of the cross as he stared down at his nephew. He breathed heavily, hunched forward and clutched Rocco's arm, Quasimodo anguishing among the Gargoyles.

"Jesus Christ," he said in a low, trembling voice, "Jesus Christ, I swear on this body, I swear to God I'll get whoever did this . . ." He let go of Joey's sleeve and turned back to the police officers.

"What happened?" Noto's eyes snapped in his swarthy face as he bit out his question. "What the hell happened?"

"We need you to identify the body, Alderman," Commander Gleason answered. "Then we'll tell you what we know. Maybe we could go to another room."

"Fuck that, fuck that!" Noto's rage broke loose and Joey reached over to place an arm on his heaving shoulder. The alderman pulled away and looked back at his dead nephew's face. "He's my nephew. Joey can tell you. You tell 'em, Joey, you tell 'em." His voice had fallen to a whisper and, as he straightened up, some of the tension drained out of him.

"We're sorry about this, Alderman," Gleason said, "but there are some things you ought to know about your nephew's death."

"What the hell do you mean?"

"Well," Captain Vincent interjected, "it's not the same pattern as some of the other homicides we've had."

Noto stared wide-eyed as the two officers explained the homosexual aspects of the killing. The alderman's face began to twitch halfway through their recital. He exploded before they were quite finished.

"What the hell, what the hell is this? Jesus Christ, what am I gonna tell his mother? For Crissake, what am I gonna tell her! Her boy was out fucking with fairies? Is that what you want me to tell her? What you think she's gonna do, she'll throw herself in the grave, too . . ." He paused ominously and tears began to work their way down his swarthy face. "You tellin' me he was a fairy, a goddamn fag? Mother of God."

Noto looked at his nephew, twisted in shameful death like a wrestler straining to throw off an opponent. His toad-skin face twitched.

"You tell me my nephew was maybe a cocksucker, that he was queer, and he gets killed in a fucking by some sons of bitches. Who ever heard of that? Nobody. That's who. Nobody for Crissake." He sighed and looked directly at the police officers. "You gonna keep this outta the papers?"

"The M.E. is already cooperating," the commander answered. "We'll keep this as quiet as we can."

Noto waved his arm in disgust and stepped back from the table. "You remember something. My people know how to keep their mouths shut. We don't talk family with others; they don't need to know. You Irish, you talk all the time, you talk too much." He paused as he put his hand on the doorknob. "But I swear to God, you talk about this, you two'll be in shitville with your badges up your ass." Then he pulled the door open and strode out without bothering to close it behind him.

Back in his office on the fifth floor of City Hall, Tom Cullen was relaxing with Cap Malloy, an old aide with a veined poorhouse face, the court jester to whom the aldermen would hand their coats as they went in to see the Mayor.

"I tell you, Mayor"—he pronounced it "Mare"—"I understand now why they call us dirty old men."

"Speak for yourself, Cap," Cullen said with the beginning of a chuckle.

"Just so, just so. But you mustn't think I'm talking of sex, or desires for young maidens in dried-up old fellows like me. I could tell you about that another day. Another day. I'm talking about making water, Your Honor. That's what makes dirty old men of us, even after the prostate operation." He pronounced the word "prostrate" and Cullen started to giggle.

"Yessir," Malloy said, lowering his voice even though no one else was in the office at the time, "it's that you can't stop the dribble, call it what you will. Like I said, I passed water this very morning, while Your Honor was reading the budget. I had a good stream, and thought I shook all the drops off. But by God, Your Honor, I still wet my pants. At my age, Mayor, I'm a dirty old man."

Cullen laughed out loud. "By God, Cap, I believe you are. What do you hear around the Hall these days?"

"Nothing too much, Your Honor, just that we're all expecting you to run again. That's the talk I hear all over the Hall. They talk of little else. 'When will the Mayor be announcing?' that's what they ask me. 'When will His Honor throw his hat in the ring again?'"

Cullen waved his hand at him to staunch the flow of flattery.

"Did anybody ever see me take my hat out of the ring?" he asked, giggling again. "I thought I might just leave it there permanently."

His phone rang and as he lifted the receiver his features fell back into solemn folds like a suddenly loosened set of drapes.

"What?" the Mayor said calmly after a pause. "All right, all right. Come to my office and we'll talk about it." He replaced the phone and

looked up at Cap Malloy, who was standing in front of his desk waiting
to continue his late-morning's entertainment.

"Sorry you can't stay, Cap," Cullen said pointedly and Malloy, accustomed to such dismissals over the years, turned to leave.

"Let me know, sir, when you're going to make the announcement of
your next candidacy so I can let your many friends and supporters here
in the Hall know the good news before they read it in the papers."

"On my word," the Mayor said gravely. "You will be the first to know."

Mark Richler, disheveled and distracted, entered as Malloy wandered
into the outer office.

"What's this all about, Mark?"

"I just heard it, Tom, and I can't believe it, it's so dumb. The *Times*
has a man working on Wendel and they're close to going with a story
about a deal he's worked out on a cable TV franchise. They say he's taking a percentage for swinging it to some group called Ardi-Vision."

A stranger would have been unsure of Cullen's reaction. He had long
ago perfected a fixed expression of seeming indifference to all reports.
He did, however, drum his fingers on his desk as he nodded Richler into
the chair by his desk. Richler, an unlighted cigarette dangling from the
corner of his mouth, opened a folder on his lap.

"Tom, we have to get on this quickly."

"Yes, the old Richler strategy. Anticipate the worst and beat the
papers to it." Cullen sighed. "How much do you think this will hurt us?"

"Are you kidding?" Richler answered as he held a match to his cigarette. "They'll murder us with a story like this. It's just what they're looking for, a scandal to tie onto the administration. There's too much out in
public on this."

"Yes, yes," the Mayor said distractedly. He clenched and unclenched
his fist as a column of pain rose in his left arm.

"I thought Wendel was smarter than this myself," he said, forcing a
grim smile. "There are two things here, Mark. First, there's the money.
Big money. A chance for him to get out of the stiff business." Cullen
paused and shook his arm, which now felt normal again. "But it's more
than the money. It's me, that's what this is all about. He's making a
move against me, trying to show he can swing a big deal on his own,
that's the story here. He didn't know some newspaper reporter would get
nosy . . ."

Cullen rubbed his chin with his left hand. "It's never ceased to amaze
me how some small men can see themselves getting so big." Cullen
laughed unpleasantly. He had seen his low expectations of human nature
fulfilled again.

"We've got to break this story before the papers," Richler said urgently. But Cullen sat as if lost in contemplation of Alex Wendel's at-

tempt to seize some of his own power. Was Cullen slowing down? Was
he tired of these battles with would-be Davids?

Cullen grunted, stood up, and walked around his desk. Richler inspected him carefully but he looked okay as far as he could see.

The Mayor circled the desk and sat down again. He would never tolerate impropriety with a situation as public and sensitive as cable television franchises. That kind of deal had to be handled out in the open.
Now Wendel, out of his goddamn ambition and his greed, had begun
something that might harm the Democratic Party and, of course, its local
leader, Thomas H. Cullen. That would never do, Cullen's head and
stomach agreed on that. The Mayor turned toward Richler, who had
inched forward in his chair to quash his cigarette in the ashtray on the
edge of the Mayor's desk.

"What do you want to do, Mark?"

"Well, I think this is important enough for you to speak out, have a
press conference on it. You'll need to appoint a blue ribbon committee to
oversee the awarding of franchises. We need to make it absolutely im-
partial, nonpolitical. We'll have to have a speech about our shock at dis-
covering this and the need to protect the interests of the people."

"Yes, yes, Mark, your usual good recipe. You get started on the talk.
Use that line . . . what was it? The one you wrote for the last campaign.
How did it go? 'Square deals or no deals.' I like that. That's my idea of
government."

Cullen was more animated as he spoke these words, more like the man
Richler had worked for through a whole generation. Richler closed his
folder and stood up.

"Any ideas for the blue ribbon commission?" the Mayor asked.

"I'd like to see somebody like Harding, the President of the University
of Chicago," Richler replied as he stuck another cigarette into the corner
of his mouth, "or maybe Fulton of Transfer Trust . . ."

"No, Mark, no bankers. We've had attempted theft already. And I'm
not too sure about the university presidents. We want to get these franchises settled someday." He held Richler with his bright-blue eyes. "I've
got somebody for you."

Richler paused, holding a lighted match beneath his cigarette. "Who?"

"That woman who spoke for the Missing in Action people this morning. O'Brien is her name, Ann Marie O'Brien."

"Jesus, Tom." Richler shook out his match. "What do we know about
her? She hasn't had any experience that I know of."

"What do you mean," Cullen said, pink and hearty again. "She's an
outstanding young woman, her husband is a hero, she's made a name for
herself in this MIA cause."

"But, Tom . . ." Richler broke off, recognizing that, as far as the
Mayor was concerned, the matter was settled.

"She's a fine woman, Mark. And, besides, she's got no sponsor, no constituents but the missing soldiers, no ties to any political leader."

Richler understood why the Mayor looked so pleased. If appointed to this blue ribbon commission Ann Marie would owe her position only to Cullen, she would look good in the press and her only loyalty would be to him. In other words, the classic Cullen move.

"Call Monsignor Fitzmaurice. He's her cousin; he'll tell you about her. See if you can't get her right away."

Richler turned to go. "And, Mark," the Mayor called after him, "tell Helen to call Wendel's office. I want to have a little talk with him."

4

Why couldn't I come?" Matthew asked in direct little-boy fashion. Ann Marie didn't have an answer, not one that would convince him, even if he were only eight years old. She really didn't know why she had not brought him to the City Council meeting. And now, after her talk had gone well, she felt guilty that she had left him at her Aunt Molly's house. She had been through this emotional drill many times in her life. She protected her own feelings and felt depressed immediately afterward. Then, with another sliver of scar tissue added to her psyche, she would push forward. Pushing forward could have been inscribed on her coat of arms.

"Matt, this was just a meeting of grown-ups," Ann Marie said as she hunched down and placed her hands on either side of his face.

"But it was about Daddy. You said it was about Daddy . . ."

"Yes, everybody remembered what a brave man he is. And, until he comes home, you have to be just as brave . . ."

"But why couldn't I go then?" Matthew was back to square one.

"Next time, Matthew, next time Mommy will take you."

"But why couldn't I go today?"

Ann Marie looked into her son's eyes. He was only eight and his concrete question was about something fundamental, the invisible husband and father around whom their lives had been led, the man she had tried to keep and bring back alive in the cause which for years now had been the focus of her quicksilver energy, her restless feelings.

Matthew was right but she didn't know how to agree with him.

Anger was the one emotion of which Ann Marie was absolutely sure. After all the work, all the pleading and praying, nothing came back from the jungle stillness, just cruelly collapsing stories. The Americans who were suddenly sighted turned out to be Dutch traders. Other promising reports were part of a scheme to get money out of the waiting wives. They all hurt, the way the anonymous telephone callers sometimes did, getting off on the special misery of those who were not quite widows but were no longer wives either. Close your eyes. Grit your teeth. Push forward.

"Next time, Matt, next time Mommy has to go to City Hall for something, I promise you can come too." Matthew looked uncertain, as though the ambiguity that had filled their lives since his father disappeared had left him permanently hesitant about believing any promises. He stared at his mother for a fraction of a second and put a finger in his mouth and pulled his lip forward. Then he smiled and nodded and she pecked a kiss at him.

"I like Aunt Molly," he said, and Ann Marie was not sure what to make of his reaction. He seemed too young to have learned how to change the subject, by introducing a distraction about her aunt who had taken care of him while Ann Marie was at City Hall and at lunch.

"Aunt Molly lets me play with the trains," Matthew said, slipping away from his mother and rattling off a list of the different kinds of toys that Aunt Molly, good old unmarried Aunt Molly, kept on hand for the visits of her grandnephews and grandnieces. Every family needed a great-aunt Molly. Every Irish Catholic family in Chicago seemed to have one.

The phone rang and, as Matthew moved off still reciting the inventory of playthings at his great-aunt's house, Ann Marie picked up the receiver.

"Monsignor Fitzmaurice calling," a reserved woman's voice said with sanctuary softness. Ann Marie hated the way her cousin had his secretary put through calls for him. But it matched his wanting-to-be-a-bishop style, an ecclesiastical big shot opening cemeteries like they were shopping centers, but no miter yet. Tough nuts. Catholics were good at waiting; it was a religion based on expectation, on things getting better. Ann Marie waited for Charlie. Molly, even at sixty-five, waited for a husband of any kind, and Cousin Morgan waited for the letter from Rome making him a bishop.

"Ann Marie?" Monsignor Fitzmaurice's voice was subdued, subtle, expectant.

"Yes, Morgan," she said. "I'm sorry I didn't get to talk to you more this morning."

"Yes, Annie, so was I." Such pleasantness. He wanted something. "I'll tell you why I'm calling. I just had a call from the Mayor's assistant, Mark Richler. The Mayor is interested in seeing you. He'd like to talk to you."

"About what?" Ann Marie asked warily.

"I'm not sure of that." The hell he wasn't, Ann Marie judged, for it was clear from his tone that he wanted her to respond positively to the City Hall invitation; it was as natural as breathing for diocesan officials to operate in harmony with municipal officials.

"He probably wants to thank you again for coming down today. The Mayor is a great gentleman and very patriotic, too." The good monsignor paused. "I think he was quite impressed with you."

"Then why didn't he invite me himself?"

"Oh, I think he will. Or Mark Richler will. I just wanted to let you know that they'd be in touch with you."

"Well, I'm glad you called," Ann Marie said flatly.

"I think it would be worth your while to go and have a visit."

It would be worth *his* while, that's what he's thinking. Without giving her cousin a yes or a no, she hung up. She sighed. It might be interesting after all, something different, something new at least for a few hours in her life. And she liked the old Mayor, she really did. Maybe she would go down to City Hall again. Maybe she'd see that reporter who had given her the twice-over this morning. Why had she promised to take Matthew with her on her next trip there?

She only talked to Mayor Cullen for a few moments when he called with a courtly invitation to come to see him at City Hall. She hadn't felt the kind of attention old Cullen conveyed since those golden days when she was a young girl and knew how to get what she wanted out of her father, that handsome Irishman, who, until he had that stroke after her mother died, had been the most romantic man she had ever known. Her initial hesitation about returning to City Hall vanished. The erotic excitement that trailed off the possibility of seeing that reporter again receded too. The Mayor wanted to talk about some kind of job. She felt better about herself than she had in a long time.

City Hall, like a humming and trembling transformer, gave off shimmers and vibrations of every kind. Matthew was wide-eyed and shy as they walked through the marble concourse hung with old-fashioned lights in brass-fitted lanterns. The light was as soft as it was in a museum or an aquarium. Near the entrance a blind newsman made change as accurately as a bank teller, and beyond him a sign invited passers-by to have their blood pressure taken free. The intricately designed bronze doors of the elevators opened and closed in syncopation with the pace of the hallway.

A moustached policeman whose dully glinting revolver practically hypnotized Matthew directed them to an elevator that would take them to the Mayor's office on the fifth floor. With three women employees carrying Styrofoam cups of coffee and talking about lottery tickets, they rose quickly to the much more sedate atmosphere of the level where Thomas H. Cullen had presided over Chicago for so many years. The city workers moved nimbly in and out of their offices, like athletes who had played together through many hard seasons. The policeman receptionist inside the glass-doored outer office nodded and asked her and Matthew to wait while he called the Mayor's secretary down the gallery-like hall.

She and Matthew took chairs against a wall that was filled with framed pictures of all those who had served in the office of Mayor of the city. Matthew watched the policeman while Ann Marie, for the first time on that tingling morning, glanced down at a newspaper that had been left on a table next to her chair. The bold headlines spoke of the Mayor's budget message while another one, halfway down the page, read "Alderman's Nephew Murdered."

Matthew picked up a copy of the Police Department newsletter and looked at the pictures to see if the officers' guns were showing, while Ann Marie read the account of the slaying that had been discovered out at O'Hare Field. There was no mention of the peculiar details of the crime, but there were two paragraphs of citations about other recent car trunk murders. One last sentence noted that the victim was not known to have had any connection with organized crime. She glanced up as the policeman beckoned her and Matthew and directed them to the large outer office in which three middle-aged women, as contented as cows grazing in a familiar meadow, bent over their secretarial tasks. Helen Morrison, the one nearest the door to the Mayor's office, hung up her phone and signaled for Ann Marie and Matthew to come over to her desk.

"You're Mrs. O'Brien, aren't you?" she asked in a motherly way. "And this is your son? The Mayor's expecting you." She ushered mother and son into the room where Mayor Cullen was already rising from behind his absolutely clear desk to greet them.

"Mrs. O'Brien, I'm happy you could come down. Is this your boy?"

"This is Matthew," Ann Marie answered as the Mayor bent down and took one of Matthew's hands in his own.

"Will you grow up and vote Democratic, Matthew?" Cullen asked with a chuckle. Matthew looked confused and shy. The only older man he had ever spent much time with was his grandfather, who barely managed a sweet grin when they visited him at the nursing home. He had none of the vitality of this big bear who was smiling down at him. Matthew looked at the floor and moved closer to his mother.

"Good lad, good lad," the Mayor said heartily as he straightened up. "You'll go far in the party if you know how to keep quiet. Not many do. Mrs. O'Brien, this is Mr. Richler." Cullen extended his arm toward his aide, who was standing by the windows, a thick manila folder tucked under his right arm. One of Cullen's hulking bodyguards came through a side door and Cullen beamed at Matthew.

"This is Sergeant Berrigan, Matthew. He's going to show you around while we meet with your mother."

"Can I see your gun?" Matthew asked, suddenly enthusiastic, as the officer, with a slightly forced smile on his face, escorted the boy out of the office.

Ann Marie glanced from the Mayor to Mark Richler, who had, without a word, taken a chair a little off to the side of his boss's desk.

"Mrs. O'Brien," the Mayor began, "you made quite an impression on everyone yesterday, yes, a fine impression." Cullen immediately invested young women like Ann Marie with virtues just a level below those of the Blessed Virgin, seeing in them ideals of purity and innocence that at some other level of his old lion's soul he recognized as unrealistic and present, if at all, in slightly worn fashion. Politics called for living by such pleasant fictions. It gave a chauvinistic, patronizing edge to his courtliness.

Still, Cullen possessed a kind of magic and an Arthurian grandeur and Ann Marie relaxed as he bubbled along about the great work she had done for the missing-in-action. He seemed to combine the characteristics of the two men she had lost, her father and her husband. The old Mayor stood bobbing his white-crowned head, laughing and gesturing, intensely alive, immediately and fully present. He could have asked for just about anything and she would have said yes.

"Mrs. O'Brien, to get to the point. That's what the old Irishwoman said to the priest, you know, 'I like your talk, Father, but what's the point of it all?'"

Ann Marie smiled. "Yes, I did wonder what you had in mind." She had been taken into the councils of the mighty. Did her enjoyment of it show? Mark Richler surveyed her steadily as he searched for a package of cigarettes in his suit pocket. Cullen had already unfolded his storyteller's cloak.

". . . So they thought making a retreat would be good for their souls and nobody was more pious than George McGraw, and his wife was so glad he was going because it would keep him away from the racetrack for a few days. And, by God, it did until he went into the monastery garden to make the outdoor stations of the cross. George had taken a paper with him to kneel on, and at the twelfth station he looked down and saw that it was the racing form. He saw the names of two horses and it came to him like a vision and up he got—he never did finish the stations—and ran into the monastery, called his bookie, and bet them in the daily double. McGraw made two thousand dollars that afternoon and never missed a retreat again." Cullen laughed charmingly, seductively. A wink of the eye. What's the harm in a twice-told tale? Plenty of them in the business of politics.

"Well, I'm not a horse player and not a politician either," she said with a smile. Cullen's face grew more serious.

"Exactly, exactly," he said. "That's one of the things I liked about you yesterday, the way you got right to the point. That's why I wanted to talk to you."

Cullen cleared his throat and Mark Richler opened his folder and placed it on the edge of the Mayor's desk.

"Mark has a lot of background material here on a project that's important for the city. It has to be handled properly for everybody's good. And we want you to chair a blue ribbon commission we're setting up to oversee the matter."

Ann Marie felt flattered but mildly uncertain. More committees? More meetings? She had her fill of those in the MIA work.

"It's got to do with distributing the franchise rights for cable television in the city," Cullen said softly, the lilting charm of his old pol stories toned down for the moment. "I want to tell you, Mrs. O'Brien, that great fortunes are going to be made in this cable television thing. And there are parties out there who want to make them. They'd do anything to control this, or even to get a small portion of control over it. This is a big order and I want you to think about it. Mark here will give you all the background you need."

"Has there been some trouble about this?" Ann Marie asked. "Isn't a blue ribbon panel a kind of special thing, something you only have if there's some difficulty?"

"Sometimes, Mrs. O'Brien, but in this case it's because we want this to be done right."

"We're trying to avoid trouble for the city," Mark Richler broke in. "We want this to be as aboveboard as possible."

"Yes," Mayor Cullen added, "doing it fairly is doing it right. That's the only direction for government to go in something as important as this."

The phone on his desk rang and Cullen picked it up, gesturing toward Richler to take over the conversation. Richler listed some of the other names proposed for membership on the committee. It was an impressive catalog of business and educational leaders in the city. The Mayor hung up his phone and, smiling broadly, spoke again. "All we want is for you to think about it and let us know. We would like to know quickly, of course, since we want to make an announcement soon."

"Tomorrow, if possible," Richler added from inside a haze of cigarette smoke. "Do you have any questions?"

Ann Marie looked from one man to the other and said quickly, "I'll take it. It sounds interesting and different from what I've been doing. When do I start?"

Cullen beamed again. "I'm glad you said that. Mark will take care of the details and we'll make an announcement either today or tomorrow."

"We'll hold a press conference," Richler added. "How about this afternoon, so we can make the six o'clock news and tomorrow morning's papers with it?"

Ann Marie nodded in assent. She felt good about her quick decision, but deadpanned it, remembering what she had learned dealing with Far

Eastern ambassadors. "I think that could be arranged. Can I make some calls?"

The Mayor smiled and rose to shake her hand. "We're very pleased about this. Mark will take you to an office where you can make whatever calls you wish. We'll see you this afternoon." A genial hand-off play, a well-practiced gesture by an old master of the art of moving people along. Ann Marie didn't mind at all.

"I want to thank you, Mr. Mayor," Ann Marie said, as she leaned suddenly toward him and kissed Cullen lightly on the cheek. He beamed and walked to the door with her, launching into another anecdote as Mark Richler, tucking his folder back under his arm, swung around to her other side to see her out.

Thomas Cullen, shielding his best cards, had gotten exactly what he wanted. He had told Ann Marie nothing of the real nature of the cable TV problem. Alex Wendel was due to come to his office in a few minutes and Cullen had the blue ribbon committee snugly in the dark of his pocket, with the noble chairperson he wanted. Smart, too, but safe. Richler remained against it on the grounds that the woman lacked political experience. But Cullen's instincts told him what he wanted to know, that she would cooperate with him, that, in the long run, she would not come up with radical recommendations or do-gooder plans for the city. And she would be totally loyal to him since he was the only one to whom she owed anything. With a touch as deft as that of an old blues pianist, he had played her perfectly. Cullen wasn't interested in sex from these idealized young women; he couldn't have fit it into his schedule. He wanted devotion, he wanted women to be there, the way his own daughter Maureen was, when he needed them. It was a thoroughly Irish sentiment.

Wendel had done the unthinkable the previous afternoon: he had been unavailable when he heard that the Mayor was looking for him. Stiffing Cullen the afternoon before had been a necessary step in his plan to force the old man to recognize him as a prime contender for future power. Nobody else had the psychopathic nerve to launch such an assault on Cullen's position, even though there had been whispers about the Mayor's health and the impossibility of his living forever.

For his part, Cullen understood—and grudgingly admired—what Wendel had in mind. It took more drive than some of his Irish protégés had to lay down a challenge that combined such a spurious purity of intention, lofty wickedness, and high-style political larceny. Well, Cullen smiled inwardly, we'll just see how this comes out. While he waited for Wendel to arrive he took another phone call. It was Alderman Noto and he wanted to talk to the Mayor personally about the death of his nephew.

"How's his mother?" the Mayor asked with a genuine concern for the
woman who had lost her son.

"Not good," Noto responded. "Crying all the time. Goddamn shame, a
terrible thing, the whole thing's a terrible thing. You know the kid was
clean, he never done nothing wrong."

"I'm sure you're right," Cullen answered guardedly. "Who's handling
the arrangements?"

"Barone. You know, Richie's brother. Terrible thing." Noto paused before he placed his next question. "The mother, she'd appreciate if you
could stop by. You know what I mean?"

"Yes, I do," Cullen answered ambiguously, "but I'm afraid I won't be
able to make it. The party will send flowers and there'll be plenty of
people there . . ." Cullen felt bad for the mother—he had great sentiment for mothers, just as he had for putative virgins—but he wanted
nothing to do with this situation.

"I'm sorry for these troubles, Sam, and I'll have a Mass said for your
nephew. Give my best to his mother." With that he signed off and
shifted in his chair to compose himself for his next visitor.

About a minute later Alex Wendel appeared at the doorway wearing a
white suit. Cullen nodded toward a chair by his desk. Wendel sat down,
adjusted his red tie, and took a gold penknife out of the pocket of his
vest. Cullen, his features as massed and motionless as those on Mount
Rushmore, folded his hands in front of him like a dutiful schoolboy at
his desk.

"You wanted to see me?" Wendel finally asked in flat tones.

"It's your move, Mr. Wendel," Cullen responded without inflection.

Wendel eased sideways in his chair and straightened the flaps of his
suit coat beneath him.

"I'm interested in the future," he said, snapping his penknife open
while studying the fingernails of his left hand. "I'm young and strong
and I work hard. I deserve something for that."

Cullen did not blink. He continued to regard his visitor calmly. He
had nothing to gain by responding to Wendel. A man did not keep
power by giving some of it away. He kept it by not giving any of it
away at all.

"So, I figure," Wendel said, after another awkward pause, "you can
count on me. I play ball. You're going to let me make something on this
deal." He looked into Cullen's eyes as he would at an old animal that
was bound to yield territorial rights to a challenging young buck. Cullen
still said nothing.

"What's more," Wendel added in a conversational tone, "I don't think
you'll make anything of this because the election's only two years off.
You don't want any bad publicity for anything in the party right now."

"You're a nice young man, Alex," Cullen said slowly, "but you've forgotten something. You think old men scare easily because they're old. The funny thing is, when you're old you've seen so much of life that you don't get scared at all." He stared coldly at Wendel, who stopped fiddling with his penknife, dropped both hands into his lap, and looked intensely at the Mayor.

"I'm not trying to scare you," he said quietly.

"And you're not. You see, the other thing is, that if you get scared too easily, you never get old at all. That's how it is in this business. You understand, I'm sure." Cullen pushed his chair back and stood up. He walked around his desk and past Wendel as though the alderman were not there. He went slowly over to the windows, holding his hands loosely together behind his back. He had gotten up because he was beginning to feel miniature skyrockets climbing up and then fading away in his arm, and he was more comfortable if he moved a little. Besides, he did not want Wendel to see his face if the perspiration began to flow, as it often did when he experienced these episodes. He spoke without turning back toward his visitor.

"I want you to know what I've decided to do so that you can make decisions as you see fit. You know, the cable television franchise is very important and has to be handled correctly. That's why I thought you'd be the right chairman for the committee to handle it in the Council. Smart fellow, that's the kind needed for the job. Well, you're smart enough to know that you don't control the votes on your committee. I do. How do you think those men got on the committee in the first place?" Cullen's arm felt better and his face seemed free of sweat; he turned slowly and walked back to his desk.

"The man who controls the votes also controls the committee, no matter who or how smart the chairman is. I'd think a fellow like you was smart enough to know that." Cullen walked around behind his desk again and eased himself down into his chair. Wendel, his mouth slightly open, watched him carefully.

"Now, in a situation like this where a chairman has begun—so I hear— to make promises to certain companies before anything is decided, what can a fellow do?" The Mayor folded his arms and stared straight ahead as though he were musing to himself. "Well, you might ask the chairman to resign because of a conflict of interest. And if he wouldn't do that, you might have to look into other business arrangements the fellow has and kill all those contracts. That would be easy. Businesses like to cooperate with the Mayor of the city. Then it's always possible to reduce his patronage, or take it away altogether so that he doesn't have any jobs to give away as political favors. All those are things that could be done. But they would be very embarrassing to a chairman, very embarrassing indeed." He shifted his eyes toward the alderman, whose calm had begun to disintegrate. "And I wouldn't want to embarrass anyone, not unless it was absolutely impossible to handle a situation differently." He paused and wet his lips. "So this is what we're going to do. This afternoon we're holding a news conference at which you'll be present when I announce that at your suggestion the cable franchise business is being taken out of the City Council and handed to a blue ribbon civic committee. Then I'll announce that you are introducing a bill to establish rules by ordinance for competitive bidding so that the public will get a square deal in all this. Then we'll announce the new committee and you'll have your picture taken with the head of it—Mrs. O'Brien, the one who worked for the Missing in Action groups." Cullen paused. The contest was over.

"That way, there's no embarrassment for anybody. It's good government. And you'll get some of the credit for it. Probably you'll get a couple of editorial mentions. Along with me, of course. There won't be any party squabble and no scandal. Now don't you think that's a prudent way to handle all this? It'll do wonders for your reputation. And it will keep all your business arrangements and patronage intact."

Wendel did not know what to say. It was bad enough to get nothing but, Jesus Christ, he would have to do business with some broad in the bargain. He swallowed and looked again at the Mayor. The old bastard hadn't lost his touch at that. But he couldn't live forever. And Wendel would be heard from then. He stood up, replaced the penknife in his vest pocket, straightened his suit again, and, without a word, walked across the office and out the door.

Cullen smiled, pleased with the accomplishments of the morning. He picked up his phone and asked his secretary to get Mark Richler. He wanted to be sure everything, including an ordinance prepared by the Corporation Counsel, would be ready for the afternoon news conference.

5

*A*nn Marie, excited at the prospect of this new adventure, first called her aunt and then Mother Francis.

"Cable television? But, Annie, that's one of the biggest deals the city will have. Did they go into detail on what you would do?"

"The Mayor's aide, Richler, Mark Richler, was very nice and helpful. You know him, he's the Jewish one who's so close to the Mayor. Well, he explained that the City Council would pass an ordinance requiring all the cable companies to place competitive bids and that the panel I'm going to chair would make the decision on awarding the franchises. All on merit, that's how he explained it . . ."

"Whom do you report to?"

"We didn't get into that. The Mayor, I suppose."

"Oh, I'm sure it will be the Mayor all right." Mother Francis's tone grew slightly skeptical and trailed off.

"Do you think you can make the press conference? Molly is coming. My father can't, of course. But I'd love for you to be there. They're sending Matthew and me home in a car to get freshened up and then we'll pick up Molly back here at about three. We'll be in Mr. Richler's office if you get here early."

"Wonderful. Then dinner's on me. Well, I mean on the college. In honor of a distinguished alumna. Don't argue. I'm happy for you and I must say the best thing is that your voice is full of life again."

"I feel good about it, I really do."

"Tell me one thing. What do you think of my old friend, Thomas H. Cullen?"

"Well," Ann Marie felt a gentle current roll through her being, "I can certainly see why you like him. I had never seen him so close up before. He's, well . . . I can see why you think so much of him."

"Yes, Annie, he's quite a man."

The older woman paused for a split second. Her voice, which had been filled with the melodies of enthusiasm, became that of the watchful old eagle of a nun: "Annie, I think this is the beginning of a new life for you. I think you're coming into the sunshine again after a long period in the shade."

"I'm looking forward to it, I really am," Ann Marie answered, and she quickly ended the conversation.

At four o'clock promptly, Thomas H. Cullen escorted the committee members and their guests through his outer office to the room that had been set aside for press conferences. The Mayor smiled into the pop and glare of the lights and raised his hand for silence.

"Ladies and gentlemen . . ." Cullen giggled. Everybody knew that he thought the members of the press were anything but ladies and gentlemen. One reporter applauded. Others joined in and Cullen laughed out loud. The room was suddenly filled with good humor and Max Day, the dean of the crowd of newsgatherers, stood up in the front row as if to shake the Mayor's hand. General laughter broke out as Cullen, smiling broadly, leaned forward and grasped the reporter's hand.

"Here, get a picture of this," the Mayor called out. The laughter subsided as Cullen pulled back to take his place directly behind the microphones again. "I don't want anybody to get the wrong idea," he said, his eyes twinkling. "My mother used to tell me to watch out who it was I hung out with." The laughter picked up again and everybody, even the bankers and educators who were to constitute the blue ribbon panel chaired by Ann Marie, loosened up and smiled nervously.

The good-humored sparring was a sign, read accurately by Richler and a few others, that the Mayor was comfortable with the arrangements that he was about to announce.

Ann Marie stood just to the Mayor's right. The give and take of the moment, which, as she saw it, enhanced rather than diminished the way Thomas Cullen dominated the group, was different from and more exciting than anything she had participated in for years. As the Mayor spoke, Ann Marie studied the reporters, who were scribbling away in their notebooks, even though copies of Cullen's remarks were being passed along the jumbled and crowded aisles. Afterimages from the lights danced in her eyes and she turned her glance aside, just in time to see trench-coated Paul Michael Martin come through the door. Was he grinning at her, or at the spectacle of the news conference? He edged along the wall until he had worked himself to within ten feet of the slightly elevated platform on which Cullen and the committee stood. He settled himself against the wall and took up his inspection of Ann Marie's body again.

Ann Marie felt protected by the bulwark of Mayor Cullen, who stood just forward and left of her. Still, her flank was exposed to Martin's appraising eyes. She fixed her eyes on Cullen's broad blue-suited back for a moment, then glanced toward Martin, who had not shifted his eyes at all. His unused notebook propped up the flap of his side pocket. Okay, she would take him on; she wouldn't let him feel her up with his eyes.

They locked in on each other. It was visual Indian wrestling, a kind of amusing foreplay. Martin grew irritated as he realized that her eyes sparked with disdain and that she was besting him, humiliating him in the staredown. The hell with foreplay. This was a contest for the championship. He wouldn't blink at the bitch even if that were the cheap price he would have to pay to pop her into bed. The hell with her. This was life and death, a dogfight at no altitude with the blue ribbon queen herself.

The duel was interrupted by Mayor Cullen as he introduced the members of the committee whose duties he had just explained. As the Mayor turned toward Ann Marie she took a step forward, smiled into the cameras, and stepped back. She did not look at Martin after she returned to her place but followed the Mayor's gestures toward the other committee members, who stood like earnest children waiting for good conduct pins. Cullen beamed again at the members. "Now, I want Alderman Alex Wendel, who has worked closely with the administration in developing this plan, to explain to you the ordinance that he will introduce in a special session of the City Council tomorrow morning to establish the rules for submitting bids on the cable television franchises."

Wendel forced a smile as he stepped up onto the platform. It was not in his makeup to be repentant; he had merely decided to plan more carefully, to be more sure of his execution of the correct plays the next time around. Wendel would have to deal with the companies to whom he had already promised cable rights; that would all work out if he kept his coolness now. He made his brief remarks and moved aside.

"I'm sure you'll all agree that this is a great decision on the part of the subcommittee," a poker-faced Cullen said, "and Alderman Wendel, in the great tradition of his family, has given leadership on this and deserves credit for working out the details. Now, we'll have questions, if you please."

A dozen hands shot up and Cullen fielded most of the inquiries himself. No curves, no high inside fast balls, either. Cullen knocked each one over the fence easily. He recognized Paul Michael Martin.

"Mayor Cullen, isn't it true that blue ribbon panels are often invoked when there has been some serious doubt about the propriety or legality of some transaction? And if that's so, why have you brought this group together? Is there something improper or illegal in the way the Council subcommittee has been handling things?"

"Now that's several questions," Cullen responded, his good humor unsoured by this perennially hostile questioner. "You get a blue ribbon yourself for that." The other reporters chuckled. "Now, to take them one by one. The answer to the first and the third is the same, no. The answer to the second one is that this is the greatest group of citizens we could have gathered for this important job. Any other questions? You got another three-parter?"

"No, Mr. Mayor, those questions don't elicit much information." His words fell like acid rain on the crowd of reporters and dignitaries. "I want to ask a question of Mrs. O'Brien, the chairperson of the panel." The Mayor turned toward her and, for the first time since their indecisive staring contest, Ann Marie looked Martin directly in the eyes.

"Mrs. O'Brien," Martin began sarcastically, "just what qualifications could you possibly possess to be chairman of this committee, especially if it's as important as the Mayor says it is?"

Ann Marie cleared her throat as Mayor Cullen, sensing her uneasiness with this direct attack, intervened. "Mr. Martin, certainly you know of Mrs. O'Brien's great work with the Missing in Action movement."

"Yes," Martin shot back, "but I'm not convinced that this qualifies Mrs. O'Brien for what you yourself describe as a very important job."

"I'll answer," Ann Marie said in a low voice to Cullen as she stepped to the microphones. The room became quiet as Ann Marie, her concentration fixed on Martin across a laser beam of tension, pushed back a wisp of hair from her forehead. The television cameras focused in tightly on her and, as she often did, she made an accidental discovery. If she paused the room grew even quieter. All the attention was fastened on her and not on her questioner.

"You've asked what qualifications I have to chair this committee on franchises for cable television?" She paused again. "The answer is simple. I don't have any qualifications." The squeak of a chair counterpointed the room's utter silence. "I don't know anything about the technicalities of television or of the cable systems. I am not an expert on franchising. I admit all that. And that is why I am qualified. I have no connection with, no interest in, and do not stand to profit in any way from any of the parties who may be involved in this business. I am truly disinterested."

All this with the same compelling emphasis that had marked her address the day before. And with the same kind of effect on the crowd.

"I did not seek but I was glad to accept a commendation for that work yesterday. I believe Mr. Martin is connected with a television station that might be interested in a cable franchise. His question would not prejudice me in the slightest in making judgments if the station were eligible. I believe that covers everything." She stepped back to her place as a few people applauded. The members of the commission joined in and the Mayor, grinning happily at the way his appointee had handled herself, reached over and shook her hand. He held her arm aloft in the gesture of a winner.

"Thank you, gentlemen," Mark Richler said, and the press conference ended swiftly as the television lights went out and Mayor Cullen, after thanking Ann Marie again, slipped back through the door that led to his outer office.

Vintage Chicago, the press conference had everything—intrigue, tension, and the battle of the sexes right out in public. Reporters sensing that Ann Marie would be good for a story a day if only because of her good looks and her directness, swarmed about her, while Aunt Molly held on to Matthew's hand. Mother Francis stood at the edge of the group of reporters who were asking Ann Marie questions about her background and about when she learned of her appointment and how she planned to carry out the commission's work.

Max Day slipped his notebook into his pocket and stopped to say a word to Paul Martin who, still leaning against the side wall, had continued to watch Ann Marie as she answered questions and posed for pictures.

"Well, Paul," Max said dryly, "you wanted to get to know her."

"A star is born," Paul replied, wrinkling his brow and shrugging his shoulders, "and I was the fucking midwife."

"Seems to have been a successful delivery."

"She won't like the birth announcement I put on television tonight," Martin said grimly as the two men turned and walked slowly out of the room.

Ann Marie loved the excitement of the event. She let the experience wash over her, let it wash down, as sensuous and satisfying as a good bath, a cleansing of the dust of the past. Ann Marie had not pushed with her shoulder against the leaden wheel of time to make it turn. It had moved all by itself and she felt cleaner and lighter, ready for everything new.

It didn't seem so grand later that evening when Paul Michael Martin's face loomed up on the television screen as it had out of the crowd that afternoon. She could not answer him back as he sardonically commented on the "untrained and inexperienced woman who has been appointed to head the blue ribbon committee on television franchises. She admits that she knows nothing about it. Why, then, was she appointed?" The camera pulled in close on Martin's ruggedly handsome features. His eyes mocked her again. Fury ate away at her earlier delight as Martin continued his abrasive commentary.

"What is Mayor Cullen trying to hide? Why does he need a blue ribbon commission for this? He hasn't appointed one since the sewer contract scandal. Does he really think we are going to buy his vague explanation? Or his appointment of a chairperson whose only distinction is that she admits that she doesn't know anything about the subject of the committee's concern, cable TV franchising in this city? There's a big story here, ladies and gentlemen, and I'm going to keep asking questions until the truth comes out." He seemed to sneer as he uttered his customary sign off, "Sincerely, Paul Michael Martin."

But, dammit, there was something attractive about him. No matter what he said, he was handsome. That made her madder. The telephone rang and shattered the icy rage that had consumed her. The television screen blinked a commercial from Martin's sponsor, a downtown bank.

"Hello," a hearty voice said, "this is Mayor Cullen. Is that you, Mrs. O'Brien? Have you been watching that fellow, what's his name, Martin, on the television?"

"Yes," she answered, feeling better just to hear the old man's voice.

"Well, one thing you have to get used to is things like that. And you don't want to pay any attention to those fellows. The thing is, Martin has to think of something to say every night, and tearing things and people apart is his business, and you're the piece of meat for today. You should hear some of the things he's said about me. You don't want to let this upset you and you don't want to answer him either."

"I feel like knocking his block off."

"Say, you really are Irish, aren't you? Save your fight for the committee work. It's very important for the public and for the city. Guys like Martin want to get you mad just to get you to say something you'll regret."

"I suppose you're right." Ann Marie sighed, feeling better, feeling protected by this extraordinary man, feeling that Cullen did know best, that she might be able to give him what she had not given away for years—her trust.

"But you'd still like to knock his block off, right?" The Mayor laughed and Ann Marie smiled.

"I sure would."

"Well, there's nothing he'd like more. My mother used to tell me, 'Don't do your enemy's work for him,' and, you know, she was right." Then he added, as though it were something not too important, but he'd throw it in anyway, "By the way, I wouldn't say much to any reporters while we're organizing and getting this ordinance passed. And you might save yourself a lot of trouble if you got your telephone number changed."

Ann Marie assured him that she would follow his advice, and when she hung up her phone the hurt Martin had inflicted was almost gone. Talking to the Mayor was as good as going to Lourdes for the cure. Better, maybe. She had been there once and prayed for Charlie. But she hadn't gotten any answers. She hadn't gotten Charlie either. She shook her head. Martin was still trying to win the staring contest, that's all. The ring of the phone interrupted her reverie almost immediately. It was a reporter wanting a comment on the remarks made by Paul Michael Martin. "I have no comment," she answered brusquely, "none at all."

"Well," the reporter continued, "what about his charges that there must be something funny behind all this for the Mayor to appoint a blue ribbon committee at all?"

"I have no comment on that either." Then she broke off the conversation but, as she replaced the telephone receiver, she realized that she really did not know the answer to that question, that the Mayor had never explained it fully to her, and that, in his comforting call, Thomas H. Cullen had chuckled and quoted his mother, he had been as charming as hell, but had never brought up that part of Martin's commentary at all. She shook her head again, removed the phone receiver from its base, placed it in a drawer, and slowly undressed for bed.

. . . .

6

*A*nn Marie hoped that these new, lighter tones in her feelings would not disappear. She had known exciting moments of hope when her juices surged at the prospect that Charlie might climb out of that distant cloudbank in which the MIA's seemed to wander endlessly. There had been disappointments every time and she had finally adopted the strategy of relentlessly pushing forward, just to keep herself functioning, to keep the parts of her mind from rusting together the way they do in abandoned machinery.

Ann Marie had blocked the parts of her body out completely, wearing dark or neutral colors to match the numbness that had set into her at every level of physical reaction. Desire had gone fast asleep until very recently, when she had passed from failed hope into despair and then into an almost crawly restlessness. That had come on when it looked like she might stand forever in the beige world of women who were not quite widows.

As she undressed that evening, however, she looked at herself again to inspect the body which, for the last four years, might as well have been a saint's hidden in a hair shirt. Except that Ann Marie had lost her touch with the life of the spirit too, along with the Catholicism which had once seemed almost instinctive to her. Maybe it was too many prayers unanswered, like those at Lourdes, too many candles that had guttered out without results, too many cruelties that all the reassurances of the priests could never explain away. Religion had become lifeless and she did not think this reaction was the dark night of the soul. Yet she lived in her disowned flesh as in a tower and did not understand it at all.

As she looked at her body in the full-length mirror of her bedroom, she felt a nudging of life, some early spring feeling. She felt that it was hers again. She glanced away quickly. Her identification with her flesh was uneasy, still uncertain. She was looking at a stranger, someone she had not seen in a long time, perhaps a distant relative with whom she had never been on completely easy terms. Ann Marie ran her hands down her sides, reached up and touched her breasts. Who was this person? What was this body anyway? She pulled away from the mirror dazedly and slipped into a shapeless nightgown.

She climbed into bed and opened a folder that Mark Richler had given to her that afternoon. It contained background information on the nature and structure of cable television as well as a draft of the proposed ordinance. She was good at leading the charge. This paperwork was about as intriguing to her as looking up numbers in the telephone book. Ann Marie closed the folder, dropped it on the floor next to her bed, switched out the light, and dreamed of lions stretching in the sun and of old men, hunters, crouching by their fires in the darkness.

On the West Side of the city, in an area from which most of the Italians had long before moved away, stood Angelo Barone's funeral home, a square stucco-covered box with a neon sign sputtering above a small parking lot. Angelo was, in a sense, an importer, handling the funeral arrangements for many Italian families who had moved away to other places. They liked to come back to Angelo; they even flew withered old ladies and men back from Sun City and St. Petersburg to have Angelo apply the finishing touches for their final journeys. It didn't hurt, of course, that Richard Barone was his brother or that he handled many syndicate funerals with a Sicilian gusto that matched the ornate Italian restaurant finishings of his parlors.

It was ten o'clock of the first night of the visitation for Noto's nephew and, although it was a chilly evening, it was about one hundred degrees in the crowded and noisy room where the young man lay, as sweet-looking as a Vatican choirboy, in a coffin that would outlast a time capsule. A sickly smell rose from the baskets and flower arrangements to fog the air with sweetness.

One union had sent a floral piece of gold mums shaped like a chalice, and a contractor had sent one of tiny white and blue flowers fashioned into a facsimile bust of the Blessed Mother. A few mourners wailed and cried with the parents up near the casket while the milling crowd scene that followed the recitation of the rosary filled the rest of the large room.

Sam Noto, wearing double knit black and looking weepy, stood at the door of the parlor shaking hands with the visitors. Monsignor Fratianni, the eighty-nine-year-old patriarch of the neighborhood who had just led the prayers, was talking to Noto before he left for his nearby rectory. A spearhead of white collar rose out of the back of his threadbare cassock.

"We wanna thank you, Monsignor," Sam said loudly, "very much. We wanna thank you very much for coming." He slipped an envelope into the splotched hand of the aged priest, who looked at him through thick glasses. "A good boy," the old priest said, "a good boy. Not like that goddamn young curate I got. Lazy good-for-nothing, not like him. He looks in on me the other morning. I'm sleeping good. He calls me, I don't hear. So he calls the Chancery Office and tells them I died in the night. What the hell. Goddamn dumb, not like your nephew." Then the old man stuffed the envelope in his cassock pocket and made his way out of the funeral home.

Angelo Barone, eager to please, was next in line.

"Everything all right, Alderman?"

"Yeah, very nice. The family is all broken up but everything is very nice."

"You got any idea who did this? I mean, this was not, what can we say, not . . ."

"Angie, we don't want any talk about the condition of the body. You understand?" The tone of a blood threat rose in Sam's voice. "I don't want you to talk even to me about it. You understand?"

Angelo nodded and, attempting to regain his usual composure, he signaled to two young men a few feet away. "Alderman," he said unctuously, "I want you to meet two of my sons. This is young Angelo and this is Anthony."

Noto looked at the sturdy young men in dark suits and nodded a greeting. Then he leaned closer to Angelo, "They know about this? They know what you know?"

Angelo shook his head. "Don't worry. On my mother, nobody knows but me."

"Keep it that way," Noto said as he turned to greet Alex Wendel.

"You know Angelo?" Noto asked his fellow alderman. "You guys are in the same business."

"Yes, we've met," Wendel answered, nodding at Barone as the undertaker moved off with his sons to begin the process of closing down the parlor for the evening. It was going to take a while for them to get everyone out and Sam would have to help them with the mother, who had already declared her intention of staying at the side of the casket all night.

Wendel and Noto exchanged the formalities of concern about the homicide. Wendel had heard about the homosexual aspects of the killing from a policeman from his ward who worked on the airport detail. Rumors traveled fast in Chicago and half the city administration already knew the facts. Wendel, however, had no intention of bringing them up. He wanted to talk to Noto about something else.

"What do you think of the old man putting that bitch in on the cable television business?"

"No good, Al, no good. A woman? No good. What happened? I been tied up, you know, with the kid and the family . . ."

"Of course," Wendel said, moving closer, as the departing mourners filed past.

Wendel waited while a black-shawled old lady tearfully wailed into

Noto's ear. Then he said, "Sam, I want to talk to you about the whole thing. I know you can't be on the floor tomorrow when I introduce this ordinance . . ."

"What did the old man do, put the arm on you?" Noto asked, looking directly into Wendel's eyes.

"He's still tough, Sam, but we have to talk about this. Things won't always be this way, you know. We've got to think of the future."

Noto looked beyond him into the room where his brother and sister-in-law stood by the casket.

"One thing we've got to do," Wendel said earnestly, "we've got to get control of this cunt, this whore he's made head of the committee. We can't let this whole thing get away from us."

Noto pouted his lips out and then patted Wendel on the shoulder. "We can't let no goddamn woman fuck us. You're right. Right now we gotta go with the ordinance, right? We'll see about her later."

Richard Barone emerged from the thinning crowd. "What's the matter, Al," he asked sarcastically, "you becoming a reformer? I hear you're introducing a big ordinance in the morning."

Then Sam Noto's sister-in-law began wailing loudly; she was resisting the undertaker, who wanted her to leave. Sam shrugged his shoulders and moved swiftly toward the stand-off scene by the coffin. Wendel and Richard Barone watched in silence.

At midnight on the near North Side of the city the park that filled the block in front of the Newberry Library was almost empty. Fallen leaves scuffed along the intersecting sidewalks and a few young men, their hands shoved into their jacket pockets against the icebox-cold night, loitered near the corner where Walton and Clark streets met. Bughouse Square was the center for young homosexuals on the lookout for someone to sell themselves to for the night. Cars cruised by slowly, their drivers trying to get a look at the kind of meat that was on the hoof, the drill that was as old as buggery itself.

A station wagon slowed down and pulled to the curb next to a slender young man in a leather jacket who moved a few steps toward the car and leaned down to listen as the window on the driver's side was lowered.

"Want a ride?"

The young man peered in but could only make out the outline of a man and see the glow of his cigarette.

"Twenty bucks," the young man said.

"Get in," the man in the darkened car answered, snapping the electric locks open. The youth in the leather jacket, glad to get in out of the cold and to make some money, hurried around and slipped into the front seat. The locks snapped again and the car eased around the corner and south onto Clark Street. Without saying a word to his new companion, the driver headed several blocks south, turned right into Ontario Street and in a few minutes was on the Kennedy Expressway that threaded north by northwest out of the city. The young man had been on dozens of rides like this one and, since the older man did not speak, he leaned back and dozed off.

He awoke as the automatic doors of a garage clattered down behind the car. They were in a house, God only knew where, but that was the nature of the business. Places and faces, names and addresses, they weren't important to either party. He yawned and looked at the driver who had just switched off the ignition and popped up the door locks. He was a sturdy young man, not much older than he was himself, and he was dressed in a navy pea jacket.

"This is home base," the driver said softly as they both swung out of the car. The pickup could see that the driver had a moustache and dark curly hair. He followed him up one step, through a door, and into the house. There were lights on and stereo music was playing softly. They passed through the kitchen and into a living room. The young man looked around the neat room as the older man took off his navy jacket and tossed it onto the couch. He loosened his own jacket and looked expectantly toward his host, who was lighting another cigarette.

"You come from Chicago?" the older man asked, blowing a jagged ring of smoke into the air.

"Naw," the younger man answered, "I'm from out of town." That was the answer he gave to all these fags. "I'd like the twenty in advance."

"Okay," the other man said, reaching into his pocket and pulling out a gold money clip wadded with bills. He removed a crisp new twenty, folded it paper-airplane style, and flipped it free so that it spiraled down to the floor. The young man stepped forward and bent down to get the money. Then he felt a crunching blow to the back of his head and dropped like a dead weight onto the nubby surface of the carpet.

7

Ann Marie was enraged by Paul Michael Martin's front-page story in *Eyes,* the sensationalizing newspaper that showed up at every check-out counter in Chicago on Friday afternoons. "Who Is This Woman?" the banner headline asked, above a picture of her and Mayor Cullen that had been taken just as he gave her a fatherly kiss after she accepted her City Council Award.

"Chicagoans are talking about Ann Marie O'Brien," it led off, "who, although admitting her lack of qualifications, recently accepted an appointment by Mayor Thomas H. Cullen to chair the powerful committee that will oversee the awarding of cable TV franchises in the city. The Mayor's wife has been dead for two years and some suggest that Mrs. O'Brien, whose own husband is still listed as missing in action, has proved to be an agreeable companion to him. A close observer of City Hall has told this reporter that the attractive Mrs. O'Brien heads a committee whose main job is to cover up a serious scandal in the city's initial negotiations with Ardi-Vision and other cable television companies . . ."

Ann Marie could have killed. Even Mayor Cullen, who laughed the story off, had to draw deeply from his stores of blarney to calm her down and to reassure her about the integrity of the commission she was heading.

"Annie," he said, "you know what Lincoln said, that if he read all the false stories written about him, he wouldn't have time to get any work done."

Ann Marie was not in a mood to be cajoled, even by the old prince of charm. "It's a lie, the whole thing is a lie. I can't shrug it off as easily as you can."

"Now, now, Annie," Cullen said soothingly, "the important thing is the wall you're going to build, that's what my mother used to say, not the mud somebody's going to sling against it. These fellows have been trying to get me for years. You know that. Why Franklin D. Roosevelt never used to read the newspapers for two weeks before every election. Said it would be too upsetting and he didn't want to lose sleep."

Ann Marie still could not smile. Her acceptance of public service had been greeted with a ferocious onslaught. How could she ever have fantasized that Martin might mean something to her, that he might be a savior lover? She could have killed him; she was not kidding about it at all. She would get him someday.

"Mister Mayor," she asked primly, "what about these charges, these innuendos, or whatever you want to call them, that there was something scandalous going on in the city's negotiations about cable television? This man Martin says the committee is a cover-up . . ."

Cullen put on his how-could-you-think-that-of-me look, which involved a rearrangement of his great thrust of Irish face into Basset hound folds. He didn't want Ann Marie O'Brien, who had become "Annie" to him over the weekend, looking into anything beyond the committee's surface charge—she was sharp-eyed enough to find something. He explained the need for her to be a strong executive and to push the work of the committee along. She was supposed to keep those bankers and educators focused on the bull's-eye, and not let them stray to the outer rim of the target. Her misgivings began to dissolve under the tide of the Mayor's reassurances.

"Now, Annie, to avoid political implications to this work, you ought to get started right away. Before Thanksgiving. You see the party'll do its slating for offices the week before Christmas and it would be good if you could get the commission to finish the work before that happens. It'll guarantee that there's no connection between what you're doing on the commission and the upcoming political campaign."

"You mean, get this all finished before Christmas?" What would she do after it was finished? Was this brief term going to be the whole of her public service? Was she being used for a short season and turned out again just at the blues-laden holidays, to contemplate the boring stretch of another year in limbo?

"Now, Annie, I don't want you to think this is all I'll have for you to do. I know this will be a success and Mark and I'll have something new for you to take on right away. We're thinking of opening an office called 'The Neighborhood Advocate.' That might be just right for you. But right now just get this commission to do its work."

Ann Marie's hesitation disintegrated under the magic dusting of the Mayor's words. She would not question him further about the matter. She would get the job done and she wouldn't let the professors hold things up in the process.

"One thing, Annie," the Mayor said, "or maybe two other things." Ann Marie, who was organizing her purse in preparation for leaving, became attentive again. "Follow what Mark Richler tells you about handling the press. He knows how these things should be done."

She nodded. She liked Richler, who had already been very helpful to her. He was unassuming and always got right to the point.

"And there's one other thing. I'd like you to do me a favor this morning. I'd like you to accept a picture for me that some old artist has painted. It's of me and Mrs. Cullen. I just don't feel up to doing it. It will only take a few minutes and you won't have to say anything. All you have to do is say that you're representing me and thank them. Do you mind?"

Ann Marie did not mind at all. It gave her a feeling she liked, a part of his family feeling. It was the kind of thing an old man would ask a daughter to do.

"I'll be glad to," she answered. "When is it?"

"Well," and the old man grinned apologetically, "it's actually the next thing on my schedule. So if you can wait here, I'll just slip out the other way. You can leave when you're done. It won't take long."

After the Mayor stepped out of the office it seemed quite empty. Ann Marie wandered behind his desk. This was his view of the world flooding through his office door. Standing behind his chair, she imagined all the politicians, dignitaries, and presidential hopefuls who had sat there during the years that Cullen had been in office. She ran her fingers down its leather back, liking the sensuous feel of the place where Cullen had rested, sensing some communication of his presence rising off the smooth surface. She slipped around and sat down in the chair, enjoying the feeling that she had broken some unspoken rule by doing so. Would Cullen come back later in the day and ask, "Who's been sitting in my chair?" Would he laugh, the way a father might at finding his daughter in such a position? Would he be delighted with her and hug her as he picked her up and placed her on the edge of the desk? Or would he be angry, displeased at what she had done, and would he tell her never to do it again? She closed her eyes and settled back, letting her fantasy build like a great summer cloud within her.

Then the office door opened and Helen Morrison poked her head in. Ann Marie bolted upright.

"Mrs. O'Brien," she said in tones from which all possibility of surprise had been wrung years before, "the Korchows are here with the picture. Shall I bring them in?"

"Yes, yes," Ann Marie said quickly, as she rose from the Mayor's chair and came around the desk and toward the door.

Cap Malloy entered carrying a large package wrapped in brown paper. Then a bulkily built man and woman trundled through the doorway like great freight cars easing over a difficult part of the track. The man, who had long springy white hair, wore a flowing black tie at the neck of an unpressed shirt. The woman had the flat gray hair and the puffy face of the wives of Russian premiers. Cap Malloy breathed heavily as he lowered the package to the floor.

"So vere is he?" the old man asked of nobody in particular. "Vere is da Mare?" He moved toward the desk as though he expected to find Cullen crouched underneath it. Ann Marie stepped sideways and blocked his path. "I'm Mrs. O'Brien. I'm representing him," she said nervously.

While she ran uneasy interference with the old man, the woman unwrapped a huge framed canvas. An official city photographer came in the room and stood next to Cap Malloy, who was still getting his breath. Helen Morrison, who had been through a thousand drills like this with everybody from Boy Scouts to Chinese acrobatic teams, moved with an air of relief out of the Mayor's office.

"Who are you? You're not da Mare, da Mare who said he would see me, Igor Korchow, yes, and my wife, vere is he?"

Cap Malloy opened his mouth to speak, but Ann Marie cut him off.

"He's been detained at an important meeting," she said hurriedly, hardly noticing how easily she had shifted into the argot of mistruth that was practically the mother tongue in City Hall. She was more aware of the fact that Mayor Cullen had stuck her with a couple of looneybirds who had apparently been hounding him for this moment of presentation. She was a surrogate daughter all right, for a daddy who had pulled a fast one on her, the same way her own father had once done, leaving her with the crazy relatives while he went out to play golf.

"Ve have letter," Korchow said, waving one in the air. Ann Marie grabbed it just as Mrs. Korchow, a small smile of achievement curling itself into place, tore the last paper off the painting. The Mayor's face was a sunset-in-the-Keys color; and above his wife's head a small aureole of gold shone brightly.

"A lovely pitcher," Cap observed while Ann Marie studied the document.

"This letter just invites you to the Mayor's office. It doesn't say anything about the Mayor being here," she quickly improvised, pointing to the paper as Korchow looked quizzically down at the words.

"Ve could hang it. I haf some nails. Dere, over dere," he said, pointing to the wall behind the Mayor's desk as though it were a newfound continent. Cap Malloy was absorbed in studying the painting.

"No, no," Ann Marie said, cutting Korchow off again. "You need a permit for that. A permit from the Building Office." She marveled at how well she was putting together a story to repel this invader.

"You got hammer?" he asked as Mrs. Korchow pushed the canvas across the carpet toward the wall.

"You got permit?" Ann Marie asked Korchow, doing a fairly good imitation of the painter. Korchow blinked at her.

"No permit," Ann Marie said firmly, "no hang picture. You get your picture *taken*. But no *hang* it. *Understand?*" She would show Cullen that she could handle blue ribbon committees and nutty artists, too. She would show him, as she used to show her father, that she could take on the challenges that he would lead her into accepting.

Korchow's voice contained a thousand years of Middle European resignation.

"No hang?"

Ann Marie shook her head vigorously. "No hang. I'm sorry, Mr. Korchow. You can leave the picture. Mayor Cullen will be glad to have it, but you can't hang it. Now let's get the photo taken . . ."

She posed Cap Malloy, a grinning Korchow on each side of him, behind the painting and instructed the photographer to get his work done swiftly. The Korchows beamed and Cap maintained a dignified look as the photographer flashed away.

"Cap," Ann Marie said as though she had often given him orders, "please see Mr. and Mrs. Korchow out. All the way out."

Cap nodded. "Just as you say, ma'am, just as you say." He propped the painting against the wall and escorted the Korchows out.

Was this an initiation rite? Ann Marie glanced back at the Mayor's chair and made a face at it. Then she collected her purse and walked toward the door. She turned and the primitive, brightly colored painting caught her eye again. Was Mayor Cullen smiling at her?

She heard the real Mayor's giggle. He was standing by the partially open door from which he had made his exit before the Korchows arrived.

"Annie," Cullen said, gesturing for her to come back and sit down, "you did get a great job . . ."

"Did you . . . ?"

"Only part of it, only part of it. I usually let Cap take care of these people. You'd be surprised how many busts and paintings and other souvenirs I've got in the attic. Well, I thought you'd enjoy it." He laughed again.

"Well," Ann Marie said, "*enjoy* isn't exactly the right word."

"I knew I was right about you," Cullen said as he regained his composure. "I knew that you could take charge."

Ann Marie felt flattered. The incident had drawn her closer to the old man and made her regard him more warmly. She could not help herself.

"Was this a test to see how well I would do?"

"No, no," Cullen answered, "it just kind of came up. Cap would have hemmed and hawed and had them here for half an hour. I've been ducking that artist for years." Cullen straightened his tie. "I got a kick out of what you did. And all in five minutes. That's the same kind of speed we need with the blue ribbon committee."

Ann Marie smiled. "If I'm in charge, I'll run things."

"Good, good," the Mayor said as he picked up his phone. "Helen, have somebody come in and get this picture out of here." As he put the phone down he looked across at Ann Marie. "You go down and talk to Mark Richler now. Okay? And keep in touch."

Ann Marie smiled, feeling that she had won a mixture of paternal and governmental approval. In a building in which she had felt like a stranger the week before, she now felt quite at home. She said her good-bye and as the old Mayor gallantly rose she smiled over her shoulder and walked toward the door.

Cullen watched her depart. She was a nice girl and he had been right to trust the instincts of his innards. She would, whether she knew it or not, finally make the recommendations that would please him.

8

Ann Marie convened her committee on the Monday after Thanksgiving, using space at the Bismarck Hotel, which was only across the street from City Hall. The other members of the committee were pleasant enough, although the college president was a colossal fussbudget about the matters that they had to review. Ann Marie began to understand what Cullen meant when he spoke of "the do-gooders who undo the good" in city government. She let the educator talk as much as he wanted so that he could never complain that he hadn't been able to get his views expressed. In another week they would finish the preliminary sorting out of the proposals that had been forwarded from several production companies, newspaper organizations, and the other groups that wanted at least a strand of the available cable franchises that the city would grant some time early in the new year.

As the days of discussion proceeded, Ann Marie enjoyed being in charge but was bored by the details that dangled like Christmas decorations from the tree of proposals set before them. She was half-glad that the banker Franklin Barnes was obsessive enough to immerse himself in the fine points. She could listen to him instead of plowing through everything herself.

She was walking back to City Hall on Wednesday afternoon for a meeting with Mark Richler when Alex Wendel hailed her as though he had accidentally run into her, which, of course, he had not.

"Madam Chairman," he said, turning on a first-class undertaker's smile, "I hope everything is going well with your work."

Ann Marie had only spoken to Wendel on the afternoon of the press conference when he had announced that he would introduce the ordinance that would establish her committee. She still knew nothing of his previous negotiations with Ardi-Vision or of his frustrated attempt to force the Mayor to grant him additional power in the cable matter. Ann Marie had heard that Wendel was ambitious and tough and she liked his erotic swagger as well as the fact that, although it was a brisk day near the end of November, he wore a well-styled brown three-piece suit and no overcoat.

"Things are going fine," she answered. "There's a lot to it."

"Yes," Wendel said as he moved into step beside her. "We should talk about your present work," he said as they turned the corner onto LaSalle Street.

"What's that?" Ann Marie asked, lowering her head into the gusting wind.

"Well, I was chairman of the original City Council subcommittee. I have a lot of background you might find helpful. Would you like a cup of coffee?"

Ann Marie glanced at her watch. Richler was waiting for her. "Fine," she answered brightly.

"Let's go in here," Wendel said, turning graciously and making a slight bow toward a restaurant that was almost directly across from the entrance to City Hall.

After they had ordered their coffee, Wendel smiled. It made Ann Marie uneasy.

"Mrs. O'Brien, you've never dealt with the Mayor before, have you?"

Ann Marie stared at him, sipped her coffee, and said nothing.

"He's quite a guy," Wendel said, laughing like a man recalling a brush with death. "I've watched him for years now. What I think you ought to know is that people are beginning to take these stories by Paul Michael Martin seriously. You know what Goebbels used to say about throwing enough mud . . ."

"You don't believe . . ."

"No, no," Wendel answered airily. "Hell, I know you're not the Mayor's mistress." He let the word hang in the air.

Ann Marie forced herself to remain silent.

"But, seeing that you're in this sensitive position, heading a committee that will make final recommendations directly to the Mayor himself, well, I just thought you should know what the talk is."

"It's filthy talk and it's not true."

"You can't afford to be labeled as his patsy, as the woman he controls. That's what I'm trying to tell you. All you know is the gospel according to Cullen. He's your patron. You ought to get to know some other people in this town and in this party."

"I'm not in politics, Mr. Wendel. You seem to forget that."

"The hell you're not. That's what I mean about how you need a wider outlook. Do you think Cullen picked you just because you're young and pretty? Cullen picked you because he could run you. He'd rather run you than lay you any day, do you understand that?"

Ann Marie started to rise. Wendel reached over and took her arm.

"Excuse me, lady," he said smoothly. "Now just hear me out. You may very well stay in politics. Knowing Cullen, I'm sure he's got something in mind for you. So you ought to know more than I think you do. It's true, isn't it, that your whole political education has come from just the fifth floor of City Hall?"

"I suppose so," Ann Marie said, settling back uneasily in her chair. There was an irritating grain of truth in his statements—just a grain. Dammit, she had to be loyal to Cullen.

"I thought so," Wendel said as he broke open a packet of sugar and let its contents drop into his coffee. "Martin knows very well the Mayor didn't appoint you out of the blue or because he intended to leave this entire business of issuing cable franchises to your committee. You may not know it, lady, and you may not feel it yet, but Cullen's got you in the palm of his hand. You'll end up doing just what he wants, don't you know that?" He raised a hand to fend off any response from Ann Marie.

"Listen, for Crissake, I like you. I don't want to see you get a terrible surprise someday. Like the one the old man gave you when he let you handle that crazy painter last week. That one went all over the Hall fast. People were laughing like hell at you. You didn't know that, did you?"

"Unless you've got more to say, Mr. Wendel, I've got a meeting to go to."

"Probably with Richler. Right?"

Ann Marie did get up this time. "I think I've had enough advice for today, Mr. Wendel." She dug into her pocketbook, pulled a dollar bill out and dropped it on the table. "Here's for the coffee. I wouldn't want anybody spreading rumors that you were spending money on me."

Wendel smiled up at her.

"You're mad, Jesus, I can see that you're mad, lady. You know I'm telling you the truth. That's what gets you, isn't it? You know the Mayor is a master at using people and right now he's using you. But you're so stuck on him you can't let yourself admit it." He dropped another dollar on the table and stood up.

"You ought to be glad there's somebody else watching out for you." Wendel kept at her side as she moved, without looking at him, toward the door.

"Lady, you're going to need friends one of these days. You'll see. You'll be glad to know Alex Wendel when the times comes."

She went through the door without saying a word and marched directly across the street and into City Hall. Wendel stood on the sidewalk laughing as he watched her disappear through the glass entry doors.

Mark Richler sat in his shirt-sleeves behind a large cluttered desk. His tortoiseshell glasses were propped high on his forehead. Without a word of welcome, he handed a sheet of newspaper to Ann Marie as she came into his office on the fourth floor of City Hall.

"This is an advance proof of Martin's front page of the next issue of

Eyes," Richler said with the calmness of a man who understood that part of his daily job was damage control. "Did you ever speak to this Martin?" he asked as Ann Marie began to read the story. She did not answer as she stood, with her coat on and her handbag dangling from her arm, scanning the proof sheet. Its banner headline read, "Mrs. O'Brien's Secret Role in City Hall."

It embroidered the story of the Korchows and their painting with several quotes from them and additional quotes attributed to Ann Marie herself. It was all insinuation, but Martin left the impression that Ann Marie O'Brien acted as Mayor Cullen's hostess, that she had assumed the duties of the "first lady" in City Hall, and that this seemed to prove that she had a relationship of intimacy with Cullen. The story alleged that Ann Marie had blocked the hanging of a painting of Cullen's late wife because she wanted no memory of her around City Hall. "Is Mrs. O'Brien in charge?" the story concluded. "An exclusive interview in the next issue of *Eyes.*"

Ann Marie felt slightly dizzy. She was angry and confused about the obvious lies and the gross suggestions of the story. She handed the paper back to Richler. "Can't you stop that? Can't you do something about it?" Her voice was tense with irritation.

"Now, now," Richler said, "sit down and we'll talk about this." He popped a cigarette into his mouth as he waved toward a leather chair by the side of his desk.

"Did you ever give an interview to this Martin? Ever talk to him about this?" Richler asked dryly.

"No, never. I try to avoid the man."

"Good." Richler lighted a cigarette. "Good, leave it that way."

"Can't we get him to print a retraction? Can't you get him to withdraw this? I mean, it's only Wednesday. The paper doesn't come out until Friday."

"I know that. But in this business you've got to remember something. If you don't respond to a story that's false, it'll die right away. If you get involved, especially ahead of time, you'll just make people curious, and you'll repeat the charges. You'll also make them wonder how much truth is in it. Nothing helps a false story more than honest people trying to explain themselves. It can't be done. Not even a saint could do it. It just gets you in deeper."

"Are you saying that we can't do anything about this?"

"No. There's plenty we could do. What I'm saying is there's nothing that we're going to do. Open yourself up to questions about this and the press'll really murder you. Just give them a chance to ask you a question about the Mayor's wife. There's no way you can give an answer without leaving yourself wide open to a lot of meanings that aren't there. What I'm saying is that we make no response, especially not ahead of time.

And if anybody asks you about it, just say, 'This is a new low in gutter accusations.' That's all. I promise, it'll blow over in a few days."

"But these are lies. That's not the way it happened at all."

Richler exhaled smoke and his tone turned philosophical. "Face it, Mrs. O'Brien. Some of these reporters are trying to get at the Mayor. It's the favorite sport in this town. You take the bait and start defending the Mayor and Martin'll have you in deeper."

He paused, flicked an ash from his cigarette, and leaned back in his chair. "I know you feel offended. The Mayor is boiling too. Hell, I've been restraining him for the last hour. But, underneath, he knows the right thing is to ignore this." He pointed to the page proof that was now spread out on his desk. "If we don't say anything, they may not go with this on Friday. They may pull it. They didn't send us an advance proof to help us with our side of the story. They want us to react, to overreact if possible. Martin wants to provoke you into giving him that 'exclusive interview' he promises for next week."

Ann Marie felt a little better after Richler had finished talking. She could be tight-lipped.

"There's a lot of people resent you, you know that, don't you?" Richler asked.

"I'm beginning to find that out. And I haven't done anything to any of them."

"You don't have to," Richler responded. "This is their business. You're important because so many people are interested in cable TV. Getting Cullen's scalp would be the biggest thing they could do, bigger than finding a cure for cancer. News, Mrs. O'Brien, is essentially negative. That's its nature. And Martin has just papered something together here to get your goat. It'll blow away, if we let it."

Ann Marie liked Richler. There was something disinterested and objective about him. Maybe it was because he was an outsider, a Jewish observer inside the walls of an Irish Catholic government.

"Mark," she asked, "what kind of man *is* the Mayor anyway?"

Richler pulled on his cigarette and flipped his glasses down from his forehead. "That's a big subject, Mrs. O'Brien," he said good-humoredly. "He's one of the most unusual men I've ever met."

"Does he really control everything in this city? Is that part true?"

"Somebody has to," Richler responded, hunching his shoulders as he leaned forward on his elbows. "Let's put it this way. He's used to being in charge. That's been his way of life. He doesn't think about it when he gets up in the morning. That's because when he gets up in the morning, he is in charge, the same as when he went to bed the night before. It's a habit. Being in charge is a habit."

"Mark," Ann Marie asked almost plaintively, "is he trying to control me too, me and the committee?"

Richler paused and drew on his cigarette.

"Let's put it this way, Mrs. O'Brien. He appointed you. You accepted. The committee is to report its recommendations to him. That's in the ordinance. There's nobody else to report to." Richler smiled and quashed his cigarette in his desk ashtray. "Does that sound like control?"

Ann Marie knew that Richler would not go beyond this enigmatic statement. She was not entirely sure of what to make of what he had said. She thought of Wendel and of what he had said. She decided to put the whole thing out of her mind. She was doing her job. She liked the Mayor. Thinking more about him was like trying to think about Charlie out in the jungle. She could only take so much of it on any one day. Right now she wanted to like Mayor Cullen. Right now she couldn't let herself think about anything that might make her change her opinion.

9

*R*ichler had been right about *Eyes*. They went with their story that first Friday of the last month of the year but they had dropped some of the innuendos and cut out the promise of an interview with Ann Marie, or A.M., as she was getting to be called around the Hall. She had followed Richler's advice, stayed out of places where reporters might surprise her, and refused to return any of Paul Michael Martin's phone calls. The story sputtered and died. Martin kept digging but he wasn't able to come up with anything but a rehash of the charges he had already made. His editor at the paper told him to develop a new angle or change the subject. And his television producer, under pressure from the bank that sponsored him, suggested that he comment on something else besides Ann Marie and cable television.

Ann Marie could honestly tell herself that Thomas Cullen had never made one suggestion about any of the applications that had been reviewed by the committee. So much, she thought, for the rumors that he controlled her. She had parlayed the banker's stupefying attention to detail and her own ability to scan and quickly get the gist of things into an effective chairing of the committee's work. Now it was all done except for a day of public hearings, and Ann Marie felt exhilaration and depression alternately. She looked forward to the official windup of the committee's labors but she held her breath about her own future. The old Mayor had said that he would come up with something, but she hadn't talked to or seen him in days. Maybe he had grown wary of her after Paul Michael Martin had made his commentaries and published his articles. Maybe she would start the new year the way she had started so many, waiting for something or someone to turn up, Charlie out of the jungle, the Mayor out of his office with a Christmas present of a job, something, somebody, anybody . . .

Had she played the Mayor wrong? Was there some unspoken expectation that she would let Cullen have his say before the committee wrapped up its work? Men always wanted something, no matter what they said. Was that true of Cullen too? It made her depressed and anxious to think that, in the explosion of events that had brought her so swiftly into the eye of the public, she might have missed a signal that the Mayor had expected her to catch. She shook her head and got herself under control. She had been through a lot. She would get through this too.

Ann Marie felt that she had been on the right track, if only because Wendel, who was obviously no friend of the Mayor's, had been putting so much pressure on her to give Ardi-Vision the first place all by itself. He had called her a couple of times and Sam Noto had asked to see her, "to fill her in," as he said on the phone. When he arrived, however, it was more of the same kind of stuff she had heard from Wendel. The old Mayor was using her whether she knew it or not. She ought to take their advice. They could be very helpful to her. Did she want everybody in the city saying she was Cullen's whore? Noto had, however, started her worrying about the whole process again. Ardi-Vision seemed a reputable firm without all this extra pushing. Why? Everything seemed in order. And yet . . .

At the hearings themselves Ann Marie worked out the last wrinkle of doubt. She did it, as she did many things, by accident. The hearings were not supposed to add anything to what the committee had already learned by studying the written proposals. *Pro forma* all the way, window dressing to guarantee the public nature of the deliberations, the wrap-up before the reports went to the Mayor.

The witnesses were generally dull and Ann Marie shifted uncomfortably in her chair. All this talk about numbers, on-line projections, and subsidiary rights generated little drama. She glanced across the room as Paul Michael Martin swaggered in. He was not bad-looking, not bad at all. He was certainly more interesting to look at than the current witness, the wizened accountant for Spectrama, Inc., who kept unfolding long sheets of paper, scraping the microphone as he did so.

"Could you move those materials back a little?" Ann Marie asked, schoolmarm-direct.

"Yes'm," the accountant answered. "It's just that the projected cash flow charts are so important."

"We'll take your word for it," Ann Marie shot back. The witness, Uriah Heep to comply, dropped all his papers on the floor. Everyone laughed, including Ann Marie.

"I have just one more section to go," the beleaguered accountant called out as he dipped below desk level to retrieve his documents.

"Fine," Ann Marie answered. "You go right ahead."

Paul Michael Martin smiled at her. Not hostile, not testing, just a human smile inspired by the bungling accountant. Ann Marie smiled back and looked down as the witness rattled off his last projections. Martin seemed different. For the moment at least, he was not the hunter. She looked up again. He nodded slightly and their eyes held each other's briefly. An interval of peace in what had been a running war between them, a truce over the head of the droning accountant, a shared sense of incongruity at the ways of bureaucracies. Maybe he wasn't so bad, maybe there was something there after all. The witness, noisily rolling up his charts, thanked the chairperson for her time. Ann Marie and Martin relaxed their grip on each other's attention.

"Thank you, Mr. Kaufmann," Ann Marie said matter-of-factly. "Our next witness will be Mr. Garrison Curtiss. From Ardi-Vision, is that right?"

"Yes, Madam Chairman," answered the velvet smooth-looking man who had just slipped into the chair vacated by the accountant. He placed a Hartmann leather briefcase on the table, snapped it open, and removed a manila folder.

"Mr. Barnes," Ann Marie asked, turning slightly toward her fellow commission member, "do you want to begin the questioning?"

The banker nodded and cleared his throat. "Just a few questions, Mr. Curtiss . . ."

P. M. Martin smiled at Ann Marie. The hint of an invitation this time. We could be friends. You're a good-looking woman. You can't give up on life just because your husband is missing. Come on. Don't be mad at me. I'm a nice guy, really I am . . .

A.M. looked at him steadily. She got the message. Oh, Christ, I can't do this. Charlie, Charlie . . .

"We're looking into that," Garrison Curtiss said sonorously. "We have plans for special educational services to the school systems. That, I might add, is one of our distinctive features . . ."

God, another boring witness. But smooth. Ardi-Vision. Wendel and Noto interested in special features for the schools? God, this is dull.

"Our investors want to make a special commitment to education . . ."

Wendel and Noto pushing education? Something was out of synch here. Ardi-Vision was not a nonprofit operation, not with those two aldermen endorsing it. A.M. looked more carefully at the witness, a $250-an-hour lawyer in a $500 suit. Franklin Barnes finished his questions and thanked the witness. Curtiss slipped his folder back into the Hartmann case.

"One moment, Mr. Curtiss," Ann Marie said, picking up a yellow wooden pencil and pulling a pad of paper closer to her. "I'd like to ask a question. Or maybe two." She was flying by instinct. Something wasn't quite right here. Ardi-Vision made itself sound like the Peace Corps and the Salvation Army rolled into one. Curtiss smiled blandly and sat back in his chair. Ann Marie didn't like the slightly imperious way in which he relaxed. She didn't like his expensive attaché case either.

"Mr. Curtiss, Ardi-Vision is in this to make money, isn't it?"

"Ardi-Vision is interested in providing a service to the people of Chicago."

"At a price."

"Service, Madam Chairman, of genuine value. It would be hard to put a price on real value."

"Service of value, then, at a profit."

"Our investors must expect some return on what they are doing for culture and entertainment, for broadening the public's right to choose their own programming. And, as I've mentioned, a contribution to education, a unique contribution."

Curtiss was as slick as he looked. Ann Marie touched the pencil to her cheek and looked intently at him.

"Your investors, yes, of course." Then, quite by accident, Ann Marie asked the right question. "Just who are your investors?"

Silence from the smooth lawyer. A slight stir of interest in the hearing room.

"Perhaps you didn't hear me, Mr. Curtiss. Who are your investors?"

"I do not feel that private investors should have their names revealed at a public hearing of this nature, Madam Chairman. We are here to discuss the technical aspects of our propositions and the nature and scope of the services we are prepared to offer." Curtiss hadn't even blinked but something had changed in the atmosphere. It had become absolutely quiet. Paul Martin pulled his notebook from his pocket.

"Mr. Curtiss, the committee would like to know the names of your investors." Ann Marie accented her words by jabbing the pencil in the air. "Surely they have nothing to hide."

The television crew that had yawned through the hearings came to life as unexpected tension bubbled out of the flatness of the afternoon's testimony. Their lights went on as they panned back and forth between the urbane witness and the sharply inquisitive chairwoman.

"It does not seem to be within the purview of your committee," Curtiss answered through a fake smile.

Ann Marie glanced at Franklin Barnes. A perfect blank. God only knew what he was thinking. He was not wearing his your-loan-is-approved face, however. Not at all.

"Mr. Curtiss, we understand your role as a spokesman for Ardi-Vision. But what can you expect to gain from keeping the names of your investors secret? The committee has every right to know these names before it makes its final recommendations. I'm asking you again. Please name your major investors."

"Madam, I'll do that in executive session. But not with reporters present. Not with cameras rolling."

"The reason for this commission, Mr. Curtiss, is to make sure the public knows what is going on. We do not have executive sessions. We would like that list of names."

Curtiss studied her carefully. This was impossible. This woman was causing enormous trouble over something that was none of her business. He smiled.

"I must respectfully decline to do so," he said with cold geniality, "as not being in the best interests of the firm I represent."

"And it is in the best interests of the City of Chicago for us to find out."

"May we have a brief recess?"

"Not until you answer the question."

"Madam, I only want the recess in order to try to get the information you have requested. I do not think that is asking too much."

"How much time will you need? We planned to conclude these hearings today."

"It's hard to say. I want to discuss this with those whose interests I represent."

"Do you know their names?"

Curtiss stared back at her unsmilingly.

"Mr. Curtiss, certainly you can answer that question." Ann Marie didn't know exactly what she was driving at. A fine instinct for the jugular moved her forward. Curtiss looked less comfortable than he had before.

"Madam Chairman, there is no need to pursue this in this fashion. We are entirely cooperative. But surely you must understand my position."

"I understand it perfectly. You came here to answer questions for us. You came here to convince us that your firm is the best one to handle cable franchise in this city. In not answering the question, you raise doubts about Ardi-Vision."

"Madam, a recess would be helpful."

"Maybe to Ardi-Vision, but not to this commission. Who is behind your company? Can you tell us that?"

"I will submit a full statement on that if you give me some time to prepare it."

"One hour recess," Ann Marie declared. "No more, no less."

The room exploded as Curtiss pulled back his chair, picked up his bag, and turned to leave the room. He was besieged by reporters as he struggled toward the door. Paul Martin ignored him, heading instead for Ann Marie.

"What have you got on this guy?" he asked, smiling broadly.

Ann Marie ignored his question and turned to Franklin Barnes. Martin stepped closer to the table, his notebook flopped open in his left hand. Barnes whispered something in Ann Marie's ear and they both rose to leave the room. Other commission members did the same. An air of puzzled expectation lifted off them. They had stumbled onto something. But what was it? Martin tagged along behind Ann Marie.

"Mrs. O'Brien, would you comment on Mr. Curtiss's refusal to name the investors in Ardi-Vision?"

Ann Marie paused by the door. Curtiss had left the room, and the television crew and the other reporters turned their attention toward her. She waited while they shifted their cameras into position.

"If Ardi-Vision has nothing to hide, they can tell us the truth. That's what we expect to hear when Mr. Curtiss returns. That's all I have to say now."

She turned her back on the crowding reporters and left the room.

"What the hell's the matter with you? You're a lawyer, for Crissake. We didn't hire you to get us publicity."

Garrison Curtiss held the telephone away from his ear. It had been hard enough to find a quiet office in which to make some phone calls. The reporters were outside waiting for him. He didn't need Sam Noto yelling at him.

"Sam, this woman is one-track. I can't put her off. She's made so much of this now, there's bound to be a follow-up. I can't very well deny that Calco has 51 percent of Ardi-Vision. And if I mention that, she'll want to know who owns Calco. Do you want to come down and testify yourself about who owns it?"

"Christ, I knew this whole goddamn thing was trouble. Never let a woman into things. Christ, I told Wendel this would never work . . ."

"Do your people want to have their names mentioned in connection with a cable franchise? Where will that lead? You may recall the advice I gave you about this a long time ago."

"Who the hell knew we'd have a blue ribbon commission? And who the hell knew where this woman was coming from?"

"Well, what do you want? Calco and the chance papers will call it a syndicate operation? Do you want that, or do we withdraw for the time being and try to work our way back in at some other level?"

There was a long pause while Noto thought about the situation. The last thing he could allow was public notoriety for the owners of Calco. That would not go down well with them. But neither would the idea of their losing the bid for cable. It was nonetheless the only choice possible in the circumstances.

"Take it out. That's all we can do. We'll get back in when this god-damn woman returns to her fucking missing soldiers. Make something up. Anything you fucking want. But keep Calco out of it. You understand?"

"Perfectly," Curtiss said as he made a notation with his pencil on the manila folder. "I'll cover it, don't worry. I'll make it an invasion-of-rights issue, totalitarianism versus free enterprise. It'll sound good. But your friends are out of the running this round. Blame the woman if you want, but this could have been structured differently."

"You just make like a lawyer on this. We'll worry about everything else."

It was Ann Marie about whom Sam Noto and his associates were worried. There would have to be a day of reckoning with this woman who had almost uncovered—by dumb luck or a witch's intuition—the very thing they wanted to conceal the most, the syndicate share in Ardi-Vision. Temporary retreat was their only option. But Ann Marie was a woman to be watched and dealt with sooner or later. She had scared them. And they couldn't make any loud protests. She had stirred the media up and even though Curtiss had withdrawn the Ardi-Vision application reporters all over town were digging through records and following up leads in some effort to trace the origins and financing of the cable company.

Cullen was delighted. Ann Marie, quite by accident, had done just what he wanted. She had made it easy for other companies to be given proper consideration. He knew very well the kind of companies Franklin Barnes would end up endorsing—that was why he had appointed him. And now Ann Marie had made it all easier. Wendel, Noto, and the others had been taught a lesson, at no cost to Cullen. They could be mad at Ann Marie but there was not much they could do about it. And Barnes, master of detail, had come through as Cullen expected.

He had known the stuffy old Wasp for years, and understood his thought processes better than Barnes did himself. Barnes was, in essence, a conservative crook who belonged to all the right clubs. He picked well-managed organizations with good credit ratings and with proof of previous cooperation with the city. He also knew which ones would do business with his bank. The committee, including Ann Marie, thought they made their selections all on their own. That was because its members were naïve in exactly the area where Barnes was wise: how things worked in the big city.

Ann Marie was just fine, Cullen thought, because she would always want to please him. Loyalty was everything in politics. She would be perfect for the next assignment he had in mind. Richler thought that Cullen would follow through and make her "The Neighborhood Advocate," a kind of ombudsman for complaints about garbage collection, broken streetlights, and potholes, just the kind of activities Mrs. O'Brien would be able to dramatize successfully. But Cullen had a surprise for Richler that afternoon. It was another of the Mayor's instinctive moves.

"Mark," Cullen said almost piously, "I'm going to have Mrs. O'Brien slotted for alderman in place of Matty Hogan."

"What?" Richler responded in a startled tone. "Alderman? I thought you were going to give her the neighborhood job . . ."

"We'll have to call her alderwoman," the Mayor said with a distracted smile, letting his decision roll around like wine inside his mouth.

"What about Hogan?" Richler asked in amazement. "He's been with you a long time. He's got a following up there."

"Don't worry about Hogan. He'll play ball. He's a professional." The Mayor smiled brightly. "The slating's next week, so I want a release on Hogan's retirement. And a dinner set up for him. A citation, everything first-class. We'll go with this day after tomorrow."

"But, Tom," Richler said, "Mrs. O'Brien has no real political experience. She's made a lot of headlines. But she made some enemies with that commission, too."

Cullen raised his hand. "Mark, you don't understand. She's got enough to get along. Hell, we've been looking for the right woman, you know that. We can't run somebody who looks like a librarian or one of those tough dames who's always complaining about women's rights. Nobody can complain about Annie . . ."

"Hogan certainly will. He's meant a lot to the party and to the city. Are you certain he won't make a stand and run for the nomination in the primary on his own? It's been done before."

"Mark, Matty has done very well by the city. And he won't be forgotten. How does *Judge* Hogan sound? He wouldn't be the worst man on the bench in Chicago, I'll tell you that. Close, but not the worst. We'll see if we can announce the judgeship when we put out the release. You can handle that. You've done it before. Besides, Hogan will much prefer being on the bench to standing in front of it. That could happen too."

"Day after tomorrow," Richler said, half to himself. "Does Mrs. O'Brien know about this yet?"

"No, Mark," Cullen replied, his elfin smile returning. "It will be better to get this cable TV report out, let that fill the papers tomorrow, and then announce her candidacy for Hogan's spot the next day. You always said not to use all the headlines up on one day."

Richler shook his head but could not refrain from smiling. Cullen was old and sometimes he did not seem well, but he was in top shape these days. Cullen was using power, exercising himself with it as though it were a barbell. No wonder he was in good spirits. Richler left the office as Cullen's phone rang.

Ann Marie was excited as she met for the last time with the members of the blue ribbon committee the next day in a hearing room in City Hall. In a few minutes they would go together to the press conference in the room off the Mayor's office to announce their recommendations. All the members, especially Barnes the banker, seemed delighted with the work they had accomplished. My, she had stirred things up with her questions! She looked at Franklin Barnes, this staid, dry man with the slightest of twinkles in his eyes, and thought well of herself for pushing him along so vigorously. They had worked well together and neither had any insight into the way the other really operated. They had both gotten what they had wanted.

"Ann Marie, Ann Marie." It was Aunt Molly, clutching Matthew by one hand, advancing through the crowded room. She was supposed to be waiting upstairs for the news conference. Ann Marie's heart stopped for a split second. There was something wrong. Something would always go wrong just when things started to go right. She involuntarily reached out and took her aunt's arm.

"What is it, Molly? Is it Charlie?"

Molly nodded, biting at her lip. Matthew looked up at his great-aunt and his mother, his eyes wide in anticipation of whatever it was that had disturbed first Molly and now his mother.

"We were downstairs waiting. With the Monsignor. And a call came through to the Mayor's secretary. It was for you and it was from the government . . ."

"Yes? What, for God's sake, Molly, what was it about?"

"It was a Mr. Potter and there's a number he wants you to call. He says they've just been notified that there are some remains being returned. It wasn't expected. That's what he said, it wasn't expected, nobody had any idea. And they think maybe Charlie is one of them . . ."

"Daddy?" Matthew asked. "Is Daddy coming home?"

Ann Marie stood perfectly still, her mouth partly open. She could hear the conversation around her but, for the moment, she could make no sense of it. Charlie's coming home. That's all she could think of, Charlie's coming home for Christmas. She took a deep breath as a void swelled open within her, pressing against her heart and lungs. She leaned down toward her son and kissed him on the forehead. She could hardly breathe as she spoke to him. "Yes, Daddy's coming home, Matthew, Daddy's coming home at last."

"Here's the number you're to call, Ann. It's in Washington." Molly reached toward Ann Marie the way she had so often when she had been a child, the way she had when the news first came that Charlie was missing. Ann Marie pulled back and squared her shoulders. So intense and subdued had their conversation been that they had not disrupted the flow of talk around them. Nobody seemed to notice, Ann Marie thought to herself, that our little world just caved in on us.

Everything was ending, the committee, the year, her hopes for Charlie. She remembered the stories her father used to tell her about the Irish Catholics who had lain starving in the holds of ships with only the toughest living through it. The Irish as survivors, that's what her father had always talked about. She was a survivor; she had always expected Charlie to survive too. But Charlie was dead. The committee members milling about her froze into grotesque shapes, like disintegrating memorials for a life that had almost become normal for her. She was a survivor too, goddammit, and she would survive this, she would survive whatever life threw at her . . .

"Ann Marie, are you all right?" Molly asked apprehensively.

Ann Marie struggled to get back to the surface, to get out from under the weight of the drowning pool in which she had been submerged. If she could push herself just a little more, she would break the surface and find fresh air again. She exhaled and the crowd stirred into movement and noise around her. Charlie was dead, Charlie really was dead. Charlie was gristle and bone in the belly of a cargo plane high above the Pacific.

"What did you say, Molly?"

"You looked a little funny. Are you all right? Do you want to call that number? It was a Mr. Potter."

"Yes, yes," Ann Marie said deliberately, "I'll call. Let's see. You take Matthew and meet me up at the press conference."

"Are you going to go ahead—?" Molly broke off her question as she saw the rock-hard expression on Ann Marie's face.

"Of course, I'm going ahead. Charlie's dead. But we have to stay alive." She looked down at Matthew, who seemed confused. "Remember that, Matthew. Your father may be dead but you have to stay alive. You have to fight to stay alive."

Tears welled up in Matthew's eyes at the statement that his father was dead. Ann Marie bent down and hugged him. "Fight, Matthew, fight for life. That's what your daddy wants you to do. And Mommy has to too." She kissed him lightly on the forehead. "Now you go with Aunt Molly. Mommy will be with you in a few moments."

She turned to Molly, who had become weepy herself.

"Please, Molly, please, for all our sakes, don't break down now." Ann Marie's voice was remarkably controlled. "Take Matthew upstairs while I make this call. And don't mention this to anyone. Not to anyone. Okay?"

Molly nodded and, pressing Matthew's hand back into hers, led him through the gathering and out the door.

"Mrs. O'Brien," Franklin Barnes asked, "is there something wrong? I couldn't help noticing how intense you look." She must look terrible, she thought, for the dried-up banker to have noticed.

"It's nothing new," Ann Marie answered steadily. "I'm fine. I just have to make a call. I'll meet you up at the press conference." She turned from the banker and headed out of the room.

10

*A*nn Marie carried the press conference off in high style. Her face was a little flushed and she seemed tense but nothing out of line for such an occasion, especially since the great interrogator, Paul Michael Martin, sat in the front row of the reporters. When he asked for the specifications of the bids, Ann Marie rattled off a series of figures that she was surprised that she could remember. She drew on all her resources to maintain control, to get *this* job finished before she finished the job she had both dreaded and expected for four long years. Martin asked her another technical question about viewer projections and she handled that smoothly too. He was less hostile than he had been at the first news conference. He was giving her a chance to prove she had the qualifications for the job; he smiled roguishly at her prompt and complete responses. This was an interesting woman.

"I'd like to thank the whole committee," Mayor Cullen said, stepping forward after the questions petered out, "for an outstanding job in making their recommendations to the administration. The whole city is grateful for this effort." He grinned. "I don't think we ever had a committee get its difficult and trying work done so fast. Maybe we should have women as the heads of all our committees." Cullen giggled and the reporters laughed and the news conference broke up on a mellow note. As Cullen turned to use the back door that led through the waiting room to his own office, Ann Marie touched him on the arm.

"Do you mind if I go out this way?" she asked in a low voice.

"A pleasure," the Mayor said, extending his arm in a gentleman's gesture. "You don't think that Martin fellow will think we're slipping off for the afternoon, do you?" Cullen asked playfully. He was mildly surprised when Ann Marie ignored him and moved swiftly through the door in front of him.

When they reached his office Ann Marie explained briefly about Charlie and of how she had called Mr. Potter at the State Department just before the conference. Charlie's remains would be flown into O'Hare Field the next afternoon. The government had made a positive identification. She would have a funeral Mass the next morning and Charlie would be buried at last.

Tears formed in the Mayor's eyes as he watched and listened to Ann Marie quickly recite these details. The sorrowful Catholic wife and mother, brave as the Blessed Virgin, and a good American whose husband had made the supreme sacrifice. Cullen felt a warm river of sentiment flow through his entrails. He put an arm on her shoulder and spoke in an almost inaudible voice.

"Annie, you're a brave girl. Can I do anything for you? We'll get a car and driver for you for the next several days."

"Can you have someone drive my aunt and Matthew home now? I've got to think a little." Her voice was clear, her face set with determination. She didn't really feel anything. Maybe her tears were used up long ago. Maybe she never had any. Ann Marie watched the old Mayor dab at his eyes with his handkerchief. That's one thing he can do for me. Let him find the tears, wherever they are. She felt dry, scoured out. She felt sure of Cullen's concern. God knew she needed it. She would like to have him hold her, care for her. But not right now.

"It's been a long wait for you, Annie, hasn't it?"

"Yes, yes, it has." She stepped closer to him, pecked a kiss at his ruddy face and pulled back. She would take advantage of the car and driver but right now she needed to be by herself. "Thank you," she said softly. "I think I'll walk a little before I go home."

"It's dark already," Cullen waved his arm toward the December night beyond his office windows. "Are you sure you'll be all right?"

"Yes, yes, I really will. I've known this would come. At the bottom of my heart, I always knew that this would come someday." She looked directly into the old Mayor's eyes. "I just didn't expect it to come at Christmas, that's all."

She turned quickly and exited through the side door of the Mayor's office. The great white-haired bear of a man watched her leave. He sighed and went to his desk and dialed Mark Richler's office.

"Mark, Mrs. O'Brien's husband's body has been found. It makes that job all the more important. We'll hold off announcing it for a few days." His feeling bad for Annie O'Brien had not clouded his practical political judgment. Pictures of her at the arrival of her husband's flag-draped remains would only enhance her already splendid image. Let the papers and the TV run with those for a few days. She would make a great successor to Matty Hogan . . .

Ann Marie decided to walk down the five flights from Cullen's office. The huge stairwells were not used very much and their atmosphere was quiet and church-like on this cold, shadowed evening. She was on her own, despite the week's excitement, despite the headlines, despite the fatherly interest of the Mayor. Even if he did give her a job, she would have to make good by herself, just as she had with the blue ribbon committee. But it was different now. Charlie wasn't wandering in the jungle. He had long ago disintegrated into a cage of ribs and dust. It was all over. So were the years that she had built on some kind of hope, the years whose activity had been fueled by anger, first at the enemy soldiers, then at the Army, then at life in general, and, finally, at Charlie himself. That was over too, she thought as she slowly descended the steps; she couldn't be mad at poor Charlie anymore. The anger had been there before Charlie disappeared; it had been there before she even met him. Now a stone had been rolled away from the tomb in which she had buried it. She didn't have to try not to be angry anymore.

"Hi, there." Paul Michael Martin was standing on the landing of the third floor, leaning on the wall as though he had been waiting for her. "I thought you might come down this way when I saw you duck into the Mayor's office."

Ann Marie had been through too much to be surprised at finding Martin. She walked slowly past him and turned to start down the steps to the second floor.

"Wait. Please," Martin said as he moved to catch up with her. "I just heard about your husband. I want to say I am sorry. Sorry I've been so tough on you, too. That was strictly business, nothing personal." They were halfway down the stairway to the next floor. Ann Marie gave him a quick sideways glance. Bars of shadow fell across his face, shifting with each downward step.

"Mrs. O'Brien, you've been through a lot." Martin touched her face with his right hand. She pulled back but did not object as they stepped onto the concrete quadrant of the second-floor landing. The light behind her spread a delicate aureole around her red hair.

"I really am sorry. I thought maybe you could use a cup of coffee. Maybe a drink." He looked directly into her eyes. "It's a cold night. Maybe it would be good to talk a little."

Ann Marie looked him up and down, appraising his sincerity. "Maybe," she said softly, lowering her eyes.

"There's a quiet place at the Bismarck. It's just across the street." His tone was first-date earnestness, almost boyish. Ann Marie nodded. He took her lightly by the arm and they walked silently down the remaining stairs to the ground floor. They huddled against the cold as they crossed LaSalle Street, the city a heaven of twinkling stars around them.

"Are you okay?" Martin asked. *"Really* okay?"

She nodded and they did not speak again until they had settled into the old-fashioned restaurant. People greeted each other and laughed all around them. Ann Marie studied the menu.

"I really am sorry. My father died in the Korean War. I never even saw him . . ."

Ann Marie studied his face. It seemed softened, not so brash and assertive as it had at news conferences. He was a kind of boy, mischievous, but he had known pain, too. Matthew would probably not remember his father either. Paul Michael Martin, the man who had said the worst things imaginable about her, now spoke gently. He reached across the table and put his hand on hers.

"May I call you Ann Marie?"

She bristled and pulled her hand back. Was this really happening?

"I'm sorry."

"No, it's okay. It's my name." She kept her hands in her lap.

"You're really quite a woman."

She began to cry softly.

"There, there, Mrs. O'Brien, there there." Martin rose and came halfway around the table to put his hands on her shoulders. She looked up at him but did not protest his comforting gesture.

"Maybe you ought to lie down for a while before you try to go home . . ."

She heaved a sigh, touched her eyes with her napkin, and gritted her teeth. She did not want to break down in public, not after all the waiting, not after she had given up on ever crying again.

Martin signaled the waiter, spoke a few words to him, and gently took Ann Marie on his arm and out of the restaurant. "My paper keeps a room here. You're welcome to use it." He spoke offhandedly, as though he were disinterested in her response.

"No, I think I'd better go home." She didn't want to go. Not yet, not back to that house that was so empty, not back to Charlie's ghost. She looked at Martin cautiously. He was trying to set her up. He only looked boyish. "Maybe just to freshen up."

"That's the idea," he said with a touch of gallantry. "I'll show you up. Here's the key."

In a few moments they were unlocking a room on the seventh floor.

"Seven eleven," Martin said lightly. "Lucky numbers." He snapped on the light and they entered a small well-worn suite. Two typewriters, with papers scattered on the floor around them, stood in the sitting room. A picture of Mayor Cullen, smiling through cracked nonglare glass, hung crookedly over the fake mantel.

"You can wash up in there." Ann Marie followed Martin's pointing hand with her eyes.

"I think I'd better . . ." She burst into tears and burrowed into Martin's arms. He looked down at her, patting her back. He looked like a man who had just won a prize and he didn't know what to do with it. Ann Marie shook and twisted. She didn't care about control anymore. She had to be rid of the misbegotten past.

"Oh, Charlie," she wailed as she pressed her head against Martin's chest. She sobbed and choked, gagging on her broken sentences, catching her words in her strangled efforts to breathe. Charlie—you—were—never—there—Charlie—you were dead—all—the—time—

Martin closed his arms tightly about her. He felt her slightness, the smallness of her bones, the delicacy of her shuddering body. She was firm, she was just the way he had imagined. Martin had wanted her since he had first seen her walking into the City Council Chamber. Now he hesitated. He had planned, even while offering his condolences, to get her up to this room, but he didn't know what to make of her. He had never been in a position like this before. Ann Marie pounded on his shoulders with her fists. He took them in his own hands and she looked up into his face. She heaved and bucked and finally caught her breath.

Martin kissed her full on the mouth and on the neck, on that wondrous silken neck he had examined so often from a distance. He kissed her on the throat and nuzzled down to kiss the tops of her breasts. Still, there was something different in this woman. She seemed passive and compliant, ready to yield everything to him. P.M. was getting what he wanted but not on the terms on which he usually operated. Ann Marie had the handful of trumps. This tough, beautiful woman was ready to go to bed without saying a word. But who was in charge here? He didn't seem to be running things . . .

Martin frowned and carried her into the next room. He stretched her out on the bed and sat on its edge. Her face was streaked, her eyes swollen. Why was he hesitating? There was some rock-hard strength there, some rumbling from depths he had never heard in a woman before. Had he ever listened? Had he ever had to before?

She scared him, by God, that's what it was. She scared him. She might have shark's teeth, she might eat him alive . . .

Ann Marie pulled Martin down toward her. She kissed him searchingly, intensely, as though she were trying to find something. She loosened his tie, snapped it out of his collar and slapped it against the bedboard as she pulled it free. He fumbled with his shirt, standing up to complete his undressing. He edged back toward a chair, stepping out of his pants as he did. Ann Marie slipped off the bed and piled her clothes quickly on the dresser beside it. Martin watched her as he tossed his undershorts onto the chair. She was just as gorgeous as he had expected.

He climbed into the bed and Ann Marie pulled him close. She kissed him from head to toe, nuzzling and fondling him, rubbing her hands on his sides and chest, rubbing her own body, leopard-like, along his. She pummeled him, turned him over, kissed his back and his neck, twisted her hands in his thick black hair. She pushed him to turn onto his back

and lay down beside him. Full of wonder and uncertainty, Martin stared
at the ceiling. She pulled at his arm and he moved on top of her.

It was sensational and yet Martin was not sure of what had happened.
He had started out in charge, he had planned the scene. It was supposed
to go the way they always did. He glanced at her. She had never spoken
a word. Still hadn't. But she had certainly taken him for a ride. Christ Almighty, was she in training for the Olympics? Still, she had a beautiful
body. She was good, very good indeed. But she had worked something
out on him and kept him on the outside of it. He sat up, leaned down
and picked up his cigarettes from where they had fallen. He struck a
match, lighted one, and sat back on the bed.

Ann Marie looked at Martin's muscular back. She pulled herself up on
one arm and looked around the room. Martin's clothes were jumbled on
the nearby chair, his pants, a handful of change scattered out from one
of the pockets, were lumpy tracks in the middle of the carpet. She
looked to the dresser where she had piled her own clothes. Her slip
shimmied down the side and onto the floor. From the next room Mayor
Cullen looked almost directly at them through the crescent-shaped break
in the dull glass of the framed picture. She stood up, retrieved her slip
from the floor, took her clothes in her arms and stepped toward the
bathroom. Martin shifted himself to watch her. He raised his eyebrows
expectantly as she looked at him.

Ann Marie reached a free hand out from beneath her jumble of
clothes and wigwagged, *mezzo-mezzo*. She closed the bathroom door
behind her. Martin sucked deeply on his cigarette. Why the hell had he
wanted an opinion? Martin could hear the shower running. A few minutes later Ann Marie emerged fully clothed from the room.

"You're a goddamned wildcat, lady . . ." She leaned forward, kissed
him on the cheek, then turned and picked up the wool winter coat she
had draped over a chair. Martin rose and followed her into the sitting
room.

"Hey, you're not leaving. I want to talk to you . . ." She did not turn
around as she opened the door and walked out. "Hey . . ." The door
closed on Martin's words.

Ann Marie pulled her coat tightly around her as she rode down in the
elevator. Was she better or worse off? What had she done anyway?

It wasn't a sin, no matter what her cousin, the Monsignor, might think.
Had she gotten rid of some demons? The elevator doors opened and she
strode quickly across the almost deserted lobby. She stepped into the
shapeless cold of the night. The car and driver would be across the
street in front of City Hall.

Ann Marie waited for the light to change. Christmas colors, the traffic
lights had Christmas colors.

Charlie. It had something to do with Charlie. But Charlie was dead. Charlie was a necklace of calcium resting on velvet in the hold of a cargo plane. Had they quivered when she and Martin had made love? Charlie, it was nothing. It's part of burying you. That's all. Just part of burying you at last.

11

*T*he next few days were dream-like for Ann Marie. The Mayor had been solicitous, had even said that she should not worry about the future, that he would have something for her to do. Cullen did not go into details, however. His plans to put Matty Hogan on the bench went forward quietly and Mark Richler drafted the appropriate statements and Cap Malloy was delegated to arrange for the testimonial dinner. Even if Ann Marie had been sure of a job she would have put it aside for the next forty-eight hours. She was about to cross the last barrier to a totally different life.

Matthew had cried and Ann Marie had sat up with him after she got home from City Hall that dark and eventful evening. She held him in her arms and explained that they would go to the airport the next day and that they would have to be brave. Matthew turned his cowboy hat in his hands and grew silent. Ann Marie let him watch television and sat with him looking at, but not comprehending, an old movie. It was scratched and parts were missing so that the actors jumped suddenly from one side of a room to another. Like her own life up until that day— something spliced together, with pieces missing and jerky action. Matthew finally dozed off and she carried him to bed. She watched him for a moment, placed his cowboy hat on the coverlet and went back to turn off the television. The movie was over and the station was running an abbreviated version of the previous evening's news. There was a clip of Ann Marie answering Paul Michael Martin's question of the afternoon before. Had that been foreplay? Had the scenario been encoded in their genes so that it was just a question of time before they met and acted it out? The old Mayor moved into the center stage of the news conference and Ann Marie switched the set off. Whatever it all meant, life was going to be different from now on.

It was a bitter, windswept morning at O'Hare Field. Captain Vincent had been asked by the Superintendent to escort Mrs. O'Brien's car onto the landing strip. That had been a request from the Mayor himself. Vincent had selected Officer Hackman to accompany him and deployed other police officers discreetly so that the somber greeting of Captain

Charles O'Brien's body could be carried out with as much dignity as possible. Vincent and Hackman sat in a patrol car near the entrance to the military side of the field. Except for the jet planes' keening like giant airborne mourners it was dead quiet. Mrs. O'Brien's car had not yet arrived and the Air Force plane had not yet landed. But the police officers, the soldiers, and the members of the honor guard were ready for their assignments. A gray hearse was parked just at the side of one of the great dark hangars that housed military aircraft.

"Lots of waiting in this work, Captain," Hackman said as he gazed out at the airfield.

He could see Monsignor Fitzmaurice, the stole draped over his shoulders fluttering in the brisk wind, standing beside the hearse talking to a man dressed in black.

"Most of it's waiting," Captain Vincent answered.

"Say, Captain, has anything else developed on that trunk murder we had last month?"

"Noto? No, no leads that I know of. Homicide has taken over. Why do you ask?"

"Oh, I don't know. I've seen other bodies in trunks. The writing, the fag stuff, that was new for out here. And, of course, he was related to an alderman."

"One tough son of a bitch of an alderman," Vincent said. "I wouldn't want to be the guy when Sam Noto finds out who did it."

"My brother's a cop. I think you met him once. He was in on a fag killing just this week."

"Yeah?" Vincent had seen more killings than he cared to remember. News of another one did not intrigue him.

"In Everest Park. They found a kid in the forest preserve there. Young kid, attacked the same way."

"They're all attacked the same way. They don't vary it much."

"And there was writing on him . . ."

Vincent turned his head. He had never seen that before the Noto case.

"Where, on his ass?" Vincent was surprised at his own interest in a subject that had, until Hackman's last remark, been boring to him.

"No, on his chest. Same kind of marker, that's what my brother said. Somebody drew circles around the kid's tits, like they were bull's-eyes, and the word 'kill' was printed up here." Hackman made a gesture toward the area just below the neck.

"I didn't hear about that. Didn't read about it either."

"There wasn't much in the papers. I only knew it from my brother."

"Who was the kid?" Vincent asked.

"Some runaway, that's what Dave said, some kid who'd been out of the house for about a year. They just identified him yesterday. I forget his name. Spanish, I think."

Vincent rubbed his jaw. Something bothered him about this. But why? He had no opportunity to think about it further. The radio squawked a message from the Mayor's car. Mrs. O'Brien's party had just turned off the expressway and would be arriving in about three minutes.

"That's us," Captain Vincent said. "Let's get going."

"It all went very well," Monsignor Fitzmaurice said to Mother Francis. They stood in the shadows at the rear of the medium-sized parlor of Shaughnessy's Funeral Home in which the flag-draped casket, a picture of Charlie on top of it, rested against a bank of flowers.

"It was heartbreaking, wasn't it, when the honor guard took the casket."

"Ann Marie bore up well. And so did Matthew."

"Annie seems to be in a daze," Mother Francis whispered. "She's had a hard time. She's a brave woman."

Ann Marie was in a dreamy state. She had blocked out of her mind the view she had been given of Charlie's remains. No wonder the casket seemed light. But seeing the remains had been a termination point. The hope she had lived on, the fantasies she had nourished, the promises she had made about her life returning to normal—one look in the casket and they all died too. They had to be buried along with Charlie so that her new life could begin. She pulled herself back to the moment to greet those who had come to console her. Many of them were total strangers. They were city workers carrying out the orders of the Mayor to show up at the funeral home and to bring Mass cards if they could.

The Mayor came about nine o'clock. His daughter Maureen, who was about Ann Marie's age, was with him. She looked a lot like Cullen, a little on the chunky side. Ann Marie had never met her before, although she understood that she had three children and a drinker of a husband, whom the Mayor kept busy on some job in the Sanitation Department.

"Mrs. O'Brien," the Mayor said, bowing slightly, "this is my daughter, Mrs. Coleman. We all grieve for you and your family. Is this your dad, then?" Cullen turned his attention to an old man sitting in a wheelchair. The old man smiled crookedly up at the Mayor as he shook his hand. He worked his mouth but was unable to say anything.

"I'm really sorry for you to get such news right at Christmas," Maureen said. She seemed clear-eyed and direct, a commonsense woman, and Ann Marie did not dislike her. They looked at the white-haired charmer of a Mayor kneeling, head bowed, by the casket. He seemed so alive, so powerful next to her vaguely smiling father in the wheelchair. Ann Marie didn't have any feeling beyond slight envy for Maureen; she was just not really interested in her.

"And where is Matthew?" Cullen asked after he had straightened up and turned back toward Ann Marie.

"He was here earlier. Aunt Molly took him home a little while ago. He'll be sorry he missed you."

"No, Annie, I'm the one who's sorry." Cullen smiled. "He'll be at the church, of course?"

Ann Marie nodded.

"And is my old friend, Monsignor Fitzmaurice, going to say the Mass?"

"Yes, he will. And Cardinal Meehan may preside."

"Now, Annie," the Mayor said, pulling closer to her, "I want to talk to you after this is all over. I have a big responsibility for you, and I think you'll like it."

"What is it?" Ann Marie blurted out the way she had when she was a child and could not wait to find out what her present might be.

"Well," the Mayor said softly as he looked around to make sure that he would not be overheard, "there's a vacancy coming up for you in City Hall. We'll give you all the details next week."

Ann Marie smiled and took the old man's hand in her own. She didn't know exactly what the job was but she felt instantly better about the new year. The job was something concrete, like remains, something you could touch, something that was real. There was something to look forward to after the funeral the next day.

"Not a word," the Mayor said gently. Then he turned and bent down toward Ann Marie's father again. "You're a great lad and you've a grand daughter." Ann Marie's father's mouth churned again but nothing came out but a little drool. The Mayor took out a handkerchief and touched the other man's jaw with it. "There, there," he said, "we old fellows have to stick together."

The Mayor and his daughter made the rounds as though it were a political meeting. In a few minutes they were gone. Ann Marie returned to greet the steady stream of callers. But the dream state had loosened during Cullen's visit. He had made her feel like a princess.

There was a light, icy snow the next morning as the limousines pulled slowly away from Holy Name Cathedral. The cemetery was a half hour's drive in the best of weather and the long procession, even with a police escort provided by the Mayor, would take almost an hour to get to the chapel where the prayers for the deceased would be read. The casket was only taken afterward to the actual gravesite. It avoided a lot of trouble, as Monsignor Fitzmaurice, a great proponent of the custom, used to say, and enabled funerals to be scheduled more efficiently.

Captain Vincent had been asked by Commander Gleason to take over for him at the chapel. Vincent did not mind, since it was a short drive from O'Hare Field and Gleason, of the 16th District, was an old friend. Vincent asked Officer Hackman to drive him and they were already in place when the first cars of the O'Brien funeral cortege came through the gates of the cemetery. The weather had slowed everything up and the earlier funerals had been delayed.

A cemetery official in striped pants huffed across the parking lot, punching chugs of breath into the frigid air, to advise the driver of the hearse which bore Captain O'Brien's body that there would be a few minutes' delay. The whole procession stopped, a long string of lights against the drab background of the winter day. The headlamps of the limousines shone into the lightly falling snow and the amber and blue lights of the police cars and motorcycles turned slowly. Steam rose from the exhaust pipes of the caravan that was spread out along the winding road that led to the chapel.

Captain Vincent and Officer Hackman got out of their car and stood watching as the mourners from the service that had just ended came slowly out of the building. About a dozen people climbed slowly into two battered cars that had been covered with a layer of snow while they were inside. A mean, small funeral for some poor bastard, Vincent thought, as one of the mourners climbed out of the car with a piece of newspaper to clear the windshield. The waiting O'Brien funeral was a puffing juggernaut compared to the two dilapidated cars that were preparing to pull away.

The cemetery official in the pinstripe pants caught sight of Captain Vincent and hurried toward him, sliding, but keeping his balance successfully. He was dismayed and thought that Captain Vincent looked official enough to receive his apologies.

"I'm sorry about the delay," he said, catching his breath, "but we've been running late today."

"It's okay," the captain replied. "Everybody'll understand."

"Oh, thanks, Captain. It's been a hard morning." The official, perspiring despite the weather, took out a handkerchief to wipe his face. "And that was such a sad little funeral. The mother was very upset."

Captain Vincent was listening absently, his eyes on the long procession that was poised at the edge of the parking lot.

"Yes, very sad. They found the poor boy in the forest preserve the other day."

Vincent jolted to attention. Hackman moved a step closer to the pinstriped man.

"Very sordid. One of those things, Captain. You must deal with it all the time. Ah, here they come." The two cars had driven away and the hearse immediately moved forward, an engine slowly pulling a great train behind it. In a few moments all the cars had coiled into the parking lot. Captain Vincent and Officer Hackman moved forward through the veil of snow, too busy to talk about their common thoughts.

12

*T*he slating for the elective offices went off just the way the old man wanted it. When wouldn't it? Matty Hogan knew that Cullen held some trump cards about a block of real estate that the old alderman owned under a blind trust. The gag was that Hogan was involved in so many blind trusts he needed a Seeing Eye dog to find his real estate. Hogan wouldn't have wanted the papers to learn that he was a slumlord for a bunch of broken-down flats. The judgeship seemed a good alternative.

Slating Ann Marie for the alderman's job caused a lot of bad feeling in the ward organization and in the City Council, too. The professional politicians, however, understood exactly what the Mayor was up to. After Ann Marie buried her husband, she had received even more favorable publicity than when she chaired the blue ribbon committee on cable television franchises. She was unbeatable and almost uncriticizable. Publicly, that is.

So Cullen had overwhelmed the opposition on two scores, cable television and a new face in the City Council, continuing his monopoly on power through these moves. He beamed as he rode down in the elevator exactly one week before Christmas to light the city's Christmas tree in the square of Daley Plaza.

With him were his daughter, Maureen, her husband, Lawrence Coleman, and their three children. The Mayor always sniffed the mousy Coleman to see if he had been drinking. A weak character, Cullen had always thought, but in life, as in politics, you made the best you could out of things. It never occurred to him that his own forceful personality might have contributed to his son-in-law's somewhat sad and frustrated life.

"Well, Maureen," the Mayor said jovially, "the kids look fine." He bent down and patted the heads of his grandchildren. "Are you going to help Grandpa light the Christmas tree?" he asked heartily. But the children, looking up at the huge figure of their grandfather, were as intimidated as their own father was of him. Although they loved him, they often did not see him for weeks at a time, except for his almost nightly appearances on the TV news. Then suddenly they would be washed and combed, dressed in their Sunday best, and transported to some place filled with light and noise where Grandpa was the center of attention.

"Come on, now," the Mayor cajoled, "you want to help light the Christmas tree so Santa will know how to find Chicago, don't you?"

Little Kevin, who was five, nodded eagerly, and Thomas, who was nine, said, "Sure, Grandpa." Sheila, who was eleven, just smiled sweetly and her grandfather kissed her on the forehead as the elevator opened on the main floor of City Hall. The Cullens, flanked by bodyguards, headed east down the long corridor, crossed Clark Street in the icy black evening, and mounted the stand that had been set up on the edge of the huge plaza across the way. The Fire Department band was playing Christmas carols and the mood of the approaching holiday lay gently across the crowd of several hundred who stood behind the blue wooden barriers stretched out below the platform. Cullen took his place, his great thatch of white hair lifting slightly in the stir of air, as the woodwinds and brass gave a Salvation Army character to the familiar melodies.

Every politician or city official who could squeeze onto the platform anywhere near the Mayor was there that evening. Cullen scanned the crowd. Sam Noto, his face in scarred repose, looked almost pious as the anthems of Christmas drifted over him. Richard Barone stood next to him looking directly up at Cullen. The Mayor gave no signal of recognition but turned his eyes across the faces of the ordinary citizens, many of whom were singing along with the band. Down to his right, where the arc of the crowd ended at one of the barriers, Mrs. O'Brien and Mother Francis huddled together over the blanketed form of Ann Marie's father, who sat in his wheelchair, his woolen-capped head moving ever so slightly in tune with the music.

Martin was standing fifty feet away, preparing to tape his television commentary against the background of the Christmas tree lighting ceremony. He had watched Ann Marie as she wheeled her father across the plaza. Just viewing her, even bundled up in her heavy coat and scarf, had excited him. He wanted to have her again, on his own terms. He hadn't really had his turn at the plate yet. Martin wanted to even the score as soon as possible.

The music ended and Cap Malloy, his watery eyes sparkling in the television lights, raised his hand like an aged preacher. "Ladies and gentlemen, the Mayor, the Honorable Thomas H. Cullen." The loudspeaker system squealed and Cap pulled back as if he had been given an electric shock. Laughter rippled across the good-natured crowd as Cullen, pushing his shaggy hair back from his forehead, stepped to the microphone.

"My good neighbors," he began, "Christmas is special in this city. We have much to be thankful for. And many of us can remember when we were so poor that we had no tree and no presents either." Laughter rose from those anxious to please him. He raised a hand and smiled. "I'm serious, I really am. That's why this tree is for all the kids who can't have a real one of their own. My grandkids are going to help me light this." He gestured toward the children, who, shepherded by their mother, walked the few steps to where the Mayor stood with an electrical switch in his hands. As he grouped the children around him and helped them get their hands on the switch along with his, Alex Wendel whispered hoarsely to Raymond Carney, "That's the only power he's shared since he's been in office." Carney smiled but did not reply.

The large tree came alive with light and everyone on the platform stood in its transforming glow. The oohs and ahs were drowned out as the band struck up "O Come, All Ye Faithful" and the crowd applauded. Standing high on the spine of the dying year, Cullen was truly the powerhouse, the source of light, for the city.

Ann Marie applauded along with everyone else. She watched the Mayor's beaming face for a moment and then looked down at the wrecked old man in the wheelchair in front of her. "Doesn't the Mayor look well?" Mother Francis asked against the huffing tubas as they negotiated the last chorus of the Christmas song.

The Mayor did look well, especially in the roseate hue of the twinkling lights. Nobody could see that he had grown suddenly pale or that, despite the frigid evening, he had begun to perspire. Cullen tried to steady himself. It was a strange feeling for him to be out in public, to be in everyone's view, and yet not to be noticed at the very moment he needed some attention. There was nothing nearby for him to grasp for support. The song was winding down and he would be able to take a seat shortly. He felt weak and turned his head toward the crowd. Dozens of openmouthed singers were finishing off the words of the carol. His vision became distended and darkened at the edges. He felt himself falling free and far down, away from the lights and the noise.

In his almost barren office two floors beneath the main concourse of O'Hare Field, Captain Vincent had stayed late to read again some clippings that he had gotten from Officer Hackman's brother. There was a copy of the police report on the young man who had been buried on the same day as Captain Charlie O'Brien. Vincent had tried to dismiss it all, but his wonders had returned about the similarities between it and the Noto case. He sipped cold coffee from a Styrofoam cup, silently arguing himself out of thinking about the subject anymore.

He sorted out the clippings. They did not come to much. One was a story about the dead young man, the twenty-year-old kid who had left home more than a year before. The family hadn't heard from him until the police called them with their bad news. The other clipping was of an ad in a neighborhood newspaper. It was about another missing young man, a sixteen-year-old, five feet ten, 150 pounds, black hair, last seen at a shopping mall not far from the airport just before Halloween. Vincent shook his head, crumpled his empty cup and tossed it into his waste-basket. He placed the clippings into a manila folder and slipped it into his top desk drawer. He stretched and yawned. His phone rang and the officer outside buzzed him. It was Commander Gleason from the 16th.

"Something's happened to the Mayor—we just got it on the radio. He collapsed at the Christmas tree lighting. They were putting him in an ambulance the last anybody heard."

Vincent hardly knew how to respond before Gleason hung up. It did not seem possible that anything could ever happen to Mayor Cullen. A chill ran down Vincent's back. At some level he felt that all the events of the past several weeks were connected with each other. But the thought crumbled away as he hurried into the outer office to see what further news he could get of the Mayor's condition.

What was to have been a routine taping of his evening news commen-tary had suddenly become for Paul Martin eyewitness reporting of the collapse of Mayor Cullen. Martin stood only a few feet from the plat-form describing the startling scene as the video cameras sent a live feed of images out over the air. They had not been able to televise much beyond the sudden moving and shifting that goes with an emergency. There were no clear views of the Mayor but repeated shots of people's backs or their suddenly looming faces as they moved awkwardly away from the event around the now-forlorn Christmas tree.

"To repeat," Paul Martin said, "Mayor Thomas H. Cullen collapsed at approximately six ten this evening. We have no word on his condition as yet. He was taken immediately by Fire Department ambulance to the University of Illinois Hospital. A team of medics was giving him emer-gency treatment as the ambulance pulled away from Daley Plaza. Mayor Cullen had just lighted the city's Christmas tree when he toppled to the platform . . ."

Ann Marie was near panic inside. There was nothing that she could do but stand, protecting her father against the unpredictable movement of the stunned crowd. Mother Francis stood next to her, holding on to the rear of the wheelchair as she moved her lips in prayer. Shock had struck the crowd like a radiation blast, eating away at the onlookers' strength, making them shaky and unwilling to move very far away from the site of the incident. They could not look away from the part of the platform where the Mayor had fallen, as if some afterimage of the event continued to rise and fall on that now-empty space.

Ann Marie held on to the wheelchair. She felt numb. Life was nothing but abandonment and loss, being used and put aside by husbands, fathers, and lovers. Goddamn these men who had slipped away from her, each one under the cover of darkness, each on a cold black night. She prayed for Cullen as best she could, but that was mixed up with her efforts to maintain her calm, to hold on under yet another onslaught.

Alex Wendel had gone back to his City Hall office with Sam Noto and Raymond Carney. They had hailed Felix Ramirez out of the crowd and all had taken seats around Wendel's desk. Tension and expectation charged the air. Wendel switched on a small radio by the side of his desk. He turned back to his fellow aldermen.

"This, gentlemen," he said acidly, "calls for a plan."

"Christ, Al," Noto mumbled, "don't curse yourself. You wanna curse yourself at a time like this?"

Carney pursed his lips and wrinkled his brow while Ramirez blessed himself and mumbled something in Spanish. Then the room fell silent except for the staccato radio reports, none of them with any additional news about the Mayor's condition.

Wendel leaned back in his chair. "Gentlemen, this is a fine time for a plan. We'll only curse ourselves if we don't think one out. Don't you understand that? You're afraid to think about the fact that we're going to have to be ready to carry on without Cullen."

The others were still too stunned to respond. They stared separately into space.

"Cullen's liable to be dead by morning. Maybe he's dead now, for all we know. How the hell are we going to run this thing if that's true? What the hell do you think will happen to you if you don't have some idea now of what we'll do to replace him?"

"Al's right," Carney said softly. "We have to think about this. If we don't, 'The Rosary' or somebody else will."

"You smart guys talk," Noto said like a man standing in the shadows of a great curse, "you smartass guys talk. I'll listen. For now, for now, I'll listen."

Ramirez signed himself again. "You are right, Al. But it seems funny, talking about the Mayor. He ain't dead yet. Your radio didn't say he was dead yet."

"Look, put away your superstitions for a minute. The people who have a plan are the ones who can take over. There'll be a fucking vacuum, you know that. What happens if Cullen does die? Ray, you know all the fine points."

"Well," Carney said in a more comfortable tone than he had used before, "there's a Vice-Mayor who takes over until the City Council elects a successor to finish out his term."

"Christ Almighty," Wendel said, "Matty Hogan is the Vice-Mayor.

And we just threw him off the ticket and made him a judge. He's not a judge yet, though, is he?"

"No, that was scheduled for next week," Carney responded. "That was part of Cullen's strategy. He was going to appoint that bitch O'Brien to fill out his aldermanic term. She's already been slated for the next election."

"She's one hard lady," Ramirez said slowly.

There was an interval of silence as the men, now caught up in the task which a few minutes ago they spurned, thought about what to do. The radio continued to chatter without imparting any hard news about the Mayor's condition.

"You would think they would know something by now," Ramirez said. "They ought to know something by now."

Wendel sat upright and pulled his chair toward his desk.

"This is the opportunity we've been waiting for, gentlemen. We can make our plans and get rid of the bitch at the same time!"

"How?" Noto asked flatly. "How the hell you gonna do that?"

Wendel folded his arms and leaned forward on his desk.

"It's perfect. Matty Hogan is the Vice-Mayor. Don't you see? He postpones becoming a judge. Hell, he's got the right to be Mayor by ordinance. Until the City Council elects a successor. Well, he's not a bad man to fill out the rest of Cullen's term. Two years isn't very long. And if we can't make some other switch, we'll have him stay on the City Council and let him run as an independent against this dame. Without Cullen's support she'll have her brains beaten out."

"Christ," Noto interjected, "Matty's okay as far as he goes. But we can't let him go too far."

"Let's use him for the transition, until the next election is set, or we can use him to knock this broad off," Carney said, as though he were settling the matter.

"Then what?" Ramirez asked. "Then what? That's what I want to know. I want the Finance Committee if you want me to go along with this."

"Take Rafferty's place? That's a high price," Wendel replied.

"You want a plan? That's part of the plan."

"Rafferty might not be bad until the next primaries. We could dump him then," Carney said enthusiastically. "If we play this right, we can take care of everybody with the right moves. We don't have Cullen anymore. We get rid of the O'Brien dame. Then we can reexamine the cable TV issue all over again. Accuse her of malfeasance or something. What the hell would she know, anyway?"

"The people like her," Noto said softly. "War hero, all that shit."

"They'll forget that in this situation. What we've got to do is to get busy on this tonight. We may not have much time." Wendel paused as a bulletin was announced on the radio.

"A spokesman for the hospital has just announced that Mayor Cullen is conscious and is undergoing tests at the present time. Monsignor Morgan Fitzmaurice, Vicar-General of the Archdiocese of Chicago, has administered the sacrament of the sick . . ."

"There," Wendel said, snapping off the radio, "give 'em the last sacraments, that's as good as greasing the slide for him."

"*Madre de Dios,*" Ramirez said, signing himself again.

"Don't be so certain," Noto said, raising a protesting hand. "Lots of times, those things, the oil and all, they work. Don't be so certain."

"Well," Wendel responded in his best mortician tones, "I have had some experience. And we'd better be ready. Who can you contact? Sam, you'd better get hold of Hogan right away. Get him in line for this. He may have the right to take over already . . ."

A half block away Richard Barone sat in his Cadillac talking with Francis Rafferty. Their eyes had met at the tree lighting ceremony just as knowingly as they had over many real estate deals. Once the old Mayor had been driven away in the big red-and-white ambulance, they knew that they should get together for a talk. Not that Rafferty dropped his guise of piety.

"Glory be to God, Dick," Rafferty said, "can you imagine the dear man stricken at such a beautiful scene, when we were commemorating the very birth of Our Lord himself? It takes great faith to understand the divine mysteries. Great faith indeed."

"What about tomorrow?" Barone asked in a tone with an edge sharp enough to cut through the crust of religiosity.

Rafferty sighed. "Yes, tomorrow, we'll have to give some thought to tomorrow and what, with God's help, we can do to maintain balance and continuity." Rafferty knew better than anyone else in the city the issues that would be involved in a transfer of power. "May God grant the good man a long and prosperous life, Richard," he said unctuously, "but we do have to think of the good of the city."

"Fuck the city," Barone said as he shifted slightly on the squeaking leather seat, "we've got arrangements to protect. The city'll be okay if we take care of those. But let things come loose, let there be a split in the party, let guys start fighting with each other and things will come apart pretty fast. Look, Francis, you're the glue to keep this show stuck together."

For years Rafferty had wanted to become Mayor of the city, but Cullen was always the obstacle. Now, even though he was seventy-one, the goal of his ambition was just the length of his arm away from him.

He had not survived so long, however, by saying too much or admitting anything even to close business associates like Barone. He understood that Matty Hogan, soon to be Judge Matthew Hogan, glory be to God, would be Vice-Mayor for the brief period before the City Council elected a Mayor to fill out Cullen's term. He would have to secure that position for himself. That was the first step. Then he would have to get the party's slating to run in the primary for the official nomination to be the candidate in the next election. He understood that Barone wanted him to make sure that this plan, even though it remained unspoken between them, would be carried out successfully. He would have to contact Wendel, Carney, and a half dozen other members of the City Council, push the right buttons, and all would be well. All, as Rafferty knew, except for one thing.

"You know, Richard," he said philosophically, "the Mayor is not dead yet, thanks be to God."

Barone grunted as he pushed in the cigarette lighter.

"Now, Richard, if you don't mind, I have a little work to do. And I might just go light a candle at St. Peter's." Rafferty opened the door and eased himself out. "Good night, Richard," he said as he grasped the car door to close it. Barone's hand reached out to prop it open. He leaned across the front seat, holding a glowing cigarette delicately between his splendidly capped teeth.

"One last thing before you go."

Rafferty leaned down as though he were about to hear a confession.

"Get rid of that dame O'Brien. She fucked up the TV franchises and she'll be nothing but trouble in the City Council."

"Why, Richard," Rafferty said, in tones of admonishment, "she's the candidate of the party for Matty Hogan's seat. She's the people's choice." Rafferty smiled and walked off into the night.

In the waiting room off the Cardiac Intensive Care Unit at the University of Illinois Hospital the Mayor's daughter Maureen sat on an uncomfortable plastic chair while her jumpy-looking husband paced back and forth. Whether his father-in-law was on the way out or not, Larry Coleman needed a drink or he felt that he would die himself. But he couldn't leave the waiting room. The children had been taken home by some friends and the great beast of the media was snorting and restless in a temporary news center that had been set up in a conference room on the first floor of the hospital. Everyone else—except Monsignor Fitzmaurice—had been kept away from the reception area. A team of Cullen's bodyguards stood outside the door to make sure that the curious kept their distance. The door to the unit opened and Dr. George Barton, chief of cardiology, came out and walked over to Maureen.

"Mrs. Coleman," he said gently, "it's not clear that your father has had an actual coronary attack. We're going to continue monitoring him very closely, of course, and we can't predict too much. But he's holding his own and would like to see you—just you—for a few moments."

Maureen followed the doctor through the door and down the hallway to the room in which, surrounded by a bewildering array of winking and ticking instruments, the Mayor lay, an old battleship in drydock. His eyes were half-closed but he smiled as Maureen approached. She leaned down and kissed him on the forehead.

"Who hit me?" he asked, with a smile.

Maureen started to cry at this evidence of his good humor.

"How are you, Daddy? Do you feel all right?"

He nodded. "Considering everything, not so bad." He spoke softly so that Maureen had to draw closer to hear him.

"Maureen, you've never given me anything but happiness."

She gritted her teeth to control the tears of affection that welled up in her eyes.

"Listen, Maureen," the old man said, "I'll lick this, I really will. Tell the kids I'm a tough old man." He paused for breath. "And, do this, will you? Keep in touch with Mark. You're the only one I can trust. Find out what's going on for me . . ."

"Yes, Daddy," she answered softly. "Don't worry."

"Good girl. Those bastards'll be selling the sidewalks if we don't keep an eye on them."

13

*P*aul Martin ignored all the usual City Hall contacts. They were suffering bad cases of nerves and believed every rumor they heard. Instead of checking with this unreliable lot, he called Ann Marie.

"Ann? This is Paul Martin." His charm mustered, he spoke as though they had never shared more than a passing greeting with each other. "I'll just bet you could find out Mayor Cullen's real condition for me."

Cullen's hospitalization had put everything into a different perspective for Ann Marie. She regarded her fling with Martin as a cheap and shameful episode. Maybe she needed it at the time, but she despised it now. Ann Marie was as uncomfortable with herself as a cradle Catholic could be. Even though she didn't believe everything the Church taught anymore, why, she wondered, why couldn't she shake loose from its power? And what nerve Paul Martin had in calling her.

"I'm sorry, Mr. Martin," she said coldly, "I'm not in the news business. I don't have any information."

The distance in her voice did not dissuade Martin. Overcoming resistance was his business. His hobby, too.

"Come on, Ann, who the hell are you kidding? You just have to smile a little and you can find out anything you want to. You owe me . . ."

"What the hell do you mean, *I* owe *you*? I don't *owe* you a thing."

"Temper, temper. I'm not asking for much, just the straight story on the old man's condition. You can get it better than anyone in town, and you know I'm right. Is that too much trouble for you?"

"Goodbye." She bit the word out and slammed down the phone.

But she did call Mark Richler, who was coordinating many of the activities at City Hall with one hand and dealing with the media with the other. He was on a call and as she waited she wondered again about Paul Martin. There was something about him; dammit, there was so much "little boy" in his insistence on attention. She wasn't really calling Richler because Martin had asked her to do it. She just wanted to know how the Mayor was. Wouldn't anybody?

"Mrs. O'Brien," Richler said wearily, "I'm glad you called. The Mayor was asking for you. Wanted to know if you could spend some time with his daughter, give her a little moral support. The Mayor'd feel good if he knew you were doing it."

"Sure, Mark, I'll do whatever I can. How is the Mayor doing?"

"Not as bad as they thought at first. He's picking up. The doctors think it was just a minor episode. He may get out in time to be home for Christmas."

"He'd like that."

"He also told me to tell you to stay away from any aldermen who might try to contact you while he's sick."

"What did he mean by that?"

"That's all he said. Sometimes he doesn't explain things. He figures people are bright enough to understand what he means. And if they aren't, that's their lookout."

"Should I contact Maureen?"

"We'll send a car for you and you can spend some time with her in the hospital waiting room. That's the tough part, all the waiting."

Ann Marie frowned. Maureen Coleman was Cullen's real daughter. Now that Cullen's wife was dead, she had the first place in the Mayor's heart. Maureen had the Cullen blood in her, the inside track, too. But she was a good scout who had her share of life's problems. Just think of that drinker of a husband of hers. How could she have ever found a man who was her charmer father's equal for a husband? Larry Coleman was not missing in action. That was the trouble, he was around, ticking and smelling of drink. Would Maureen become a kind of stepsister, another uncertain relationship in Ann Marie's life? She seemed genuinely glad to see Ann Marie when she arrived at the waiting room.

"Thanks for coming, Mrs. O'Brien . . ."

"Your father will do fine," Ann Marie said with as much warmth as she could manage.

Maureen glanced at the shadow of the policeman that fell across the frosted-glass reception door. It was safe to talk.

"He *is* doing much better. I think this scared him. He never expected that any illness would have the nerve to attack him, least of all in front of City Hall."

"He's tough," Ann Marie said, forcing a smile. "He's as tough as they come."

"You know, he said that about you this afternoon."

"About me?"

"Yes, yes, he did. He was talking about his illness and its effect on city government. It would really kill him if he had something that laid him up so that he couldn't function. And he's concerned about what some of the City Council members might be doing now that he's in the hospital."

"About what?"

"Well, he thinks they may try to put in an acting Mayor . . ."

"They wouldn't dare . . ."

"Sure they would, if they had the slightest chance. Haven't you gotten to know what they're like yet?"

"Well . . ."

"I know you learned a lot about them when you were on the blue ribbon committee. Some of them put a lot of pressure on you. That's when my father said you showed you were tough."

A nurse poked her head in the door and smiled. "The Mayor just complained about the food. That's a good sign. He's looking better all the time."

Maureen smiled back and the nurse disappeared. "They're wonderful here." She looked around again. "You know, it's good to be able to talk to another woman about this. My father trusts me. And I think he trusts you too. He says that you have to be careful not to get drawn into any discussions with people like Wendel or Carney. Or Sam Noto either. And Francis Rafferty would give up a lot of real estate to get my father's job. He's always wanted it."

"I thought they were great friends."

"None of these men are really friends of my father's. I'm not sure how many he has. I'm not sure how many any of these men have. Richler is very close to him, but they've never been social friends. But Mark is probably the closest man to him."

"Do you think they can really put somebody in, some acting Mayor?"

"Not unless we let them. We have to hold the fort, protect my father, and, as Mark Richler says, just carry on as if there isn't any great concern about my father's health. There are good men in the City Council too—Schroeder and Cutler and others we can count on for help." She drew a breath. "There will be lots of rumors. People will want to believe the worst. So keeping it calm, keeping up a good front, all of that is very important. My father's relying on us because he doesn't trust many others."

So, Cullen trusted her and thought she was tough. Ann Marie felt better than she had earlier. The depression that had dogged her since the Mayor collapsed at the Christmas tree lighting began to lift. She and Maureen would do the job that the Mayor asked of them.

"Can I see him?"

"Come in on the hour with me. We'll only stay for a few minutes." Maureen smiled at Ann Marie. They had made some pact together. They were almost friends but they were not quite friends, not yet. Whatever their relationship with each other, they shared a common cause, protecting Mayor Cullen. Even through this vaguely uncertain alliance with his daughter, Ann Marie saw a way of protecting her own security and her own future. She was smiling when she left the hospital a half hour later.

"The Mayor's doing fine," Ann Marie said cheerily into the phone, pleased that she could drop this firsthand morsel onto Paul Martin's plate. She did not let herself think about whether she was violating the Mayor's trust or not.

"You sure of this? There are rumors all over the place that he's going to step down for a time and let Hogan take over until he feels better. And there's a story that they discovered cancer and that he'll never get out of the hospital."

"Look, you asked me to find out and I did. I'll tell you something else nobody knows yet either." She paused.

"Yeah?"

"The Mayor is going to leave the hospital sometime tomorrow morning and go directly to his office to show people that he's in good condition."

"Are you sure of that? That sounds risky to me for a man of his age. There's been no announcement of it, nothing like that, not even a rumor about it."

"Paul," she said slowly, "you believe what you want to. I've just given you an exclusive. Why don't you check it out with one of your other sources? Maybe some secretary, or a girl reporter, I understand you know a lot of them very well."

Martin remained skeptical. "That's too good a story. If I go with that and it doesn't pan out, I'll be the laughingstock of the city."

"Well, you make up your own mind about what you want to believe . . ."

Martin was in a quandary. He did not trust the information because he wanted to believe that the Mayor was really too sick to leave the hospital. Besides, Barone had told him that Rafferty and others had used the last few days to put a plan together to replace Cullen with an acting Mayor for a while. They wouldn't try that unless they knew what they were talking about.

"Put it this way, Annie. You'd believe anything the old man says. I've never believed half of anything he's said. We'll see who's right."

But Ann Marie was right and the reporters, including Martin, were caught completely by surprise when the Mayor's limousine pulled up to the LaSalle Street entrance to City Hall at ten o'clock the next morning. Cullen had signed himself out of the hospital despite his doctor's cautions and left on a service elevator that enabled him to use the emergency room exit and avoid the media. The newspapers were only alerted after his car had started its brief trip across the center of the city. Cullen had followed his stomach. If the doctors said he could go home in a few days, he could go home safely today. An arrival at City Hall at mid-morning would guarantee that he would dominate every edition of the papers and every newscast for the rest of the day. Dozens of reporters, television and news cameramen crowded the curb as Cap Malloy opened the back door of the long dark-green limousine. Cullen swung himself lightly out onto the sidewalk with no assistance and stood bareheaded as the cameras whirred and clicked. His broad face looked ruddy and his eyes twinkled above his half-moon grin.

"Gentlemen, gentlemen, what did you expect to see? A reed shaken by the wind? I'm sure this probably disappoints some of you, but as you see," and he made a thumbs up gesture, "I have returned." Cheers and laughter rose from the reporters. All except Paul Martin, who stood impassively at the edge of the crowd.

"And now, gentlemen, I must get to work. I'll have some news for you in about an hour." Cullen moved swiftly into the Hall and to the elevator that stood waiting to take him to his office. The reporters trailed noisily after him, shouting questions about his health and plans. Cullen smiled contentedly back as the elevator doors closed against the glare of the television lights.

Seated once more at his desk, the Mayor felt a combination of fatigue and exhilaration. He had not only stunned the reporters but also sent "The Rosary" Rafferty into shock. Wendel, Carney, and the rest of the aldermen who hoped to manage the expected transition worked hard to shed their conspiratorial look. That was not easy for them. Cullen had counted on the impact of his sudden return to shatter the alliances that had been constructed during his five-day absence. Maureen and Ann Marie had taken soundings for him. When Ann Marie reported that Rafferty had called and suggested a meeting, he was sure of what was going on. It was good medicine to disconcert his enemies just before Christmas.

"Glory be to God, and don't you look good, Tom," Rafferty said as he entered the Mayor's office to welcome him back and to assure him that he had kept a close eye on things while the Mayor was in the hospital. The sight of Rafferty's straight face cheered Cullen.

"I am good, Francis," Cullen said. "I hope my return has not been too much of a surprise to you."

"A present, Tom, a present worthy of being placed under the Christmas tree, a present right along with the gifts of the Wise Men."

"Yes, Francis, the story of the Wise Men is a good one." Cullen's smile faded away. "They followed the right star. A man has to be careful what star he follows, isn't that so, Francis?"

"Glory be to God, yes, Tom, I was thinking that myself." Rafferty's tone grew confidential. "I'm a little concerned about some of the younger men around the Hall. Very ambitious, some of them. Men to be watched, God help us."

Cullen smiled. "Francis, you have no idea how well I slept in the hospital knowing that you were watching things for me."

"Yes, yes, and your lovely daughter keeping me informed. A saint, Tom, Maureen is nothing less than a saint. And Mrs. O'Brien right with her. Who will find me a valiant woman? That's the Bible's question, Tom, and there she is. She's already to run for Matty Hogan's seat and we're all pleased about it, thrilled you might say, to have her joining us in the Council. We'll have a strong ally there."

"Yes, Francis," Cullen said as he stood up and rounded his desk to put his arm around his old colleague's shoulder, "that's the very thing I want to talk to you about. Francis, we've known each other a long time. What is it, thirty-five, forty years?" They walked together toward the windows. Cullen dropped his arm away and the two men stood silently for a moment, their eyes fixed on the shadowed avenue below.

"You probably won't believe this, Francis, but I heard that Matty Hogan was cooking up some plan to exercise his title of Vice-Mayor while I was in the hospital."

"Glory be to God, no," Rafferty gurgled.

"I knew it would come as a shock to you." Cullen turned and walked back across the room. Rafferty continued to stare out of the window. "So, Francis, I wanted you to be the first to know. The demands on the courts are so great that I've decided that we cannot postpone Matty's elevation to the bench. Not a day longer. *Judge* Hogan, what a lovely sound it has! A kind of a Christmas gift for him. I've arranged to have him sworn in this afternoon."

Cullen sat down and smiled at Rafferty's back. "So, Francis, we have to fill the vacancy in the ranks of City Hall. And I'm sending Mrs. O'Brien's name for Council approval to that position today as well. It should be a popular move, seeing that she's already received the party's slating for the post anyway."

Rafferty looked pale as he turned toward the Mayor. But he did not lose his composure.

"Tom, are you sure you want to do this?"

"I've no doubt of it. It puts our house in order for the holidays. There's only one other question. This means that we have no Vice-Mayor. It's not much of a title or a job anyway. So I'm asking the Council to give that to Mrs. O'Brien as well. The people of the ward might not like it if the title was taken away from their representative in the City Council. I wanted you to know all this so that you could pass the word. A unanimous vote would be lovely. I'm going out for a news announcement about it shortly. I think it would look good if you appeared with me. Matty'll be there too, unless he's busy collecting rents."

Rafferty gritted his teeth as he regarded the man who had been his political boss and rival for so long. It did not seem possible that Cullen could have collapsed and come back to play his tricks on them all once more. But that woman! Rafferty cringed as he thought of the inexperienced Mrs. O'Brien's imminent entrance into the City Council. The vote would never be unanimous, not if Wendel and Noto had their way. It wouldn't matter.

"Glory be to God, Tom, if that's what you want. She doesn't have much experience, God help us."

"No, that's true. But neither did Wendel when he left the family undertaking parlors to enter government. And Carney was a cop. And nobody knows exactly what Ramirez did . . ." Cullen clasped his hands across his stomach. "She'll be just fine, Francis, just fine . . ."

Cullen leaned back after Rafferty left. He was tired and he would go home after the news conference. There was something to having women watching out for your interests. It was especially helpful if the women were in competition with each other for your attention. That just added to their vigilance and their desire to please you. He felt better than he thought he would. It would be a merry Christmas after all.

14

*C*hristmas slipped by in a shimmer of twinkling lights and New Year's barely shone through a crust of snow. Ann Marie spent her first holiday season as a widow and the first as a member of the City Council. Her anger at the fates was tempered by the sweetness of the adventures of the last six weeks. She had entered Thomas Cullen's kingdom and had been declared a court favorite by the old man. She liked being an alderwoman even though she had not yet attended any meetings. She even enjoyed Paul Michael Martin, who pursued her during the Christmas interim, pressing her for dates and for more information about Cullen's health and the failed coup attempt during his hospital stay.

For Christmas she had splinted her fractured family together—her father in his wheelchair, Monsignor Fitzmaurice, Aunt Molly, Matthew, and Mother Francis—and held a good-humored dinner and a present exchange. Routine was death for Ann Marie, and as the fresh year began she felt a dizzying stimulation generated from City Council work and the campaigns that lay ahead. There would always be something to do; she would never wonder about how to fill her days.

The Mayor and his daughter and her family had gone to Florida for two weeks on Christmas Day. Cullen had called Ann Marie on New Year's Eve and told her that he was enjoying the sun and feeling fine and wished her well for the new year. The first week of January was very quiet. The city seemed to have turned over under its blanket of snow and gone to sleep again. Chicago was having a hard time starting the new year.

"That's because his nibs is away, Annie," Paul Martin said across the lunch table he had persuaded her to share to celebrate her City Council appointment. "After Cullen got wind of their plans to put him on the disabled list, he got them all so scared by replacing Hogan right away they don't even dare think about doing anything. You were one of his spies during that, weren't you?"

"Spy? No, no, nothing so romantic as that."

"That's what I hear. Rafferty thinks you told Cullen about his call to you. Among other things, that is. You and Maureen. Boy, those sons of bitches really hate you now."

"So what?" Ann Marie enjoyed the status that being disliked by Cullen's enemies conferred on her. "I've never done anything to them."

"That's not what they feel. Christ, Annie, you killed Ardi-Vision. You're the Mayor's choice to take Hogan's place, you're thought to be one of those closest to him, and you helped finger their little gunpowder plot. They say that, except for the knowledge that Rafferty was beginning to maneuver, Cullen would never have hiked his ass out of the hospital so fast. Haven't you heard that?"

"No comment, as they say to the journalists. Just what is it that you're driving at anyway?"

"Nothing much. I'm damned curious about how Cullen is doing. How he's *really* doing. He's going to run for another term next time and shrug his illness off as though it didn't mean a goddamn thing. He won't give out any medical reports, no information about the true state of his health. That's a dangerous thing for a man to do to a city. And he's doing it just to hold on to power for himself."

"Would you rather have Rafferty in his job?"

"Hell, no. That's not the question. What I'm saying is this: if Cullen's not really healthy, he ought to play fair with the city, retire, and let a new Mayor be elected before he kicks off or strokes out. Otherwise, he's leaving it to these jackals to settle things after he's gone. I think he owes it to the city to play it straight now."

"He seems to be healthy enough as far as I can see."

"Hell, Annie, he's got you so bamboozled with his fatherly charm you probably can't see it straight either." He paused for effect before he spoke, "But you're not number one for him. You know that, don't you?"

"What do you mean?" she bristled. "I've never thought I was number one."

"The hell you haven't. All anybody has to do is watch you when you're looking at Cullen. But you'll always be behind Maureen, second in line. Hell, he's playing you off against his own daughter. He's got the cats with the sharpest claws in the city keeping their eyes open for him." Martin paused to sip his coffee.

"You'll make something up just to tear it down the next day." Damn him, playing on her insecurity about where she stood with Cullen. "You tear things down all the time."

"Hold it there, Annie. My job is trying to find the truth beneath the press releases and the political arrangements. I'm just doing my day's work, ma'am." He patted his lips with his napkin. "What you don't like is the part where I tell you that he's using you just like everybody else. That's the truth and you're better off knowing it than not."

"Just what do you want out of all this? You make yourself sound so noble."

"First, I want to know just how sick the old man is. That's all I want." He flashed his charmer's grin. "Well, maybe that's not all that I want. But I want it. You know, Annie, you've got to get over this schoolgirl crush you've got on Cullen. Always remember that with the Cullens, the Cullens come first. You're nice, but you're window dressing, a convenience, a woman in a showy job."

"Stop it," Ann Marie cut in angrily. "Stop it right now."

Paul smiled again. "Ann, I want you to remember one thing. My job is to sift through the garbage. You don't even want to smell it."

"Then we've both found our right places in life. And, if you'll excuse me, I'm going back to where I won't have to smell this conversation anymore." She rose partially from her chair. Paul Martin put his hand out to restrain her.

"Now, now, Annie. You're already a public figure. You've got to learn to handle questions and statements that you don't like. Just look on this as good practice."

Ann Marie sat down again and finished her lunch. But she was troubled by Martin's hammering at her relationship with Cullen. She was still troubled after the Mayor, his snowpile of hair setting off his newly acquired tan, arrived back from Florida. Maureen seemed to be with him all the time. Ann Marie saw Cullen regularly enough, but she knew that she was in second place.

Cullen had slowed down, although that was hidden from the public. He napped on a couch in his office every afternoon and more than once Ann Marie had been with him when he had dozed off momentarily. "The medication, the medication," Richler would say to her, and, although she could accept that, she was surprised at how much she worried about the Mayor. She knew that Rafferty and the others were watching him closely too, that they were ready to move against him on short notice.

Cullen had lost fifteen pounds and bragged about it, pulling on his loose waistband at the news conferences which he still held regularly. But he rested immediately after them and the mass of detailed paperwork that once crossed his desk was now largely routed elsewhere. He had two or three important appointments in the hours before lunch and saw two or three more people after the nap. But he cut down on the dinners and the wake-going, and under Maureen's watchful eye—she had practically moved into his apartment—he was in bed before ten every night.

Running for a term of her own as alderwoman kept Ann Marie fully occupied during the month of March. Her Republican opponent didn't have any money or any political organization to support him, but she

pushed as energetically as if the election were not a sure thing. Ann
Marie took Matthew with her on some of her daytime campaign trips,
visiting shopping centers and clubs, schools and union hiring halls, shaking hands with ladies in hair curlers and men in hard hats, smiling in a
fixed way at everyone in sight. It was just such a trip that brought her
into a dining room at the Hilton Hotel at O'Hare Field.

The airport is tied to the City of Chicago by the Kennedy Expressway
like a balloon on a string. The slender corridor of highway is part of
Chicago even though it is surrounded by suburban Cook County. It
touched the ward which Ann Marie represented in the City Council.
The stop at the Hilton was to make an appearance at a testimonial luncheon for the Honorable Matthew Hogan, former alderman of the area
and now judge of the Circuit Court.

The luncheon had not yet begun and Ann Marie circulated around,
Matthew at her side, to shake hands with as many people as possible.
The room was large and bland, but the crowd was sprinkled with char-
acters she had come to know very well. Sam Noto was there smoking a
ragged cigar. So was Richard Barone, whom she had come to recognize
by sight and know by reputation since she had assumed her City Council seat. Judge Hogan greeted her with worked-up warmth and Alex
Wendel was undertaker suave to her. Larry Johnson smiled broadly and
Raymond Carney turned on his Irish charm as they circled past each
other after the luncheon broke up.

"Hey, Mrs. O'Brien," Richard Barone called crudely, "don't hurry
away. I've never had a chance to meet you." Matthew had become restless after he finished his dessert and now tugged at his mother's hand
for freedom. She looked into the dark rugged features of the real estate
investor.

"This is my son, Matthew. Come on, Matt, shake hands with Mr.
Barone."

Barone, a giant regarding Jack below the beanstalk, thrust a hairy fist
down to Matthew. The little boy stepped back instinctively, pushing
himself against his mother's body.

"Hello, kid," Barone said heartily. "Got the same name as the judge,
eh? Maybe you'll grow up to be a judge too." Then he laughed and
promptly forgot the boy, who continued to gaze uneasily up at him.

"Hey, Mrs. O'Brien, I'd like you to meet one of my relatives. You
ought to know him anyway. He's one of your precinct captains." Barone
made a signal and a dark-haired young man in a navy blue suit detached
himself from another group and edged through the crowd toward them.

"One of my brother Angie's boys. Good boy. You can count on him."
He put an arm around his nephew's shoulder. "This is Anthony Barone.

This is Alderman O'Brien and her little boy, Matty." The young man grinned shyly and shook hands. "You work for Mrs. O'Brien, right?"

"Do what I can, yes. We've got a good organization."

"So I've learned," Ann Marie answered. She liked the young man's sensuous good looks. "We'll meet often, Anthony, I'm sure."

"Anthony, why don't you take Matthew here—Matthew just like the judge—and buy him an ice cream or a nice toy, you know, something nice. Mrs. O'Brien and I have a few things to talk about."

Before Ann Marie could raise a protest Anthony took the suddenly revived Matthew by the hand and moved away. She pouted her lips slightly in disapproval.

"What's the matter? Don't you want to talk?" Barone asked.

"I like to make my own decisions. And I don't want Matthew spoiled by big spenders."

"Big spenders? Don't worry about that. Look, we've got a lot to talk about." He drew closer to her. "Listen, don't be afraid."

"I'm not," Ann Marie shot back, "just cautious."

"Well, I understand that. I understand that very well. You're new to this. You don't know everything that's involved. It'll take you some time to get acquainted. Hell, there's lots of other precinct captains you haven't met. But they're very important to you, you know that, don't you? They keep in touch with the neighborhoods for you. Would you like a drink?"

"No, if you want to talk, we can do it right here."

"Well, I mean, it's a little crowded, people will be coming up to say hello."

"That's how I keep in touch with the neighborhoods."

"Okay. Listen, what I wanted to say was simple anyway. I know you don't know some of the other aldermen too well. Guys like Noto and Wendel."

"How about Rafferty and Carney?"

"Yeah, them too. And I have no interest here, I'm just concerned that you don't have some misunderstandings that will keep you from working together."

"Keep talking." Ann Marie enjoyed the tension, the hint of threat, that drifted like haze around Barone. She got a kick out of standing toe to toe with him. It was a turn-on.

"Well," Barone said, adjusting his tie, "you all have to work together. Don't get these guys wrong. Especially about the time the Mayor was sick. They were thinking, what do we do if he dies, what do we do to make sure the city has continuity, you know, that things run smoothly. That's all they were doing. Some of these bastards in the papers have hinted that it was a takeover, like a goddamn South American revolution or something."

"It was close," Ann Marie said, letting a half-inviting smile ride on her lips. "It was pretty close."

"No, no. Look, you think that, you'll never get along with these guys. You want a future in politics, you've got to work with these men. They're elected just like you, they're concerned, just like you. You think Cullen's the only man cares about the city? These men care too. And you don't want to forget that."

The hulking man had gotten her attention. She was loyal to the Mayor. But there was something in what Barone said. It distressed her, but she could not deny it. She would have to work with these men. That was just practical.

"Look, Mrs. O'Brien, you're the Vice-Mayor now. What does it mean? Not a goddamn thing. Just a technicality. Does it mean because we have a Vice-Mayor that people are plotting to overthrow the Mayor? Christ, this whole thing was blown out of proportion. You think about it."

Anthony Barone had hit it off with Matthew, and the little boy, traces of ice cream on his upper lip, was clutching a plastic model of a jet passenger plane when they returned.

"Mom, look what Tony got me!" Matthew said happily. It was one of the few times recently that Ann Marie had seen a genuine smile on his face. Maybe these people were not as bad as she had thought.

"I'll think about it." She looked at Barone's icy dark eyes, pinpricked with light. "Thanks," she said curtly. "Matthew and I have to go."

"Let me see you out," Barone said, feeling that he had made some headway. They had made some unspoken promises to each other. There had been an exchange of erotic signals, he was sure of that. He liked her looks. He put his hand on her arm and she did not pull back. There was something possible here, there were deals to be made on many levels. As they worked their way through the crowd he imagined what she looked like with her clothes off.

"This is Captain Vincent," Barone said, snapping out of his tingling reverie as they reached the main entrance. The captain, in civilian clothes, had come over from his airport office when the hotel security men had called about a protest being staged by a group of older citizens in the lobby. They were retired people carrying signs that bore variations of the legend "Save Our Apartment House." The protesters had heard that a number of politicians would be at the hotel and had organized to stage a peaceful demonstration.

"You may not remember, Mrs. O'Brien, but we've met before," Captain Vincent said diffidently.

Ann Marie, distracted by the line of grizzled protesters circling the lobby, looked curiously at the police captain. "When was that?"

"On the day of your husband's burial. I was at the chapel out at the cemetery."

Ann Marie looked more closely at him. "I don't remember much," she said. "I remember it was cold and dark. Sorry." Captain Vincent was not bad-looking at all. She liked the attention that she was getting from all these strong-looking men.

"What's the picketing about?" She did not mind tarrying for a while with Barone on one side of her and Captain Vincent on the other.

"These people are part of a Gray Panther group, ma'am. There's some plan for a new parking garage that will take the place of the apartment house a lot of them are living in."

Ann Marie had heard about the project but had not as yet visited the neighborhood in her ward where it was to be developed.

"I want to meet these people," she said impulsively.

"Now, Mrs. O'Brien," Barone interjected swiftly, "you don't want to jump in here. This is a situation you want to check out first. With your captains, with other members of the organization."

"No," she said firmly. "If I represent these people, I want to talk with them." She looked around and saw that Matthew, the shy Anthony Barone watching over him, was playing with the toy plane near the registration desk.

"Captain, you get them outside. Tell them I want to hear what their troubles are."

"Mrs. O'Brien . . ." Barone broke off as she turned and went out through the main entrance of the hotel. The baker's dozen of elderly protesters filed out after her. Captain Vincent stood by the side of the door and watched as they gathered around Ann Marie and began to tell her of their grievances. Barone remained inside the lobby and shook his head at the scene. What Ann Marie did not know was that Barone owned the apartment house in question and that he stood to make an enormous profit if the complex deal, of which its demolition was only a part, finally went through. It meant a huge development, millions of dollars. "Goddamn," he whispered to himself, "this goddamn woman is going to be a lot of trouble."

He mumbled his way past Matthew and his nephew Anthony without looking at either of them. He would have a more serious talk with this dame. She was dangerous not because she knew too much but because she didn't know anything at all.

Ann Marie listened earnestly as an older man in a fishing hat ticked off the group's problems. They had no place else where they could live, they were getting by just where they were, the city didn't really need a new parking garage on that site. Her face grew stern as she heard them out. "You'll get action," she promised after they had finished. "I'll look into this right away. I promise you that."

"Every door seemed to close on us," a woman of about eighty said as she dabbed at her eyes with a handkerchief. "We're just about out of hope."

Captain Vincent folded his arms and watched the older people talking animatedly to Mrs. O'Brien. She seems like a nice lady, he thought to himself, and really interested in these people's problems. He glanced up at the dark expanse of the parking garage that rose a hundred yards beyond the discussants. He thought of the Noto boy, and then of the other young man whose pitiful funeral cortege had delayed the splendid train of limousines that had followed Captain O'Brien's remains to the cemetery chapel on that snowy day in December.

He remembered the manila folder of newspaper stories in his desk drawer. Vincent had clipped at least eight ads looking for information about young men who were missing from villages that sprawled beyond the airport. Where were the young men? Were they lying dead someplace with writing all over them? He shook his head. Hell, kids disappeared and reappeared all the time. Maybe he had been thinking too much about all this. He had to file these grim thoughts along with the clippings. The crowd broke up, the old people smiling as they scattered, and Ann Marie signaled to him. "Captain, would you mind getting my little boy for me. He's in the lobby. There's a nice young man watching him."

Vincent nodded and laughed at himself for daydreaming about mass murderers. This was what police work was like these days: getting aldermen's kids out of hotel lobbies.

15

*A*nn Marie's political education proceeded rapidly during the next few weeks. Angered, she felt the senior citizens deserved a better hearing than they had received. Getting angry was a form of release for her; she loaded the nameless conflicts and frustrations of her soul onto the ark of a cause, and loosed her hostility in the process. This time it was for the soon-to-be-dispossessed older people. She would talk to Mayor Cullen immediately.

"Annie, Annie," the old man said gently when she had finished her presentation, "I'm glad to see you so interested in the older people out there. Grand, Annie, just grand." The Mayor leaned back and folded his arms across his chest. "But, Annie, have you researched this question? Maybe the city's been more helpful than you think. Have you checked the history of this? Have you been to the Building Department? Or Human Services?"

"No," Ann Marie answered hesitantly. "The facts seem clear enough for me."

"And they may be, they may be. Annie, government exists in order to manage life for everybody together. Sometimes rights are in conflict. This is very important business, but you can't attack it like a crusader. You ought to do it like a member of the government. Pardon me for saying this, Annie, but this isn't the same as an MIA issue. You don't win it by dramatizing it. Headlines are not the same as winning what you want."

Ann Marie felt chagrined. Daddy was sending her back to finish her homework. "I thought . . ."

The Mayor raised his hand like a traffic cop. "I'm sure you have. And you care about these people. Maybe you ought to work through the process. That's why we have a City Council. And departments. And committees that oversee things like this. That's where you begin. Get the facts on this thing, and then proceed to do what you think is right."

"I thought you could just do something directly about this."

"Maybe I could. Maybe I should. But that's not my idea of how to run a city. I work through the various committees and departments. You can't get people into government service and then bypass or ignore them. I mean that, Annie. You're bright but you're a little impulsive."

Ann Marie did not know what to say. She had been gently dressed down, she had been shamed by this revelation of her naïveté, by this swift exposé of her blind-in-one-eye emotional style. The old Mayor had caught her trying to manipulate him into doing what she wanted, caught her at what she had been so good at doing with her own father when she was growing up. She felt herself blushing.

Damn the Mayor! He wouldn't budge. She couldn't get her way and he refused to make an exception for her.

"Annie," the Mayor said gently, "people come through that door by the dozens every day to see me. Half of them want to ask me for something. Half of them want to tell me something about somebody else. You can't rush into anything. You can't respond as though there were no other parts to the government. Do you understand what I'm saying?"

"Yes," she said softly. "I've got some work to do on this."

"Exactly," Cullen replied, a benign smile lighting his face. "And now, Annie, I'm afraid I have to take a pill and see Mark Richler, not that such events are connected . . ."

The brush-off. She hated to be reminded that there were other things and people in the old Mayor's life. Maureen would probably have stayed if she had wanted to. And Richler, she thought to herself as she crossed the office on her way out, that little Jew could get in any time he wanted. He was just entering as she left. Richler had a sheaf of papers under his arm and smiled a greeting at her. Ann Marie walked past him without a word.

"What's the matter with Mrs. O'Brien?' Richler asked as he spread the papers out on the Mayor's desk. Cullen popped a pill into his mouth and sipped a glass of water. "Mark," he said slowly as he placed the glass back next to the vacuum jug on his desk, "Mrs. O'Brien, as you once said, has very little political experience. She's got a lot to learn. Now what do the figures look like?"

The head of the Building Department was a professional engineer named Charles Tobias. He told Ann Marie on the telephone that he could see her briefly at five o'clock that afternoon. He would study the file on the project. A square, bustling bank teller of a man, he was all business when she appeared in his office. A folder lay open on his desk.

"Mrs. O'Brien, this project has been under consideration for several years. We were only responsible for the design concept and the integration of this into other city projects. As far as I can see, this was thoroughly researched, need was demonstrated, and the project was awarded to Hansen Construction as low bidders."

"But these old people have no place to go . . ."

"That may be, but I have nothing to do with it. I don't have that responsibility. You probably ought to see the Planning Department . . ."

"And that's the best you can say?"

"That, I'm afraid, Mrs. O'Brien, is all I can say. From our department's viewpoint, everything is in good order. I'm sorry."

"I'll bet you are," Ann Marie said angrily. "I'll just bet you are."

Tobias arched his eyebrows in surprise at her hostility. He was not, however, moved by that or by the erotic swing she gave to her backside as she marched out of his office.

The next morning she spoke to Arthur Larson in the Planning Department. What the hell is the matter with this place, Ann Marie asked herself. Why aren't there some Irishmen around instead of these coldhearted Swedes? Larson was affable, however, as he heard her out and he did not seem to be upset at her display of impatience. But everything was in order as far as he could see. All the elements had been considered, including the relocation of the tenants of the building that was to be demolished. Ann Marie could check with Human Services about that. There was nothing more that he could do.

"These things are complicated, Mrs. O'Brien," Larson said in a mellow voice, "but they are not done without thought, I assure you. And we are not as hardhearted as some people think. There is a committee of the City Council on this. You might speak to the chairman, Sam Noto—I'm sure you know him."

Ann Marie barely controlled herself as she thanked him and left his office. There were old people out there in her ward and nobody seemed to care about them. The goddamn bureaucracy was blind and dumb and full of Swedes. She was in a rage as she headed back to her own office on the third floor. She did not even notice Paul Martin walking down the corridor toward her.

"Annie, what's the matter? You look pretty steamed up."

Ann Marie's hardened face did not relax as she recognized Martin. "I'm beginning to think there's something in your approach," she said coldly. "There are lots of hardhearted bastards in this building."

Martin loved her hell-for-leather mood. He also lusted for her. He sensed that she would have been willing to go to bed with him on the spot, but how the hell could he swing it? These wonderful opportunities were all coming at the wrong times.

"What's the problem, Annie?"

Ann Marie brought him into her office and explained, in icy tones, the frustrations of her efforts to explore the new parking garage.

"Well, I hate to be the one to say I told you so. But I did. You know you could make quite a story out of this. Old people about to lose their home and the city bureaucracy remains indifferent. What the hell do the fat cats care? Mayor studies polls while senior citizens are evicted. Great stuff. Hell, we could make a great story out of this."

Ann Marie leveled her gaze at Martin. "Are you serious? Would you do that?"

"Sure." Martin crossed his legs and wrinkled his brow as though he were thinking deeply about the ethics of the matter. "We could make these sons of bitches uncomfortable. That's one of the powers of the press. Will you talk on the record?"

Ann Marie bit her lip. She was supposed to get the facts and work through the channels. She couldn't ignore Cullen's orders.

"No, not yet. Later maybe. Let me see this through my own way for now."

"Chances like this don't come around every day. You'll get lots of ink on this issue."

"If I'm right," she said in a surprising tone of caution. "I've got to be sure of that first."

"How about dinner? Doing anything, Madam Alderwoman?"

She rooted through her top drawer, searching for the directory of City Hall offices. "I'll tell you later," she said as she held the book open with one hand and dialed Sam Noto's office number with the other. "I'll call you later."

"Promise?"

Ann Marie nodded as Martin stood up to leave.

"This is Mrs. O'Brien," she said. "Is Alderman Noto there?"

Noto sat behind a large mahogany desk smoking a rope-like stick of cigar. He did not rise from his chair as he waved Ann Marie to a seat.

"Well, Mrs. O'Brien. I saw you at the luncheon for Matty Hogan, you and your kid. Nice kid."

"I want to talk to you about a building that's to be torn down in my ward in order to build a parking garage. Seventy old people live in it. They don't have any place to go. I want you to help me stop this." She said all of this matter-of-factly as if she did not expect Noto to help her any more than anyone else had. Noto puffed on his cigar and smiled.

"Sure, I can help you," he said almost graciously.

"You mean you can stop this project?" Ann Marie asked uncertainly.

"Start. Stop. What the hell's the difference? I can do it, yeah."

"Will you?" Ann Marie was wary, as though she were speaking to an easily ruffled animal.

"Maybe." Noto sucked on his gnarled cigar. "That depends."

"On what?"

"On what you can do in return. What the hell do you think we're running here? This is business. I help you. You help me. Easy."

"What do you mean exactly?"

"Well, little lady," Noto said, studying the cigar he held aloft in his right hand, "this is how we have to work together. It's like a business. I help you today, maybe I need you to help me tomorrow. You never know what might come up."

Was this a trap, a Sicilian cave filled with corpses? Ann Marie wanted to save that building but she couldn't sign a blank check for it.

"You don't want me to help? Fine. You come back when you make up your mind." Noto picked up a paper filled with figures and examined it as though Ann Marie had already left the room.

"I'm not sure I understand your proposition," she said firmly.

"Well, I don't understand your proposition either." Noto lowered the paper and let it fall carelessly back onto his desk. "You come in here. You tell me what you want. You don't have a goddamn fact or figure, nothing to back you up. I say I can help without asking any questions. Then you start asking me all kinds of questions. Who the hell is helping who around here?"

"How could you stop the building from being torn down?"

"Lots of ways. Shift the site. Buy the building back. Nothing to it. Easy when you know who to talk to."

"Will you really do that if I say I'll help you later on something?" she asked tentatively.

"I can only tell you something so many times. You make up your mind, come back."

Ann Marie rose silently from her chair. She had gotten what she was looking for and she was not sure now that she really wanted it. What would the price be, what would this toad of a man want in return? She thanked him for his time and left. He grunted a goodbye as he picked up the page of figures from his desk.

They might as well have been talking about a piece of meat or a sack of stone. It was all the same to Noto. Should she really try to save the building? It wasn't all as clear or as easy as she first thought. She would go back to the Mayor's office and tell him that she needed more time to think about it. Maybe she could get him to intervene directly. It was worth another try. These details were getting her down.

As she reached the fifth floor, however, Cullen was just leaving through the glass doors of the main entrance of his office. Maureen was on his left and Mark Richler was walking behind them. Ann Marie paused halfway down the corridor to watch them. They were laughing unselfconsciously about something as they moved together toward the elevator. She envied their easy intimacy with each other. Richler stopped at the elevator door as the Mayor and his daughter entered. Two body-guards moved in after them. Ann Marie could hear the Mayor's voice boom a last comment. They all laughed again. She felt desperately on the outside of their group and the government.

She watched Mark Richler as he walked back into the Mayor's office. She was suddenly angry at him for all the frustrations and disappointments of the day. Why wouldn't the Mayor just pick up a phone and save her all this trouble? Why did he give so much time to Richler and so little to her? Did Cullen really care for her? Or did he just use her? Somehow or other she was going to get action on this matter. Even if she had to go to Sam Noto for the help she needed to do it.

16

Ann Marie followed Mark Richler through the main entrance of the Mayor's office. If Richler was so close to Cullen—and as wise as everybody, including Paul Martin, said—then he ought to be able to help her. Richler was in Cullen's private office when Ann Marie caught up with him.

"Mark, do you have a minute?"

"Sure," Richler answered as he scooped up a pile of loose papers from the Mayor's desk and tucked them under his arm. "What can I do for you?"

Ann Marie described her efforts to get something done about the old people's apartment house. She omitted the part about Noto, as well as her conversation with Paul Martin. Richler hunched on the edge of Cullen's desk as she recited her tale in a voice seeded with irritation. When she had finished he smiled.

"You're getting a real introduction to municipal government, aren't you?"

"It seems like an advanced course to me. Those old people are in trouble. What can I do for them?"

Richler shrugged his shoulders. He had not survived as Cullen's chief aide by being drawn into situations like this.

"It seems to me you're going about it the right way. You say you haven't been to Human Services yet. That might clear up a lot of your worry. They do a hell of a good job in cases like this."

"Mark, that's what's wrong with city government, these delays, these procedures." The grinding edge of Ann Marie's anger was plainly audible now.

"What do you want me to do? You've talked to the Mayor and he told you how to handle it. For what it's worth, I think you ought to go along with his ideas."

Ann Marie was in no mood for sweet reason. She wanted something done now and to hell with departments and procedures, to hell with Richler's caution.

"Mark, you're supposed to be the man closest to the Mayor. Everybody says that. Couldn't you say something to him for me?"

Richler shook his head and eased himself off the desk. He started for the door.

"Mark, wait a minute." She closed the distance between them and put her hand on his arm. "You can help me if you want to."

Richler, uneasy at Ann Marie's move, pulled away. "Mrs. O'Brien, I'd help you if I could. I sympathize with you . . ."

"There're mostly Jews who live there . . ."

Richler was startled. "It doesn't matter who they are. It wouldn't matter to the Mayor if they were second cousins from Ireland. He'd still want everything to go through channels. The chances are you'll get what you want if you move that way. You're a member of the City Council, there's a lot you can do." They were at the door of the office.

Ann Marie stared coldly at Richler. Another man brushing her off, another man missing in action. Goddamn them all.

"I'll remember this, Mark. As you say, I am a member of the City Council . . ."

Richler opened his mouth, thought better of it, and walked through the door.

The next morning, the head of the Department of Human Services, Gordon Garfield, explained that preliminary efforts at relocating the old people had begun and that he expected that sixty percent of them would be settled in new quarters within a few months.

"What about the rest?" Ann Marie asked petulantly.

"Most of them will go with some other family member, a son, a daughter." Garfield smiled reassuringly. "I assure you, Mrs. O'Brien, we're handling this as sensitively as we can. It isn't as if this is news to these people. They've known this was going to happen for a long time . . ."

"That's not the way I heard it. And I heard it directly from them."

"We've had case workers interviewing everybody. This is a big project. That whole neighborhood is changing."

"Yes. It's falling down on top of the old people."

"Mrs. O'Brien, if this doesn't happen now, it will happen a few years from now. Redevelopment is taking place. To postpone that would merely make it harder when these people would be forced out later. It's inevitable."

"I'm sorry you feel that way, Mr. Garfield," Ann Marie snapped as she stood up abruptly and clattered defiantly out of the office.

Everybody was so reasonable, so goddamn reasonable. She fumed as she stomped noisily down the corridor. The Mayor and the system! She hadn't asked him for much. Against the soft corridor light the previous evening's images of the old Mayor and Maureen laughing together reappeared. They vanished as they had into the elevator. And Richler! He was really no help at all.

She stopped suddenly as she reached one of the building's broad stairways. Ann Marie was good with the press, everybody said that. Fine. The press would be her channel of assistance to these elderly constituents. She hurried down the stairs to the floor where her own office was located. She passed through the outer office without greeting the half dozen or so people who were waiting to see her. Her secretary lifted her head up away from her typewriter as she glided by but failed to get her attention. "Mrs. O'Brien . . ." she called firmly but all she saw was Ann Marie's back as she hurried through the door of her own office.

Ann Marie sat down and reached for the telephone. She dialed a number swiftly.

"Paul? This is Ann Marie. Can you drop by for a chat?"

"Christ"—Sam Noto coughed through the pollution of his now stub-sized cigar—"I know the deal's connected. What the hell's the difference if we wait awhile? The whole thing is going through within a few years anyway."

"I don't trust this goddamn woman. You want me to swallow the apartment house and you're not sure whether we'll be able to hold on to her or not. A woman like that, Sam, Christ, a woman like that, you don't know whether she'll keep her word or not." Richard Barone chopped gestures in the air with his right hand as he spoke. "What'll Rafferty think about this?"

"I already talked to him . . ."

"Hell, it wasn't easy to get this land together. Christ, we spent a fortune just getting those variances. We've got the whole fucking city finally cooperating. They're working on moving the old people now . . ."

"Rafferty says he'll go with it." Noto squashed the smoking knuckle of his cigar into his desk ashtray. "Worth it to get this O'Brien bitch."

Barone still looked unhappy. "But the parking garage. We'll need that when the shopping center gets under way." He scowled skeptically. "What makes you think she'll play ball?"

"Just say I got a feeling. Okay?" Noto searched in his pocket for another one of his evil-looking cigars. "My idea is this. Cullen's been stiffing her, throwing her back into the system. She don't like that. She's used to getting what she wants out of men. You know what I mean?" He laughed hoarsely, revealing brownish teeth. "She's been a real pain in the ass so far. Look the way she fucked up the cable television. So we do her a favor. She owes us. She owes somebody besides Cullen. We begin to collect. Christ, she's better with us than against us. She could help us in, shall we say, future business plans?"

Barone shook his head slowly. "You say Rafferty'll go along?"

"Rafferty says with the fucking inflation, you'll make twice as much in eighteen months as you will now. All we do is help her out, make her feel she can get things done without the help of the big turkey. We got a real whore here, that's my bet. And a real whore stays bought."

"Well . . ."

"There's one thing you can do. It's important. Get your friend Martin. Christ, he owes you a few favors. I think he's laying her anyway. Tell him to put in a few good words, tell him we don't want to see our names in the papers."

"Sam, that ain't as easy as you might think. These press guys, they don't push so easy."

Noto began to cackle derisively. "Don't shit me. You cut him in on a few good deals. What are you trying to do, kid your blood brother? You just don't want to pick up any of your chips with him yet. That's the truth, Christ, I know you, Richie . . ." He laughed until he coughed.

"I'll see." Barone had wanted to keep the reporter as an ace up his sleeve for some day when he really needed a good story or some inside information that only Martin might be able to provide. "I'll see, Sam."

"Good," Noto replied as he struck a match and held it below his fresh cigar. "Good. I tell you, it doesn't cost much. It'll mean a lot in the long run."

"Okay, Sam, I'll talk to Martin. I'll give him a call right away. But if this bitch double-crosses us, you heard it from me first."

"You'll see. I'll bet you fifty that I hear from her by this afternoon. She's tired of talking to these fucking professors in the different departments. You'll see . . ."

"Let me use your phone, Sam, I'll call Martin now . . ."

Martin was in the City Hall pressroom when Ann Marie reached him. He had been propositioning a girl reporter from a suburban newspaper when his phone rang and, after he hung up, he promised to contact her later. She was only twenty-two and there was a lot to be said for twenty-two-year-old girls. He could have filled a trophy room with the smooth hides he had brought home from hunting among the twenty-year-olds. The fantasy of a later meeting with the young woman reporter played pleasantly in his imagination as he hurried up the steps toward Ann Marie's office. A bird in the hand, he thought . . .

He passed through the waiting room where the clutch of glum-looking favor seekers still sat expectantly and went directly into Ann Marie's office. She did not waste time. She wanted a story, she wanted him to blast the planners and the engineers, she wanted him to find out who owned the building and whether there was a big profit involved in its sale.

"Now, Annie," Martin said smoothly, "you've got a great story here. We can run with it. There's no doubt of that." He paused as he remembered the telephone call from Barone he had received a few minutes before Ann Marie had reached him. Barone had done him a lot of favors. He had to protect him but he had not expected to get called on to do it so quickly.

"What's the matter, Paul?" Ann Marie asked, snapping the thread of his reverie. "Crusader Rabbit would have more enthusiasm than you. You were just talking about what a great story this would make. Now you look funny . . ."

"Have you thought this through, Annie?" Martin asked as he eased himself around to her side of the desk and leaned back against it. He looked down at her, his arms folded. Their legs rubbed against each other. "I mean, how do you want to play this? Is the city the villain? Is Cullen the bad guy?"

"Oh, no," she interrupted. "I don't want him in it."

Martin had found the vein he was looking for.

"You can't leave him out, Annie. It's his city. You think he doesn't know about this? Fat chance . . ."

"He doesn't have to be part of this. Who are the builders? Who are the people who are liable to make a profit out of this, out of dispossessing old people?"

"What the hell, you want pinpoint bombing. The Mayor would have to be in the target area in a story like this . . ."

"You've lost a lot of steam since yesterday. What happened to you?"

"I've fallen in love with a beautiful alderwoman and can't keep my mind on my work." He leaned down and kissed her full on the mouth. She was taken by surprise and her chair rolled backward under the impact of Martin's pressure. She put her hands up to push him away but Martin took them into his own and kept his mouth pressed firmly against hers until her chair bumped against the credenza by the wall. He pulled away from her mouth but held on to her hands.

"Paul, you're changing the subject . . ."

"The subject? What was the subject?" He leaned forward and kissed her again. "The subject was roses," he whispered. Ann Marie did not protest. After the frustration of the last few days this was not the worst thing that could happen to her.

He lifted her out of the chair and held her as close to himself as he could. He kissed her again and she pressed back against him. After all the frustration this was at least a response, something she could feel. It didn't require explanation. She was ready for Martin, she didn't care where they were, and she didn't care about her secretary or the little band of citizens waiting to see her. She would get around to all that and she would get around to the old people too. But first she was going to do something for herself. She reached down and picked up her phone. "Hold my calls."

They edged across the room holding each other like marathon dancers on their last turn on the floor. They found their way to the couch and descended slowly onto it. Martin would show her how a man took charge. He tugged her blouse free of her skirt. He struggled awkwardly to get his pants off without falling onto the floor. A handful of coins spilled out onto the carpet. That's the kind of goddamn thing that's always happened. Ann Marie laughed at his fumbling. This wasn't coming off the way he had planned it. She was still in charge. The lights on the desk phone blinked off and on as he struggled to get on top of Ann Marie without slipping off the couch. He braced his right foot against the lower arm of the couch, put his weight against it in order to pull himself up. His foot skidded on the buttery leather and Martin fell halfway to the floor, his legs splayed out painfully beneath him. "Goddammit," he howled, "my ankle, my fucking ankle." He twisted down onto the floor, reaching toward his right foot.

Ann Marie propped herself up on her arm and watched Martin writhing uncomfortably. "Oh, you use your *ankle* these days." She laughed.

Martin glared over his shoulder at her as he massaged his foot.

"Wait a minute," Ann Marie said, slipping off the couch, "I'll get you something cold." She tucked her blouse in and hurried barefooted across the room. Martin was sitting on the couch when she returned with a towel she had soaked in cold water in the bathroom off her office.

"Here, lover," she said, "this'll make you feel better." She picked up her purse and returned to the bathroom.

Martin was putting on his shorts when, makeup reapplied, she came back into the room.

"How's it feel?"

"Okay, it'll be okay," Martin said edgily.

"You really looked funny, you know . . ." Ann Marie laughed again.

"Cut it out," Martin said sharply. "What the hell are you trying to do, make a fool of me?"

"Oh, Paul, it wasn't my doing." She affected a nurse's smile of concern. "I think you'll recover."

"We could finish this. The hotel, yeah, the hotel. You remember 711, our lucky number? How about later this afternoon?"

"This isn't our day," Ann Marie said. She felt strangely satisfied anyway.

"I'll get a nice place," Martin said eagerly. "Wait. You'll see, you'll like it. I know just the place."

Ann Marie smiled at him as he tested his weight on his ankle. He was a big boy, that's what he was. That's what most men were.

"What do you say, Annie?" Martin had regained his composure. He slipped his shirt on.

"Maybe we ought to finish our other business first."

Martin pulled on his pants and reached down to pick up the change that was scattered in an arc at the edge of the couch.

"I want that story, Paul. You said you could do it. Now you've gone soft on it." She laughed again.

"Very funny," he snarled, picking up his tie. He stood in front of her desk. "Did anybody ever tell you that you put impossible conditions on things?"

"You're not going to do the story, are you?"

"No," Martin answered, turning away from her as he secured his tie. "Annie, the story I need from you isn't about some apartment house in your ward. You know that."

"You want something on the Mayor," she countered.

"Exactly. Something about his health, something about his money." Martin picked up his jacket.

"Not from me," Ann Marie answered. "No deal."

"Come on, Annie."

"Forget it."

"How about somebody close to Cullen."

"Like who?"

"Oh, I don't know. His daughter or that boozing husband of hers. Somebody inside the castle walls. Richler, maybe Mark Richler." Martin slipped his arms into his jacket and buttoned it.

Ann Marie hesitated. Richler, the inside man. Annie could never take Maureen's place. Richler was something else.

"What would you want to know about Richler?"

"Anything. Does he have business interests outside the office? Is he on the take? Does he screw trees? There's a hundred things he could be doing. Hell, he's been around forever."

"If I knew something about Richler, would you help me on the apartment house?"

What an odd deal. "Maybe."

"Maybe's are no good," Ann Marie said firmly.

"All right, I'll help you. If you've got something, that is. What did you have in mind? Do you have a lead on something?"

Ann Marie made a notation on her pad. "We'll see what shows up," she answered vaguely. "It may take some time."

"Well, I'll wait. You come up with something, you'll see a big story." He paused and pulled out his cigarettes. "There's nothing I can go with on the apartment house thing, not right now. It's too thin." He struck a match. "Now as to our unfinished business . . ."

Ann Marie liked Martin's utter lack of sentimentality. They had been through a low burlesque scene and they were bartering about stories. None of it made any difference to him. There was some relief in knowing a man with whom one could have such a relationship. "I may not need you at all," she said brightening up. "I may just save that property completely without your help."

Martin puffed on his cigarette. She wasn't going to finish their other business. He thought of the twenty-two-year-old girl back in the pressroom. He walked to the door and turned. "If you get anything on Richler, or anybody else, let me know." He flashed his rogue smile, "See you," and was gone.

17

*T*hings quieted down and Ann Marie settled into a new routine. She won the special election, the Mayor seemed fine and, after so much excitement in such a short time, life had again become slightly boring. She felt more comfortable with Paul Martin. He suited her well. He was romantic, sensual, and he had no interest in marriage. Martin had also gotten the keys to a Lake Shore Drive apartment from Barone. It was a much better place to meet.

A standoff had been reached about the project in her ward. Barone, on Noto's advice, held off in pushing Ann Marie to cooperate. Everything remained quiet until one September day, after leaving Paul Martin, Ann Marie studied the calls that had come in while she was out. She found one from the Gray Panthers tenants' group. A Mr. Solokowski had phoned. Ann Marie returned the call and was excited by what he proposed.

The old people were planning a demonstration that afternoon at the airport. They had waited long enough for help. They would make a human chain out of themselves on one of the runways.

"I'll be right out to stand with you," Ann Marie said enthusiastically. After all the trouble and all the miserable deals that had been offered to her by everybody from Sam Noto to Paul Martin, deliverance had come from the ranks of the spirited elderly themselves. Solokowski's plan would attract every television station in town. And she would be in the middle of it. Ann Marie told Solokowski to meet her in an hour with his group on the baggage level of terminal two.

To passersby the thirty old people standing around the attractive redheaded woman on the lower level of the terminal building might have been members of a package tour group clustered around their guide while the baggage was sorted out. Some of the men and women used canes, one had arm crutches, and a brightly blue-eyed man with a freckled bald head sat placidly in a motorized wheelchair. Nobody paid any attention to them.

"Now, Mr. Solokowski," Ann Marie said into the ear of the gray-haired man who bent his head to hear her, "where are the signs?"

"Later," he said in reedy tones, "they'll bring them here later. We couldn't make a human chain if we had to carry signs. We got a special group coming later with the signs."

Ann Marie nodded. "Well, then, let's go." She felt wonderful. Their plan of attack was simplicity itself. All they had to do was to wait for someone to open the door leading to the baggage area from the inside. They would pass swiftly through to that dark region that gave them direct access to the airfield. Mr. Solokowski would commandeer a baggage truck and drive out to the busiest intersection he could find. The others would follow on foot.

Because the plan was simple and bold and was built on a foundation of enormous surprise, it worked very smoothly. A baggage train operator slipped out of his seat, leaving the cart motor running, while he checked a list taped on a wall. He was startled when the train jerked away, an old man at the wheel.

The baggage handler stood, too amazed to pursue the carts that rumbled swiftly away. In a few moments Mr. Solokowski, his long hair streaming behind him in the wind, had negotiated the baggage train out past the planes which were lined up along the terminal building like animals at a trough. The driver hurried to notify the police but, by the time he did this, Solokowski had rounded the far dogleg of the green glass building and was heading for open concrete. It was a few moments before groundworkers noticed his strange maneuver and realized that he was not one of them. He sped between two passenger jets standing near the end of a long line of planes waiting patiently for their taxiing directions.

"Tower, this is American 234. There's an old man driving a baggage cart out on the taxiway."

"Roger," the reply came back. "Unauthorized vehicle sighted."

Ann Marie and her followers were spotted quickly. They were halfway down the length of the wing of the building, the old man in the motorized wheelchair riding point, moving in and out of the shadows of the parked jetliners.

"What?" Captain Vincent responded as he received his first phone call. The band of elderly men and women had already brought the activity along one side of the terminal to a halt. "What the hell is going on? I'll be right up."

He was in such a hurry that he left his manila folder open on his desk. He had just cut out a suburban newspaper ad inquiring about a seventeen-year-old runaway. That made thirteen clippings in ten months. He had no time for that now. Highjackings he had expected, more bodies in car trunks were always possible, but old people taking over the airfield! What was this job coming to?

Mr. Solokowski parked the baggage truck square in the middle of the main runway expanse, removed the engine key and tossed it as far as he could into the weedy growth alongside the concrete. Police and other emergency vehicles closed rapidly in on him as he sat fingering the cane that lay across his lap. He adjusted his thick glasses and smiled contentedly.

Near the end of the terminal the police and other airport personnel formed a ring around Ann Marie's marchers and, like a collapsing lasso, closed in gently on them. Captain Vincent arrived just as Ann Marie's group came to a halt inside the ring of police officers.

"Where are the signs?" Ann Marie asked the old man in the wheelchair as he pulled up beside her.

"Probably upstairs"—the old man nodded—"we've got a team inside, too."

"Mrs. O'Brien," Captain Vincent said as pleasantly as he could, "we've met before."

"Hello, Captain. You remember these people from my ward. We're here to save their apartment house."

"Mrs. O'Brien, we can't do that by tying up the airport."

"It may be the only way we can do it," Ann Marie answered defiantly. Cheers rose from the old people standing around her.

"'We have to ask you to disperse peaceably."

"There is no law above the law of justice," Ann Marie responded quickly. "Besides, what would it look like for you to be on television arresting people old enough to be your parents?"

"Yeah, what about that?" the lady on the arm crutches called. "You wanna look like Nazis?"'

On the concourse almost directly above this confrontation, six elderly couples held banners by the windows. Shortly after this demonstration began the first television vans arrived at the airport. Soon all aspects of the event were within range of the cameras.

"We'll give you back your airport," Mrs. O'Brien said to Captain Vincent, "when the city gives these people back their homes."

"Now, Mrs. O'Brien, we don't have anything to do with this. You know that. Why don't we all just march upstairs? I'm sure there are plenty of reporters around by now. You can talk to them."

"I'll have to talk to my people," Ann Marie answered. The captain backed off a few feet as the aged men and women huddled around their alderwoman.

They whispered back and forth and after a few minutes Ann Marie stepped forward. "You'll have to arrest us, Captain. We want attention for our cause."

Captain Vincent raised his hands in a placating gesture. "Now, I understand how you feel, Mrs. O'Brien, but we really cannot let you interfere with the operation of the airport. I want to ask you again to disperse peacefully."

"We will stand here peacefully." Shouts, like slurred endorsements in the House of Commons, sounded around her.

"You don't give us much choice, I'm afraid," the captain said. "You understand, don't you?"

"You're only doing your duty, Captain. That's what they said at Nuremberg too."

Mayor Cullen had gone into a room off his office to watch the television coverage of the airport incident. Mark Richler stood next to him, his hands on either side of his waist, a cigarette at the corner of his mouth. Paul Martin stood by a fence at the edge of the airfield as the special lenses picked up the fuzzy figures of the protesters as they were placed one by one into police vans. The old people went limp when the officers approached them. Ann Marie went into the paddy wagon with them.

"My God, Mark, the woman's gone mad," Cullen said as the scene shifted to the apprehension of Mr. Solokowski out on the runway. Cullen looked up at Richler, who continued to watch, a frown of concentration shadowing his face.

"A clever woman, Tom," Richler said without emotion, "but a very impatient one. I knew she'd been quiet too long."

"She has been quiet, hasn't she? I thought she fell in love or something." Cullen sighed, shaking his head. "And this amount of publicity will shake things up on that building project again."

"Damned right. Every older person in the city will identify with those people. She's made it a hot issue. They'll have to back off on that project now."

The Mayor stood up, leaned over and snapped off the television set, and walked, Richler at his side, back into his main office.

Cullen smiled as he sat down at his desk. He ran his right hand through his hair. "Have we taken an asp to our bosom?" he asked genially. "We'll have to tone her down a little. She's going to disturb an awful lot of people. I imagine Rafferty will be calling any minute now."

In another part of City Hall, Sam Noto was listening on the phone to the anguished wails of his blood brother, Richard Barone.

"Sam, what the fuck? You said she'd play ball. If we all laid low for a while, you said you'd get her under control. Now she doesn't have to play ball with any of us. Christ, she's had ten million dollars' worth of publicity. We'll have to delay that project again or face a hell of a lot of trouble. I warned you. I warned you you couldn't trust the bitch."

"Rich, who the hell would think she'd do this? Nobody could know.

She doesn't know the rules. That's the trouble, this cunt doesn't know the rules we play by."

"Well, goddammit, you better find out how to teach her. She's made us look like a bunch of fools. And she doesn't owe us a thing. Christ Almighty, Sam, we've got to straighten this dame out . . ."

Captain Vincent looked at his watch. Three o'clock. He stretched to loosen the kinks in his back. He had handled the demonstration as swiftly as possible; the airport traffic had been interrupted for only fifty-seven minutes. A mess, and he had not enjoyed taking the old people away in the police vans. He sighed and entered the elevator that took him down to the subterranean level where his office was located. Officer Hackman was waiting by the sergeant's desk in his outer office when he entered.

"Captain, I'm just coming on duty. I guess you've had your hands full."

"You can say that again. Mrs. O'Brien doesn't take no for an answer. Did you want to see me?"

"Well . . ."

"Come on in." He gestured for him to follow him into the plain windowless office. Vincent sat down and looked wearily at the young officer.

"My brother, Captain, my brother thought you'd be interested. He's picked up some rumors about a guy who's been seen in some of the shopping malls lately. His own chief won't listen to him, says he's crazy. In the electronic games places and the record stores. Nothing definite, but he invites kids to lunch, sometimes to dinner, sometimes two or three at a time. Says he wants to give them wrestling lessons . . ."

Captain Vincent's fatigue and annoyance drained away. "Where is this? Does he have a name?"

The old people were released almost immediately and Ann Marie, standing with a group of them on the steps of the police station, made a speech that capped the coverage of the event on the local newscasts that evening. The network shows mentioned the airport takeover briefly, treating it somewhat wryly, but Ann Marie O'Brien was mentioned by name. She had gotten home in time to watch the news program and had taken the phone off the hook so that she would not be disturbed by any telephone calls.

Matthew, who had been with his great-aunt all day, was upset and crawled up close to his mother as the television blared out the story of the afternoon's graybeard protest at the airport.

"Were they really gonna keep you in jail, Mom?" he finally asked.

"No, Matthew," she answered calmly, "they'd never do that. Some-

times you just have to make a lot of noise to make people pay attention
to something that's wrong. Mommy's all right, don't worry about that."

She left the phone wrapped in a towel most of the evening. She must
get a switch that would allow her to turn the phone off whenever she
wanted to. She didn't want any calls, she just wanted to enjoy the feeling
that had welled up in her as she led the old people down the side of the
airport building. Power had been born in her. It had not been immacu-
lately conceived, but it had been delivered at full term on the tarmac of
O'Hare Field. Ann Marie wanted to relish these moments and to replay
the excitement of the day, letting it arc through her like swipes on a
radar screen.

She had finally accomplished what she had wanted without anybody's
help. With the media as her bustling entourage she was as strong as any
of them.

She must have impressed Mayor Cullen. He must have recognized the
skillful way in which she had played this game. Ann Marie felt alive and
free in a way that she had never known before. She could take on anybody now.

18

A grim-looking Francis Rafferty arrived at 10 A.M. the next day to see Mayor Cullen. He completely ignored Cap Malloy's efforts to amuse him while he waited in the Mayor's outer office.

"Did you hear, Alderman, we were going to put waterbeds in the hallway here after the election?"

Rafferty scowled at him.

"That's so we can say that Mayor Cullen truly walks on water. Isn't that grand now?"

Rafferty did not even give a polite laugh but rose at the secretary's signal and marched into Cullen's private office. The Mayor was alone at his desk studying another sheaf of poll results. He wore dark thick-framed glasses, something he seldom did when anybody else was around.

"Francis, my friend," he said heartily, "what is the source of the fire I see in your eyes?"

"Goddammit, Tom," he said urgently, "you've got to rein in this woman. She's drawn so much public attention to that development in her ward that we've had to back off. Not once, but twice."

Cullen raised his eyebrows quizzically, delighting in Rafferty's discomfort.

"Tom, she's got some very important people upset. We need land developers, we need people ready to risk capital. To get it and then to have it interfered with by a woman who doesn't know shit from Shinola, well, they'll look other places to put their money . . ." He was out of breath.

"Now, now, Francis, I hardly think Mrs. O'Brien has undermined the fiscal integrity of the city. Have a seat. Have a glass of water." The Mayor poured water into a glass from the jug on his desk and handed it across to Rafferty.

"Francis, you yourself wouldn't have any financial interest in that development, would you? I understand there'll be a big shopping mall, town houses and apartments, office plazas. A regular city out there."

Rafferty calmed down after sipping the water.

"It just so happens that I have some interest in the property. Cast your bread upon the waters, Tom, I've always believed in that." Rafferty was beginning to sound like himself again. "But that's not the point. You can't have somebody like Dick Barone investing over two million dollars and then let some woman ruin the whole thing on him. You've got to discipline her, for the good of the party."

"Well, I'd have to think about that. It doesn't seem to me she's done so much harm. Let me give you some advice. She's an elected official. Don't fight with her. Make her your friend. You want her strength on your side, you're the one who knows just how to do that."

Rafferty looked skeptical. "What do you have in mind?"

"Well," Cullen said as he removed his glasses and rubbed his eyes, "why not include plans for senior citizen housing in your development? Low cost with plenty of federal aid. Get her to be honorary chair for that part of it. Name it after her husband, something creative like that. She can't very well fight you if you're taking her cause away from her. She'd have to support the rest of it, and it really wouldn't cost you a dime."

"Glory be to God, Tom, it is a grand idea at that." Rafferty sipped some more water. "But I'd still like you to talk to her."

"I'll have Mark chat with her about public relations. Now, Francis, you'd better get back to your devotions. We must keep the sun in the sky for a few more days."

But Rafferty was already preoccupied as he left the office. Why hadn't he thought of that?

Cullen smiled to himself. Rafferty had been dumb not to think of senior citizen housing to begin with. He asked his secretary to find Mark Richler.

"Mrs. O'Brien, the Mayor is not mad at you. He only asked me to speak to you about some of the public relations aspects of your work."

She was not sure whether Cullen had asked Richler to talk to her or not. She wanted to think that he had stopped by on his own.

"Mark," she said tartly, "I'm going to win this issue. I'm going to help the party a lot. I've dramatized us as the party of the people. That includes old people too."

"There's no doubt that you dramatized it," Richler said, allowing himself a rare indulgence in ironic counterpoint, "but you don't want to think the media is friendly just because they play you up."

"Another thing, Mark," Ann Marie cut across his comments, "I've had lots of calls. And letters. They're almost entirely in my favor. The complaints have come from people like Rafferty and Noto, people who front for Barone. These men wanted to take over when the Mayor was sick— you know that."

"I think," Richler said in a conciliatory tone, "you ought to remember that you have to work with these people. They're not devils. They're not angels either. But they are Council members and they have power. You can't just savage them in order to get on television or into the papers. The Mayor knows all about them, but he doesn't want to make permanent enemies of them. He's never believed in that. The Mayor's a great realist, you know."

Richler smiled. "Look, Mrs. O'Brien, ideals are great. I'm an idealist myself. But life isn't ideal. That's what politics is all about: negotiating your way through a life that isn't ideal."

"What exactly am I supposed to do?" She was not conceding the argument.

"There's nothing you're supposed to do. You just have to be receptive to the way things are done."

"Is that all you've come to see me about?"

"Not exactly. Let me put it this way. The Mayor feels that Alderman Rafferty wants to cooperate with you, that he will be in touch with you about the senior citizen issue. All the Mayor would like is for you to hear him out."

"Doesn't the Mayor know what kind of a man he is?"

Richler laughed and shook his head. "You know the Mayor once told me he likes having Irish Catholics around him because he understands them so well. He says he knows just how they'll try to betray him."

Ann Marie looked stonily at Richler. She would listen to Rafferty and she would do what Cullen expected of her. Was he really speaking for the Mayor? Or was he somehow using his position of influence to keep her away from Cullen?

"And there are no conditions on this?" Ann Marie studied Rafferty closely.

"Glory be to God, ma'am, it was our intention all the while to have a proper place for the senior citizens. You don't think we would have granted all the necessary variances and all the other things without holding the developers to taking care of the older people, do you? That's part of what's caused the delay these past months. We know there's a good number of them in that neighborhood. And even though most of them are not of our faith, Mrs. O'Brien, they're fine citizens, fine tax-paying citizens, and it would be a sin to neglect them, a terrible sin. Honor thy father and mother. Glory be to God, it will be a blessing for us all to have this project go ahead. And to name it the Captain Charles O'Brien Center is no more, surely, than a hero deserves."

Ann Marie did not really believe or trust him, but the plans he had outlined made sense and they achieved more than she could have by delaying further the destruction of one apartment house. She liked the

idea of a memorial for Charlie. She hadn't thought much about him in
months. A memorial would make her feel better about forgetting him so
easily. She turned a poker face to Richard Barone, who had accompanied Rafferty to the meeting.

"You stand to make a lot of money out of this, Mr. Barone."

"That's the nature of capitalism, Mrs. O'Brien. You take a risk and you
deserve the reward of the risk you take. That's the American way."

Ann Marie paused for a moment, looked back and forth between the
two men. She had beaten them. They were suing for peace.

"All right, gentlemen, I'll serve as chair for the senior citizens' complex
in the development. When can we announce it to the old people?"

"Saturday would be a good day," Rafferty answered. "It would make a
grand story for the old people to read in their Sunday papers."

"And you'll get all the good coverage, Mrs. O'Brien," Barone said, a
salesman slipping in an added feature on an appliance deal. "You'll get
all the publicity, you and Captain O'Brien. I'm sure you'll want to share
some of it with Mr. Rafferty, seeing as he's done so much of the prepara-
tory legislative work on this."

Ann Marie smiled at Rafferty. "You don't mind, do you?"

"If it was just for me, I wouldn't care about it at all. God afflicts the
proud, but He lifts up the lowly. On the other hand, it would add a note
of solidarity to the effort, it would show party harmony. I'm sure the
Mayor would be pleased as well."

"Okay," Ann Marie said, sensing her importance in the matter, "Saturday is the day."

The Thomas Cullen Fund-raising Dinner was a big night, a hotel
ballroom filled with politicians, contractors, and other fat cats with glowing eyes. As Monsignor Fitzmaurice read the opening prayer, again
representing the Cardinal, who was off preaching a charismatic retreat
in Ohio, the Mayor studied the crowd carefully. Despite the attempt at a
coup d'état the previous Christmas—and despite his own collapse and
hospital stay—Cullen had again managed to tug the blanket of harmony
over the edgy animals of government. At least they were all in their
proper stalls tonight. They had even established a working relationship
with Ann Marie O'Brien, who was more energetic than Cullen had expected. She sat at a big table—a stoneface between Matthew and Aunt
Molly. Mother Francis was there too. Where was her father? Too many
people and too much excitement for him.

Cullen looked down at his daughter Maureen. What a great help she
had been. And what a wonderful mother to those children despite that
weak-willed drunk of a husband. Look at him. Cockeyed already. Still,
things were holding together. They would be in good shape for the May-
oralty election next time around. Governing and running a political

party was like keeping order in a reform school classroom; it took all your attention and you could still get killed for all your pains.

Ann Marie watched the old Mayor carefully as he rose in a storm of applause to speak. Not far down the dais sat Judge Matthew Hogan. A typical Cullen touch, with his co-opting philosophy of always making friends with his enemies. Had she really pleased him, going in with Noto and Rafferty on the housing project? Anyway, those aldermen who thought they were so tough had a new respect for her. Rafferty and Company had come around and saved the old folks after all. Of course, the old people were surprised to find out that, after all the fuss, Ann Marie had agreed to let their building be torn down. But there would be new quarters rising soon. That main battle was over. What kind of fight would she face next? She enjoyed those more than the details of law-making.

Paul Martin sat next to Max Day eyeballing all the women, with spe-cial glances at Ann Marie. He couldn't figure it out. He was really get-ting to like her. Maybe not exactly to love her, but like her as he never had any other woman. He treated her well in his broadcasts and col-umns. Barone's suggestion, but he would have done it on his own. And she was a good lay, better in some ways than that twenty-two-year-old reporter. What the hell, she had had more experience. There was some-thing about her that, despite the ups and downs of their relationship and the lies he sometimes told her, kept him intrigued. He and Ann Marie seemed to hit if off well in a curious nonbinding way. He liked her, goddammit, and he never thought he'd hear himself say that about anybody.

Sam Noto fidgeted in his seat. The goddamn fools, he thought, they've struck an alliance with a woman who's dangerous. Fuck with women, they can give you bad sicknesses. Well, let Rafferty and that crowd do it their way. Those dumb bastards would be back for his advice soon enough. Only a goddamn fool thought he knew how to handle women.

". . . and so we pledge again, as we have before, our complete dedica-tion to the work of governing and improving this great city." The Mayor smiled broadly at the audience as he put aside his text. "Let me add a few words," Cullen said in his deep baritone. "In the last year, there has been a lot of speculation about my health. Let me say to my friends— and to any Republicans who are here—I've never felt better in my life." Thunderous applause filled the ballroom and Cullen smiled and waved into the cameras. He called his daughter and her family up to join him. That's when Ann Marie took Matthew by the hand and began to move out through the tables toward the exit. She did not need to witness an-other display of the Cullen family intimacy.

Ann Marie hurried out of the hotel with Aunt Molly and Mother Francis trailing about a hallway behind. She would take Matthew home and then return to the hotel for the private party that followed the banquet. She suggested to Mother Francis that she go directly to the party with Monsignor Fitzmaurice. Mother Francis was dying for a drink anyway. Aunt Molly would stay home with Matthew.

As Anne Marie reached the night air and searched around for her driver, she realized that the future was no longer uncertain. She was in politics, she was a real part of the Cullen administration. She hoped things would stay lively.

Captain Paul Vincent's wife, Mary, told him that he was getting too wrapped up in something that was none of his business. He had nodded and said that he just wanted to check something out. It was okay—he smiled as he kissed her on the cheek—he would be home by ten o'clock. That was why he was sitting with Officer Hackman in the "Hi-Tec-Rec Arcade" at the Fruitful Plains Shopping Mall. They pretended to be playing a sophisticated electronic war game while they watched the flow of customers. The room echoed with the pings and bells and whooping sounds that accompanied the electronic encounters in the machines all around them.

"Well, Captain, that makes two games out of three. Can we fake our way through another one?"

Vincent searched in his jacket pocket for more quarters, inserted them in the slot. The display glowed beneath them once more.

"Do you like this stuff?" Vincent asked.

"It's not bad. I wish I had a beer."

"Well, kids like it, that's certain. We haven't seen anybody who looks suspicious yet, unless you count the manager over there. And he thinks we look suspicious."

"It's a funny thing about this," Hackman replied, leaning closer to Vincent as a shower of explosive noises rose out of the machine next to theirs. "This place is filled with kids. And a few adults, most of them in their twenties or early thirties. It's a natural place for a guy to make a pickup. They say this guy has a lot of change, he loans out quarters to the kids that are hooked on these things. A guy could make contacts easy in a place like this."

"You know," Vincent said wearily, "I'm beginning to wonder. What the hell am I, a grown man, doing here at nine o'clock at night? Hell, maybe I should forget this whole thing. My wife says I'm crazy . . ."

"I know what you mean. My wife's not happy with me either."

The men smiled at each other.

"And yet"—Vincent grinned—"I learned long ago that this is what police work is like. Sitting in a dumb place waiting for something to happen." They laughed and began to play their electronic game again.

They did not notice the man at first. He seemed a part of the place, like somebody who worked there. He was about thirty, sported a cowboy's moustache, and he was watching two teenagers who were tensely engaged in some interstellar war game at the far corner of the arcade. He caught Vincent's eye when he pulled up his left arm. Dangling by a leather thong from his wrist was a small bag. The captain had glanced up just in the split second that it took the man to poke it open with his right hand and to remove a handful of coins and spread them across the glass surface of the game. Then he dropped his left arm immediately. Vincent had just caught the essence of the swift gesture, the sweeping move of the friendly stranger loaning the boys some money so they could keep playing. Vincent touched Hackman on the forearm.

Hackman turned slowly. The kids—they could not have been more than seventeen—looked hesitant. The money lay untouched on the top of the game. The stranger, his face lighted with animation, continued to talk, making gestures of "Go ahead, don't worry about it, glad to help you" with his right hand. He was dressed in dark clothes. Everything about him was dark.

It was a curious dumbshow played against the muffled futuristic sound effects that rose and fell in this strange place of recreation. The sturdily built man in the dark clothes was being too friendly. One of the teenagers stood up and the other rose a litttle more slowly from his chair. They weren't taking his money, they were breaking away, leaving his quarters where he had spread them. He reached out and took one of the youth's arms. It was clear that the kids were not buying whatever it was that the stranger was trying to sell them. Finally they pulled away and headed for the door. The man in the dark clothes quickly scooped up the coins, slipped them into his bag, and turned to leave.

"You take the kids," Vincent said curtly. "I'm following him."

They hurried out onto the sidewalk. The teenagers were looking in a window a half dozen stores away. Hackman turned and walked toward them. Vincent peered out into the dark of the parking lot. Where was the son of a bitch? About a hundred yards away a car door opened. A solid, dark figure stood outlined in a frame of light. He raised his left arm and leaned it against the car roof. A small pouch dangled from his wrist. He slipped into the car and closed the door.

Captain Vincent hurried to his car and caught up with the stranger's vehicle as it turned right onto the main highway that fronted the mall. Vincent followed it for about five miles. The stranger followed a road that led through a band of trees to a development of English Tudor tract houses. The captain stayed about a city block behind the other car and stopped as it turned onto the driveway of a corner house. Vincent started off again very slowly. As he passed the house the garage doors were clacking down behind the car he had been following. A decorative mailbox stood on a mock farmpost at the edge of the driveway. It read "Phillips, 111."

The captain was not happy the next morning to discover that George Phillips of 111 Riverview Circle was an active member of the local Democratic organization, Alderwoman O'Brien's organization.

19

*F*all entered the city that year like a road company ballet, grace under strain. That was Ann Marie too. She settled down for a while, but sitting through hearings and doing paper work set off a consuming restlessness in her. She had two antidotes.

One of them was Paul Michael Martin, whom she saw regularly. "Noonsies," Martin termed these sessions, which in their raw and indifferent intensity made up for what they lacked in depth of emotional commitment. They weren't competing so much with each other any more, either. Paul Martin felt very relieved.

Ann Marie's second solution was to cause trouble. Championing the old folks' cause was only a warmup for her sudden descents on various businesses in her ward. Ann Marie loved nothing better than to stage a confrontation with some mechanic or butcher about whom she had received a complaint. She always invited the press along with her, so she popped up regularly on the evening news and in the papers. She loved to make a well-publicized accusation. The people called her "Joan of Arc."

Following through was something else. There was nothing exciting in that and she delegated follow-up to a member of her staff. On one or two occasions, the affronted businessman proved his innocence, too late to do him any good.

The Mayor didn't mind. He had other matters to consider, including a reorganization of the city transportation system, trouble with the schools, and plans for running again eighteen months later. Ann Marie charged hard, but she was only affecting small fry. Near the end of the year, she involved herself in police matters.

George Phillips had made an appointment with her. He had been a member of the Democratic organization for five years, he had raised money and helped to deliver the vote for Ann Marie and all the other Democratic candidates. As a reward, he had a supervisor's job in the Sanitation Department. And he had a good record there. She could look it up, she could call up if she wanted to. Judge Hogan could tell her.

"So, Mrs. O'Brien," he said across the battered desk in her small ward headquarters office, "I object to being followed by the police. And I've been followed, I'm no dummy. What is this, Hitler's Germany, a man can't walk the streets as a law-abiding citizen anymore?"

"You're sure there's a policeman following you?"

"Yes, in plain cars and plain clothes. The reason I'm sure is because I got a good look at one of them the other afternoon. His name is Paul Vincent, he's a captain, for God's sake, and he's supposed to be in charge of the airport. He's got no business tailing me."

"I know this Captain Vincent. I've met him a couple of times. Let me have a talk with him." Ann Marie liked the idea of baiting a police captain, especially the one who had arrested her and her band of protesters at the airport. Captain Vincent was a good-looking guy, just the kind with whom she could generate a little playful tension. Why would he be following somebody in her organization? Was somebody spying on her for Rafferty or Wendel? Carney had a lot to do with the police. Maybe he was involved in this. She didn't like the idea of policemen keeping an eye on her party workers. Were they trying to keep an eye on her? She would put a stop to that immediately.

Ann Marie arrived at O'Hare Field on a cold December day. The whistling roar of jet engines drowned out Captain Vincent's sidewalk greeting to her. She smiled and followed him into terminal two.

"Why don't we go up to the Airline Club?" the captain asked. "It's a good place to talk."

Vincent waved at the hostess at the desk as he led Ann Marie back to a conference room and closed the door behind them. Ann Marie seated herself at the small round table and tugged off her gloves. Vincent looked at her warily. He had not seen her since the Gray Panthers' demonstration.

"Captain Vincent, I want you to stop following George Phillips."

"Who said I was following him?"

"He's complained to me about it. He recognized you on one occasion. It's been going on for months. Maybe you're not as good at shadowing people as you think." Ann Marie enjoyed nettling the police officer.

"Mrs. O'Brien, I've seen people make all kinds of mistakes in identifying people. They do it in the lineup all the time." Vincent's voice was calm and steady.

"Captain, I'm not here to argue about this. Mr. Phillips is a law-abiding citizen and he objects, rightly I think, to being followed and having his home watched. This is a democracy and, unless you can prove that you have good reasons for this surveillance, you'd better discontinue it."

"There are sometimes confidential matters that can't be discussed," Vincent replied.

"That won't do here, Captain. You've got to either put up or shut up

on this matter. Who told you to do this? Was it Rafferty? Are you working for somebody who wants to get something on me?"

Vincent blinked and pulled back from the table.

"I don't spy for anybody."

"Well, see that you don't. And stay away from Mr. Phillips." She
smiled sourly at the captain. "Stick to arresting senior citizens. It's more
your line of work."

Vincent reddened but held his tongue. Trouble with her was not
something he needed and, dammit, he was vulnerable to her complaints.
He didn't have anything on Phillips, nothing but suspicions and that
nagging feeling that he was a man to watch. If he watched him long
enough, Phillips would make a mistake. Phillips could tell him where
those disappearing kids were. A cop's intuitions? He really didn't have a
thing. Maybe he had let himself get carried away.

Ann Marie rose from her chair and Captain Vincent opened the conference room door.

"I appreciate your coming all the way out here," he said as she walked
past him. "I do understand your concern and I'll take care of it."

Ann Marie flashed him a satisfied smile. She had accomplished what
she had wanted. Now she could turn on a little charm. "I hope, Captain,
that we can meet again when we're not involved in a problem of some
kind."

He nodded and escorted her out of the club and downstairs to her
waiting car. "Goodbye, Mrs. O'Brien," he said, as the car pulled away.
He turned to walk back into the building. If he didn't know better, he
would have sworn that Eve lived again in the alderwoman's last smile.
Was she ready to pick out a tree under which they could frolic? Jesus
Christ, I need some time off. He shook his head and headed for the elevator at the far end of the terminal.

Ann Marie tingled with satisfaction. If they thought they could spy on
her by spying on her organization workers, they had another thought
coming. If it wasn't Rafferty or Wendel or one of that crowd, who could
they be? Captain Vincent seemed genuinely surprised when she had
challenged him about them. Who else would want to find out about her?
She watched the towers and steeples blur by the window of her car
as she headed down the expressway toward the heart of the city. Part of
Cullen's meaty face beamed off a peeling brick wall display that had
survived a former campaign. Some vandal had whited out the letter R
from one of the words. Now it read THOMAS CULLEN YOUR
F IEND. Mark Richler wouldn't like that, not at all. Mark Richler was always so goddamned worried about the Mayor's image.

Mark Richler.

Mark Richler, of course. He was always cautioning her, always warning her, always running interference for the Mayor and keeping her away from him. Richler had been around forever. He knew everybody, including cops. Martin had told her that the grapevine said that Richler had opposed her being named to the blue ribbon committee. Richler had always emphasized her lack of political experience. Richler didn't like her. It was as simple as that. Why hadn't she understood that before? He never helped her when she wanted it. He was always referring her back through channels. Mark Richler wanted her out of City Hall, that was certain. He only helped her because Cullen had made him do it. Secretly, he would do whatever he could against her.

Besides, he was a Jew.

Late that afternoon as she lay in bed with Paul Martin she began her counterattack. She reached up and touched Paul's hair with her hand. She curled a lock of it around her forefinger as he began to lower himself onto her.

"What are you trying to do, break my rhythm?" he asked as he awkwardly pushed her hand away.

"Wait, Paul," she whispered.

"Some things can't wait."

She turned her face away from his.

"What the hell do you want?"

"I want to talk a little."

"Christ, there'll be plenty of time for talk afterwards."

"Paul, you once asked me to tell you something about the Mayor. And if I couldn't do it about the Mayor, to tell you something about Mark Richler."

Martin's interest sharpened. For perhaps the only time in his life he let curiosity overwhelm the tide of lust that flooded through him.

"Have you got something?"

"Maybe. Depends on what you can do with it. I think he's using police to spy on city officials."

"What?" Martin pulled up away from Ann Marie and leaned on his elbow. "That could be a hell of a story. How do you know?"

"I think he's trying to find out about me. Richler's had people tailing members of my organization."

"Have you got names? Dates?"

"I can get them. Do you need all that for a start?"

Martin swung himself up and sat on the edge of the bed. "Maybe not, maybe not. Tell me what you know about this."

He rose and, stark naked, walked over to the chair where he had placed his coat. He took a pad and pencil and came back to the bed.

"I'll tell you more afterwards," she said in a half-teasing voice.

"What the hell is this?" Martin said, dropping the pad on the floor and climbing back between the sheets. Ann Marie rolled swiftly to the other side of the bed and Martin hurried after her. He took her by the shoulders and wrestled her back toward him. "First things first," he said as he leaned forward to kiss her.

"Mark, Mark," Cullen said soothingly as he studied the advance copy of *Eyes* that had been sent to his office that Thursday afternoon, "I know there's nothing to this. This story is all innuendo, it's all conjecture. They don't name any names, they don't give any real facts."

Richler wrinkled his forehead. "They've wanted to get you for a long time. Getting at me is second best." Richler was nervous and uncomfortable. The attack was so vague that, although he was the expert at dealing with such onslaughts, he really did not know what to do to protect himself.

The Mayor spread the paper out on his desk and rubbed his chin thoughtfully.

"Mark, we'll just have to ignore this. I mean, here's a story suggesting that you have policemen spying on Democratic workers in certain sections of the city. The closest thing he's got is a quote from this unnamed organization worker claiming that he's been followed by a high-ranking police officer. But no names, no names. And no real connection with you . . ."

"I understand all that. But there's no way to answer a smear without repeating it, and this Martin can certainly make things sound bad."

Cullen glanced through the story once more in silence while Richler lighted a cigarette.

"Mark, forgive me for asking this." The old Mayor frowned at himself for what he was about to do. "There isn't anything in this, is there?"

Richler was hurt but not totally surprised by Cullen's question. If the old man found out that there was something they could pin on him, Richler knew that the Mayor, despite their years of closeness, would separate himself from him quickly. That was one of Cullen's fundamental rules of survival.

"Of course not. Why would I want to do such a thing? It's crazy. That's what bothers me about this. The whole thing is crazy. That's what makes it dangerous. And this Paul Michael Martin will be on television tonight raising the same questions. It doesn't make me feel too good."

"Of course, of course." Cullen sighed. "Shall we make a statement?"

"You'll get plenty of questions. I think we have to use our standard approach. Just say that it's another example of gutter tactics and that's all."

"Yes, Mark, you're right. I'm sure this will blow over in a few days." But Cullen sighed as he spoke these words. There was none of the old booming confidence in his voice. Cullen sounded like a man expecting the worst. As Richler rose to go he realized that if any more stories came

out about his old adviser he might have to do something about it. He
wouldn't like that, not after all these years together.

Martin did hit Richler hard a few nights later on his television show.
The story dropped into a yawning news vacuum. There wasn't even a
good horse race or golf tournament scheduled for that weekend. So the
charges against Richler were juicy tidbits for the carrion to swarm over
for the next few days. Richler was like a man who had been hit by a car
that had run a red light. Right seemed to be on his side, but he was the
one sprawled on the pavement. Nobody even came out to pick him up.

The story gathered momentum. Over the next few weeks papers
turned up some old photographs that had been taken of Richler and a
group of police commanders at the scene of a riot a few years before.
Richler was fair game and the journalists swarmed over him. "Did
Richler Buy Property Secretly?" inquired the ominous headline of the
papers on the first Sunday of February. Was Richler a man of mystery?
A story, based on real estate transfer records, suggested that the Mayor's
chief aide might have acquired parcels of land in a suspicious manner
during his years of work in City Hall. It was true that Richler had
bought land. He had done it seven years earlier as an investment. There
had been nothing unusual about it. But he hadn't made any public announcement either. The land had, in fact, appreciated three times in
value since its purchase. Richler had also purchased two condominiums
and sublet them. There was nothing wrong with that either; it was
strictly business but it was made to sound faintly illegal or improper in
the news stories. The papers also printed maps of his property and pictures of the building in which he had purchased the condominium apartments. They had pictures of him and his family, of him and the Mayor,
displays of everything but his fingerprints.

Ann Marie followed the explosion of news about Mark Richler with
mixed feelings. She was glad to stick it to this man who was on such
close terms with the Mayor. But she felt some crude semblance of guilt,
some suffusing shame about how she, with a little pillow talk, had
caused all this. She had set the city blazing when she only meant to play
with matches. On the other hand, if Richler had been dabbling in real
estate, he deserved what he was getting. She could override her distress
by letting herself be angry at Richler. She could not feel half-sorry, half-
mad; it had to be one way or the other. For Richler it would be
unrefined dislike.

By the beginning of March, questions about Richler had been given a
fatal twist. "Did Cullen Know About Richler's Land Deals?" "Did Mayor
OK Richler Sweetheart Contracts?" Joining the Mayor to Richler's distress increased the pressure on him and Cullen enormously. Now it
wasn't just the Mayor's aide who was being questioned; it was the

Mayor himself. It was a poisoned moment and the atmosphere in Cullen's office was anything but friendly when Richler arrived to discuss the matter.

"Mark," the Mayor said with a calm that told Richler that he was about to be cut loose, "I don't see how you could have done these things." He seemed hurt by the fact that Richler owned real estate in the city. A heavy silence, like that which invades a disintegrating marriage, lay in the space between the two men. Richler had always known that the last thing Cullen would permit was the association of his own name, even in a remote way, with a scandal. He was not even surprised that Cullen pretended not to know about his relatively modest real estate holdings. Cullen had, in fact, urged him to get into the real estate market in order to build up a nest egg; the Mayor had encouraged him to put some of his money into land. But Cullen sat there without any recollection that Richler had told him about it. Maybe the Mayor doesn't remember, he's had some memory trouble since he had that spell over a year ago. There were other things he forgot, like signing letters or checks. Maybe he had a lot of blank spots, maybe that's why he can't remember.

Richler's throat was dry around a swelling Adam's apple. He knew what he had to do.

"I'd like a leave of absence," Richler said, watching himself, hearing himself living out a nightmare. "I'd like a leave until we can get this cleared up."

"That sounds wise," Cullen answered, the patriarch calling down from a mountain fastness.

"I'll give out a press release this morning. It's being run off now. I'll clean out my desk for the time being . . ." His voice faltered and broke. Richler felt enormous pressure in his chest, but he was not going to break down. He was, after all, an innocent man, Chicago's Dreyfuss headed for miserable exile on rumor. Was there an Émile Zola out there somewhere who would champion his cause? Or was he, like countless other Jews, elected to be the scapegoat to be sent off for the sins of others? It did not matter. The notoriety that had enveloped him in the last few months left him no choice but to wrench himself loose from the side of the man with whom he had worked for a generation. Richler stood up and turned to go.

Cullen watched him move slowly across the office. He wanted to call out to Richler, he wanted to say something to the man who had worked so long with him. Richler's shoulders sagged as he walked in slow motion toward the door. Cullen's features softened but he said nothing. Richler put his hand on the knob as he had on thousands of occasions. This might be the last time he ever did it. He turned his head sideways so that he could see Cullen sitting stolidly at his desk. Richler nodded and quickly raised his right arm, like a conductor just before he hops aboard the last car of a departing train.

Cullen sat for a long time in the utterly silent room. He felt light-headed and reached for his box of pills. "Dammit," he mumbled to himself as he poured a glass of water, "goddammit to hell."

20

*T*he Richler story stayed close to the front pages throughout March. He remained on a leave of absence waiting for the air to clear. But who would clear it? There had been no formal charges, the State's Attorney didn't seem interested in it, there was nothing in it for the United States Attorney. It was sediment swirling through the air the way it does when a hot dry wind blows across the Midwest in June. You just wait until it settles down by itself. But Richler was neither absolved nor condemned, when the season of storms arrived.

It happened late in June on a day on which air conditioners across the city moaned and flapped under the press of the heat and the humidity. At about five o'clock the western sky boiled up green and black and the weather bureau announced that Cook, Lake, and DuPage counties in Illinois were under a tornado watch. At five-fifteen the designation was changed to a tornado warning. A funnel cloud had been sighted forty miles northwest of the city. It began to rain in downtown Chicago, a choking hot rain that brought no relief as the commuters ran and stumbled for shelter at the height of the rush hour.

Mayor Cullen was meeting with consultants on an expressway project when the eclipse-like darkness fell across the city. He rose from his chair and walked to the windows of his office just as sheets of rain cascaded down against them. Lightning turned the atmosphere eerily white for a second, then thunder exploded and shattered into sections around the downtown buildings. The lights dimmed and went out and the ventilation stopped abruptly. Cullen herded everyone back from the windows as his secretary arrived with a transistor radio, which relayed reports about the sudden fierce storm that was just striking the city.

"Get the Civil Defense on the phone," Cullen said as the lights struggled back to life. Then they flickered unsteadily and went off again. "Haven't we got auxiliary power here?" the Mayor asked as another flash bathed the city in milky light. The phones in the outer office rang wildly as Cullen ushered his visitors through to an inner hallway.

Ann Marie was in her ward organization office as the sickly colored clouds, rolling like tumbleweeds, dimmed the light of day. Savage winds, unwinding from the center of the storm, filled the air with scraps of paper and other debris.

Ann Marie went to the window and watched the slashing rain uncoil in whip-like patterns on the street. A traffic light hanging across the intersection swayed like a skip rope. Water spurted down through the roof in the adjacent meeting room. Ann Marie's nervous secretary rubbed her hands together as she paced back and forth. "Judge Hogan said we needed a new roof last year," she muttered. Ann Marie snapped on the radio and heard the announcement about the threat of active tornadoes. Flashes of lightning alternated with booms of thunder before the lights blinked and went out. Ann Marie thought of Matthew and hoped that he was safe at home with Aunt Molly. She would call after the worst of the storm passed.

The raging storm sent excitement dancing through Ann Marie's body. Anything could happen in a storm like this. Everything was up for grabs when the hulking clouds began spinning tornadoes like tops across the flat prairie land of Illinois.

"Shouldn't we go down to the basement?" the secretary asked.

"You go. See if you can find a pan for that leak. I'll be down in a few minutes."

Ann Marie was enjoying the war-like storm. Its random anger suited her; that's what the betraying world deserved, a violent purgation and cleansing. She stood by the window and watched the rain lash down. There was something mysterious and exhilarating about the way a great storm recklessly spent its energy, wasting it lavishly on the world. It was a beast having its way with the earth and there was nothing anybody could do to stop it. It was thrilling to look into the storm's rheumy apocalyptic eye and to feel its power in the trembling windowsill. She heard a rushing sound, like that of a speeding freight train, and, as the darkness thickened, she headed for the steps to the basement.

The sound of the surging freight train rose out of a funnel cloud, the jet-black spawn of the towering and spreading storm, an evil plume dancing blindly across the flat land northwest of Chicago. It zigzagged through villages, yanking out telephone poles, their lines flapping wildly, and devouring them in the column of energy at its core. Houses collapsed in on themselves and their shambles were lifted away and chewed into fragments in the maw of the tornado. The funnel, grinding hungrily across the county, stuttered for a moment, then veered through the Prairie Acres Trailer Park, crunching and discarding the mobile homes as though they were beer cans, raising their terrified occupants into the air, lifting them like Elijah, their goods spinning about them, until it threw them down again in the wreckage of their homes.

The funnel cloud cut across the military side of O'Hare Field, snatching one of the hangars away from the planes it housed, leaving them shuddering in the wind and rain, while pieces of hangar soared like dead leaves above them. The tornado then hopped the fence at the edge of the field and raced toward a housing development, devastating, as expertly as a barrage of artillery shells, a grove of old trees at its entrance gate. The spinning cloud then moved diagonally, taking the houses on one side of the street but leaving those on the other. It cut across Buxton Drive and Adobe Way and then made a swipe at the last house on Riverview Circle.

It was number 111. George Phillips was not there during the few seconds that it took to strip away the garage and then neatly skin the wall, from roofline to foundation, off its side. The howling wind plucked lamps and chairs out of the suddenly exposed rooms. A punching bag attached to a slab of ceiling lifted away from a second-floor room like a hot-air balloon being launched. The door to the closet inside the room rattled furiously for a split second and was torn away. The howling died down and the rain lessened. Then a gas explosion in the cellar shook the house. It jolted the corpse in the closet so that it swayed grotesquely, mimicking life again. It was the body of a newly dead young man. The rope around his neck held him suspended from a steel bar that ran across the top of the closet. There was another explosion and one side of the upper wall of the closet cracked and the bar pulled loose. The naked corpse slid downward on the sagging bar and hung leaning halfway out the closet door. Lazarus, white and still, had come forth, Lazarus with the number thirteen printed in thick black letters on his unmoving chest.

By six o'clock the storm, having split itself to follow paths just north and south of the city proper, had moved eastward. The lights had come back on at City Hall where the Mayor, his tie loosened and his coat off, sat receiving reports on the damage that the explosive storm had caused. There were power outages in several parts of the city, many streets and highways were flooded, hundreds of trees were down, and dozens of roofs had been blown away. Live wires lay in sparking strands in many streets and eight small planes had been overturned at Meigs Field, the lakefront airport. Nobody knew yet how many sailboats had been overturned or whether anybody was missing. First reports were sketchy, but the worst damage seemed to be in the northwest quadrant of the metropolitan area. The rush-hour traffic was tangled up everywhere, but the worst was over.

Cap Malloy entered the office bearing a cup of coffee for the Mayor. Cullen thanked the aides who had briefed him on the effects of the storm and smiled as Malloy handed him the coffee.

"Thanks, Cap. I'm going out with the Fire Commissioner in a few minutes to check out some of the worst of the damage. I'll be glad I had this."

"It was a hell of a storm, if I might say, a hell of a storm. I remember one like it back in sixty-seven, in the spring. Do you remember it, Mayor?"

"I do, I do, Cap." Cullen took the coffee and walked to the windows to look down on the glistening streets. "I've been through a lot of storms in my day," he said solemnly.

"You're a young man, Mayor, a young man to say a thing like that."

Cullen finished his coffee, handed the mug back to Cap, and smiled crookedly. It seemed odd not to have Mark Richler around during a time like this. He suddenly felt alone in a way that surprised him. He was old, no matter what Cap said in his foolish, friendly way, and he had been through a lot of terrible storms. It was a fleeting emotion, a shiver of melancholy, and he looked at Malloy for a long moment, good old Cap who always had a smile and a joke, Cap, the court jester and mascot rolled into one. Cullen clapped him on the shoulder.

"You've been a great pal, Cap. Thanks."

Cap blinked in surprise. One compliment like that would keep Malloy warm for a year.

"Your coat, Your Honor. You can't go out without your coat."

Ann Marie toured her ward in a four-wheel-drive vehicle with the local supervisor for the Department of Streets and Sanitation at the wheel. A two-way radio crackled as they drove around fallen trees toward the trailer park that had sustained severe damage. Fourteen vehicles had been smashed, three residents had been killed, one was still unaccounted for, and several others had been injured. Two ambulances and an emergency vehicle stood near the edge of the crumpled park, their red emergency lights rotating against the now-clearing sky. A helicopter from a local television station clattered low overhead. Ann Marie ordered the superintendent to drive as close as possible to the area where the medics were assisting those who had been injured.

"I'm Alderwoman O'Brien," she said to the police officer who was trying to keep things in order. "I'd like to talk to some of these people."

The officer nodded and Ann Marie headed for a small knot of sopping residents standing numbly by as their neighbors and relatives were carried out of their ruined trailers by the medical teams. She told them who she was, asked their names, and reassured them that she would do whatever she could to help them get their lives back in order. She moved swiftly from group to group, occasionally lending a hand as people sifted through the rubble of what only an hour before had been their homes. Sirens sounded in the distance and two more ambulances arrived. So did a camera crew from the television helicopter that had landed in a nearby parking lot. There would be plenty of pictures of Mrs. O'Brien in the midst of the action on the home screens later that night. Ann Marie, on an adrenaline high, moved about energetically, talking briefly with as many people as possible. Then she moved toward the television crew. They wanted her reaction to the disaster at the trailer court.

She answered the reporter's questions, quoted the Chicago slogan of "I Will" about cleaning up and helping the people, and closed by asking for prayers for the dead and missing as well as for those who were injured. She was very effective, her voice vibrant with the intense quality that such emergencies generated in her. She was good, she felt that, she was good at this sort of thing.

Ann Marie walked back to the emergency vehicle. Another helicopter passed noisily overhead.

"This is the worst area of the city, Mrs. O'Brien," the superintendent said to her. "I've been monitoring the reports. Lots of trees and lines down from the wind. We were right in the track of the twister. There's bad damage at O'Hare and a lot of houses have been hit bad too. The Mayor's supposed to be coming out for an inspection. He's been looking at the city in a chopper from the Fire Department."

"Well, in that case, we'll wait around for him," Ann Marie answered. "Do you know when he's due here?"

"Any minute from what I can make out."

Captain Vincent wiped his brow. By some miracle nobody had been killed when the storm struck the airport. There had been heavy damage on the military side of the field where he was now standing. An entire hangar was gone and the planes had been battered about. But everybody was alive. A number of small aircraft had been flipped by the wind at the Butler Aviation Terminal but, again, there had been no casualties. He felt relieved as he inspected the clean-up operations. He wanted to avoid the reporters; the last thing he needed was to be seen on television or appear in the papers. Since his reprimand about trailing Phillips, he had kept his profile so low that he hardly cast a shadow.

"Captain," Officer Hackman called to him. He was jogging toward him from a patrol car, his keys and gun bouncing up and down at his waist with every splashing step. He was out of breath when he arrived.

"Captain, I gotta tell you something. I know you're busy, I'm sorry, but you'll want to know this." Hackman did not have himself completely under control.

"Yes?" Vincent said expectantly. "Come over here." He led Hackman a few steps away from a group of Air Force officers who were assessing the damage in the military area. They sensed the urgency of the consultation as the officer pointed and made gestures to the captain. Vincent, his hands on his hips, stood rock-still, attention completely given to the young policeman. Vincent asked a question and nodded as Hackman made a reply. Then the trance in which they seemed to be held broke and they walked back past the military officers. They did not seem to see them. "Jesus Christ," Vincent muttered, "Jesus Christ."

Other newsmen and camera crews arrived at the trailer park and Ann Marie gave two more interviews, one for radio and one for Channel Two. It was beginning to grow dark and all of the dead and injured had been removed. There was still a man missing. She winced inwardly as she thought about that. Life was the war. This was an engagement with the enemy Death. Oh, Charlie, goddammit, Charlie, did the wind take you too? Ann Marie shuddered and hunched her shoulders.

"Anything on the Mayor's arrival?" she asked the supervisor who had driven her.

"I can't figure it out. I've been getting mixed-up messages. The Mayor's chopper turned back . . ."

Ann Marie's heart raced. "What do you mean, mixed-up messages?"

Ann Marie grabbed the edge of the vehicle's open window and leaned through to hear the radio better. Messages burst like gunfire out of the receiver. Static clouded the words, but the tension in the distorted voices was unmistakable.

"What's happening?" she asked anxiously.

The supervisor turned the volume down and looked toward Mrs. O'Brien. He took a deep breath.

"I'm sorry to say this, Mrs. O'Brien. I think the Mayor's sick again. I heard them use the word 'stroke' . . ."

PART TWO

21

A stroke. The word fell, echoing all the way, deep into the well of her memories. Ann Marie stood, still half in and half out of the window of the four-wheeler, the supervisor staring quizzically at her. "What's the matter, ma'am, don't you feel good?" The radio squealed again and Ann Marie pulled back from the window, turned around, and leaned against the vehicle.

Mother Francis had sent for her, had called for her during philosophy class. She knew something was wrong right away. You only got called out of class when there was bad news, a death in the family, a fire at home, an accident of sufficent tragedy to justify the interruption of a lecture and thus to alter the obsessive routine of Our Lady of Peace College. Ann Marie could see the long, shadowed hallway, the gleaming floor, the pictures of past presidents peering down severely out of their wimples as she made her way to Mother Francis's office near the main entrance of the building.

Your father's been taken ill. Mother Francis reached out to take Ann Marie's arm. He's been taken to the hospital. Your aunt is coming to pick you up. No, we don't know any more. We'll have the sisters all praying for him, child, you mustn't worry. God works things out for the best . . .

A stroke. First her father and now Cullen.

A stroke. My God, they'll start all over again, the Raffertys, the Wendels, and the Carneys. They'll be out to take over the city again. She and Maureen would have to stand guard, protect the throne, speak for him if Cullen could no longer speak for himself.

"Mrs. O'Brien, we've had a call for you on the police radio."

Ann Marie stared glassily at him.

"They'd like you down at City Hall as soon as possible. We've got a squad car ready, Mrs. O'Brien. They said it was urgent, that you had to get there right away, seeing you're the Vice-Mayor . . ."

Vice-Mayor. She had almost forgotten that title. It meant less than being a monsignor, she had said once to her cousin Morgan when he had complimented her on it.

Vice-Mayor. It meant something now. That was the role old Hogan had the last time the Mayor was ill. Vice-Mayor was the card that the sharpies had tried to play against Cullen.

"Is there any more news on the Mayor?" Ann Marie asked as she followed the police officer to the waiting squad car.

"Not much. He's at the University of Illinois Hospital. Seems he was flying with the Fire Commissioner to inspect the storm damage when suddenly he slumped in his seat. A stroke, the doctors think . . ."

A stroke. She shook her head as she climbed into the front seat of the police car. Cullen was tough, but could he stand what a stroke would do to him? Would he stand for it? The police officer started the ignition and they pulled away from the knot of media people who had followed her to the squad car. How different from the time that her father had been stricken. Then, she sat alone waiting for Aunt Molly, gripped by the silence that had pervaded all proper Catholic institutions in those days. Ann Marie had heard the clock ticking across the room; she remembered the faded papal blessing on the wall. The parlors of Catholic schools were all the same, voids, timeless places in which nothing was ever thrown away and nothing was really ever saved, either. The old church was good at holding its breath in the space between life and death.

This was different. An unmarked escort car with two men in plain clothes peeled off a curb a block away to follow them downtown. The rooflight was turning and the driver sounded the siren regularly to move the traffic ahead of them out of the way. They were traveling at seventy miles an hour and the other cars were splitting away before them. She loved the thrill that rose off such events, that depended on them and yet had a life, like the burst of a firecracker, that was all its own. Nothing suited her better than riding dramatically into battle. She bit her lip. She had forgotten to call Molly. She had forgotten to find out if Matthew was all right or not . . .

Sam Noto waved his cigar angrily at Richard Barone. "What the hell you gonna do? Send Martin to fuck her again? Rich, I'm telling you, this time we got to take over right away. It's the only chance. This fucking woman is dangerous. We got to arrange a special election . . ."

"Sam, you must have the votes to elect somebody to finish the old man's term."

"Maybe yes, maybe no. I just know this goddamn woman is trouble. And we can't use sweet talk, we can't fuck around if we're gonna stay in business."

"Are Rafferty and Wendel coming over?"

"Yeah, and Ramirez too. And Larry Johnson, the nigger preacher. They ought to be here soon. Town's in bad shape in some places. This tornado was a son of a bitch. And now Cullen's sick again. And this woman, Rich, she's like a fucking curse . . ."

A crowd of reporters waited on the sidewalk at the LaSalle Street entrance to City Hall as Ann Marie arrived in the squad car. It had grown dark and television lights went on as, grim-faced and refusing to respond to any of the dozens of questions that were thrown at her, Ann Marie strode into the Hall. The reporters and cameramen trailed after her. Are you taking over, Mrs. O'Brien? What's the condition of Mayor Cullen? Is it true that he's paralyzed? Are you acting Mayor?

The elevator doors closed on the hubbub as Ann Marie, flanked by two huge bodyguards, rode silently up to the fifth floor. More glaring lights and shouted questions as she moved hurriedly through the glass doors marked "Office of the Mayor."

"The Mayor is paralyzed on one side, Mrs. O'Brien," the Corporation Counsel, Herbert Marx, said quietly. "We think that he may be away from the office for some time."

Ann Marie stared blankly at him.

"We think that, considering the bad storm today and the Mayor's illness, you should make some kind of statement. My legal opinion is that you can assume the duties of the Mayor. For the time being."

Ann Marie glanced at Cullen's desk. The room was different without him. Paralyzed. Away from the office. Missing in action.

"Call a press conference for nine." She thought of Mark Richler and what he would say if he were there. "No. Get hold of the television stations. Tell them I'll have a statement for the ten o'clock news. From here."

"Alderman Rafferty asked for a meeting with you this evening. He said he thought you two should talk before we made any decisions."

Ann Marie looked harshly at Marx. "Get the television stations on the line. I want to talk to the hospital. Do you hear me? Move it."

Marx mumbled something and edged back toward the door. Ann Marie moved to the Mayor's desk. No, she wouldn't use that yet. She would call from the outer office. She followed Marx through the door. Two of the secretaries had just returned to the office, summoned back with other staff members by the Corporation Counsel as soon as the news of the Mayor's stroke was received.

"Get me the hospital," Ann Marie said in business-like tones. The room filled up around her as she picked up the phone and spoke with the doctor in charge of the case. Mayor Cullen was indeed on the critical list. The hospital chaplain had anointed him; there had not been time to call the Cardinal. He was paralyzed on one side and, although conscious, had not been able to speak.

"Can he govern?" Ann Marie asked in her point-blank, let's-get-this-settled-right-now fashion.

That wasn't, the doctor said, for him to say. That was not a medical question. Ann Marie asked to talk to the Mayor's daughter. While she waited she looked at the secretaries who, slow-motioning their way around the large room, were listening intently to her conversation. She should have called on Cullen's own phone. No, then they would say she had taken over prematurely. Let them all hear what she said.

"Ann Marie?"

"How's your father?"

Maureen's voice was pressured. "Not good." She began to cry.

"Listen, Maureen, we've got to think of the city."

"Yes?" Maureen was stunned by Ann Marie's directness.

"You remember Christmas. We've had tornadoes today, we've had people killed and lots of damage. Now the Mayor's sick. I have to speak to the people at ten o'clock, I've got to reassure them . . ."

"But we don't know how my father's going to be. You know sometimes they come out of these things very fast. Look how well he did at Christmas time."

Ann Marie saw Francis Rafferty enter the outer office—Cromwell come looking for his kingdom. She spoke so that he would be sure to hear her.

"I'm going to speak as Vice-Mayor. At ten. We can't wait, we can't leave anything up in the air. There's a bad band of men down here and they're not going to take over the city government. Do you understand?"

"Don't you think this is a little quick?" Maureen felt as though Ann Marie were not letting her in. They were not guarding the Mayor's room together. Not this time. Ann Marie was going to do it her way and have no discussion about it. "I mean, do you have to . . . ?" Maureen's voice broke.

"That's my decision," Ann Marie snapped. "I'll pray for your father." She hung up the phone and looked up into the shaken features of "The Rosary."

"You wanted to see me, Alderman?" she asked curtly.

The secretaries, as stiff as wax figures as they listened to the telephone conversation, began moving again. The other officials and the alderman stirred out of the stop-action poses they had assumed while Ann Marie was on the phone.

"Yes," Rafferty said in a subdued voice, "yes, Mrs. O'Brien. God help us, Mrs. O'Brien, we don't want to act impulsively in matters like this . . ."

He waved a hand toward the Mayor's office as though it would be the natural place for them to talk.

"Helen," Ann Marie called to the Mayor's secretary, "get your pad. I want you to take notes. And we'll talk here, Alderman, if you don't mind. Out here where everybody can see there are no secret deals going on." Ann Marie glanced at the other officials who were standing around the waiting room.

"Draw up chairs, gentlemen. There's an open government in this city tonight." Rafferty choked and gasped, swallowed a stillborn sentence, and sat down heavily in the chair next to Ann Marie.

"And, Helen, get somebody to see if Paul Martin and his camera crew are outside. I want them in here to record this too."

The surrounding officials moved like dazed men on a battlefield. They took chairs. They did exactly what Ann Marie, feeling in top form in the midst of the growing tension, told them to do.

"Now, Alderman Rafferty, what was it you wanted to talk about?"

Rafferty wiped his forehead with a handkerchief, and paused as Paul Michael Martin, a minicam unit in tow, shouldered into the room. Shouts from other reporters back down the hall followed him.

Ann Marie watched Martin as he helped the cameramen select the best possible position to record the informal discussion that was about to take place. He took a microphone from a black leather case and looked at Ann Marie. Martin felt sexually excited, he felt the vibrations, transmitted on the field of stress that filled the room as though it were the natural conductor for erotic investigation. Ann Marie was the center of everyone's eyes. She was in charge even though she was not sitting in the Mayor's chair; she was in charge of the attention in the room the way a stripper with good timing was in charge of her audience.

The minicam was finally in place, the television lights went on, and Ann Marie spoke. She sparkled whenever television lights were trained on her.

"We're all here because of two tragedies that have struck our city. As Vice-Mayor, I've summoned members of the City Council and department heads for a planning meeting. In a few minutes I'm going to address the whole city on television. What I want is your input so that our citizens will know that while Mayor Cullen is ill, and while we clean up from the storm, we have unity and continuity in city government"—she looked directly at Rafferty, who was sweating profusely—"and that we have nothing to hide."

Alderman Wendel, followed by Carney and Ramirez, came in and stood against the far wall.

"I think it is the consensus of all of us that we must put the city first. We pray for Mayor Cullen and we'll do what we can to keep things going while he recuperates. Second, we will extend every assistance we can to the people who have suffered during today's storms. We're all agreed on that, I think."

Alderman Rafferty nodded. There was little else he could do. Christ Almighty, this woman has us trapped. We're on television. In an emergency. We can't disagree with her. Christ Almighty, she's liable to say anything, anything at all. Better to humor her, the way you would a crazy man with a gun.

"May I congratulate Vice-Mayor O'Brien on the leadership she is showing our great city?" Rafferty had his breath, and his voice, although dry, remained calm. Let's get this over with, that's all, butter her up, grease her up so she could swim the Channel. But let's not talk in public. "And we all support her in prayers for that great leader, Thomas H. Cullen, that dear man who has given so much of himself to the city for so many years."

Wendel raised a hand and spoke even before Ann Marie recognized him. The minicam lights swept around to illuminate him.

"I think we should—I think there are enough of us here from the City Council—to pass a resolution about this." Let's keep talking bromides, let's not let this woman talk any more freely than she has. We're all out in the open, for Crissake, so she can't disagree with us either.

"I second the idea of a resolution," Carney piped up beside him.

"May I put it in the form of a resolution then?" Carney asked.

Ann Marie nodded and, as the assembled officials rustled as they shifted positions, a resolution was improvised and a vote taken. It passed unanimously. Everybody was in favor of everything.

Ann Marie glanced around the room and then at her watch. It was nine-twenty. She had promised to speak at ten. She would do it right from where she sat with aldermen and department heads grouped all around her. Like a broadcast from a busy newsroom. Live from the waiting room where she was assuming temporary command of city government. Instinctively she felt that it would be difficult for anyone to challenge her power if she spoke to the citizenry while surrounded by the command structure of the City Council. She had them all in the open; it was perfect.

"Call the other television crews in," she said sharply. "We'll speak to the people while we're all together."

It took several minutes for the equipment to be hauled in and set up. Rafferty did not know what to say. Let it happen, glory be to God, let it happen, for what she does in the light we can undo in the dark.

Wendel moved uneasily as Carney leaned toward him.

"What the hell do you make of this? This is showboating."

"Let her do it, let her have her little drama. We have to go along with it for now. But we'd better have some meetings later."

Ramirez, who had moved close to them to listen to their conversation, nodded gravely. "She's loco, this lady, she's fucking loco."

Rafferty decided to engage Mrs. O'Brien in conversation once more.

"Ma'am," he said deferentially. He had watched Disraeli talk to Queen Victoria that way once on television. "Ma'am, I'm sure you've thought about what you want to say. But surely you want to be careful and not overcommit yourself one way or the other."

Ann Marie, who had just hung up from talking to the doctor again—no change—stared coldly at the head of the Finance Committee.

"I mean, you don't want to say too much. Or promise too much. You know, before we have complete information about the damaged areas. And about the Mayor's condition."

Ann Marie ignored him. She looked at her watch again. Nine-fifty. A television producer made his way through the congested room to her side. Rafferty stood there a moment until Ann Marie's glare made him feel as if he were intruding. The producer blocked out the area, moving the secretary's desk Ann Marie had been using for a better camera angle. "We'll lead with this at the top of the hour." He smiled and then worked his way back behind the cameras.

Ann Marie picked up the phone, dialed a number, and waited, serene in the midst of the nervous and uncertain crowd of officials.

"Hello, Molly . . . It's a long story . . . How's Matthew? Put him on, will you?" She talked briefly with her son, who told her he wished that she were home. Can't you come home, Mom? Can't you come home now? She would be home late, very late, and Matthew was not to wait up. Did he understand?

"Ready, Mrs. O'Brien," the producer called out. The crowd grew hushed.

"Good night, Matthew," Ann Marie said, hanging up the phone as the television lights flashed on. She looked into the cameras. There was dead silence in the room.

"This is Vice-Mayor O'Brien. I want to talk to all of you because of the sad and tragic events that have taken place in our city today . . ."

Ann Marie sensed that she was giving an Academy Award performance as she moved briskly along asking prayers for the Mayor and the tornado victims, assuring the citizens of the aid that would be coming, and then recounting the resolution that had just been passed. She did not smile.

She gestured at the room around her.

"We can be proud that the city government, men like Alderman Rafferty here, and others have worked together tonight to make sure that the city runs smoothly during the time of the Mayor's illness. Government cannot go on vacation. Neither can any of the city services we all recognize as vital . . ."

At seven minutes past ten she was finished, the lights were killed, and the members of the crowd, most of them unwilling participants in an event that reinforced the Vice-Mayor's image, like sailors hallucinating after being on submarine duty too long, staggered wearily down the hallway.

Ann Marie crooked a beckoning finger at Rafferty. He approached, more Barkis than Disraeli this time.

"I think we'd better meet at nine in the morning, Alderman. I want the heads of all the Council committees. We'll meet down in my office."

Rafferty nodded and backed away. "You spoke very well, ma'am, very well. I'm sure we'll all be able to work together during this trying time."

She snapped a glance at him and turned to the Mayor's secretary. "I want complete reports on the tornado damage. Round up whoever you have to. I'll meet them right here."

About a dozen officials remained in the room. Cap Malloy, who had stood dazed at the edge of the corridor that led out of the office, stepped forward unsteadily. He had not quite absorbed the events of the day. The Mayor was in the hospital. The Mayor was paralyzed. The world had changed suddenly on him.

"Mrs. O'Brien," he said hoarsely, "Mrs. O'Brien . . ."

Ann Marie looked up at him from a damage summary that had just been handed to her. "What is it, Cap?" she said impatiently.

"Well, Mrs. O'Brien, I wanted to tell you I saw the Mayor just before he went out. So I did. And he looked at me and he said I'd been a great pal. Can you imagine it, Mrs. O'Brien? And him almost forgetting to wear his coat . . ." Cap snuffled and blew his nose.

"I'm sorry, Cap," Ann Marie said brusquely, "I haven't got time for all that now . . ."

22

*T*hank you, gentlemen. We'll meet again here in my office tomorrow at the same time."

"Mrs. O'Brien," Alderman Rafferty said impatiently, "I have a few questions." He hunched forward at the table that had been placed against Ann Marie's desk to accommodate the crowd of city officials at the meeting. The atmosphere was tense—Ten Downing Street with the Queen on the verge of forming a new government.

"Yes, Mr. Rafferty?" Ann Marie said absently. Later, she would be touring the damaged city, then visiting the damaged Mayor. Cullen was still mute—that was the report—and half-paralyzed. Maureen was there. Of course, Maureen was there . . .

"Yes, go on," Ann Marie answered abruptly, "what is it you want?"

"Mrs. O'Brien, we're grateful that you have assumed leadership at this difficult time. As chairman of the Finance Committee, I would like to know if you plan to go ahead with the regular Council meeting . . ."

"Why not?" Ann Marie snapped. "It's next week. Wednesday."

"Yes, of course." Rafferty pried a slit of smile open in his leathery face. "It's just that in these unusual circumstances . . . God be good to the Mayor and bring him back to us. Naturally, that is the prayer and wish of all of us. But, seeing that he may be incapacitated for some time, it might be important for us to have a special meeting to discuss the question." Rafferty crinkled a sheaf of paper noisily in the heavy quiet of the room. Ann Marie stared coldly at him. She knew what he was up to. Rafferty meant to move against Cullen decisively this time. Have him declared incompetent, get the Council to elect him acting Mayor until a special election could be called, and push Ann Marie out into the cold.

"We'll meet next Wednesday as scheduled," Ann Marie said with finality. "Thank you all for coming." She stood up and the men scraped their chairs back, murmuring goodbyes as they shuffled out. Rafferty, treacle dripping from his smile, gestured confidently toward Aldermen Carney and Wendel to remain behind.

"Mrs. O'Brien, a word in private, if you please."

Ann Marie waved her secretary out of the room. Her face was stiff and expressionless.

"Mrs. O'Brien, you are Vice-Mayor of the City of Chicago," Rafferty said coldly. "That is an office which, in itself, is meaningless. And, I might add, powerless."

"I haven't claimed any power, Mr. Rafferty. I am fulfilling my legal obligations."

"It's past the time to get this straight, ma'am," Rafferty said, spreading his bony, spotted hands out on the desk before him. "We do not govern this city in front of cameras and with reporters present. You have a great talent with the media, Mrs. O'Brien. It should help you considerably when the regular election for your City Council seat comes up."

"What Alderman Rafferty means, Annie," Wendel cut in sharply, "is that we have a serious situation. Cullen's a beached whale. I'll admit you did a great job in the emergency last night. Kept the city calm, got all the pieces together. Now we have to move ahead and fulfill our legal obligations. Within five days of the Mayor's being declared incompetent to govern, we have to select an acting Mayor and set a date for a special election."

"I understand that." Ann Marie folded her arms and tilted her head back slightly. "I have no problem with that."

"Ma'am," Rafferty interjected, sweetening his tones, "that is exactly why it is urgent to hold a special Council meeting. Tomorrow would not be too soon."

"This is not like that time the Mayor got sick at Christmas," Carney said softly. "The Mayor is not going to show up at City Hall with the big laugh and the wave. Not this time."

"Is that all you want to say?" Ann Marie's eyes scanned the faces of the aldermen. Their intention was clear as the Waterford crystal bud vase that glittered on the side of her desk. This was an ultimatum. Either she stepped out of the picture quickly or they would throw her out. Rafferty stared at her evenly and opened his mouth to reply.

"Thank you again," Ann Marie said abruptly. "I'll get back to you on this. Now, if you'll excuse me . . ."

Ann Marie stood impassively at the center of the storm of news conference questions. How is the Mayor? Are you taking over? Short answers. Deadpan. Focus on the day, what had to be done for the city in the aftermath of the storm. No speculation about Cullen's condition. Thank you, gentlemen.

"One more question." It was Paul Michael Martin, a lock of black hair tumbling down his forehead, his best lover's smile in place.

"Mrs. O'Brien, when the Mayor was sick a year ago last Christmas, there were stories that some influential aldermen wanted him to step down temporarily in favor of then Vice-Mayor Matthew Hogan." He paused and glanced around at the other reporters. What's the matter with you guys? Afraid to ask the big question? He smiled again at Ann Marie. The members of the crowd were extras watching the stars play a scene together. "Have any aldermen made this kind of suggestion to you today? If so, what was your response? And would you name them, please?" Barone, his patron in many ways, wouldn't like Martin's question at all. The hell with it. Only he could play this card with Ann Marie.

Ann Marie waited until all eyes were on her. Nobody expected her to give a straight answer.

"Nobody has asked me to take over," she said flatly, "and I have no intention of doing so. I am merely carrying out my legal obligations." The tension in the room relaxed. "However," and the atmosphere stiffened under the wind-up tone of her voice, "however, I have been approached by aldermen who think that the Mayor should be replaced. They have suggested, rather strongly, that I hold a special City Council meeting in which they could carry this out." The reporters froze, stunned by her directness. "I think such talk is premature and in bad taste. Our only thoughts about Mayor Cullen are for his complete recovery. I will fight any effort to stage a *coup d'état* as long as I have the responsibility of Vice-Mayor."

"Names, Mrs. O'Brien?" This from Martin through the bustle of the suddenly alert reporters.

"You ought to be able to figure that out for yourself," Ann Marie snapped and turned away from the microphones as a dozen reporters hurled follow-up questions at her. She went through the rear door into the Mayor's outer office and asked Helen Morrison if there were any messages.

"All the networks have called. Lots of calls from all over." Helen Morrison lifted a sheaf of notes from her desk. "George Ohland is handling the press office. He can take care of a lot of this for you . . ."

"I'll look at them in the car," Ann Marie chirped brusquely. "Get your pad, Helen. You're coming with me."

"The Governor wants to talk to you. He called during the news conference."

"We'll get him later," Ann Marie said as she turned toward her waiting bodyguards. "Let's go. This is going to be a long day." She turned back toward Helen, who was stuffing a stenographer's notebook into her large pocketbook. "Okay, Helen, let's move it."

"You mean, there's been no sign of Phillips yet?" Captain Vincent's impatience rasped against Commander Gleason's irritability.

"Paulie, I don't like this any more than you do. Christ, homicide's sent a team in and they're still finding bodies. We've had to cordon off the area. A special team from the M.E.'s office is there. Christ, there's bodies all over the place . . ."

"He can't be far, Walt . . ." Vincent took a breath. Phillips had been a dark adversary in his mind for months. A dark man. Everything about him had been dark. Even the leather pouch dangling from his wrist. Now he had burst into the light, his secret graveyard of a house sheared open by God Himself, God riding the whirlwind. The naked body strung out like a bowsprit from the upstairs closet, staring sightlessly from Phillips's wrecked home, was only the freshest of the kills that had taken place at 111 Riverview Circle. Vincent had never seen anything to compare with what he looked at with Commander Gleason in the shattered house the evening before. It took his breath away.

"Paul, are you there?"

"Yeah, I'm here . . ."

"Look, Paulie, I know this thing's been eating at you. I heard about how you were trailing him last year. I heard the whole thing. You been a cop long enough to know the score. It's out of your hands now . . ."

"Who's going to catch the son of a bitch? You, Walter, are you?"

"Calm down, Paulie. You've got a job. I know O'Hare isn't easy. You'd like to be back in the action. No way on this deal. You hear me?"

"I hear you. Does that mean I can't keep an interest in Phillips? Want me to stop reading the papers, too? City Hall isn't going to protect their old precinct worker anymore. Nobody'll be on my ass now."

"Just stay away. What do you want to be, a hero or something? Look, I've got to go. I'll keep in touch . . ."

Ann Marie checked through the messages as she rode in the back of an unmarked police car to the hospital.

"No to these." She dropped a half dozen of the call memos into Helen Morrison's lap without looking at her. Helen shifted the stenographic pad awkwardly.

"Yes to 'The Noon Show.' Call them when we get to the hospital." She let the note flutter down on top of the others.

"We'll call these when we get back to the office." She leaned forward, poking one of the bodyguards on the shoulder. "Tell them I'll need a car with a phone in it. I want it waiting when I leave the hospital." The officer shifted his bulk as he turned quizzically back toward the Vice-Mayor. Ann Marie's attention was back on the still-thick packet of messages. Everybody wanted to talk to her, interview her, get to see her, everybody.

"Call Paul Martin while I'm in with the Mayor. Tell him I want to see him at lunch. Tell him one o'clock."

Helen Morrison, attempting to balance the papers and her pad, dropped her pencil on the floor. As she bent forward, the memos showered down around her feet. Ann Marie paid no attention as Helen wheezed herself upright. "Where do you want Mr. Martin to meet you?"

Ann Marie glared at her. "Call Franklin Barnes, too. Tell him to come by my office around five."

Maureen Cullen Coleman was in the Intensive Care waiting room. Her husband, restlessly tapping his right foot, sat smoking a cigarette as Cap Malloy told him stories of the old days. Aimless, sad stories, the merriment pressed out of them long ago. The Mayor's daughter was talking to Mark Richler when Ann Marie entered. Maureen stood up quickly and embraced her. Richler rose and stepped back without saying anything.

"Maureen," Ann Marie asked before they broke their tight hold on each other, "tell me how your father is."

"It's not so good this time." Maureen separated gently from Ann Marie's arms. She was calm but haggard-looking. Stray hairs played out from the sides of her head. "It's serious. My father is partially paralyzed. He can't speak . . ."

"That can come back . . ."

"The doctors have said that. But it's too early to know anything for sure. He'll be a while recuperating."

"Is there anything I can do?"

Maureen looked for just an instant as if she might collapse from within. She swallowed hard. "Nothing more than you're doing. Mark told me what you said at the news conference this morning." She nodded toward Richler, who watched the women in disengaged fashion. Ann Marie did not look in his direction. She focused directly on Maureen, who seemed hesitant and unsure about what she wanted to say. Keep up the fight, watch out for Rafferty, we're depending on you again . . . None of them was quite right. "I'm sure my father will be fine. He's strong. You know how strong he is . . ."

Ann Marie wanted more than that. She wanted thanks for what she had done. She had barred the door already. Maureen was cautious with her, a little too measured in her tone. What had she and Richler been talking about? How were they planning to handle this one?

"I'd like to see the Mayor, Maureen. I want to be able to tell people that I've been in touch with him."

Maureen led Ann Marie wordlessly through a door that led to the special room where Thomas H. Cullen lay. Richler stepped out of Ann Marie's path. He recognized the *pas de deux* that Maureen and the Vice-Mayor had danced around the almost-spoken possibility that Cullen would not be able to govern anymore. Were they still allies, the woman's movement against the corrupt pols? Or was there a hint of something different there this time? Anything could happen when power might shake loose at any moment. Richler looked down at the floor as the women moved past him.

Two nurses watched the snowmass mound of the Mayor. His slack features beneath the splash of his white hair were as pale as his hospital gown, as expressionless as the sheets that covered him. And he was silent, like Lake Michigan deprived of its roar by the grip of a bad winter. The magnetism, the animation of the great public figure had been drained away. Ann Marie remembered visiting her own father in the hospital. The memory was dark and smooth. Long, dark, tiled walls along polished hallways in the hospital, a room that seemed dark even though it was daytime. Had someone drawn the blinds? And her father struck dumb and drooling by the same force that had now come close to turning Thomas H. Cullen into a ghost of himself. Another one of her men had crossed the barrier into silence.

Maureen bent low over her father's head. "It's Annie, Dad, Annie O'Brien." She took her father's right hand in her own. Ann Marie moved closer. She looked down into the Mayor's face. Recognition and a hint of fear rose off Cullen's eyes, watery blue boy's eyes in an old man's face. Ann Marie—remembering her own father caught tight in the winding sheet of his stroke and pleading with her through his terrified glances—bent down and kissed him. Cullen came to the edge of making a sound, and then let go of it.

"I don't want you to worry, Mr. Mayor," Ann Marie said loudly, as though Cullen were deaf. "You'll be back soon."

Cullen looked up at her out of the coarsened shell of his body. What was he saying? What would he say if he could? Ann Marie had learned to listen hard for words from men who couldn't speak.

"Maureen, I don't want to tire the Mayor. I've got to get going."

Maureen pulled away from the bed without speaking as the nurses moved in around her father.

Richler was sitting in a corner. Maureen's husband had slipped out and Cap had gone to the bathroom. Maureen walked Ann Marie to the door. Richler, puffing on a cigarette, wrinkled his forehead as the women, their right arms touching tentatively, looked into each other's faces.

"We're counting on you, Annie," Maureen said softly.

"We'll all be praying for your father. You know that." Ann Marie turned and opened the frosted-glass door. Helen Morrison was standing outside next to one of the bodyguards holding her notebook filled with new messages.

Ann Marie did not look at anybody as she strode down the corridor to the elevator.

23

*P*rairie Acres Trailer Park. The mood of death's sudden visitation still hanging in the air. Ann Marie, thinking of the old Mayor—a still life in white—thinking of what she could or must do in the few days she would have as Vice-Mayor, thinking of what was at stake for her as well as Cullen, walked grim-faced past the jagged concrete foundations from which the mobile homes had been wrenched by the storm. The sight of Richler and Maureen together had set off an alarm in her. Suppose Maureen and Richler kept Cullen out of sight like Woodrow Wilson after his stroke? Who would hold the power then? Where would she be if that happened?

"Mrs. O'Brien!" A clutch of newsmen waited for her near what had once been the clubhouse of the trailer park. She walked automatically toward the bank of microphones. Maureen had held back a little, she knew that. Did Richler have a plan already?

"Mrs. O'Brien!" A half dozen reporters called in unison.

"One at a time." She pointed to a blond-haired reporter in a red blazer. "You, what's your question?"

"Mrs. O'Brien, we understand you've seen the Mayor. How is he?"

"I saw him for only a few minutes. He recognized me. I told him all the citizens of the city were praying for him."

"But how does he look?" another reporter broke in.

"Like anybody in the hospital. Nobody's at their best in the hospital."

"What about your comments this morning that certain aldermen were pressing to have him declared incompetent? Do you want to elaborate on that?"

"I stand by what I said earlier. There are certain aldermen who obviously want to make an assessment of the Mayor's condition. I can only guess about their motives." All of this, flatly, matter-of-factly.

"Would you like to name names?"

"No."

"Is Alderman Rafferty one of them?"

"Ask him. Now, gentlemen, I'm sorry, but I have to get back downtown."

"Mrs. O'Brien, one last question." A sandy-haired reporter from one of the daily papers stepped forward. "On another subject." Ann Marie stopped in the half-impatient, half-hesitant way of one who wants to go but doesn't want to miss anything. "Yes?"

"Do you have any comment on George Phillips, one of your organization workers, the man who is suspected of being a mass murderer?"

"I didn't know him. We have a big organization. That's a police matter." She ducked into the car that had been drawn up beside the clubhouse.

"There's a story that he once complained to you about police surveillance," the reporter called after her, "and that you spoke up for him."

Ann Marie looked blankly up out of the car window. The reporters had crowded around to catch her comments. She pressed the button and the window lowered halfway.

"I've heard the complaints of hundreds of people in the last year. I don't remember anything about him."

"But . . ."

"It's a police matter." The window glided shut as the police driver pulled the car—a sedan with a telephone—away from the newsmen and out of the trailer park.

The sights of the Kennedy Expressway unfurled past the windows of the speeding car. Ann Marie was on the telephone.

"Put him on. I don't care if he is at a meeting." Ann Marie fumbled in her purse for a notebook to which a small silver pencil was attached.

"Mrs. O'Brien?" It was the Corporation Counsel.

"Yes. I want a briefing on something. What are the laws governing the situation we're in right now?"

"Well, Mrs. O'Brien, the City Council has a lot of authority and responsibility in a situation like this."

"You're saying they run the show, is that it?"

"What I am saying is that, in our system of government, the City Council is very strong. They have the power to select from among their members an acting Mayor. The idea of having a Vice-Mayor came up after Daley died. It was merely meant to cover a short interim between the vacancy of the Mayor's office and the action of the City Council."

Ann Marie was a temporary caretaker, that was all. While she kept things going for a few days, other people were making plans. Maureen and Richler. Rafferty, Wendel, and their colleagues. Bankers, union leaders, Cousin Fitzie too. Everybody was cutting some kind of a deal. There wouldn't be room for her in any of them. She had tied her star to Cullen. She had helped save him once. Now he had plunged down silently beyond the horizon, and Richler was back with his foxy advice. Richler had never liked her . . .

"Is that all, Mrs. O'Brien?"

Ann Marie was jolted back into the moment. "I want the citations for all these. And for something else. Who has the power to declare the Mayor too ill to carry out his duties?"

"I've been researching that, Mrs. O'Brien. It's all in the Municipal Code."

"Just a minute. I want to write this down."

"I'll have copies for you when you get to your office."

"Fine, but I want the citations anyway." Ann Marie crooked the phone at her shoulder and adjusted the small notebook on her knee.

"Page 108, Mrs. O'Brien, Chapter 24. Paragraph 3 dash 4 dash 5 discusses vacancy. Then the next paragraphs explain the City Council's obligation to elect one of its members. It depends on how much of the Mayor's term is left before the next election. If it's less than a year the Council elects somebody to fill out the whole term. If it's at least a year, there must be a special election within six months. That's the gist of it."

"And the City Council makes all the decisions."

"The City Council makes all the decisions."

"Thanks." Ann Marie hung up the phone and closed the notebook. She sat tensely on the edge of the seat. She wished she were already back in her office, back where she could at least do something, before something was done to her. She picked up the phone again and dialed her own office. Busy. She dialed again. Still busy. "Can't this damned thing go a little faster?" she asked petulantly.

The driver nodded and picked up speed. Ann Marie felt tightness throughout her body. She wouldn't relax until she could hack free of the web of frustration around her. She glanced out of the window at the jumble of the city flashing past. Brick everywhere, bricks of every age. Bright-red bricks, pale-yellow bricks, dark, flaking bricks on old churches and apartment buildings, hard, unyielding walls everywhere. Where would she be after the dust settled? An alderwoman from the Northwest Side with a voiceless mentor? Ready to be dropped from the ticket in the next slating? Whoever became Mayor would only serve until the scheduled election next April. Ten months . . .

She dialed her office again.

"Helen? Never mind about that. I'll handle that when I see you. No, no . . . Now call Channel Two and cancel me off the noon interview . . . I don't care what you say. I'm busy, tied up . . . Anything. Got that? Did you get any message from Paul Martin? . . . Good. I'll see you in an hour or so . . . A prayer service at the Cathedral tonight? Six o'clock. Okay."

Ann Marie hung up just as the driver took the North Avenue exit that led to the Lake Shore Drive address Mrs. O'Brien had given him earlier. The driver had heard that Alderwoman O'Brien and Paul Michael Martin fucked at this address. He inspected her in the rear-view mirror.

Well, there were City Council members fucking all over town. At least these two were the same color . . .

"Molly? Yes, yes, I'm fine . . . No, I got some sleep, a couple of hours. Is Matthew there? Look, there's a special prayer service scheduled tonight at the Cathedral. I'll send a car to pick you up a little after five . . . Yes, put him on."

The car crossed the sprawling intersection at LaSalle Street and the green mounds of Lincoln Park rose on the left. Roller skaters and runners everywhere.

"Matthew? Yes, yes, Mommy's fine. Are all the lights back on? Yes, it was a terrible storm. You were a brave boy, Aunt Molly tells me . . . You're okay, right? Listen, now. Mommy's very busy because the Mayor is sick . . . No, no, Mommy's not going away. You're coming to see me tonight. In a police car . . . I don't know. If Sergeant Berrigan is around, maybe he'll come and get you. I'll see. You be good now . . . Yes, that's right. Be brave. Like Daddy was . . ."

Paul Michael Martin held Ann Marie in his arms.

"Relax, Annie. You're tight as a drum . . ." He ran his hands over her body. He never wanted her more than on these days when they had enjoyed some foreplay at a news conference. All part of the excitement he now felt fiercely. "Come on, baby, relax. Have I ever failed to take good care of you at noon?"

Ann Marie pulled away. She could only think about the plans and the planners huddled around the city at that very moment. She needed a plan for herself. God, she needed to be able to *do* something. The urgency for that closed down all her other systems.

"Come on, Annie." P.M. put his arms around her again. "Did I ever tell you how pretty you look when you bite your lip that way?" He leaned down and kissed her. "My turn to bite it." She pushed him away with her right arm. He did not let go of her completely. "Temper, temper . . ."

"Paul, for God's sake, I've got to decide what I'm going to do."

"I know what to do. Come on, Annie, we can have a deep, serious discussion later on . . ."

She folded her arms. "No, Paul. Not now. Cool yourself off. Go take a cold shower."

Martin dropped his arm from behind her back and stepped a few paces to the coffee table to get a cigarette. He surveyed her as he lighted it. She was coiled and tense. Very sexy.

"Okay, baby, let's talk." He flicked his lighter closed and walked across to the windows that opened on a panoramic view of Lake Shore Drive. He looked down at the sweep of the roadway and at the escarpment of sand, the Oak Street Beach, just where the drive turned east by the

Drake Hotel. Hundreds of people were on the beach on the warm June day.

"Look, Annie, lots of people are enjoying themselves today. Why don't we? Then we can discuss all this business that's bothering you. What is it, the succession business? Who'll take Cullen's place, is that it?"

She stood, her arms still folded, drawing him into her focus from across the room. Everything was matter-of-fact to Martin.

"No, that's only part of it. I just feel that I'm on the outside of whatever is happening today. I'm minding the store. And somebody else is going to take it over anyway."

"Who?" Martin asked languidly as he tilted the blinds to darken the room slightly. "Rafferty and Company?"

"Of course. They're making deals right now."

"Who else?"

"Maureen, the Mayor's daughter. She has Richler with her. I felt she was getting ready to work out some kind of front for her father. She'd keep him in office and run the city from behind the scenes."

Martin exhaled cigarette smoke and walked back to Ann Marie.

"You worried they're going to leave you out in the cold? Is that it?"

Ann Marie nodded slowly and leaned against Martin.

"You're Vice-Mayor, Annie."

"That doesn't amount to anything. The Council's got the power. You know that."

Martin held her with one arm and with the other dropped his cigarette into an ashtray. He began to laugh. Ann Marie, annoyed, glared up at him.

"Come on, Annie," Martin said boisterously, "let me help you." He reached toward her.

"What's so funny? Just what the hell is so funny?"

"You worried about your future? Come on, Annie. Don't you know that at this very moment, at this goddamned instant, you're the most powerful person in the city?"

"My office doesn't mean a thing."

"That's the least of it, Annie, that's what's so funny. It's you that's important. Think about it. You're the city's heroine. Took over in the wake of the worst storm that's hit the city in years. Cullen has a stroke. You calm the people, reassure them, keep the government going. You're on the tube practically every minute. You're on every newspaper's front page. Christ, Annie, do I have to spell it out for you in capital letters?"

Ann Marie's looks softened. Martin hugged her. She still felt taut. He touched her breasts with one hand. Christ, they were like sentinels on guard.

"Annie, Annie, I don't care what the City Council's power is. You've got the power of the media. Didn't we prove that this morning? Hell, you've got these little bastards on the run. You're worried about them? Hell, they're worried about *you!*" He leaned forward and kissed her on the mouth. She was more receptive.

"Don't you see, Annie?" Martin laughed again. "Hell, don't you remember years ago how Jane Byrne set those old toads to flight? Momentum, that's what she had. And she knew it and rode it right the hell into City Hall. And you're prettier than she was . . ."

Ann Marie felt the rigidity in her body lessen. Alertness to new possibilities was born in its place. There *was* something she could do after all. She wasn't just caught helplessly while these forces worked around her.

"Annie, come on back to life. This is P.M., in person. In the flesh, as they say. Come on, we can talk more in bed . . ."

"No," she said decisively, "we'll talk right now."

"Come on, Annie." Paul flashed his most sensuous grin. He loosened the knot of his tie.

"You're right, Paul." Ann Marie moved quickly back to the entrance-way and retrieved the pad from her purse. "There are things I can do to save myself."

"Hell, Annie, saving yourself isn't the problem. Rafferty and that crowd are the ones who have to save themselves."

"Sit down, Paul. I want to talk about this right now."

Martin let go of his fully loosened tie and took a chair opposite the one Ann Marie sat in. She held her notebook on her knee.

Christ, she was all business. Martin leaned forward and plucked another cigarette from the coffee table. "You're important to the city right now. Hell, the public loves you. They'll love you more when they know you've blown the whistle on the aldermen who want to put Cullen out to pasture. Believe me, Annie"—Martin lighted his cigarette and inhaled deeply—"if the election were today, you'd win in a landslide. Don't you understand how powerful you are politically? Hell, you're a Joan of Arc right now. They can't shove you out of the way, no matter how weak your office is. You scared hell out of them on cable television. You move your finger and the media jump. You have the city in the palm of your hand. Don't you know that?"

Ann Marie listened carefully. She felt calmer. The wailing sirens of distress that had sounded the alert inside her earlier trailed off. "But I have to support Cullen to do this. Is that right?"

Martin shrugged, pulled his tie off and tossed it onto the coffee table. "Maybe. Maybe not. You're the one in the limelight. Depends on what his condition is. *Really, is.*" He unbuttoned the top of his shirt. Ann Marie was taking this so fucking seriously. Now if she would only be serious about the fucking . . .

"You'd have to deal, let them know you were ready to do business.

That you're ready to use your public popularity against them. They'll get the message." Martin leaned back and drew on his cigarette.

A key sounded in the door of the apartment. Both Ann Marie and Paul, startled by the unexpected noise, turned their heads. The door opened and closed. Richard Barone came around the corner of the foyer. Blue suit. Solemn look.

"Well," he said in his deep oily voice, "the birds are in the love nest." He did not seem amused as he advanced across the carpet, huge and unfriendly in every aspect of his being.

"Well, Rich," Martin said nonchalantly, "how nice. You've never dropped in before." He waved an arm expansively.

"No," Barone answered as he dropped onto a white sofa on the far side of the coffee table. "No, I stay away when you people have the courts signed up." He grinned falsely at Ann Marie. She didn't change her expression. Barone looked toward Martin.

"I've never had a friend do what you did at the press conference today either. What the hell do you think this is, anyway? You two playing games with each other on the television screen? Setting your friends up? Hell, that's all there is on the news right now."

Martin laughed. "Come on, Rich, what do you want me to do, nominate you for Mayor?"

Barone shook his head in disgust. "You two have enjoyed this place, haven't you? I've been good to you. Right?"

Martin nodded, a grin still on his face. Ann Marie felt uncomfortable but remained silent.

"Then you fuck me. Right in public. Paul, you ought to treat Richie better than that." Barone cracked his knuckles. "I thought I'd find you here. Both of you." There was nothing friendly in his tone.

"Come on, Rich," Martin said coolly, "don't try to scare us."

Barone raised his eyebrows and looked first at Martin and then at Ann Marie. Ann Marie felt calm but fascinated with the flashy Barone. Everything about him was excessive—smile, cuff links, the sound of his voice. Bad taste from head to toe. Whatever happened, she would have to deal with him during the next day or two. She felt better that it was happening here, in the privacy of the apartment that Barone owned under the name of one of his land companies.

"Mr. Barone," Ann Marie said evenly, "are you chastizing us? Or do you just want to tell us your troubles?"

Barone cracked his knuckles again. "You wanna talk straight, I can talk straight too." He shifted his position on the sofa so that he looked more directly at Ann Marie. "Whatever happens this time, Mrs. O'Brien, whatever you've got on your mind, you have to be reasonable. You aren't some big star, not yet, not all by yourself."

"Read the newspapers," she replied. "Watch television."

"Yeah," Martin interjected, "you'll see how big a star she is."

Barone raised his hands in a calming gesture. "I do read the papers. You think I don't know your power with the press? That's why I'm talking to you. I understand what's going on in this city. I understand it better than some of my friends in the City Council. They're upset, by the way, they're plenty upset about your news conference this morning."

"You've been talking to Rafferty?" Martin asked.

"Listening, mostly," Barone answered. "You know, he wants to dump you, Mrs. O'Brien . . . Annie, he thinks we can take over without you."

Ann Marie did not feel that she *had* to say anything. She'd listen, she could wait to hear what Barone had to say. Martin opened his mouth and Ann Marie gestured toward him to be still.

Barone reached forward and took a cigarette but continued to talk as he placed it in his mouth and lighted it. "The last time the Mayor was sick these guys were too hungry. And too much in a hurry. Me too, at the time. I've talked sense to them now. We can take over. But we can't, this is my point, by electing Rafferty the acting Mayor. The people wouldn't have it, not with you running around all over the place, on the news every five minutes." Barone inhaled deeply. "Annie," he said, exhaling the smoke, "what I'm offering you, what I'm a spokesman for, is a deal. No fight, no more name-calling, no more questions and answers between you and lover boy here." He waved a large open hand in Martin's direction.

"What do you want," Martin asked, "and what are you giving?"

"It's simple. So goddamned simple." Barone leaned forward. "Mrs. O'Brien—Annie here—goes on television and announces that, in view of the Mayor's grave condition, she's calling a City Council meeting to decide whether he can continue to carry the heavy burdens of office. We want you to lead the charge."

"You want me to get Cullen declared incompetent, is it that?" Ann Marie's voice trembled slightly as she asked the question.

"That's what it comes to, yes. You take responsibility for the decision. The people might take it from you, for the good of the city, all that shit. The way I see it, you're the only one who could get away with this, seeing you've been Cullen's little darling . . ."

"What does this get me in return?"

"The Council'll elect you acting Mayor."

"What about the slating next fall?" Martin asked.

Ann Marie pursed her lips and watched Barone carefully. Turn in Cullen and side with Barone? She took a deep breath.

"Nobody can promise that," Barone said. "Hell, we have to replace Cullen as party chairman, too. We might be able to put Rafferty in that job. Wendel wants it like hell, though. Anybody who's acting Mayor has a hell of a shot at the nomination, the way I see it. Well, Annie, what do you say?"

"I'll have to think about it."

"How do we know you're talking for Rafferty and the others?" Martin asked, as he picked his tie up off the coffee table.

"Come on, Paul," Barone answered in irritation, "for Crissake, do you think on something as important as this that I'd shit you? We don't have a lot of time to put the votes together. We have to have a firm *yes* by to-night."

Ann Marie pulled a stray hair back into place at the side of her head. "Mr. Barone, maybe you people need me. I can believe that. I'm not just so sure that I need you." Barone's mouth fell partially open. "I'm serious. I am in a position of power right now. What makes you think I can't make a deal with the Cullens? What makes you think I can't pull this off on my own? Paul, here, can be a great help with the media. And you're right, I get a lot of attention these days."

"Annie," Barone began . . .

"I do prefer 'Mrs. O'Brien' . . ."

"Whatever the hell you want. You goddamned women are all alike. You want as much as you can get. What the hell is it, some instinct in you? Don't you know when you're getting as much as you're ever going to get?"

"What do you mean?" Martin asked, draping the tie around his shoulders.

"I mean you need an organization. You need votes. You can't get anywhere without the Council's cooperation. You need Rafferty. You may not like him, but you need him. And Wendel and Noto and the rest of them." Barone heaved himself up from the sofa and walked to the window. He slotted the blinds so that the room was filled with light. He turned back toward Ann Marie and Paul Martin.

"You're not so fucking clean as you think, Mrs. O'Brien. You took on the chair of the Captain Charles O'Brien Senior Citizens Center. You remember that? Thought you were winning a big one then, isn't that right? Well, that made you a partner with the rest of us. Your name—and your husband's name—they're involved with my company already. You're a fucking partner with Rafferty and Noto. How do you think that'll sound if it comes out?"

"I have no financial interest in that project," Ann Marie answered curtly.

"Maybe not, maybe not, but you've got something better. Your good name is in it. Won't make any difference to the media, not once it's leaked properly. You ought to know that. Look what happened to Richler, for Crissake."

Ann Marie felt a coating of acid shimmering down inside her. She had made no promises to Rafferty or Noto. She had taken no money. But Barone was right. She had given her name. And Charlie's. Ann Marie cleared her throat.

"You're saying you're prepared for bad publicity just to give some to me?"

"You're the one it would be news about. After all, you're the one who led those old birds out on the airport runway. You're the one who made this whole project an issue."

"But the papers know that Charlie's name is on the project . . ."

"Sure, sure. What they need is a little hint of money being passed, a few hints is all they need for a good headline. Fucking hard to prove the truth, Mrs. O'Brien, when stories like that get around." Barone's voice crackled sardonically. "How did the story about Richler get started? Maybe it would be good to get that out too? Maybe it would be good to let them know where you two've been fucking each other all these months. In *my* apartment. You think I don't have pictures of you two coming in and out of here? Mrs. O'Brien, you just haven't noticed how involved you've gotten. And nobody's pulled the switch on you until now. How's it feel? Pardon me saying this, Mrs. O'Brien, but you're too impulsive sometimes."

"Get out," Ann Marie said sharply, "get out of here."

"Out? Christ, I own this place. Look, you're not working for the MIA's anymore. I'm not some fucking foreign ambassador. This is big stuff. I figure you owe us. We can help each other. Or we can destroy you. Take your choice."

Ann Marie looked at Paul Martin. Barone was right. There wasn't much of a choice.

"Come on, Paul, let's go . . ."

"Wait, wait, we haven't even . . ."

"Come on, Paul." Ann Marie stood up and walked around the coffee table toward the foyer of the apartment.

"We need to know by suppertime," Barone called after her.

"I'll be at the prayer service for the Mayor," Ann Marie said without turning around. Martin watched her, then turned back to Barone.

The big man cracked his knuckles. "So will we, Annie, so will we . . ."

24

*C*aptain Vincent had not thought of attending the prayer service for the Mayor. But when Deputy Superintendent O'Hanlon called from downtown he readily agreed to be at Holy Name Cathedral by five o'clock. He had to do something besides think about George Phillips. His wife Mary was right. He had been a policeman for twenty years; they would have two children in college in the fall. He couldn't afford to spend his time obsessed with a mass murderer who was truly beyond his grasp. So the idea of constituting an honor guard with a dozen other high-ranking uniformed officers—and giving a hand if the crowd got as big as some expected—sounded fine. He checked himself in the mirror. He did not often dress in full uniform these days.

"You look like a real police officer," Mary said as she watched him from the doorway of their bedroom.

"And I still fit, you'll notice." He walked over to his wife and gave her a kiss.

"Paul"—Mary flicked a piece of lint from the sleeve of his uniform—"you really do look handsome."

"Mary," he said, grinning, "you're glad to see me in this because you know I can't go looking for Phillips in any of those game arcades dressed in my uniform. Right?" He kissed her lightly again.

"I hadn't thought of that, Paul," she answered, "but I'm happier knowing that you'll be at the Cathedral instead of in some shopping mall . . ."

He made a playful swing at her with his right hand, kissed her again, and, arm in arm with his wife, walked down the stairs to the front door of their house.

Ann Marie had finally left the apartment without Martin, who stayed behind to talk further with Barone. She was angry, deep down, won't-go-away angry at Martin and Barone talking deals while she had to face the problems. Damn them all. She returned to her office to handle the questions and messages that waited with her own secretary and with Helen

Morrison. She would still stay far away from Cullen's own office today. She would stay clear of seeming to move in and take over.

She saw Franklin Barnes at five. Stuffy, elegant Franklin Barnes talked in vague terms about the future of the city. When Ann Marie asked him directly about the old Mayor, Barnes smiled faintly and said, "Well, that's a difficult matter for you and the City Council to decide." Barnes didn't speak up for Cullen. The crusty banker knew that the Council was getting itself together to declare Cullen incompetent to govern. Barnes also knew what was expected of Ann Marie. "Stability, Mrs. O'Brien, and continuity. These are the things the city needs. A prolonged period of uncertainty, well, that would raise questions in the credit markets . . ." They had gotten to Franklin Barnes. The WASP counterpart in pious hypocrisy to Francis Rafferty.

The call from Louis Fairfield, head of the Chicago Teamsters Union, was also clear. Keep things on an even keel. Sure, it's too bad about the Mayor. But life goes on, doesn't it, Mrs. O'Brien? Ann Marie tightened up inside again. Goddamn these men anyway. Half the men in her life couldn't speak, the other half wouldn't shut up. And where did it leave her? She felt achy after hanging up from Fairfield's call. Ann Marie cat-stretched and ignored the buzzer from her secretary. The buttons on her telephone danced with lights. Ann Marie rose from her chair and walked over to the windows. She gazed dreamily down at the streets, gloomily shadowed by the buildings on the eve of summer. The buzzer sounded insistently. She walked back to her desk.

"Hello," Ann Marie said curtly.

"Ann Marie? This is Maureen . . ."

That's all she needed. "Yes?"

"Ann Marie, I want to talk to you about my father."

"Yes, go ahead."

"You sound so faraway."

"Busy day, Maureen. Not much sleep. How's your father?"

"I think he's doing fine."

"But what do the doctors say?"

"They seem very pleased too. They say with luck and some therapy he could do very well."

"How long, did they say?"

"Several weeks, I'm not sure. They say he has a strong constitution. My grandfather—his father—lived to be eighty-eight. Did you know that?"

Ann Marie held the phone numbly. Maureen wanted her to front for her father, make it sound like the second coming was right around the corner. The Cullens were not used to having people say no to them.

"Ann Marie, we've heard that the Council wants to declare my father incompetent. We're depending on you to fight for us, to hold the fort for a few more days."

"Maureen, there may not be much I can do."

"What do you mean, not much you can do? If they don't have a Council meeting until next week, that would be something, that would be a lot."

"Maureen, this isn't so simple. This isn't like the last time."

There was an uncomfortable pause.

"They've got you lined up, is that it?" Maureen's directness surprised her. The Mayor's daughter was defending her nest. Ann Marie was trying to defend hers. And the old Mayor lay in the hospital, quiet as a village after a snowfall. Everybody wanted Ann Marie to act in their behalf. The politicians, the builders, the bankers, the unions. Hold our coats, Ann Marie dear, while we divide the pie. Throw Paul Martin in and count the media too. The Captain Charles O'Brien Senior Citizens Center. Rafferty. Wendel. Barone. Pictures of her and Martin leaving 1325 Lake Shore Drive together . . .

"Maureen, I have to act for the good of the city."

"You wouldn't be there where you are except for my father. You know that, don't you?"

"Your father always told me to put good government first, to put it ahead of politics."

"What do you think he wants you to do now?" Maureen was as strong as her father.

Ann Marie paused. "Maureen, there's no point in talking about this now. I feel bad about your father. I'm going to the Cathedral to pray for him in a few minutes. But I'm going to have to do what I think is best. Now, you'll have to excuse me . . ."

"That's *all* you've got to say?" Maureen was angry.

"There's nothing more I can say right now. Life has to go on. Goodbye." Ann Marie lowered the phone slowly to its cradle. Was Maureen still speaking as Ann Marie hung up? She stood there gazing down at the flashing buttons. The buzzer sounded again. Her secretary was on the line. "The car is ready for you to go to the Cathedral now."

Life has to go on. Everybody said that. Ann Marie had said it herself. The sedan eased onto State Street just north of the Loop for the trip to Holy Name. It was almost the longest day of the year. A pretty evening with the streets filled with people walking home from work. The traffic thickened as they approached Holy Name Cathedral. The prayer service was going to be a media event. And she, Vice-Mayor Ann Marie O'Brien, widow of Charles, mistress of Paul Michael, St. Joan of Chicago, would be the star. At least, everybody would be looking at her.

And everybody wanted something from her. She bristled with irritation as the car eased against the curb.

The car door opened in front of the Cathedral. Monsignor Fitzmaurice, splendid in the purple robes of his office, stood at the center of an aisle across the sidewalk that had been sectioned off by wooden horses to keep the media and the curious away from the important guests as they arrived for the liturgical service. He half-bowed and pecked a kiss at his cousin's face as she stepped out of the car.

"Good evening, Ann Marie. I'm sure this has been a hard day for you."

Ann Marie looked quickly past her cousin to scan the steps of the church. Lines of uniformed police officers were spread out on either side of the textured-bronze main doors. Lots of brass around. Even the Police Superintendent was in uniform. White gloves and as many stars as Eisenhower used to wear.

"You know the Superintendent." Ann Marie nodded and shook the hand of the florid-faced man who headed Chicago's Police Department. "And you know Captain Dyra from the Chicago Avenue district." Ann Marie shook the captain's hand perfunctorily, her eyes still searching the crowd.

"Shall we go in? Matthew and Molly are already seated." Monsignor Fitzmaurice took Ann Marie's arm and they climbed the eight broad grooved steps to the entrance.

"This will be a big night for you," her cousin whispered as they mounted the stairs. Ann Marie glanced to her left down the line of police officers. She recognized a familiar face. The captain from the airport. She did not have time to react, however, as she passed into the marble-clad vestibule.

"This is Bishop Roache, rector of the Cathedral," the Monsignor said as another handsome Irish face beamed at her above a mantle of purple. The Cathedral proper was already crowded and the organist filled the old structure with familiar hymns while the last of the important guests were being seated. People turned to look as Ann Marie marched, as though to her first communion, down the aisle.

"You have an important decision to make, Ann Marie." Monsignor Fitzmaurice moved his mouth no more than a ventriloquist as he paced solemnly at her side. Ann Marie shot a hostile glance at him and then turned her face back toward the sanctuary. Strains of the "Ave Maria" washed over them. So they had gotten to Fitzie too. "I'll pray for you," he whispered through his unmoving lips as he left her at the first pew on the right and passed on up into the sanctuary proper. Ann Marie genuflected and made the sign of the cross, the quick knee bob and the blurred hand motion of the lifelong Catholic, and knelt down. She kissed Matthew and bussed Aunt Molly. She held her finger to her lips as Matthew blurted out a question.

Directly across the aisle sat Maureen Cullen Coleman, her sallow-faced husband Lawrence, and their children. Cap Malloy, a black rosary twined in his fingers, sat next to them, his head bowed. The organ shifted into Mozart and the Governor, a smiling young man who always looked like he had just returned from a skiing holiday, slipped in next to Ann Marie. He introduced himself and settled back on the bench. "Bad knee," he whispered hoarsely to Ann Marie. She raised her eyes to the huge crucifix suspended above the main altar. Beyond that, high in the splayed light above the sanctuary, she could make out the round flat red hats of Chicago's dead cardinals suspended in space. She had been intrigued by them, hanging like stuffed birds above a museum hall, since she was a little girl, their once-powerful wearers gone to dust long ago. Life did go on. The organist wandered into reedy arpeggio on the high range of the scale as the Lieutenant-Governor, sausage-skinned into a khaki summer suit, edged into the pew.

"Is this long?" Matthew whispered to his mother. She looked down at him. "No, Matthew, you just be good. Don't fidget so." He made a face, part resignation and part restlessness. Cathedrals were no places for little boys on almost-summer evenings. Ann Marie looked at Matthew again. He had changed a lot. He was getting big. Had she missed his growing somehow? How much longer would he be a little boy?

"Pardon me, Mrs. O'Brien." A young priest in black cassock and white surplice stood in front of the pew. "Since you'll be doing one of the scripture readings, we thought it would be better if you moved next to the aisle. It'll be easier for you to get in and out." Ann Marie looked up into the priest's youthful face. He could hardly be thirty. My God, Matthew was getting older and the priests were getting younger. She nodded, rose, and as the state officials shunted their knees sideways, she made an awkward passage to the aisle seat. She looked across the profiles of the Governor and his Lieutenant at Matthew. He was looking back at her, his eyes wide, as though a border gate had been lowered between them.

At the front door of the Cathedral a steady stream of cars passed by, pausing to allow judges, aldermen, and a variety of other dignitaries and celebrities to debark. They then rounded the corner onto Chicago Avenue to search out places to wait until the service ended. Routine on big occasions at the Cathedral. Captain Vincent had little to do but to stand up straight, a member of a gold-braided praetorian guard strung across the front of the old limestone structure. He watched Sam Noto shoulder out of a blue Lincoln Continental. Noto bulled up the steps, his eyes lowered, his skin lizard-coarse in the natural light of evening. Wendel and Carney had come together. They had shaken hands along the edge of the penned-off crowd before entering the Cathedral. Larry Johnson climbed out of a limousine the color of lightly creamed coffee. He had flashed a big smile and waved as he climbed the steps. Francis Rafferty oozed by on his own slick piety. Vincent gazed above the heads of the large crowd beyond the wooden horses that spilled down and around the steps and sidewalk. When was this parade of cars going to end?

The same routine for each. The car pulled up. The driver hopped out and came around to open the door. Like Oscar night in Hollywood. A lot of these guys were actors, anyway. Vincent glanced at his watch. Two minutes to six. He looked over at the television crews. Even they looked bored as they panned across the scene. Still the cars arrived, depositing the assorted shapes and sizes of Chicago's power structure at the church doors. Not one of them seemed to walk straight. Vincent smiled at the gimps and hitches of gait that afflicted so many influential people. The captain's mind wandered.

Then he noticed it. He was not even sure who had gotten out of the car. The passenger was already gone when he saw it. But Captain Vincent *had* seen it. A man's hand on the door of a car. A man's left hand, the wrist exposed as the dark suit sleeve was pulled back when the man's arm stretched forward to close a car door. Push, pull, there it was. A small drawstring pouch dangled from the wrist for just an instant. A single frame in a movie. The arm had pulled back, the sleeve had pushed forward again, and the wrist and the suspended sack had vanished behind the people moving across the sidewalk.

Vincent had the impression of a man's back moving away to the right. Had the man gotten back into the car? Had he moved into the crowd at the edge of the wooden horses? The car had pulled away swiftly. A large dark car like twenty others that had come and gone. He could not see the license plate. It had all happened so swiftly. But, Christ Almighty, he *had* seen it. He couldn't break the ranks now, not now, not with the Superintendent standing a few steps away. Not to yell "Stop, killer!" into a big crowd. Not after having been told to stay away from the case. Not here in public with the television cameras rolling. Not on the meager evidence of seeing a drawstring pouch on a man's wrist. Besides, what the hell would Phillips be doing out in public anyway? Everybody was looking for him.

State Street was clogged with people and cars. Where had the man with the pouch gone? Would he be back later? Would he stretch his hand out again for everybody to see? What the hell was Phillips doing, taunting the whole police force? If it was Phillips . . .

"Paul!" It was Miller, the officer who had been standing on his left. "Wake up, Paul, we've got to go inside now . . ." Startled, Vincent turned and, scanning the street once more, joined the converging lines of his brother officers as they slowly entered the Cathedral.

The organist struck an introductory chord, repeated it like a man getting his balance, and filled the Cathedral with an entrance hymn, "O

God, Our Help in Ages Past." A double line of priests, followed by
scores of monsignors, three auxiliary bishops, and Monsignor Fitzmaurice preceded Francis Cardinal Meehan in procession out of the sac-
risty at the side of the Cathedral. The organ boomed and the string of
clergymen hooked across the front of the church and back up into the
sanctuary.

Monsignor Fitzmaurice bowed to the Cardinal and cut solemnly back
across the sanctuary to the lectern, a bronze slab supported by miniature
bronze evangelists, clustered like a team of gymnasts.

"My dear friends," he said smoothly, "we welcome you to this service
of prayer for the return to health of our beloved Mayor, Thomas H.
Cullen . . ." He droned on unctuously as Ann Marie studied him from
beneath a lowered brow. He would be in line with the rest of them if
she accepted Barone's plan. Ann Marie looked back at Matthew, who
was leaning against Molly. Relatives everywhere she looked. A patched-
up family, all right. She turned her head to watch Maureen Cullen
Coleman, who was speaking softly to one of her own children. Ann
Marie didn't harbor any doubts about what Maureen would do if she
could get her hands on the power of the Mayor's office. She might talk
sweetly, but there wouldn't be much room for Ann Marie. The Cullens
didn't give anything away easily.

This first reading is that by the Honorable Matthew Hogan, representing the judiciary . . ." Monsignor Fitzmaurice stepped down from the
pulpit as the judge took his place and opened the red-bound book that
lay on the slanted lectern. He fumbled for his glasses. "A reading from
the letter of James . . ." Matty Hogan, my predecessor as alderman and
Vice-Mayor, Matty the slumlord in judge's clothing . . . "If anyone of
you is ill, he should send for the elders of the church, and they must
anoint him with oil in the name of the Lord and pray over him . . ."
Matty sounded very ecclesiastical. Judges and bishops. Was there a
dime's worth of difference between them, anyway?

Captain Vincent ended up without a seat. The pew reserved for police
officers was already overcrowded. He drifted back down the aisle and, as
Judge Hogan concluded and the assembled people responded, "Thanks
be to God," he edged into the vestibule at the rear of the church. If Phillips was around, he'd be outside. He had driven somebody, or ridden
along as a batman to some big shot or other. Captain Vincent was in the
crowded foyer as Monsignor Fitzmaurice intoned the responsorial psalm.
"You saved my life, O Lord; I shall not die . . ." The congregation
repeated it as Vincent pushed against the massive main door and
stepped back into the warm, bright evening. Phillips would have parked
somewhere; he'd be near the car he came in.

Vincent walked across the top step, just beyond what was left of the
onlookers, and descended to the sidewalk and hurried past the side of

the Cathedral through a courtyard and alleyway to Wabash Avenue. The limousines and other large cars that had borne the officials and dignitaries were lined up along either curb, their drivers reading the papers or napping. Cars were also lined up on the avenue beyond the intersection of Superior Street. In a few places the drivers had stepped out of their cars to chat casually and smoke in groups of two or three. Where was the son of a bitch? The goddamned drivers all looked alike. Dark suits, dark hair, full moustaches. He couldn't very well ask them to raise their left arms. The captain stepped off the curb and looked south. He began to walk in the street, looking from car to car. Phillips was here somewhere, the son of a bitch. He came to taunt me . . .

Monsignor Fitzmaurice stepped away from the lectern and smiled at his cousin, who was being escorted from the first pew to read a passage from scripture. She did not look at him as she stepped to the lectern. She glanced out into the vastness of the Cathedral. Maureen Coleman looked up at her stonily. Rafferty, his lips pursed above folded arms, sat a few rows behind her. City Council members were scattered throughout the congregation—Wendel, Noto, Carney, Johnson, Ramirez looking expectantly toward her. Richard Barone grinned almost obscenely up from the sixth row of pews. She turned and looked back at the Cardinal. He also smiled, the only pleasant smile she had received all evening. The Cardinal seemed jovial, friendly, a man too innocent for Chicago. Where had they ever found him? Ann Marie turned back and looked down at the book spread open before her. She pulled a green ribbon placemarker aside. The church breathed expectation; everybody was waiting for her to do something.

"A reading from the gospel according to Luke." She paused and again scanned the rows of faces, as varied as pawed-over vegetables on a grocer's counter. "Jesus left the upper room to make his way as usual to the Mount of Olives, with his disciples following." Her voice was firm and clear. "When they reached the place he said to them, 'Pray not to be put to the test.'"

Meanwhile, Captain Vincent was feeling foolish. Where was this goddamn Phillips? He would have to watch for him when the service broke up.

Ann Marie cleared her throat. "Then he withdrew from them, about a stone's throw away, and knelt down and prayed. 'Father,' he said, 'if you are willing, take this cup away from me. Nevertheless, let your will be done, not mine.'"

These quotations were scalding echoes from her Catholic girlhood. They did not fit her now and she knew it. But they did speak to her. Everything seemed to have a message for her. The Mayor's job was not a cup she wanted to pass away from her. As she read she felt keenly that she wanted to hold on to it, to take it for herself. She didn't want to let go of anything. If she did, what would be left for her . . . ?

Ann Marie concluded the reading, the congregation responded and, escorted by an acolyte, she walked back to her seat.

It was like a dream. What in God's name was she doing, reading the scriptures about Jesus to this crowd? She didn't like herself for doing it, she didn't like the scattered officials who wanted her to cover their take-over, she didn't like Maureen or anything much about the Cullens at the present moment. But she couldn't say, she wouldn't say, "Let this cup pass . . ."

Captain Vincent wasn't happy with himself either, as he turned west on Superior and paced under the leafing trees along the sidewalk toward the front of the Cathedral. "Holy God, We Praise Thy Name" drifted out of the side doors of the church. The television vans were parked along the Cathedral side of the street and their cables trailed up along the broad main steps. The television crews. Of course. The television crews had recorded everybody arriving. Somewhere on one of their tapes they had a picture of the man with the pouch hanging from his left wrist. Maybe even a picture of the car he had been in. Maybe even a license number . . .

As Captain Vincent climbed up to the top steps, Captain Dyra waved him toward the main door. "Glad you're back, Paul. They're just about to come out. You take that side and I'll take this." The massive doors of the Cathedral slowly opened and the first trickle of the congregation spilled through. He would have to talk to the television crews later on.

The dignitaries poured out rapidly, spreading out and down the steps, turning to shake hands with each other while they waited for their cars to pick them up. Vincent tried to keep an eye on the arriving herd of limousines, but the steps became so crowded within a few minutes that it was impossible to watch the line of vehicles carefully. As several other policemen arrived, things began to move more smoothly. A trio of plainclothes bodyguards emerged from the doors, signaling for a clear path. Maureen Cullen Coleman, her husband and children, hurried quickly out and down the steps to the Mayor's official limousine, ignoring the questions shouted by reporters over the heads of the crowd.

Another wave of handshakers emerged and dispersed down the steps. Matthew and Aunt Molly followed a policeman out of the church. Then, in the company of her cousin and a police officer, Ann Marie, her face as ungiving as the façade of the Cathedral itself, stepped through the doors. She paused a few feet from Captain Vincent.

"Captain," she said firmly without really looking at him, "tell the television people that I'd like to make a statement." She turned to her body-guard, gave him an order, and waited serenely while Captain Vincent called for a patrolman to deliver the message to the television crews. The crowd, like a millipede brought suddenly to attention, held its position and shifted back around Ann Marie. The camera crews pushed through the sluggishly parting bystanders. Other news reporters struggled to make their way closer to the Vice-Mayor. Did she have word on Cullen's condition? Was she going to name names about the aldermen she had mentioned at her morning news conference? Paul Michael Martin emerged from the Cathedral doors behind her, waving a signal at the camera crew from his channel. Captain Vincent felt his stomach tightening. How the hell could he ever spot George Phillips if this O'Brien woman was going to have a press conference on the Cathedral steps? He could not move away from the position he was in, anyway, not even if he had a clear look at Phillips . . .

Ann Marie bit her lower lip lightly as she waited for the cameramen to get into position. Was it tension or concentration? Monsignor Fitzmaurice raised his eyebrows uncertainly as he watched his cousin. Headstrong. Everybody had always said that about her. Sam Noto was halfway down the main steps. He watched Ann Marie sullenly, holding a crumple of unlighted cigar in his hand. Richard Barone had almost reached the curb when he noticed the puff of excitement spread out around Ann Marie. He waved his driver off and watched the Vice-Mayor attentively. Rafferty forced a smile as he looked across at Ann Marie from the place he had taken next to Monsignor Fitzmaurice.

Ann Marie looked directly into the cameras.

"I have an announcement I'd like to make." She paused on the edge of the diving board. Life, as everyone told her, had to go on. "We have just concluded a prayer service for the good health of Mayor Thomas H. Cullen, a man greatly admired and loved in our city. Because he is so highly regarded it is difficult to say what I have to." She paused again as the impact of her words struck those near her in the crowd. People strained forward to hear her. "We all want Mayor Cullen to return to full health. I have visited him in the hospital. I know that he cannot return to his office for many weeks, perhaps months, at the earliest. As you know, I have opposed those who want to make his health an issue prematurely. Nevertheless, I am now convinced that something must be done. I want it clear that I make this statement on my own initiative."

The crowd surged closer to her. Captain Vincent struggled to keep a space open around her. He searched the crowd clustered along the curb. It was no use. If George Phillips was out there, he was well protected. If he was out there . . .

"Sadly, and with a heavy heart, I must face the fact that the city needs a Mayor. For his own health, Mayor Cullen cannot serve at this time. He may never be able to return to his duties. We cannot have a makeshift interim government. We love the Mayor, but we must do what he would want us to do: put the city and its people first. I have been praying about what he would tell us if he were here. I am, therefore, asking the City Council to convene tomorrow morning at ten o'clock for the purpose of declaring the office of the Mayor vacated because of illness according to the Municipal Code, Chapter 24, Paragraph 3 dash 4 dash 5. I will propose that they elect from among their members a Mayor who will serve out the remaining months of Mayor Cullen's term. I am saying this now because I think it is in the best interests of Mayor Cullen and of our great city. I will not take any questions. Thank you, gentlemen."

Ann Marie turned away quickly as her bodyguards and a number of patrolmen led by Captain Paul Vincent formed a moving cordon around her and escorted her through the stunned crowd to her waiting car.

On the top steps Paul Michael Martin had taken a microphone and moved into camera range. "And so, in a dramatic move on the steps of Holy Name Cathedral, Vice-Mayor Ann Marie O'Brien has made one of the most startling statements in the history of the city, a move that may alter the face of Chicago politics and government permanently . . ." The clip and its clone on other channels were repeated a dozen times that evening as the city, like a great organism, recoiled under the impact of the news and then began to react.

Captain Vincent pulled the door of Ann Marie's car open. She looked directly at him as she climbed in. "You," she said abruptly to him, "you get in. I want you along . . ."

25

*A*nn Marie did not know why she had impulsively commanded Captain Vincent to climb into the car with her. "I'd like some brass around when we get back to City Hall," she explained tersely. Captain Vincent, wedged into the front seat with two bodyguards, nodded uncomfortably. Ann Marie looked at him. A handsome man, she thought, and, although she couldn't explain why, she felt that she had done the right thing. She wanted somehow to keep Captain Vincent under her control. Did it have anything to do with being asked about George Phillips out at the trailer park? No, of course not . . .

"Captain, I want you to take charge when we arrive. There'll be a big crowd. I'm not answering any questions. Do you understand?"

"Yes, ma'am," Vincent replied, turning three quarters profile as he spoke. How the hell had he ended up in the front seat of this car? Had he really seen George Phillips outside the Cathedral?

The rush hour traffic had thinned. It was after seven and the Loop had settled down in the still-bright evening into a black village under the sputtering neon of the theater marquees and the fast-food restaurant signs. A crowd of reporters waited at the LaSalle Street entrance to the hall. The mobile television units were just arriving as Ann Marie's car crossed the intersection of Randolph Street.

"Pull up to a side entrance!" she blurted out suddenly.

The driver slammed on the brakes, reversed jerkily, and turned up Randolph against the light. He stopped at the entrance halfway up the block and Ann Marie, with Captain Vincent in the lead, and a bodyguard on each side of her, darted into the building and up the central stairs that led to her second-floor aldermanic office. The reporters caught on to the diversion almost immediately and charged noisily down the central concourse of the building after her. She beat them to her office with time to spare.

"Captain, you stay out here. Tell them there won't be any further statements this evening. Got that?"

Vincent nodded as Ann Marie slipped through the door to her office. The boisterous reporters pounded down the hallway. Vincent smiled at them as they shouted questions. The hallway snapped with electric excitement—the war room after the missiles were launched. "I'm sorry, everyone," Vincent said calmly, "Mrs. O'Brien will have nothing further to say this evening."

Ann Marie's office was empty except for her secretary, who had stayed to do some extra work and had been caught in the explosion of phone calls that came in after Ann Marie's announcement after the prayer service. Ann Marie tingled. The response that flooded back within her justified the position she had taken. She felt alive, at the center of things, in charge, a queen with an entourage of men who backed away meekly when she spoke. She had shrugged off the weight of deadness that she experienced inside when things became routine. That was why she had been able to take over after the tornado, why she had been able to remain calm when the Mayor was stricken, why she had wrested the initiative back when everybody was set to use her and toss her away. Excitement was her medium. God, this was better than sex.

"Get me Alderman Rafferty on the phone."

"He's holding on two already."

Ann Marie went into her inner office and reached for the phone. Her eyes caught the photograph of Matthew, a much younger Matthew than the boy she had seen at the Cathedral just an hour ago. Matthew, Matthew . . .

"This is Mrs. O'Brien."

"Ma'am, this is Francis Rafferty. I want to congratulate you on your forthright action. Much as we love dear Mayor Cullen . . ."

"What is it you want?"

"Nothing, ma'am, but to thank you. We appreciate your cooperation."

"I'm glad you called," Ann Marie cut in, excitement rising in her, "I want a few things clear. I expect your support in the Council to be elected acting Mayor. Do you understand that?"

"Mrs. O'Brien, there are those who feel that, although we are grateful to you, you haven't had the experience for the job . . ."

"Look, Rafferty, I know you want the job, I know you'd practically kill for it. Of course, you'd have a Mass said for your victim . . ."

"Ma'am, I don't think that's fair . . ."

"I didn't think you would. But listen to me. I need your help. I understand that, I know where you stand among all the people in power around here."

"But that's why . . ."

"Listen, will you? I'm the one the media will play up. I'm the one the papers will write the editorials about. I know exactly what my strengths are. Face it, I've got the people and the press with me."

Rafferty, stunned, remained silent. Would they have to support Ann Marie, let her have the job until the next election? Maybe something could be worked out. She was right about her public popularity . . .

"Alderman, I've got a proposition to make to you. You support me in the City Council and I'll support you to become chairman of the Cook County Democratic Committee."

This woman was more shrewd than Rafferty had expected.

"Nobody's thought about that. But if Cullen is too sick to be Mayor, he's too sick to run the party too . . ." Ann Marie retreated within herself. She had said enough. Let Rafferty come to her.

"Mrs. O'Brien, you *do* need me. You know that. And it's true, I'd be foolish not to admit it, your popularity in the city gives you a lot of political leverage. Have you talked about this to anyone else?"

Ann Marie did not answer. Rafferty was silent for a moment. She had offered him a good deal, he could not deny it. There were, in politics, "moments to take the tide." He sighed, pleased with the literary allusion at the crunchpoint of the most important deal he had ever negotiated.

"I think we can do business, Mrs. O'Brien."

"You handle organizing the Council. I'll help you when it comes to the party chair. Understood?"

Rafferty had accepted enough. The schoolmarm tone of the last question rankled his soul. A woman telling him what to do! Could this be happening?

"I always keep my word, ma'am. Good evening."

"You sure this is what you want to do?" Richard Barone sucked on a toothpick and leaned back on his chair. The round table at the Villa Borghese Restaurant on the West Side of the city was littered with the remains of a half-eaten meal. Rafferty had gathered Wendel, Carney, and Ramirez for a late dinner with Noto and Barone. They had, angrily and reluctantly, agreed to Rafferty's deal. They would put the bitch in, at least for the rest of Cullen's term. But they would run the show from the City Council.

"Would you like dessert? Maybe some nice spumoni?"

Totally absorbed in their conversation, they ignored the waitress.

"Look," Sam Noto said, leaning forward on his elbows, "I warned you about this woman all along. This time, you want to fuck with her, make sure you wear a rubber . . ."

"In a way, Sam," Carney said thoughtfully, "we really don't have much choice. Politically speaking . . ."

Noto waved his hand and made a disgusted sound. He looked up at the waitress. "Espresso, Clara, just espresso." The others nodded in agreement and the waitress drifted off.

"All I'm saying is, powerful with the press or not, we got to make sure we have some control. This woman, you don't know what the hell she's gonna do . . ."

Barone extracted the toothpick from his mouth and waved it as he spoke. "Look, I think she's reacting to what I told her this afternoon. Let's not let her bluff us. She wouldn't want the pictures I've got of her and Martin, she wouldn't want them published. And she's already tied to us with the housing development. This isn't a time to be tough. I think I know this dame better than you guys."

Wendel sniggered. "The great lover speaks . . ."

Barone glared at him. "I know how to handle women. This dame needs a little wooing, a little romancing the way a man can do it if he knows how. That's the card we ought to play . . ."

Barone lowered his voice. His brother Angelo and one of his sons had just entered the large dining room. They walked up to the table to greet the aldermen.

"You know my brother Angelo?" Barone took his nephew by the arm. "And Anthony . . ." The men at the table smiled and uttered variations on the theme of having met before. At the funeral home.

"Not far from here," Angelo said. "Maybe a mile. Let me know when any of you need our services."

The aldermen smiled up uneasily at the undertaker and his son. Their silence made it clear that the father-and-son undertakers had interrupted a meeting at which they were not welcome.

"Yeah, well, me and the boy are gonna have something to eat." He backed away, Anthony at his side. Richard Barone waved a halfhearted goodbye and joined his attention again to that of his comrades. Rafferty watched Barone's relatives take a table against a far wall and then looked from one to another of the men seated around the table. He fussed with his napkin.

"Gentlemen, this is strictly a business deal. Dick, this talk of romancing Mrs. O'Brien, there's no point to that. Sam's right. This time it's strictly business. She can't get elected acting Mayor without us. In return, we take complete control of the party machinery. We also control the votes in the Council. That puts the power in our hands. We can't give any of the reformers a chance to organize. We *can* live with *her* for a year. We've got enough power to keep her under strict control. Being an alderman is one thing, being the Mayor is another. She needs us now. She doesn't have Cullen." He looked around the table again. Sam Noto picked up a glass of wine and finished it off. "Now," Rafferty asked in his more-familiar honeyed tones, "are we agreed about tomorrow?" They were silent as the waitress placed the small cups of dark coffee on the table.

"Yeah," Noto said, pinching the twist of lemon into his espresso. "I'll make my piss calls in the morning. You can always get people at six o'clock in the morning . . ."

"One thing, one thing," Ramirez said. "I go along, but I got to get more for my people. I want that clear. Right now. I don't do this for nothing . . ."

"Christ, Felix," Wendel interjected, "none of us is in this for nothing. If you put in, you'll take out. Just like a fucking bank. It's as simple as that."

"We're agreed then," Rafferty said, raising his demitasse to eye level. "Here's to the new Mayor!"

It was nine-thirty. Maureen Cullen gazed at her sleeping father. The doctors had smiled, they had even been encouraging about the long-term possibilities for the old Mayor. "A strong constitution. Good genes, Mrs. Coleman. That means a lot." No, they hadn't given any medical opinions to Mrs. O'Brien. Nobody on the staff had spoken to her at all. Maureen shivered and shrugged herself back into control. Her father had been cut loose. She had to take care of him. And the children. She would have to do it. There was no choice. She bent down, kissed her father, and walked back to the waiting area.

Mark Richler sat, a long ash building on his cigarette. He rose and greeted Maureen.

"Oh, Mark," Maureen said, loosening the cinch on her emotions a notch, "what are we going to do?" Richler did not answer. The built-up ash collapsed and feathered down onto the vest of his blue suit. Maureen paced back and forth, her arms folded.

"They're trying to kill my father." She sighed. "The men he made, the people who owe everything to him . . ."

"It's just business for them." Richler watched Maureen move restlessly back and forth. "That's the way they are. Your father wouldn't be surprised at this."

"No, but he would be hurt. Think of them. And Ann Marie. My father made her out of nothing. He gave her everything she's got in politics. Now she's stabbing him in the back."

"The Mayor wouldn't be surprised at that either."

"Oh, yes, he would. He thought she was loyal. He really did . . ."

"It's politics. Politicians never let a chance like this go by."

"I thought loyalty was the first rule of politics . . ."

Richler sighed. "The king is dead. Long live the king . . ."

Maureen stopped her pacing. She stepped closer to Richler. "Mark, what are we going to do? What are we going to do?"

Richler lowered his eyes. He had never seen the Cullens in a vulnerable position before. The old Mayor swam in his silence like a great whale just beyond their calling. Thomas H. Cullen couldn't do anything to protect himself. It was odd to think of Cullen as powerless.

"Maureen, right now there's not much we really can do."

Maureen put her arms around her father's old associate. She held on to him for a moment and, dry-eyed, pulled away.

"Someday we will, Mark. With God's help, someday we will . . ."

Ann Marie remained in her office while the reporters waited noisily outside. Captain Vincent called for additional policemen and, after an hour, ordered all the news people and cameramen out of the building. He did it with an unyielding smile, joking good-naturedly with the reporters as he supervised their evacuation. The reporters gradually retreated, then descended to the first floor, and set up camp out on the sidewalk. Captain Vincent walked over to the last of the departing television crews.

"Say, fellas, were you at the Cathedral earlier?"

"Yeah," answered a bushy-haired man wearing what looked like a prisoner's uniform.

"You shoot a lot of footage?"

"Yeah, we always do. We sent it back to the studio. The big thing was Mrs. O'Brien on the church steps at the end . . ."

"I understand that. You have other stuff though, right? Pictures of the people arriving. Things like that."

"Sure." The man snapped an aluminum container shut. "Lots of tape we never use."

"What happens to that?"

"After the editing? Well, you can use the tape over. After a few days that's what probably happens."

"Is it possible to see some of that tape?"

"I guess so. What do you want, to see yourself, Captain?" The man laughed good-naturedly as he hefted the case and turned to leave.

"Something like that."

"Call the news producer. Mark Cunningham. He can probably help you."

Captain Vincent smiled and turned back toward Mrs. O'Brien's office.

"Paul, where the hell have you been?" Ann Marie looked at her watch. Nine thirty-five.

"Annie, Annie, I've been trying to reach you. You've caused the biggest news sensation in twenty years. You know that, don't you?"

"My secretary says she hasn't been able to reach you. She didn't say you'd called either."

"Annie, everybody must have been calling you. I didn't get through. I mean I called, but I didn't get through. You're big news."

"What's the reaction been?"

"Sensational."

"I mean, how did people take it?"

"Shock, I guess is the best word. But we've had three days of shocks. I think being decisive has probably helped people. Honest to God. They loved Cullen, but they wanted somebody in charge. You know, with the storms and all . . ."

"*You* like this idea, don't you?"

"Now, Annie, you know I'm on your side. Wait until you hear my commentary tonight. I'm supporting you all the way. 'Courageous . . . against the bosses . . . a new era . . . the difficult decision that no other political leader in the city would have the guts to make . . .' You'll like it, Annie."

"Paul, your friend Barone said something about photographs."

"Yeah?"

"I want you to get them back. Negatives and all copies. No *ifs*, *ands*, or *buts*. You understand?"

"Annie, he'd never use those. You know that."

"Get them back. Tonight. I'm not kidding."

"Oh, Annie, I can't reach Barone tonight . . ."

"That's your problem. I want all of that stuff before I preside at the Council meeting tomorrow morning. Tell him it's not too late for me to change my mind about Cullen. I want those pictures, whatever they are. Do you understand?"

"Calm down, Annie." Martin paused. "Look, I've got to get into the studio. I'll see what I can do after the show . . ."

"I'm leaving in a few minutes. Call me at home."

"Want me to stop by?"

"Just get the pictures and call me . . ."

"Honest to God, Mary, that's just how it happened."

"But it's eleven o'clock, Paul." Mary Vincent took her husband's uniform jacket and slipped it onto a hanger.

"I'm sorry, I didn't expect to get summoned to City Hall. Then I had to ride with her out to her house. Then the boys drove me back downtown to get my own car."

"I was afraid you started looking for that George Phillips again . . ."

Vincent paused as he undid his tie. If he told his wife about seeing a man with a pouch on his wrist, she would get really mad. It was bad enough that "this O'Brien woman," as Mary called her, had involved him in her shocking announcement about Mayor Cullen.

"I have the feeling that woman is using you," Mary said.

"Mary, Mary . . ." Captain Vincent slipped out of his shirt and handed it to his wife. "I just happened to be the most handsome officer on the Cathedral steps, that's all." He smiled and reached toward Mary as she turned to hang his shirt in the closet. "Didn't you know that you married the handsomest man on the whole damned force?" Mary embraced him. She looked up into his eyes and fingered the hair on his chest. "There's just something about her, Paul. I mean, she wasn't very nice to you when she went out to the airport that day. And this announcement tonight. It seemed so sudden . . ." She leaned against him.

"She's full of surprises, all right." Captain Vincent kissed Mary gently. "I wonder what she'll come up with next . . ."

It was eleven-thirty. Ann Marie had been home for an hour. A police car remained in front of the rambling old house that she had begun to redecorate so many years ago with Charlie. Nothing ever seemed quite finished in her life. Things were always in between. Her father wasn't dead, but he wasn't really alive. Charlie had died in pieces, a little yielded up one year, a little more the next, until he was all gone. She had been a fill-in alderwoman and now she was going to be an interim Mayor. She wasn't a wife to Paul Martin . . . She was halfway wherever she looked. On questionnaires, the box marked *other* always fit her best.

And Matthew upstairs. What kind of mother had she been? Aunt Molly had brought him home and stayed, as she did most of the time now, in the room next to his down the hall from Ann Marie's bedroom. They were both sound asleep now. Well, she had been as good a mother as she could. She *was* a good mother. Ann Marie looked at the clutch of photographs spread out on the baby grand piano she had inherited from her mother. There were her parents, solemn-looking, their faces shadowed by some long-descended sun. Next to it was a picture of her father in an Army uniform. His face was shaded by the peak of his cap but he was smiling. A dashing man then. And there was a picture of Charlie, Charlie in fatigues on the porch of some jungle headquarters, Charlie making a V-for-victory sign. Next to him Monsignor Fitzmaurice gave off his aspiring bishop's smile from behind his Chancery Office desk. Then Matthew in her own arms when he was only six months old. Nothing quite finished about any of them . . .

The doorbell rang. Ann Marie walked slowly over and opened it. A police officer stood under the porch light. At his side stood a grinning Paul Michael Martin.

"I'm sorry, Mrs. O'Brien, but Mr. Martin here insisted that he was to see you. We weren't going to let anybody . . ."

"It's all right, officer, let him in." Ann Marie stepped aside as Martin, his teeth glistening, moved across the threshold. He had an outsized brown envelope in his hands. As the policeman closed the door, Martin dropped it on a side table and took Ann Marie in his arms. She tightened in his grasp but did not struggle.

"Baby, you really did it." He kissed her on the mouth, the eyes, the neck. She pulled free of him, but he coiled her back into his arms as if they were dance partners. "Annie, the city is yours." He kissed her on the mouth again. "I've seen the early editions of the papers. You're a heroine. They're all for you. It's wonderful. 'Mrs. O'Brien, in the best interests of the city, has made a good and noble decision . . . blah, blah, blah.' Christ, if you were a play they were reviewing, you'd run for years . . ."

Ann Marie pulled free again. "Have you got the papers?" She walked to the front windows and pulled the drapes shut.

Paul smiled engagingly. "Well, I thought we could look at those later . . ."

"Now," she said firmly as she pulled the side window drapes together, "I want to see them now. You go get them and come back."

He flashed her a humoring smile. "Sure, sure."

"Paul, are those Barone's pictures?" She pointed to the brown envelope. Martin winked and slipped through the front door. Ann Marie picked up the envelope and unsealed it. She walked over to the piano and spilled the contents out in front of the small gallery of family photographs. There were glossy prints and a packet of negatives. She glanced at the first one, a grainy blowup of her and Paul Martin emerging from the front entrance to the Lake Shore Drive building. The next one must have been taken only seconds later. She was talking to Paul under the canopy in front of the building. She could have been lecturing him. His wonderful grin generated charm even in the distortion of the enlargement. In the next he was standing behind a cab that had stopped. She must have just ducked down to enter it. These pictures were not very dangerous . . . The next, however, startled her. It was inside Barone's apartment, a blurred scene of a bare-chested Paul Martin lifting Ann Marie's bra up over her head. She was in shadows, but there was no mistaking her profile. She shuffled through the sequence of photos that showed her and Martin climbing into bed, embracing, making love . . .

"Goddammit, Paul," she said, turning in fury as he entered the front door, the newspapers under his arm, "goddammit, did you know he was taking pictures of us? Did you know anything about this?" Ann Marie's voice rose an octave in anger; she was tense, her face strained and white with rage. She crumpled the photographs and flung them at Martin as he unburdened himself of the papers and moved toward her.

"Now, now, Annie," he said soothingly, "of course not, of course not." He tried to embrace her but she pushed him away. "Paul, these are horrible, these are, are . . ." She kicked at the photographic prints on the floor. "Goddamn you, Paul, you and your friend Barone. What kind of friend would do this?"

Martin leaned down to pick up the pictures. They were already springing open from being crumpled, slowly revealing Paul and Ann Marie in their fuzzy nakedness.

"Baby, baby," Paul said, straightening up, smoothing the prints out as best he could, "we've got what you wanted. Prints and negatives. They're all here."

"You!" she shrieked. "You, with all your smooth ways. And your smooth friends." She struck out and scratched her nails across Martin's cheek. He grabbed her hand and yanked her close to him.

"For Crissake, Annie, get hold of yourself." He twisted her arm as she squirmed in his grasp. "You're going to be the Mayor, Annie. For Crissake, Annie, tomorrow you'll be the Mayor! Get hold of yourself." He pulled her close and kissed her on the mouth. Ann Marie pulled back, although she could not free herself from his strong grip. A lifetime of anger had exploded into white heat at the sight of the photographs.

"Paul, I want you to tell your friend something. I want him to know something. I'll get him if it's the last thing I ever do . . ."

"Don't talk that way, Annie. That's foolish. Dramatic, but foolish."

Ann Marie relaxed slightly, let herself go, let him hold her. She took a deep breath.

"There, there," he said, rearranging his embrace into one of comfort and support. "Wait till you read the papers. You'll feel a lot better. Does that fireplace work?" He pointed toward an elegantly screened hearth on the far wall of the living room.

"We haven't used it since last winter." She felt calmer. "It should work fine."

"Here, you look at these while I get a fire started." Martin went to the fireplace and rattled the screen open. He scooped a handful of kindling out of the wood basket next to the broad hearth. Ann Marie picked up the newspapers and found big pictures of herself and Cullen on both front pages. "Cullen Too Sick Says Vice-Mayor," read one headline; "Mrs. O'Brien Will Seek Ruling on Cullen" read the other. She got high marks for her action. The editorials praised her. She was the woman of the hour in Chicago. She felt better as she read the accounts and the comments.

"Okay, Annie." Paul Martin straightened up in front of the fireplace, the handsome lines of his face outlined by the glow of the flames he had kindled. "Time for the burning. Come on over here." He waved an inviting arm toward her. She placed the papers on a couch and, feeling lighter and warmer herself, moved slowly toward Martin. He smiled mischievously, sensuously, at the creased photographic prints.

"Look at this one, Annie." Martin chuckled as he handed the picture to Ann Marie. "Not bad, eh?" Ann Marie took the picture gingerly and studied it in the light of the fire. Paul leaned forward and kissed her on the neck, mimicking the action recorded in the photograph. He nuzzled her ear with his nose.

"We look pretty good, Annie. We look pretty good." He smiled broadly, coaxing her into a perverse and reluctant enjoyment of the lovemaking scenes. "And look at this one. Great figure, Annie." She looked at the picture of herself, naked in his muscular arms. "Maybe the shadows help," he added, nudging her with his elbow. She did look good. Ann Marie gazed up into Martin's face. Reflected flames danced in his eyes. There were welts on his cheek where she had scratched him. "You look good yourself, Paul. The shadows help you a lot."

They giggled at almost the same instant. Then they laughed, at first tentatively, then uproariously, as they regarded the pictures and then dropped them one by one into the fire. The pictures curled in the flames, flared up, and were transformed into delicate, darkened ghosts, tissues of carbon draped over the surface of the burning logs. Paul plopped the packet of negatives into the burning mass and they slowly ignited and shriveled in a glaring white eye of fire.

"I've always wanted to make love in front of a fireplace," Martin said as their hilarity subsided. "Come on. What better than love before the purifying fire? Just like a South Seas movie. A sacrifice of love to the gods." He affected a dramatic tone and then laughed again. "You white princess, me native chief."

Ann Marie felt giddy as she began to loosen Martin's tie. He fussed with the clasp at the back of her dress. "The gods will be pleased with our offering, white woman," he whispered. In a moment they were lying together on the rug. Martin kissed her, prying her lips open with his tongue, going deep within her.

They were silent afterward. She rested her head on Martin's broad chest. "Annie," he whispered against the crackle of the fire, "the bad days are all over. They really are . . ." He kissed her on the forehead. She gazed dreamily into the rising and falling flames. A portion of one of the photographs, microscopically thin and infinitely fragile, clung to a log edge, palpitating in the draft of the fireplace. Then it fragmented and rose into the flue of the chimney.

"Yes, Paul, maybe it is all over. Maybe all the badness is over . . ."

"White Princess rule all of jungle now." He affected the deep voice of B-movie village chief again. "You like to make sacrifice again?" He turned her onto her back and kissed her, beginning with her toes, working his way slowly up her legs, across her hips, and up over her breasts. "White woman taste good," he said as he lowered himself on top of her and kissed her on the mouth. Ann Marie smiled as Paul kissed her eyes, then her breasts again. She was letting herself go, letting loose, more than she could ever remember.

They laughed as they dressed. The fire was almost out. It was one-thirty in the morning.

"See you at City Hall," Martin said as he slipped into his jacket. "It's the run for the roses at ten this morning." He embraced her once more, kissed her lightly, and went to the door. As he put his hand on the knob, Ann Marie walked to him and kissed him firmly on the mouth.

"See you," she said softly. He opened the door and hurried down the steps. The police car was still in place at the curb.

Ann Marie turned, picked up the newspapers, looked at the fireplace and decided to let what was left of the glowing logs burn out on their own. She looked around the room. Charlie was still signaling his V-for-victory sign off the top of the piano. Ann Marie smiled and flashed one back. Then she turned off the lights and began to climb the stairs.

She stepped on something on the first landing, something soft. She leaned down and picked it up. It was a cowboy hat, the cowboy hat that Matthew took to bed every night, the hat he had with him when she looked in on him after she had arrived home at ten-thirty. A cold hand closed on her heart. She turned on the landing and looked back at the darkened living room. A large sofa obstructed a clear view of the hearth, but she could see some sparks rising up the flue, darting like fireflies off the glowing embers. She felt herself tremble. Had Matthew watched them, had he seen any of it, or did his hat get there some other way? He couldn't have. He mustn't have . . .

She hurried up the rest of the stairs and walked down the hallway. Aunt Molly's door was closed. Ann Marie listened carefully. Just the gentle cello of Molly's snoring. She passed on to Matthew's door and opened it softly. Moonlight lay in an elongated quadrant across the upper part of Matthew's bed. He was on his back, his mouth slightly open, sound asleep. Ann Marie placed the cowboy hat on the edge of the bed and quietly closed the door.

He couldn't have, no, he hadn't seen a thing . . .

26

*T*he soft lighting of the City Council Chamber did not dull the hard edge of tension that filled it the next morning. An overflow of reporters, many from national media, crowded the far end of the hall. A few aldermen who had been steady critics of Mayor Cullen found themselves defending him, raising questions about the need for detailed medical reports or at least for a longer time to debate fully such a grave decision. Alderman Schroeder, supported by Alderman Cutler, raised questions of law and procedure, only to be overruled quickly by Ann Marie, who presided at what one paper finally called her "coronation." The vote was 39 to 9 to declare the Mayor's office vacant. Forty-two aldermen then joined to elect Mrs. O'Brien the acting Mayor of the city. It was all over by 11 A.M.

Ann Marie felt empty during the motions and the debate, a spectator at a long-planned party that had been spoiled at the last minute. Matthew had seemed fine when he woke that morning. She had searched his face and his eyes for some signal about whether he had stood on the landing the evening before and watched while she and Paul had made love. Aunt Molly, refreshed by a sound sleep, merely seemed excited about the prospects of the day and of Ann Marie's accession to the Mayor's office. "I guess I'll move in for good," she had said at the breakfast table. Ann Marie, studying Matthew intently, had uttered a distracted "I suppose so." "Well, not if you don't think so, Ann," Molly had replied. Ann Marie had shifted her gaze away from Matthew, who was reading a sports legend on the back of a cereal box. "No, Molly, please move in. I'm a little distracted today. I don't think I can manage without you." Molly had smiled. "It's a big day, a great day for you. You must have lots on your mind . . ."

But Ann Marie had only Matthew on her mind. He was on her mind as Rafferty and Wendel, like a pair of expert volleyball players, wafted resolutions smoothly back and forth across the chamber. Was Matthew more knowing then he seemed? Had he learned the knowledge of good and evil before his time? Was he just pretending not to know anything? She could bargain with Barone and execute deals with Rafferty, but she didn't know what to say to her own son. Matthew, are you going to be

like so many of the men in my life, quiet just when I need you to talk?
She shook her head slightly.

"Ma'am?" It was Rafferty's voice.

"The chair recognizes Alderman Rafferty."

"Would the chair agree to four o'clock for the swearing in?"

"Yes, yes, of course."

"Then, Madam Chairman, I move that we adjourn."

Rafferty's motion was seconded. Ann Marie banged the gavel against a
chorus of yeas, as applause exploded from all sides. Ann Marie stood up,
managed a smile, waved her hand stiffly, and exited swiftly through the
door at the rear of the chamber. It was done, she was Mayor, she had
what she wanted, and at the moment it was not satisfying. Paul Michael
Martin stood in the passageway smiling broadly as, flanked by her bodyguards, Ann Marie passed by.

"We'd like an interview for the ten o'clock news," he called after her.

"If you've got your crew, come up now." This, curtly, without missing
a step.

Ann Marie sat at the desk in her aldermanic office. Paul Martin sat in a
chair opposite her. Ann Marie was saying all the right things. But she
seemed flat, a little held back. She would still be dynamite on television.
Just the proper note of reserve, a suggestion, after the lightning removal
of Cullen from office, of prickly duty embraced selflessly.

"What are your plans for the city?"

"We want to carry on the traditions of good management. We want to
make this the greatest city in the world. Safer, cleaner, better for everyone."

"Do you have any particular goals in mind?"

"Corruption. I want to move against it at all levels." Ann Marie had no
idea where the answer came from. It dropped into her head like change
in one of those capsules that used to shoot along wires in a department
store.

"What do you mean by that? Do you think Mayor Cullen was soft on
this issue?"

Careful, careful. Ann Marie paused. "What I'm saying is that it is a
particular goal of mine. I want to move against it. I intend to form a
special unit to investigate corruption in municipal government."

This was better than dynamite, Martin thought. When the hell did she
think this idea up?

"Mrs. O'Brien, you're suggesting that this job of wiping out corruption
has been neglected. Would you say that Mayor Cullen had plans to do
this?"

"No. I'm saying this is *my* particular goal."

"Are you saying that Mayor Cullen wouldn't have done something like this?"

"You can put any construction you want on it. When I look around city government I see a lot of things that need cleaning up. I intend to do that."

"Do you have someone in mind to head this anti-corruption unit?"

"I'm going to propose to the Superintendent of Police that Captain Paul Vincent be appointed to head this." Again, an answer from a source she did not understand.

"Why would you select him? Does he have special training for this?"

"He is an excellent police officer. He has been out at the airport. He's been outside the city, in a sense, and so he brings a new perspective to the work."

"Isn't it unusual for a Mayor to suggest a police appointment?"

"Mayor Cullen did it all the time."

"You think corruption is deeply rooted in city government?"

"What do you think?"

"One more question. Do you have any other appointments in mind? Isn't it unusual for an acting Mayor to change very much?"

"An acting Mayor is still the Mayor. And I intend to act. I will just say that everyone's work, every department's work, will be subject to review." Ann Marie spoke matter-of-factly, as though she had carefully planned the announcements which had flashed so unexpectedly into her head. She had often had such inspirations dealing with the Far Eastern ambassadors during the MIA days. She stumbled into things as she did at the cable TV hearings. What she said usually threw people around her off balance. That was fine. She liked people off balance.

The interview was concluded and, after the camera crew left the office, Martin remained behind. Ann Marie sifted quickly through the pile of messages on her desk.

"You know, Annie, sometimes I get the idea that you work strictly by intuition. Am I right?"

"I know a thing or two." She flipped through the papers before her. Matthew's face was in her mind's eye.

"Sure, sure," Martin said as he sat on the edge of the desk and leaned toward her. He touched her cheek lightly with his right hand. "That's the combination. Good basic knowledge and terrific instincts." He leaned down and kissed her. "Great body, too." She pulled her head back. What the hell had Matthew seen?

"Don't you have to get back to the station? Don't you have any work to do?"

"Annie, I just did one of the best interviews I've ever had. We'll have to go with part of it on the six o'clock. This will be big news. I'm handling the live coverage of the swearing in. But that's not what I want to talk about. I've been thinking about you, you're really something. You're dynamite. Sex appeal and guts. Annie, we could own this town. The whole state. This is just the beginning. You can go as far as you want . . ."

"Well, right now, I'm going up to the Mayor's office. I'll be moving in right after the ceremony."

"No parties? No fun by the fireside?"

Ann Marie flushed. She stood up. "My instincts tell me I should be at work. That's what the people want. We've had a lot of uncertainty in the city. Being at my desk ought to be a sign of stability . . ." She picked a folder off her desk and opened it.

"That's what I mean, Annie. Instincts! By God, you're right." Martin stood in front of her, grabbing her arms and pressing the folder and its contents in against her breasts. She looked up into his eyes. "With me giving you media advice, and your looks and instincts, we could really go places."

"I am someplace. And right now I'm going someplace else. To the Mayor's office." Her voice turned icy. "I can find my own way."

Martin released his grip. "What's the matter, Annie, what the hell's the matter with you?"

"We'll talk about it later, Paul."

"Come on, White Princess." Martin moved close to her again. "Jungle drums speak of love." He smiled his good-little-boy, I-didn't-mean-any-thing smile, "Do not be mad at noble chief." He put his arms around her. He *was* charming, goddamn him. The tension lessened within her. Ann Marie smiled. Martin kissed her until she pulled away from him. Martin knew that he had won, that he had thawed out some of the frost on her spirit.

"You can't stay mad at me, can you, Annie?"

"Try me again sometime," Ann Marie answered as she reached for her handbag. She extracted a cosmetic case, popped it open, and studied her face. "Not much damage. Lipstick will fix it." She looked back at the grinning Martin. "Your cheek needs a little work, chief. Better fix it before you go out in the jungle."

The atmosphere in the Mayor's suite of offices on the fifth floor was frigid. The man for whom the secretaries and office staff had worked so long had been snatched suddenly out of their midst. It was worse than if he had died, Helen Morrison had said to anybody who would listen. Wasn't it terrible to think of Mayor Cullen lying so ill and nothing to do but pray for him? Cap Malloy, wearing a rumpled summer suit, had come with the latest reports. The poor man just dozed most of the time, but Maureen, Maureen was a tower of strength.

There was a stir of expectation and uncertainty as Ann Marie entered the office a few minutes later. The secretaries stopped talking and looked up at her as though waiting for instructions, honorable discharges, or whatever new surprise Mrs. O'Brien might have for them. Cap Malloy struggled to his feet. "Welcome, Mrs. Mayor . . ." His voice cracked.

"Not yet, Cap," Ann Marie said calmly. "Four o'clock." She looked from one secretary to another. They were frozen in place. "At four o'clock, I'll be sworn in. I came up here to invite you all to the ceremony. I'm not planning any changes here. It's a difficult time for everyone. So we have to pitch in and work together." She turned and headed into the office of the Mayor. Cap trailed after her. The secretaries relaxed. Their jobs were safe. It was a shame about Mayor Cullen, yes, but they did have to put food on the table . . .

Monsignor Fitzmaurice read an invocation, the chief judge of the Illinois Supreme Court administered the brief oath of office, and Ann Marie, at precisely 4:07 P.M., was Mayor of Chicago. The crowd in the Council Chamber applauded long and loud. Ann Marie waited for a few seconds even after the last handclaps had trailed away. She searched the faces of the audience. There was Matthew, wide-eyed, still between Mother Francis and Aunt Molly. Her father was in a wheelchair in the aisle next to them. What judgments on her were buried in the silence of her father and her son? Ann Marie cleared her throat.

"Reverend clergy, members of the judiciary, members of the City Council, I am truly humbled by the confidence you have placed in me by selecting me to be the new Mayor of our great city. To take on this task is an enormous challenge. With your help we will build a better city." The faces of her partners in future government rose out of the dimness. Noto, Wendel, Carney, Ramirez, and, in the first row of honored guests, Richard Barone. Just below her Rafferty gazed up attentively. Did they think they had a sure thing? She would have to throw them off balance.

"The primary aim of my time in office will be to stabilize the government and to improve its efficiency. There is always a danger, when a government has been in office for a long time, for things to become routine and for the true interests of the people to be forgotten. We want the taxpayers of this great city to get their money's worth. Every dollar of taxes deserves a dollar's worth of work and service."

Ann Marie paused and looked out at Matthew again. His head was down, his face hidden, as he examined a button on his jacket.

"In order to ensure that the aims of these months will be attained, I am going to commit the administration to a clean slate in every way. This is a fresh start for Chicago. That has to be more than a slogan. I am, therefore, going to begin a systematic review with public hearings of

the performance of every department in the city. This includes the
Police and Fire as well as other administrative departments and offices."
She looked down at Rafferty. His features had stiffened. Ann Marie
glanced out at Wendel. He was frowning. They were getting the message. "In order to ensure that we have complete freedom for this intensive study of city government, I am asking for letters of resignation from
every department head. I am also asking the City Council to study itself.
If they have the same open spirit that I hope will characterize my administration, each committee chairman will also prepare a resignation.
We need to realign the city administration, redesign our committees, and
replace all the personnel who are unable to cooperate in this vast effort
to modernize our government. This is a time for service and un-
selfishness. We will begin these meetings tomorrow at 10 A.M."

A buzz of anger filled the Hall. Above a choking collar, Rafferty's eyes
were fixed hypnotically on this reckless woman whom he had just helped
to make Mayor. What was she trying to do, make a shambles of the city?
Wendel's mouth fell open as enthusiastic applause rose from the crowded
public galleries. Noto, his eyes snapping, half-rose from his chair, then
sat down again. Barone clenched and unclenched his fists as he watched
Ann Marie step away from the microphones. I'm glad I kept a set of those
goddamned pictures of her playing house with Martin. That fucking Martin. Look at him grinning like a fucking hyena with the rest of those sons
of bitching reporters.

The enthusiastic applause forecast the popular reaction to the new
Mayor of Chicago. The newspapers and television stations loved it.
Nobody would have dared to predict that Ann Marie O'Brien could
make people forget Thomas H. Cullen so quickly. Nobody ever suspected that they were impulses that had ridden in on the spur of the moment, populist impulses with the imaginative power to dominate every
headline and newscast. As one editorial put it: "In the last two days,
Mrs. O'Brien has done what has needed to be done for the last two de-
cades: she has shaken up the entrenched Democratic machine, she has
called for a crusade against corruption, she has demanded that adminis-
trators either work for the people or get out. After making a difficult but
necessary decision that Mayor Cullen was not well enough to govern,
Mrs. O'Brien has shown that she is strong enough to propose measures
that should revitalize the city government." A star had indeed been born.
What had started as the story of the unhappy ending of the Cullen years
quickly became the saga, in need of hourly updates, of the extraordinary
beginning of the O'Brien administration.

Mark Richler shook his head slowly. "It's amazing," he said, laying the
newspaper on a chair in Maureen Cullen Coleman's living room.
Maureen looked at him sadly. Her anger burned at a steady but low in-

tensity; she was worn out from keeping vigil at the hospital. She felt bereft, abandoned by the city which, until yesterday, seemed to revere her father and take special care of her. Now he was an ex-Mayor and she was an ex-Mayor's daughter. The official limousine and the body-guards had disappeared overnight. There had been a death in the family. Not a person, no, it looked like her father was going to live. Maybe even improve considerably. What had died was power and position. Maureen had not realized, until it had been snatched away so savagely, just how attached to it she had become. Power had always been there; she could hardly remember when it was not. She had always seemed to be the Mayor's daughter . . .

"Maureen, this is crazy. I mean, you can't take on a government and ask everybody to turn in their resignations." Richler clasped a hand to his head in disbelief. "But she's doing it. And she's getting away with it." He paced up and down, searching in his pockets for a package of cigarettes. "There's nothing to do about this now."

Maureen hated to hear those words. There had always been something that could be done about things. Her father had always been able to do something.

"The next thing, Maureen, and I hate to say it, the next thing they'll do is go after the chair of the party."

Maureen had not thought of that. She took a breath.

"How long do you think . . . ?"

"A couple of months, maybe more, maybe less." Richler inhaled deeply on his cigarette.

"What are you thinking about, Mark?"

"I don't know exactly," he said slowly. "I need some time to turn this over . . ." He grimaced and began to pace again. "I think they can't move your father out of the party chairmanship in a hurry. We may have time to think out some strategy of our own . . ."

"The whole city's gone crazy for her, Mark. She can't seem to do anything wrong."

"That's the kind to watch, Maureen." Richler began to chuckle. "That's the kind to watch . . ." He turned to her and grinned broadly. "Closely . . ."

27

*C*aptain Vincent had been amazed by the phone call from the Superintendent. He was being put on a special assignment at the request of the Mayor. Vincent would report only to her. No, the Superintendent could not tell him any more than that. Good luck, he had said, you may need it. Vincent had been able to see Mayor O'Brien for only a few minutes and she had been vague about what she wanted him to do. It was only her second day in office so he couldn't expect her to be more specific. She had been friendly, almost too friendly. She had spent the five minutes telling him what a great job he had done at the airport and how much she appreciated his taking on this special task.

"Just check things out. Let me know what you come up with. That's the most important thing. I want to know if you get on to anything. Now, you'll have to excuse me. Thanks for coming by." She paused. "And don't give any interviews . . ."

Vincent remained puzzled. Mrs. O'Brien just seemed to want him around. That's the feeling he got as she shook his hand. There, I've got you in place. Right where I want you. He shook his head again. He didn't need this new job, no, this was the last thing he needed. And Mary didn't like it much either.

The George Phillips case had been pushed back to page four by the outbreak of news from the Mayor's office. Nothing new. Phillips was still at large. The Medical Examiner was working on the identification of the bodies. Twelve had been removed from the shallow dirt basement of the house that had been blown apart by the tornado. Only two families had come forward to claim the bodies of missing sons. The rest might be runaways, drifters, the kids with no histories who ended up in nameless graves. Phillips was still out there, shaking his quarters out of his pouch in some arcade right now. Somewhere . . .

"Mrs. O'Brien, you don't seem to understand the delicate balance of work in city government. Not everybody working here is a crook." Alderman Louis Schroeder, Lincolnesque-sincere, had asked for a short appointment with the new Mayor. Ann Marie smiled sweetly at him.

"I never said everybody was a crook."

"No, but these stories, these plans for a special investigator to ferret out corruption, they give the public the idea that everybody in government is on the take. That simply isn't so."

"Well, then, those people have nothing to worry about."

"The morale problem is what I'm driving at. Open hearings on the efficiency of every department. Resignations from every department head. That causes serious disruptions in functioning. No company in the world, not even the best-run, would treat its employees that way. I'm asking you to reconsider some of these proposals."

"What is it you want for yourself out of this?"

Schroeder was nonplussed. Could the Mayor think that what he was saying was only to get something for himself? He opened his mouth and then closed it again.

"I really don't want anything for myself out of this. I'm trying to tell you that you can't seem to mistrust everybody who works for you."

"Thank you, Alderman." Ann Marie rose from her chair. "I don't think that anybody who works hard has anything to worry about."

"But, Mrs. O'Brien . . ."

"I think you're too accustomed to the way things used to run around here. We're opening things up. People will get used to it." She smiled again as she rounded the desk to escort the alderman out of her office. "Even *you* will get used to it." She touched him on the arm. He looked dumbfounded. "Thanks for coming by. I'll keep in touch with you."

The Landing Strip Motel was not elegant. It stood barely ready for each day's onslaught of prostitutes and customers, on an avenue crowded with similar places just a mile or so from O'Hare Field. Catalina Escobar had worked there six months. She leaned down and picked up a quarter from the hallway rug and dropped it into her pocket. Every quarter counted these days. She pushed her cart against the wall next to the door marked 208 and, without even looking, inserted her passkey in the lock and entered the darkened room. She snapped on the switch and edged into the bathroom, humming softly to herself. Her work was so routine that she did not immediately notice the red-stained towels on the floor next to the toilet. Scarlet droplets trailed away, as in a Jackson Pollock painting, across the floor toward the sink, in which lay a twisted washcloth, stiff with blood. Catalina held her heart and screamed. She stumbled out the door and ran shrieking down the corridor.

The manager entered the room a few moments later. An old man still wearing his pajamas had come out of a nearby room to watch.

"Just stay outside, please," the manager said as he moved into the room. The bed was disheveled and bloodstained. He walked cautiously around the tangle of the coverlet on the floor in front of the bed. The naked body of a man of about thirty was wedged between the bed and the wall, a fold of bloodstained sheet draped down over his legs. His throat had been slashed and his genitals mutilated. His severed penis hung like a bloodied mushroom from his slightly open mouth. On his forehead the number fourteen had been fingerpainted in blood. A darkly stained knife lay on the floor just above the thick tousled hair of his head. Blood had soaked into the carpet in a wide crescent around the body. The manager looked more closely. There were only bloody stumps at the man's wrists. He gagged, pulled back, and moved out of the room as swiftly as he could.

"Annie," Paul Marin said as he poked his head in the door and looked around the Mayor's office, "this doesn't look like a place a woman works in."

"My taste will show up soon," Ann Marie answered without looking up from her crowded desk. The only feminine touch that had been added to the severe masculine atmosphere that Thomas H. Cullen had preferred was her Irish crystal bud vase near the phone. Martin walked on exaggerated tiptoe to the edge of the desk.

"Madam Mayor"—he flourished a bunch of miniature roses that he had concealed behind his back—"it's time for some new flowers." He handed them across the desk to Ann Marie. She could not control the smile that formed at the edges of her mouth.

"Why, thank you, Paul." She placed them on the desk. "They need water."

"Take care of that later. How about a kiss?"

"Paul, you're supposed to be here for an interview." This, half-mockingly, half-seductively.

"Come on, Annie, just because you're the Mayor doesn't mean you can give up your love life."

She rose, ignoring him, and removed the fading flower that drooped in the bud vase. She selected one of the tiny yellow roses and slipped it into its place.

"Paul, we can't go on the way we have." She sounded business-like, distant. The matter was all decided, ready for filing.

"Come on, baby." He grinned like a disappointed high school boy. "You need a visit from Dr. Martin regularly. What's the matter, is being Mayor a job for virgins? Are you taking the veil? Reforming your life? Come on, this is Paulie."

"I'm serious about this. Do I have to spell it out to you? I'm the Mayor. I can't be meeting with you in that . . . in that place of your friend's, not after he had those pictures taken. We can't make love in here. Thanks partially to you, I can't go anywhere anymore without the media following me."

"Annie, you can't give up sex just because you're the Mayor." He walked around the desk and put his arms around her. "All work and no play makes Annie a dull girl."

"Paul," she said, only half-resisting him, "I have to be careful. You know that."

"Sure, sure . . ." He kissed her fully on the mouth, "There, you'll have to fix your lipstick again . . ."

She pushed him away. "Paul, you don't seem to understand . . ."

"Oh, I understand all right. You've been Mayor for two weeks, you've turned the town on its ear, and you don't need your old friend, Paul Michael Martin, anymore. It's not good to go two weeks without sex. Maybe you can take a vow, but I can't."

Matthew's face rose in her imagination. Matthew still silent about that evening two weeks before. Matthew silent like the rest of them.

"No, you don't understand. You really don't. Can't you see that I'm serious about this, that this means something to me?"

"Sorry, Annie." His tone turned more serious. "I think I missed a bar or two somewhere. What have you done, gone to confession?"

"Paul, I just can't talk about it. Can't you just leave it at that? I've had plenty on my mind anyway." Ann Marie sat down again. There was silence between them for several seconds.

"Okay," Martin said, as though conceding a chess move, "we'll talk about it later. I'll be serious. Watch me carefully now. I'm getting very, *very* serious." He distorted his features. "I am now *extremely* serious."

She could not help but smile at him. Ann Marie could never tell him her concern about Matthew. They had not made love since then. There had not, of course, been much time. But there had not been any desire, either. She had, in fact, thought of going to confession. She remembered the wonderful feeling of being cleansed that, at least for a time, used to follow after it.

"We'll work it out, Madam. Just lie down on that couch and I'll give you my special treatment. No charge. Never fails . . ."

"Paul!" She burst out laughing as he feigned a leer and then sat down in the chair next to her desk.

"Paul, you're impossible."

"You mean irresistible, don't you?"

"Maybe a little of that too."

"Well, let's change the subject for a while. We'll get back to my cure for the virgin blues later." Martin grinned and slouched down in the chair, the American male at rest.

"What did you want to talk to me about?" Ann Marie asked. "Did you have something on your mind, or was this just a friendly visit?"

"No, no. Well"—he straightened up in the chair—"maybe a little of both. I've been talking to Rich Barone. He's a little hurt that he hasn't heard from you."

"He shouldn't be surprised. Not after those pictures."

"He's a good friend of yours, no matter what you think. He can get things done. And what he gets done will be good for the city. You want people to contribute to your campaign fund? You haven't thought of that, have you? Barone's the man to line the big money up. And that's only one thing you'll need him for. Annie, there are some people in this city that it's too expensive to be peeved at. Rich is one of them."

"Did he ask you to speak to me?"

"Sure. Why not? This is business. He wants to help you. He expects you to help him. You think Cullen didn't understand that?"

"What are you getting at?"

"Well, some people think you're trying to do too much at once. Save the world, save the city, root out corruption. Hell, Annie, you want to take things a little easy."

"The media likes it."

"Sure, sure, but you can't pass laws with the reporters. They don't vote. Guys like Rafferty and Wendel, they vote. Guys like Barone, they have things they want voted on in predictable ways."

"I'm not against these men."

"That would be hard to prove, the way you've been operating." Martin reached over and touched Ann Marie's hand. "You want these men to like you. They're on your side. The danger—and don't misunderstand me —is that with all these hearings, all this insistence on the chairmen resigning, you're going to force them into a fight with you. They can stall you if they want to. They can make life lonely in here . . ."

"I can talk directly to the papers and the television stations."

"Baby, there's one thing you have to remember. The media helped to make you. No doubt of that. They can break you, too. At some level they're indifferent. What they're interested in is news. Your rise was news. Your fall would be news too. All the same to them."

"Have you been talking to Rafferty and Wendel and the others?"

"Listening, maybe. Listening would be a better word. Look, there's more to this government than sitting in this office and getting on television. Think of the Democratic committeemen, the ones who make up the Cook County Central Committee, the ones who choose the next party chairman. They haven't moved to vacate Cullen's job yet. You know why? They're not sure about you. They're not sure you'll keep your word and support Rafferty. And they're not sure about Cullen's health, either. He's been showing improvement every day."

"He hasn't talked yet."

"No, but if he does, he knows every skeleton in every one of their closets. They're still afraid of him. They still respect him. That's why they've held back on even holding a meeting to discuss replacing Cullen. Don't you realize that?"

Ann Marie stiffened. She was the Mayor now. Everybody loved her, everybody praised her. And yet influential people were still afraid of Cullen. Silent as a fossil in a glacier, he frustrated her through the power he still held over the committeemen. She thought of Maureen. Maureen would relish this frustration, however minor and however short, of Ann Marie's plans.

"Cullen's finished in this town."

"That's what you think . . ." Paul gazed steadily at her. He had seen these moods before. Ann Marie was angry and he loved her that way. He could take her right now, right on that couch . . .

"Don't these people know I'm the Mayor now?"

"Oh, yeah," Paul said, exaggerating his tones, "*they* know *you're* the Mayor all right." She tapped the desk with her right hand. He reached over and placed his hand on top of hers. "What they're doing is taking a longer look at you. You're a Cinderella Mayor. They know you're popular. But they're not going to fall down and let you walk all over them. They're regrouping. And they're tough. If you want real power—if you ever want the committeemen to come around—you'll play ball with them."

"Did they send you to tell me this?"

Martin arched his eyebrows and shrugged his shoulders like an Italian waiter.

"You've been close to Barone a long time, haven't you, Paul?" Her words had enamel edges.

"Sure." He smiled easily. "How do you think I got the keys to his apartment?"

"Don't bring that up again!" she flared. "Don't ever bring that up to me again." Matthew's face swam at the edge of her consciousness. What had ever happened to the world of Catholic innocence she had once known? Mother Francis and Our Lady of Peace and all of the girls good as nuns. Mother Francis and her ideas that she would like public service, that it was like a calling, a clean, well-formed world of Thomistic aphorisms. Had that world ever existed? Could she ever get back to it? Could she ever get back to that time, that evening Paul had come to her house, and replay it, with a different ending? Had she buried that world with Charlie?

"Annie!" Martin called her out of her reverie. "Annie, this is the real world. It doesn't stop once you get on it. You're on it now. You'd better be sure you understand it."

Ann Marie curled her lower lip. "Paul," she asked harshly, "does right or wrong mean anything in that world? Does it mean anything to you?"

Martin laughed out loud. "Annie, we're not talking about right and wrong. Those aren't the terms you use in the real world. Only do-gooders can afford to use them because they don't really have to run anything. In the real world, you talk about how things work. Either they work or they don't. If you can make them work, that's good. If you can't, that's bad. Annie, you know that." He looked at her intently. "That's the way *you* operate."

She looked surprised but said nothing.

"My God, Annie, haven't you ever watched yourself in action? That's one of the things I love about you. You do what has to be done."

"And these friends of yours . . ."

"Friends of yours too . . ."

"They've told you to tell me this?"

"More or less." Martin waved his right hand expansively. "You want to get things done, don't you?"

Get things done. Yes, she had to get things done. That's what a Mayor did. A Mayor got things done.

"Tell Barone I'll have lunch with him tomorrow."

"That's my Annie," Martin said, rising and leaning toward Ann Marie. She put her hand on his chin and pushed his face away.

"Come on, Annie, let's seal the bargain with a kiss."

"Why don't you just get the hell out of here?"

"Spunk!" Martin said, straightening up. "That's what the papers all say, the lady's got spunk." He smiled again and walked in sensuous, self-delighted strides to the door. He turned.

"I'm looking forward to your return to a sex life . . ."

Ann Marie glared at him as he passed through the door and into the outer office.

28

Walt, am I glad to hear your voice . . ."

"Look, Paul, I've got something for you," Commander Gleason replied. "There's big news gonna break this morning. Wanted you to know. Unofficially, of course."

"What the hell are you talking about?"

"We got George Phillips. Dead."

"What?" The phone trembled in Vincent's hand.

"They cut his fucking hands off, whoever it was. Stuck his fucking dick in his fucking mouth . . ."

"Who?" Vincent interjected impatiently.

"We don't know *who*. We just found out *what*. In a fleabag on Mannheim Road. He's Phillips all right. The M.E. just confirmed that. Dental records. It'll be on the air shortly . . ."

"You got anything else on it?"

"Homicide's taken over. Christ, the place was a mess. Whoever the hell did it wrote the number fourteen on his fucking head. In blood, Phillips's own blood. We don't know where the fuck the hands are. Probably in some sewer by now . . ."

Vincent was stunned by Gleason's news. Phillips was dead, the son of a bitch was dead, and Vincent had never gotten close to him . . . Or had he? That freeze frame lighted up again in his head. The forearm extended from the shiny black coat sleeve. The pouch skittering out on the drawstring like a breeches buoy riding the air between ships. Goddammit. He was obsessed with Phillips. And now Phillips was dead . . .

"It's all over, Paul. Forget it. That's my advice. I know you tailed that son of a bitch. But he's dead. They don't come any more fucking dead than he is."

"Thanks, Walt," Captain Vincent mumbled, his thoughts still racing.

"Now, about that lunch we've been talking about? When are you free?"

"Walt, did they find anything funny there?"

"The whole fucking thing was funny. Christ, a real fag killing. Couldn't kill him dead enough. They don't have lovers' quarrels, you know."

"No, I was just wondering about . . ."

"All his clothes were gone. The only thing they found was a black leather thing, some kind of a fucking purse. They found that shoved up his ass, or where his ass should have been before they tore it out."

Vincent shook his head. Everything he knew about George Phillips had been checked off. Inventory complete. Case closed.

"Now, Paul, how about the Blackhawk? Tomorrow okay? Say noon-time?"

"Okay, Walt. Noon at the Blackhawk."

"That's *tomorrow*, Paulie. For Crissake, Paul, forget this case, will you? One fag killed another, that's it. You've got plenty to do with Catherine the Great down there . . ."

"Thanks for calling. And thanks for the advice." Captain Vincent hung up the phone after barely mumbling a goodbye to his old friend. He opened his desk drawer and pulled out the manila folder he had brought with him from O'Hare Field. He began to read again the clippings he had been collecting for so many months now.

"Welcome, Madam Mayor, we bid you welcome." Patrick Bredin, the twinkling-eyed manager of the Cape Cod Room, swept an ushering gesture in front of Ann Marie, who blipped a vague smile back at him. "And Mr. Barone. So nice to see you again!" Like many other Chicagoans, Bredin was taking a second look at his new Mayor. Something in his Irish sensibility made him hesitate about giving her his full personal approval.

"Here you are. Right here. Humberto will be your captain . . ."

Mrs. O'Brien edged into the booth without looking at the manager. Richard Barone shot white cuffs from the sleeves of his navy blue jacket as he grinned up at Bredin. "What's good today, Patrick?"

"The swordfish is excellent. The prawns. Very good, all of it."

"Thank you," Barone said as he adjusted the vents of his coat beneath him. Ann Marie focused on the red-checkered table linen as she shook her napkin loose.

"Isn't it grand news about Mayor Cullen?" the maître d' asked cheerfully.

Ann Marie glared at the beaming restaurant manager.

"He started talking this morning. Got his voice back. We just heard it from a doctor from the hospital who's here for lunch . . ."

Ann Marie turned from fire to ice. The old man was talking. She hated the idea. She who hated the men who kept silence in her life felt cold rage building within her that one of them, the wrong one, had found his voice. She spread the napkin on her lap and looked with arctic blankness at Bredin.

"Great news," Barone graveled as the manager slipped away, leaving the distinguished luncheon guests to themselves.

"Listen, Mr. Barone, I'm here because I understand that you want to talk to me. I'm busy and I'd like you to get to the point."

Barone ordered a bottle of wine. "Mrs. O'Brien, we have a lot in common. We both like to get to the point. Let me make mine clear right away. You're the Mayor. Sure, that's fine. You're the Mayor for a while anyway. For several months anyway. You've started like a house afire. You're very popular. But the whole thing could go down the drain very fast. I'm here to talk about how we can keep that from happening."

Ann Marie was not listening closely. Cullen had recovered his speech. What was it, baby talk? What would he say to her? She sipped the ice water. Cullen rising like a ghost. It didn't matter. She was the Mayor now.

"For somebody who wanted me to get to the point, you don't seem to be listening much."

Ann Marie pulled her attention together, blanking out the vision of the shaggy-haired old Mayor that had formed there.

"You've been busy shaking things up. You've made a lot of speeches. Started public hearings. But, Madam Mayor, you haven't got anything *done* yet. The city is governed by the Mayor and the City Council working together. It's governed by reaching understandings with the banks, the unions, the big businesses. What the hell else do you think Chicago is? It *is* business and labor and money and deals."

"You haven't told me anything I don't know." Ann Marie held her hand over her wineglass as the captain reached toward it with the bottle.

"You know and you don't know. You sure as hell aren't going to get anything done just with headlines. And to get things done you need me." He settled back and sipped the wine.

"Have you decided what you would like?" Humberto, the captain, stood smiling at the side of the table.

"Shrimp salad," Ann Marie answered without looking at him.

"The same," Barone said, sustaining the tautness of the interrupted discussion with the lacquered hardness of his eyes.

"Who elected you?" Ann Marie asked brusquely after the captain turned away.

"Maybe it's an inherited job."

"Maybe you stole it. I hear you're good at that."

"Maybe you stole being Mayor," Barone answered angrily. He relaxed his features as if he wanted to start the discussion again, gesturing with both hands, shuffling a deck of invisible cards, as he searched for a new beginning. Ann Marie reached into the bread basket and broke off a piece of matzoh bread as carefully as if it were a Dead Sea Scroll.

"Look, there's no sense in our arguing. We've had some misunderstandings. We want to help you be a good Mayor. And you need us. Practically speaking, you need *us*."

"Who exactly is *us?*" Ann Marie nibbled at the thin bread.

"The people who can raise money for you, the people who can line up contributions from businesses, from the unions. You're going to need a war chest. The people who can get things pushed through City Hall. The people who know how to reach the Governor." He swept the air with half a benediction. "The people you can't do without . . ."

"Can you work with the committeemen?"

"Oh, yes, I forgot." Barone beamed. "They haven't fallen in line yet, have they? They're still holding back. Cullen's still head of the party." Ann Marie looked steadily at him. "I think we can help you there. Sure. They need contributions too." Barone pulled back as the waiter placed their salads before them and poured Barone another glass of wine.

Barone gestured at Ann Marie with his fork, a plump shrimp split by its tines. "What you need . . . tell me if I'm wrong . . . what you need is to have people forget Mayor Thomas H. Cullen." He popped the shrimp into his mouth and continued to speak as he chewed it. "Right?" He swallowed the seafood and looked expectantly at Ann Marie.

"I want people to know that *I'm* Mayor now." She poked at her salad but did not take any of the shrimp. "I *am* the Mayor, Barone. I want you to remember it too. You and your friends."

"Sure, sure." Barone was comfortable now. "You cooperate with us and we'll guarantee that in a few months when somebody mentions Mayor Cullen, people will ask, 'Mayor who?'" He began to laugh. He lifted his wineglass in a toasting gesture. "I knew we'd understand each other."

Ann Marie held her fork above her plate as she looked deadpan at her luncheon companion. She despised everything about him, the spicy scents and the lion's-head cuff links, the satyr's trunk of body hidden beneath the silk shirt and the cashmere jacket, the vulgarity of his carefully manicured fingernails, and the thickets of hair that could have sprouted from his ears and nostrils except for the attention of some barber at his athletic club. She hated the thought of his ever being close to her, of the possibilities of sexual advance that twitched beneath his every word and gesture. She hated this plunderer who bought and blackmailed until he had what he wanted. There seemed nothing not to dislike about him, especially his animal sense that she was still worried about, still intimidated by old Thomas H. Cullen. She hated Barone thoroughly, homicidally. Mostly because he was right. Barone had shagged the live wire that trailed sparks across her soul. She *was* afraid of Cullen.

Franklin Barnes stepped out of his limousine onto the LaSalle Street sidewalk in front of his bank. He had not been totally surprised to see Mayor O'Brien and Richard Barone at the Cape Cod Room. It would be good if they reached some kind of understanding about the true sources of the city's stability. He had also heard that Thomas H. Cullen had recovered his capacity for speech. All the more reason for Mayor O'Brien to complete her education in civics. He had thought about the staggering events of recent weeks as he rode along the sun-baked stretch of Lake Shore Drive toward the center of the city. The morning paper, with its banner headlines about the identification of George Phillips's body, lay on the seat next to him. He was preoccupied as he walked through the thick summer heat toward the bronze doors of the bank building.

"Mr. Barnes?" The questioner looked as dignified as Barnes himself. Thin, graying, he would have been comfortable at the bar of the best country club in the county. Another man, slightly younger and heavier, wearing a striped summer suit, smiled and took him by the arm.

"I don't think we've met," Barnes said, trying to push the second man's hand away.

"Oh, I think we may have," the older man said in a silky voice.

Barnes half-looked back toward his driver, who was already pulling the long gray Cadillac away from the curb. Crowds of people passed around the tight circle made by Barnes and the two men.

"We're here to help you, Mr. Barnes," the first man said.

"Who are you? What are you talking about?" Barnes asked impatiently.

The first of the two men inched closer to Barnes. "We want to talk to you. In private."

Barnes looked from one of the men to the other. "That's ridiculous. You have to make an appointment. I'm a busy man."

"We know how busy you've been. We know a lot about you," the stranger said almost casually. "We know you're gay. That's just for starters." Barnes was startled. He began to perspire.

"Mrs. Barnes doesn't know, does she? Nobody at the bank either. Except maybe Jack Grant. Jack Grant in the Bond Department? Jack knows, doesn't he? He ought to. You've been lovers for years . . ."

"This is ridiculous . . ." The hurly-burly of the early-afternoon street scene blacked out around the two men. Barnes felt faint.

"Is it?" The urbane man looked around at the milling crowd. "You look a little pale. Let's go to your office. Nice and quiet. Cool too, I'll bet."

What did they know about his relationship with Jack Grant? That was in the past now anyway. What could they know? There was a great deal they could know, even if it was in the past. Mostly in the past. Barnes nodded without speaking.

"Just introduce us as old business associates. I'm Mr. Palmer. And this is Mr. Craig. Shall we go in?"

Within a few moments they were in Barnes's private office, a darkly paneled, heavily carpeted room high in the building's tower, a citadel against the heat and sound of the city.

Palmer used the gold lighter on Barnes's desk to ignite a light brown pencil of cigar. Barnes sat uneasily in his high-backed leather chair.

"Mr. Barnes, we have sympathy for men like you. We understand you. If it came out that you had been actively gay, it might ruin your career. Or your marriage. Certainly your social life."

Barnes could feel the coldness rising off Palmer's icy calculation. Barnes had not, however, entered the inner kingdom of banking by panicking in difficult situations. He had to get hold of himself.

"The trouble, Franklin—you don't mind if I call you Franklin, do you? —the trouble is that the police have put you down as a suspect in the George Phillips killing . . ."

"What!" Barnes yelped.

"Now calm down, calm down. We know you didn't do it. But the police have had a tip about you. You can't say you haven't had some connection with the gay world . . ." Palmer puffed on his cigar. Barnes gripped the arms of his chair. "Now, if you'll stay calm, Franklin, we can fix this rap for you." He turned to his companion. "What do you think it will take us to handle this, George?"

"Ten grand," the other man said, "maybe fifteen."

"This is ridiculous." Barnes struggled to control his impatience.

"I said to stay calm. Now, as a bank president you can easily get the cash. Right?" He drew on his cigar. "Then we'll go over to the first district Police Headquarters and take care of this matter for you. But if we don't handle it now, the police might call you in for questioning. It wouldn't be pleasant. The newspapers and all. The one thing you should remember, Franklin, is that we know you're innocent." He flicked ashes from the end of his cigar into a potted fern. "So, just pick up your phone and send for the cash. It's as easy as that . . ."

"I have no connection with this George Phillips business," Barnes said firmly. He needed time to think.

"We understand that. That's why we're so concerned that this gets straightened out right away. Just a few dollars in the right places . . ."

"Suppose I don't go along with this, suppose I just take my chances . . ."

"Oh, Franklin, that wouldn't be wise, would it?" Palmer studied his cigar as he spoke. "The possibilities are terrible. Just think of Mrs. Barnes . . ."

Barnes's hand trembled as he reached for his phone. He flipped open a bank directory on his desk. "I'll dial the head cashier directly . . ."

"No you don't," Palmer said, gliding behind the desk. "Let's just see what that number is. I'll dial it for you." He checked the listing, dialed the number and, when he heard a man's voice, handed the phone to Barnes. The bank president gave clear directions about delivering fifteen thousand dollars from his special account, in cash, to his office. Head cashiers did not question bank presidents when they gave such orders. Within five minutes, a zippered leather bag had been brought to Barnes's secretary and, by her, to Franklin Barnes himself.

"Well done, Franklin," Palmer said, rising from the chair he had taken while the transaction was being accomplished. "Here, George"—he passed the packet to his accomplice—"count this before we leave."

Barnes looked at Palmer and Craig. These men were terrorists. The thought appalled his WASP conscience. Their manner—a mixture of Harvard and the gutter—offended him. This was what the modern world was all about.

"May I call Mrs. Barnes before we go?"

"Why?"

"Well, she's expecting me to meet her in half an hour. She'll be upset if I'm late."

"What's her number?"

Barnes swallowed hard. He decided to take an enormous risk. He recited a number that might, for all he knew, be disconnected now. "744-4256."

It rang on the private phone in the office of the Mayor.

Palmer held the receiver to his ear. Three rings, then a woman said hello. He handed the phone to Barnes.

"This is Franklin, dear . . ."

"Franklin who?" Ann Marie answered, astonished at the greeting.

"I just called to tell you I'll be a little delayed . . ."

"Is this Franklin Barnes? Where do you come off, calling me 'dear'?"

"Well, dear, I know you've been looking forward to this."

"Franklin, did you have too many fizzes at the Cape Cod Room today? Our meeting isn't scheduled until tomorrow . . ."

"Exactly." Palmer made a gesture for Barnes to cut the call short. "But something's come up. I have to go over to the Police Station on some business. So I'll be a little late. Goodbye, dear." Barnes hung up his phone. He was soaked in perspiration.

Ann Marie heard the click, held the singing phone in the air for a moment. She frowned. What the hell was going on? She pushed the buzzer on her desk.

"Helen, get me Captain Vincent, wherever he is . . ."

29

*C*aptain Vincent had called news producer Mark Cunningham and at the channel 7 studios on State Street was watching, over and over, and in stop action, tapes of the distinguished guests arriving at Holy Name Cathedral for the Mayor Cullen prayer service. The captain remembered that he had looked at his watch shortly before he saw the wrist jutting out of the coat sleeve and the pouch dancing in the air below it. That had been at two minutes to six.

"Could you run that section through again?" he asked the technician who was assisting him. They had worked backward from the time the police brass had joined the procession. Somewhere in that unrolling tape Phillips was opening a car door.

"Now, can we watch this very closely?" Vincent could hear the doubt in his own voice. What the hell was he chasing a dead man for? A phantom, that's what George Phillips had become, a goddamn phantom.

"There, there," Vincent said, motioning to the technician to hold a frame on the television monitor. The portly middle-aged technician did not seem to mind. The captain strained forward to examine the picture that had been taken from an angle to the left of where he had been standing.

"Take it back a little," Vincent said. The machine whirred briefly. Vincent watched the action he had observed a dozen times already. He could see the top of the limousine door open, but the bobbing heads at the edge of the crowd obscured the person who had opened it. He let the tape roll on. Another car drew up and the same activity followed. He knew that if he asked the technician to reverse the tape even further he would see roughly the same scene acted out with different players and different limousines. Somewhere in this strange ghostly life of television tape, George Phillips was tantalizing Captain Vincent.

"Would it help, Captain, if we watched this on a larger screen?"

"Can you do that?"

"Sure, we can use a projection system. It'll take a few minutes to set up."

Vincent nodded. Maybe a bigger picture would help. That was what Urban Mulvihill, his first commanding officer, had always said. Get the big picture. Big Picture Mulvihill they had called him. They had given him a huge enlargement of himself at the retirement party. The big picture. Vincent smiled in recollection. The big picture. Of course. Mulvihill was still right. Vincent had been looking too hard for the elusive wrist with the pouch. What was in the big picture around it? He put down his cold cup of coffee and his weariness at the same time.

"We'll have to go next door," the technician called from the doorway of the viewing room. "I got one of them in my basement." He seemed more animated as he led the captain into an adjoining area. "Great little suckers, Captain, great for the football season." That's the life, Vincent mused as he settled in front of a console with a separate five-foot-wide panel for a screen.

The tape began to roll. The crowded scene in front of the Cathedral swam fuzzily before him. The first car pulled up. Vincent watched intently. Not looking for the man who opened the door, he saw part of the man who got out of the car. A gray-haired man looking downward, a tall, athletic-looking man who moved swiftly across the sidewalk. The next car arrived. A couple emerged and looked neither to the left nor to the right as they moved away from the car. Vincent watched yet another limousine pull to the crowded curb.

"There's a phone call for Captain Vincent," a young man shouted through the partially open door. "They said it was important."

The technician froze the milling crowd on the screen. "There's a phone on the wall."

Vincent rose and nodded toward the technician. "That's the section I want to see again. Run it back, will you?" He walked over to the phone. Helen Morrison was on the line. Mrs. O'Brien wanted to speak to him.

"Captain, you're a hard man to find." Mrs. O'Brien sounded excited.

"Well . . ."

"Never mind. Listen, I just had a strange call from Franklin Barnes, the bank president. Called me 'dear,' said he was sorry he couldn't keep our appointment, said he had business at Police Headquarters."

"Did he have an appointment with you?"

"No, not until tomorrow. When I reminded him of that, he said, 'Exactly.' He's either gone round the bend or had too much to drink. I don't want to make a big deal out of this. And I don't want you to either. Can you get over and check it out? Then get back to me."

"We could just call Headquarters directly . . ."

"Captain, if I wanted to call them directly I would. There's something funny going on. I want you to look into it. *Now.* Do you understand?"

"Right away, Mrs. O'Brien, right away." Vincent replaced the phone on its wall perch. He turned back to the technician, who was still relishing the effectiveness of projection television. "Just like mine, Captain . . ." Vincent cut him off. "I'll be in touch with you about this.

Thanks very much . . ." The technician shrugged his shoulders as Captain Vincent hurried quickly through the door.

The lobby of the 1st District Police Station was always busy. Captain Vincent arrived about five minutes after his phone call from an agitated Mayor O'Brien. He had spent the morning looking for an image he couldn't find. Now he was looking for a man he didn't know, a man who could have been almost anywhere in the building at Eleventh and State just south of the Loop.

Captain Vincent looked around the bustling desk area of the station. A tall, well-dressed man had just approached the desk sergeant. Vincent scanned the rest of the area. In the far corner, dusky even on a midsummer afternoon, two men sat next to each other. The gray-haired man looked familiar. Very familiar. The big picture. It was the same man who had emerged from the first limousine on the tape he had just viewed. Franklin Barnes. He'd bet on it. What the hell was going on? Barnes was looking intently toward the distinguished man talking to the sergeant. Whoever he was and whatever he was doing, Barnes was giving him his full concentration. Vincent walked across the lobby and stood behind Palmer. The sergeant was speaking.

"A thing like that, it's hard to tell. You say it was a police officer on a motorcycle near Wacker and LaSalle?"

"Yes, that's right. About noontime. He was really very helpful to us when our car had a flat in the middle of traffic."

"And you didn't get his shield number . . ."

"No, I'm sorry . . ."

"And you didn't notice his name plate."

"Well, I thought it was something like Brown, or Black. Yes, something like that . . ."

"Well, you can appreciate, sir, that without some better idea, I couldn't tell you who it was. Or find out. We have a lot of officers in this district."

"Yes, Sergeant, I can appreciate that. Well, we'd like to leave him something. Maybe you can find out who it was and give him this as a token of our gratitude." He handed the sergeant a thick white envelope. "Just tell him it's with our appreciation."

It was clear what was going on. Vincent had dealt with this scam many times when, years before, he had been on the confidence detail. Men known as fruit hustlers swarmed immediately to any city in which there had been a notorious homosexual murder. They knew their marks in advance. Usually well-to-do business and professional men who could not afford to have their names associated with homosexuality. Today it had been Barnes, poor Barnes, sweating his WASP dignity away over in the corner. The fruit hustlers would tell their marks that they were suspected of some connection with the homosexual murder or that they were accessories before or after the fact. They could fix it but it would take cash. They would take their victim to a police station—sometimes right into the outer office of the State's Attorney—and let him watch from a distance while they acted out their "fix" with some story like the one that had just been given to the desk sergeant. From a distance the already nervous banker or dentist thought he was watching a payoff with the five or ten thousand he had just turned over. Instead, the desk sergeant was getting a twenty or a fifty in a thick envelope. Not many desk sergeants refused these and, if they couldn't find the person for whom they were intended, well, that's the way it was . . .

The sergeant caught sight of Vincent over the con man's shoulder. Vincent nodded. Take it, Sergeant, take it. The sergeant dropped the envelope on his desk. "We'll see what we can do for you, sir."

"Fine, fine, and thank you . . ." The distinguished-looking man turned away and walked back across the lobby. Vincent moved to the desk.

"I'll take care of this, Sergeant. Are they moving out yet?"

"Just getting up, Captain, heading for the door."

Vincent turned and intercepted the men as they reached the exit.

"Mr. Barnes?"

The trio stopped and looked quizzically at Vincent.

"Gentlemen," the captain said calmly, "the party's over. I think we'll just have a little talk. Do you mind?"

"We're here on business," Palmer said coolly.

"I know," Captain Vincent answered, "that's just what I want to talk about."

Vincent had the confidence men held in the lockup while he drove Franklin Barnes to City Hall. It was against procedure, but he had a feeling that the Mayor would want it played that way.

"That was pretty brave of you, Mr. Barnes, calling the Mayor's line." They were in the back of the plain car in which Vincent was driven around the city.

"I don't know what got into me," he said, stumbling on the words. "I had that number from Mayor Cullen. The idea just came out of nowhere. They were so vulgar. I just decided not to give up easily . . ."

"What do you want to do about it?"

Barnes looked at Vincent in alarm. "I don't want to press charges," he said softly.

"They'll just pick on somebody else."

"I can't help it. I can't afford to get involved any further in this . . ."

"You're a hero, Mr. Barnes."

"People would still think I was mixed up in this, that I was . . ."

"Gay?"

"Yes, I suppose so." Barnes swiveled his upper body toward Vincent. "We don't have to press charges, do we? This *can* be kept quiet?"

"Whatever you say. I'm sure the Mayor will handle it the way you want."

Barnes seemed relieved. He leaned back on the seat. They were only a block from City Hall.

"By the way, Mr. Barnes, can I ask you a question?"

Barnes turned his head numbly toward the captain.

"You went to the prayer service for Mayor Cullen. You know, the one when—"

"Yes, yes."

"And you went in your own limo with your own driver, is that right?"

"Yes, yes—" Barnes interrupted himself. "Well, no, as a matter of fact. My secretary called a livery service that day. Frederick had to drive my wife to Rockford that afternoon. I was going to take a cab. But my secretary had it all arranged. Why do you ask?"

"Oh, something I've been looking into. Do you remember the service you used?" Vincent tried to sound casual.

"No, not really. My secretary could tell you." The police car sat at the corner of LaSalle and Washington waiting for the light to change. "Her name is Mary Meuser. Very efficient. Mary could tell you . . ."

"You probably don't remember anything about the driver . . ."

The light changed and the car moved. The traffic policeman in the middle of the intersection waved a greeting and pointed to a space just behind the Mayor's limousine near the LaSalle Street entrance to City Hall.

"Well, Captain, he talked a lot. I do remember that. I have strict rules with Frederick not to speak unless I speak to him. I usually work in the car, even on short trips . . ." The car pulled up at the curb and the driver climbed out to open the door.

"I remember how much he talked, yes, even when he hopped out to open the door . . ."

Vincent did not move. "What did he talk about?"

"I forget. I was trying not to pay attention. That was a tense time in the city. I was preoccupied." They eased themselves out of the car onto the sidewalk. The captain and the banker walked single file through the glass entry doors of City Hall without speaking. They crossed the marble concourse to the bank of elevators on the right. Vincent glanced at the afternoon edition of the papers that were being wheeled by on a cart for delivery to the various newsstands in the building. "Cullen Talks!" bannered one, "Former Mayor Shows Improvement" the other. They entered a waiting elevator car.

"I want to thank you, Captain, for your help," Barnes said as the doors closed. Vincent watched the floor numbers wink by as they rose through the building.

"Is there anything I can do for you, Captain?" Barnes asked dryly.

"No"—Vincent smiled—"not unless you can remember anything else about your driver."

Barnes managed a smile. The captain wasn't asking for much. Most people would have expected more. The elevator doors opened on the vaulted corridor of the fifth floor.

"Oh, I really can't remember much. He talked a lot." Barnes spoke absently, as though he were trying to recall some dinner party conversation to which he had paid scant attention. "Said his family was very busy that day. All their cars were out." They were at the doors of the Mayor's outer office. "Yes, I remember he said his whole family was driving that day . . ."

The police officer at the reception desk nodded them through into the corridor that led to the Mayor's outer office. Barnes strained to recall more for Vincent. It helped to remember such inconsequential things after the near miss of the afternoon. "He had a cousin driving the car in front of us and a brother-in-law, or an uncle, or something like that, driving the car behind . . ."

"What was that?" Vincent asked, touching Barnes on the arm, making him pause at the threshold of the large room in which the Mayor's secretaries worked.

"Not much, Captain, really. I can't remember. A lot of the driver's relatives were working that day, that's all."

Helen Morrison smiled at them from her desk diagonally across the room.

"Hello, Mr. Barnes. The Mayor's expecting you . . ."

Ann Marie greeted Barnes and Vincent enthusiastically. She wanted all the details of the afternoon's excitement. This was better than the boring budget meeting that had just broken up. She listened eagerly to the details of the banker's escapade with the fruit hustlers.

"That's about the story," Barnes concluded. "I don't know what would have happened if you had changed that phone number. Or if you hadn't paid any attention to what I told you . . ."

"Well, I knew something was wrong."

Captain Vincent had not seen Mrs. O'Brien so enthusiastic since the day she had led the Gray Panther protest out at the airport. He did not know what to make of her. She was like a girl he had known in high school. "Teaser," they had called her. Old "Teaser" Healy.

"Now, Franklin," Ann Marie said, "we'll hold a press conference on this at four o'clock. I'll want you to appear with me." She glanced quickly at Vincent. "And you too, Paul."

Vincent shuddered inwardly. He could just imagine his wife's unhappy reaction if he showed up on the evening news with the Mayor holding his hand.

"We'll tell the whole city the story. How the three of us worked together. It's just like a movie . . ."

"Mrs. O'Brien, I simply cannot appear on television." Barnes flicked a hand toward Vincent. "I've already told the captain that I will not press charges. I don't want any publicity. Surely, you can understand . . ."

"Franklin, you're a hero, don't *you* understand that? You owe it to the people of the city." Ann Marie's eyes sparkled. "I've already called the press conference. Told them there would be big news."

"I'm sorry. You'll have to go on without me." Barnes was alarmed and irritated. "Surely, Mrs. O'Brien, you can understand what publicity about this would do. To have my name—and the bank's—connected with —what did you call them, Captain, 'fruit hustlers'?—well, Mrs. O'Brien, can't you see what that would do to me and my reputation?"

Ann Marie stared angrily at Barnes. Another man who wouldn't talk when she wanted him to. Was that expression of Barnes's the same one that had greeted her Irish Catholic ancestors when they had applied for jobs from his ancestors? Ann Marie turned in her chair. She glanced at the afternoon editions of the newspapers that had been placed on the side of her desk earlier. Cullen in all the headlines. The old Mayor speaks but the big banker won't. She had the perfect story to blast Cullen right off the front pages. Ann Marie felt tense, irritable, boxed in by events.

"Mr. Barnes," she said acidly, "you owe a lot to me. I took your message and passed it along to the captain here. You would have been taken by those con men if it hadn't been for me. Now you tell me you won't cooperate with me?"

"I'm grateful to you. Don't misunderstand me. I'm saying I would rather have paid the money than appear on television. I do not intend to press charges. I'm sorry if you're upset."

"Do you know how much the city has on deposit in your bank, Mr. Barnes?" The sudden, savage question was stunning. "I just went over the figures this afternoon."

Barnes nodded. Captain Vincent wished that he were somewhere else.

"Good. The funds won't be there in the morning." Ann Marie stood up.

"Larry Johnson was here telling me the city needs to put more money in banks in the black neighborhoods. It sounds like a good idea to me." Ann Marie stared directly at Barnes.

"Mrs. O'Brien," Barnes said in conciliatory tones, "surely you can understand my position. I'd be ruined if I involved myself in publicity about this incident." He cleared his throat. "And may I suggest that you don't move too swiftly on the deposits. You might lose a lot of interest."

"Good afternoon, Mr. Barnes," Ann Marie said icily. "And you too, Captain." She remained standing, glaring at them as Franklin Barnes and Captain Paul Vincent rose from their chairs and walked silently toward the door.

Ann Marie sat down. She folded her arms and rocked back and forth in her chair. The headlines swelled up off the newspapers at her. Cullen, Cullen, Cullen. And he was still chairman of the party. She picked up her phone. "Get me Paul Martin." She stood up, her arms still folded. Cullen's beefy face, the shag of white hair across the brow, peered up at her from the front page of the tabloid newspaper. She breathed deeply, snatched both papers off her desk and shoved them into her wastebasket. Her phone rang.

"This is George Ohland, Mrs. O'Brien. We're all set for the news conference . . ."

"Forget it, George. Cancel it."

Ohland was silent for a moment. "Shall I reschedule it?"

"I'll let you know." Ann Marie hung up. She sat down again. She opened a folder and, the engines of her distraction nearing the level of rage, glanced uncomprehendingly at the columns of figures. Ann Marie flipped the folder closed and picked up her phone again.

"Have you located Paul Martin yet?"

"Not yet, Mrs. O'Brien. He must be out on assignment, that's what his editor says . . ."

Ann Marie slammed the phone down. It rang again immediately. It was Helen Morrison. She spoke as though the Mayor had not just hung noisily up on her.

"Mr. Barone wants to speak to you."

"Put him on." Ann Marie shifted uneasily in her chair. A creased Thomas H. Cullen looked steadily up at her from the wastebasket. She leaned forward and pressed the paper farther down into the receptacle.

"Mrs. O'Brien? Dick Barone." The smoothness of his voice did not soothe her.

"What do you want?"

"Now, now, slow down. You don't want to get into something you'll regret later on."

"What are you talking about?"

"Do you know how much it would cost the city to transfer funds out of one bank . . ."

"You mean Barnes's bank . . ."

"Yes, okay, Barnes's bank . . ."

"It didn't take him long to get in touch with you . . ."

"Well, you made a big threat at a man whose help you'll need. Don't you realize that? Listen, if you lost several thousand dollars in interest by this move, the papers—the papers you think love you—would be all over you. Do you understand?"

Ann Marie did understand. It only increased her seething. She did not respond to Barone.

"Mrs. O'Brien, this is just some friendly advice. Don't do something you'll regret."

Goddamn these men. She mumbled a goodbye and hung up the phone without waiting to hear anything else. Where the hell was Paul Martin? Nobody wanted her to do anything. Men either didn't talk to her or were full of advice she didn't want to hear. She *had* been heroic. That's what the city wanted to hear. Why else did they call her St. Joan? Everybody wanted her to keep quiet. They all sounded like Richler. If Richler were still around, she'd never be able to talk at all. She twisted restlessly in her chair. Cullen could talk. What did he say, *goo goo*? And she couldn't tell the city how she had saved the WASP banker, the gay WASP banker, from the con men. Maureen would be on the news tonight. Yes, my father's wonderful. Yes, he'll be back to work soon.

Ann Marie blacked out Maureen's image as though she were turning off a television set. She picked up her phone again.

"Get George Ohland for me . . ." She waited while the connection was made. "George, this is Mayor O'Brien. I'm going to hold that press conference after all. Yes, yes, that's right. Four o'clock . . ."

30

I am announcing today that I will seek the Democratic nomination for the office of Mayor in the election scheduled for next April."

Ann Marie paused while the reporters froze in place as though posing for a photographer. They hadn't expected this announcement. Maybe in the fall, maybe after things settled down. But midsummer? This was big news.

"I am making this announcement at this time because, after several weeks in this position, and after studying the first reports I commissioned I realize that an enormous amount of work is needed to make this city truly great. Times have changed. Sometimes governments don't keep up with them. When that happens, municipal collapse can occur suddenly and unexpectedly. You only need to think of Cleveland and New York back in the seventies to understand what I'm talking about. In order to begin to build in the months ahead for the changes that are necessary, I announce my candidacy today, submitting it to the people for their judgment. Only that way can we ensure the continuity, the long-range planning that is necessary . . ."

She paused and sipped some water. The reports she mentioned had lain unopened on her desk for two days. By now Ann Marie believed that she had actually read them. Except for the sounds of the television cameras, the room was absolutely quiet. Ann Marie O'Brien was running against Thomas H. Cullen.

"I do not believe, in these conditions, that we can leave the choice for this important office up to the old party bosses who have been living off the city for so long . . ."

Ann Marie was taking on the committeemen even before Cullen got out of the hospital. They hadn't even regrouped since his illness. She was trying to scatter them before they could.

"I know the machinery that operates to slate candidates. My name has been submitted before. I respect that system. This year, however, I want the people to join in, I want their voices to be heard. Beginning tomorrow, I want the people of the city to express their wishes." She waited again, knowing that the next section would be the clip used on every newscast that evening. She looked directly into the cameras. "I want you to join me in the great crusade to guarantee the future of the city. I need your help to carry on the work that has to be done. I want you to vote, by phone, by mail, or on the special booths that will be set up in every neighborhood. I want you to vote for me. I want you to put your name behind mine so that we can be partners in progress for Chicago. With your voices, and your votes, the bosses will have to listen. We have a message for them." She swallowed, pushed a stray hair back into place with her right hand. "The people are taking the city back." She took one step back and lowered her head slightly, a virtuoso performer waiting for the applause to rain down.

The reporters were on their feet with questions.

"Who's your campaign manager?" Max Day asked.

"I am."

"Anybody else?"

"That may be announced later. There is one other announcement. Franklin Barnes of Home Bank and Trust will head a special finance committee to raise funds for what I think will be a long, hard campaign."

"Have you talked to former Mayor Cullen about this? He's still chairman of the Cook County Central Committee . . ."

"No."

"Is he one of the 'party bosses' you're challenging?"

"My statement was clear enough, wasn't it?"

"Are you accusing the Cullen administration of malfeasance?"

"That's your word. I've been talking about progress into the future, a new leaf, a new deal for the people."

"In effect, Madam Mayor," Max Day said, half as a question, half as a summation of her position, "you're assuming leadership of the party even though you technically don't have it. How do you think the committeemen will react to that?"

"We'll just have to wait and see, won't we?" Ann Marie rocked sensuously back and forth as she answered, bathing herself in the invisible wash of excitement. She folded her arms and repeated her plans for seeking the Mayoral nomination on the basis of established populist support. The reporters probed this notion from every angle. Finally, the drumbeat of the questions slowed. A young reporter in the first row raised his hand. Ann Marie pointed toward him.

"On another subject, Mrs. O'Brien. Our paper has information that you once spoke up for George Phillips, the mass murderer whose body was found the other day . . ."

"You don't know what you're talking about," Ann Marie snapped.

The reporter blinked but did not flinch. He waited a beat and went on with his question. "We understand that he was one of your political

workers and that you reprimanded police who were investigating his be-
havior and told them to stop bothering him."

Ann Marie regarded the reporter blankly. The atmosphere tingled.

"Now, Mrs. O'Brien, could you tell us if any of that is true?"

Another pause. "No, of course not. Phillips may have been a party
worker. There are thousands of them throughout the city. I never knew
him . . ."

The reporter sat down and another one rose to ask about her political
plans. She answered the question tersely and, ignoring a half dozen
raised hands, turned toward the rear door. "That's all for today." She
slipped through the opening as the conference room exploded behind
her. She would knock Mayor Cullen off the evening news all right. He
wouldn't be in the headlines the next morning either. Ann Marie took a
deep breath as she hurried across the outer office. All the phones were
ringing. Helen Morrison looked up at her, cupped a hand over the phone
she was using, and sighed, "Everybody, I mean *everybody*, wants to talk
to you . . ." Ann Marie shot her an automatic smile and darted into her
own office. Except for the nagging Phillips question, it had been wonderful. She stretched as if in an exercise class and walked around her desk.
They would soon know who was boss in Chicago. The whole city would
know.

But why hadn't Paul Martin been at the news conference? And why
the hell did they keep asking her about George Phillips?

Captain Vincent sighed. He was sick of Palmer and Craig and tired of
questioning them.

"Well, Palmer, you're in luck. Your mark isn't going to press charges.
Fate has been kind to you, kinder than you deserve."

Palmer smiled wanly. "Perhaps." He started to rise from his chair. "If
there's nothing else, Captain . . ."

"Sit down, Palmer, sit down."

"As you say, Captain. May I smoke?"

Vincent waved a vague gesture of permission. Palmer lighted a thin
cigar and brandished the package toward the captain in invitation to
join him. His companion shifted in his chair, a dog watching his master
for the signal that they were to take a walk.

"Palmer, what did you know about Phillips?"

The con man held smoke in his distended cheeks, then blew it out in a
rush. "He's dead, isn't he?" He put the cigar back in his mouth.

"Don't get coy on me, Palmer. If he hadn't been killed, you wouldn't
have come to Chicago."

"I suppose that's true. Something else would have come up. We never
seem to lack work."

"I'm asking you what you know about him. If you want me to call Barnes, I might just be able to get him to change his mind about pressing charges."

Palmer stared at the captain thoughtfully. "I think you might just do that. Well, Captain, I don't know much. *Really . . .*"

Vincent got up, stepped close to the con man, reached down and clutched Palmer's lapels, shirt, and tie like a horse's reins in his right hand. He jerked Palmer up off his chair. The cigar fell out of Palmer's mouth and tumbled like a falling mountaineer down the length of his crumpled suit jacket and onto the floor.

"Christ, Captain, take it easy."

Vincent pushed Palmer down onto the chair again.

"Well?"

Palmer straightened his tie, patted down his lapels. "All I know is that Phillips ran with a pack."

"What do you mean?"

"Come on, Captain, you don't think he worked alone, do you?"

"We have no evidence that he didn't. I saw him at arcades. He was always alone."

Palmer smiled. "Captain, maybe you saw him alone, but I guarantee you he didn't operate alone. There's an underworld of these guys. Haven't you learned anything about the mass murderers you've heard about for years? The ashcan murders and all the others? You think they acted alone? Come off it."

Vincent wrinkled his brow.

"Captain, there's a loose floating crowd of these boys around the country. They get their money from drugs and pornography. They scare the shit out of the gays like Barnes who are trying to live respectable lives and those groups that want gays to seem just like everyone else. These guys have done everything. Mob connections all over the place. They've run out of thrills. Christ, there's nothing these guys haven't seen or tried. So trapping a male victim, like these strays Phillips and his friends were picking up, that's the top. They assault them sexually and kill them at the same time. That's their fucking high, that's what they get off on. An orgasm while they're killing someone. Kids disappear all the time in this country. Nobody even misses most of them. Easy picking, Captain." Palmer smiled unpleasantly. "And, hell, if they get some guy they don't like, some cop following them, some guy they really want to rub out for the mob, they fuck him and kill him and make it look like the victim was a queer. That's their way of ruining a guy for good. Months ago, Captain, I heard about a mysterious killing at O'Hare. Some politician's nephew. I knew then he'd been set up by one of these gangs . . ."

Vincent's body grew tense. "What do you know about that?"

"You never have solved that one, have you? . . ."

Ann Marie's announcement struck the simmering city like a crackling storm. In one stroke she had recaptured the front pages and pushed Cullen's speech recovery back near the obituaries. Aldermen Schroeder and Cutler, joined by six other dissidents in the City Council, called a rebuttal news conference an hour later. They denounced Ann Marie for attempting to destroy the democratic process and announced that they would introduce legislation to block her efforts at setting up polling booths in all the neighborhoods. Ann Marie had been joined by an ashen-faced Francis Rafferty, whom she had summoned. She smiled as they watched the live coverage of this news conference in a room adjacent to her office. She raised a restraining hand as Rafferty began a comment.

"Listen to them," she said, enjoying their exasperation. Alderman Cutler was speaking: "We also intend to investigate the source of any funds that may be used in this, this *venture* of the Mayor's . . ." Ann Marie turned off the set. "Children," she said sardonically, "just children . . ." She moved swiftly back to her desk, sat down, and looked up at Rafferty.

"Alderman, I announced that I would be my own campaign manager at the news conference earlier."

"So I heard, ma'am."

"Well, I'm changing that. I want you to run this campaign for me. Do you understand?"

Rafferty's eyes widened. He wet his lips with his tongue before he spoke. "I'd like to think about it. Yes, God help us, and pray for guidance . . ."

"Don't give me any of that hooey. Yes or no."

"It's a big question . . ."

"I suppose so." Ann Marie motioned for Rafferty to take a seat. She picked up her phone. "Helen, any luck on that call yet?"

"No," Helen's voice sounded in her ear, "I haven't been able to locate Mr. Martin yet."

"Well, how about Captain Vincent?"

"He called a little while ago. Said he was over at Police Headquarters and would be back in a little while."

Ann Marie replaced the phone. "Now I want you to take this job. You know, Alderman, the people are going to love this idea."

"Most unusual, yes, I would say, most unusual," Rafferty answered carefully.

"The people don't call me Joan of Arc by accident. This afternoon I heard voices . . ."

"Ma'am?"

"Oh, not real voices. But I understood something this afternoon. That's why I called the press conference. Nobody's going to *let* me be Mayor in this city. It's up to me. I won't be nominated unless I go after it on my own. I'm just temporary help, a Kelly Girl in City Hall. That's right, isn't it? I mean, the committeemen—and even you—you're all waiting to hear what Cullen has to say. You'd group right behind him again if he gets better. You'd form an alliance with him in a second and get rid of me. You can't stand a woman in this office. You'd dump me, then tell me it was all strictly business . . ."

Rafferty puckered his lips and furrowed his brow, thinking hard about her proposition. A cute woman. A dangerous woman.

"So, I decided that I had better call the troops together. This is what you've been looking for anyway. This is making you a partner, you and Barone and your friends. You deliver them and we have a new working relationship in this city. It's simple." Ann Marie picked up the letter opener on her desk and balanced it between her hands. "All great ideas are basically simple. Wouldn't you agree?"

Rafferty rubbed his jaw. This woman wanted power so much that she was making a better offer than she knew. She could be the Mayor if she wanted but, if she was serious about this, Rafferty would get everything he wanted too.

"You're willing to cooperate with us? I want to be quite clear about this."

Ann Marie nodded. "My sense is that we *can* work together. That's because I'm not afraid of you. I want to do a good job. I can't do it without legislative and political support. You represent certain interests, the way my cousin Monsignor Fitzmaurice represents certain interests. You have to have a certain leeway. I understand that. That's practical politics. The end result is a new team."

"You really want to put Thomas Cullen out of business, don't you?"

"Don't you?" Ann Marie dropped the letter opener onto the desk. "You've tried, I know that, I know all about that. The great Christmas coup a year before last."

"Strictly business, ma'am."

"See what I told you? It's 'business' when you do it. What is it when I do it?" Her anger, drained off in the excitement of the day, boiled over again.

"Excuse me, ma'am, but, if we're going to work together, I want to be frank. You seem to make this very personal. I'd advise against that . . ."

Ann Marie leaned forward, uncoiling her arms, palms upright, on the desk. "Mr. Rafferty, will you serve as my campaign manager or not?"

The alderman nodded slowly. "Yes, Mrs. O'Brien, I will . . ." His voice was dreamy, his sentence unfinished.

"Good." Ann Marie straightened up in her chair. The anger left her voice and entered her stiff posture. "I want you to appear with me live on the late news tonight. We'll make a joint statement. And tomorrow I want you to get busy on these booths in the neighborhoods." The anger informed her fingers as she drummed on the desk as she finished. Rafferty rose, still regarding her uncertainly, still wondering whether he had not made a Faustian pact, feeling he had, like a soul about to be judged by Saint Peter, made a final choice.

"Meet me here at nine-thirty."

Rafferty nodded and walked slowly across the room. He had what he wanted. Why did he suddenly feel the weight of his seventy-three years?

Paul Michael Martin turned over in bed. The phone had been ringing all afternoon in the sitting room. What the hell was going on? Had war been declared? The bomb would have gone off by now. He wouldn't have minded floating up to the gates of paradise, limbs intertwined with those of the young blond reporter who lay next to him. He gazed at her breasts, erect as metal bolts. Perfect.

"Well, baby, it's been a busy afternoon."

"Oh, Paulie," she purred, digging her head into the pillow and pulling the sheet up over her.

Martin tossed back his side of the covers and swung his legs down onto the floor. He stood up and walked into the sitting room. The phone rang again. He removed it from its cradle and held it against his chest. He watched the girl as she threw the sheet back and sat up on the edge of the bed. The intersection of silken planes and curves fascinated him. He put the receiver to his ear.

"What?" he blurted into the phone as he heard Barone's harsh tones. "When?" He watched the young reporter's unblemished backside as she disappeared into the bathroom. "Okay, okay, I'll be right there . . ."

"Captain, I've only got a few minutes and I want to make something clear."

Vincent stared numbly at Mrs. O'Brien. He had returned to report about his interrogation of the fruit hustlers only to find City Hall boiling over with news of the Mayor's announcement and a displeased Mrs. O'Brien waiting for him.

"Captain, have you been talking to reporters?"

He shook his head.

"Somebody has. And I don't like it one little bit. How could they know about my visit last year with you unless you told them? I'm sick and tired of being asked about this George Phillips. I had no connection with him except for that incident. Now, answer me, did you talk about that or not?"

"No, Mrs. O'Brien, no . . ."

She waved him into silence with an impatient gesture of her right hand.

"I'm serious about this, Captain. I want that story killed. If anybody asks you, I want you to keep quiet about it. Do you understand?"

Captain Vincent, still stunned by his reception, nodded.

"I want an end of this. I can't afford to have my name associated with that of a mass murderer. That should be obvious. Another thing." She took a breath. "If you have any ideas of pursuing this Phillips thing, forget it. You're supposed to be looking for corruption in government. For wrongdoing, here in City Hall. I don't want you involving yourself any further in this Phillips case. I've been told that you've had an obsession with this thing. Is that right?"

"I wouldn't call it that. No, Mrs. O'Brien, not an obsession . . ."

"Well, whatever it is, forget it. If I hear of you stirring this up any more, I'll see that you have a change of scene. I can't afford to have *you*, who are supposed to be working for *me*, looking into a murder that I have nothing to do with. I don't want any more questions at news conferences about it. Is that clear?"

Captain Vincent felt like a little boy who had brought home a gold-starred report card only to be rejected by an angry mother. He felt taken down, chagrined, hurt by the Mayor.

"Forget Phillips. That's an order." This, acidly, from a coldly staring Ann Marie.

Vincent turned and walked out of the office.

31

*T*he committeemen were outraged by Ann Marie's announcement but uncertain about what to do. Mark Richler called a number of them after hearing the news. Stay calm, don't talk to the press. Classic Richler advice. The old man will be in touch with you soon. Paul Martin picked up the papers that came off the presses at 11 P.M. and drove out to Ann Marie's home. She was just stepping out of her limousine as he stopped his car at the curb. He hurried diagonally across the lawn. Mrs. O'Brien and two bodyguards clumped up the wooden front steps of the old galleon of a house just ahead of him. They turned when they heard the soft thump of his feet on grass. Martin bounded up the stairs to join them at the front door.

"Where the hell have you been?" Ann Marie asked sharply. One of the impassive bodyguards unlocked the front door and pushed it open. Ann Marie marched in, ignoring Paul Martin, who followed the bodyguards inside.

"The usual time, Mrs. O'Brien?"

Ann Marie nodded at the strongly built police officer standing under the hall light. "You can go now."

The bodyguards moved silently out of the house. The usual police detail would sit out the night in a car directly in front of the house. Ann Marie dropped her purse on a table and moved across the living room as though Martin were not there. Charlie, her parents, Matthew stared at her from the framed pictures that stood at slightly uneven attention on the top of the piano.

"I thought you'd like to see the stories from tomorrow's papers." Martin smiled tentatively—should he be sheepish contrite or little boy charming?—as Ann Marie turned to look at him.

"Paul, where the hell were you all day? This was an important day. You didn't cover the news conferences, you didn't return my phone calls . . ." Ann Marie felt, for the moment at least, immune to his charm, free to be angry at him. She folded her arms and stepped away.

"I covered the news conference from the studio. My producer wanted me to comment from there. We had a panel of experts . . ." He tucked the newspapers under his right arm and followed Ann Marie as she walked past the piano into the spacious old-fashioned dining room.

"Annie, I did a terrific commentary."

He reached his left arm out and touched her on the shoulder as she pushed the swinging door that led into the kitchen. She flipped a switch and an overhead fluorescent fixture buzzed and blinked light onto the white surfaces of the large room.

"They don't build kitchens like this anymore, Annie . . ." He pulled her around so that she faced him directly. "And they don't make women like you. Here, look at the headlines . . ." He flopped the papers down on the stretch of countertop next to the sink. Ann Marie, warmed slightly by Martin's manner, did not shrug his hands away from her shoulders. She studied the front pages. "O'Brien Bombshell!" on the *Sun-Times,* "Mayor O'Brien Challenges Dem Leaders," on the *Tribune.* Her picture was prominently displayed on both.

"That was a hell of an idea, Annie. Where'd you get it?"

Ann Marie turned the pages of the papers. She had astonished the street-smart old city once again. There were sidebars, man-in-the-street reactions, everything she could have wished. She flipped hurriedly to the editorial pages. One paper applauded her move without qualification. "Governing is a delicate art. Does Mrs. O'Brien possess the sensitivity to match her sensational moves? The city needs a *new* start but excessive impulsivity can lead to *false* starts . . ."

"What's wrong with these . . . these bastards?" she asked through clenched teeth. She formed a fist and slammed it down on the spread-out editorial page. The papers, a nearby drinking glass, and a washcloth jumped in unison on the Formica.

"Annie, Annie, don't get so mad. Expressing caution is one of the things publishers like their papers to do. That and 'viewing with alarm.' If they couldn't do that, they'd go out of business." Ann Marie bent slightly forward to finish reading the editorial. Paul closed his hands on her shoulders again. He could feel Ann Marie's body stiffen as she finished the next paragraph. "Thomas H. Cullen, recovering from his recent stroke, remains chairman of the Cook County Democratic Party. While this paper often disagreed with him and his policies, it remains true that his sagacity and measured judgment frequently benefited the city. Perhaps Mrs. O'Brien, whose youth and energy are so attractive, might still learn some lessons in style from her former political mentor."

Ann Marie snatched at the page, crumpled it in her right hand, and threw it at a wastebasket across the room. It hit the wall and fell silently to the floor.

"Damn them!" she snarled. "I'm sick of Cullen, sick of hearing about him . . ."

Martin turned her around and pulled her close to him. She did not yield easily, she didn't yield at all. She felt tense, coiled within herself, dangerous. "Annie, you're in charge now. It doesn't make any difference what they say." He patted her on the back. "Would you like a drink? How about a drink?" Ann Marie squirmed away from Martin's grasp.

"There's some wine in the refrigerator."

Paul opened the refrigerator door and removed a half gallon jug of Chablis. Ann Marie picked up the remains of the newspapers and took them in a jumble to the small breakfast nook off the back stairs. Martin joined her with two glasses brimming with wine. He sat across from her at the small table. She riffled through the paper, taking in the news about herself as an antidote to the poison in the tail of the editorial. Martin touched his glass to hers. "To you, Annie. The city is yours."

Ann Marie, pout lines loosening in her face, sipped from her glass. She felt at least partially restored by the other coverage in the paper. "There's only a paragraph or two about Cullen starting to talk again," she said with satisfaction.

Paul watched her as she leaned back stretching some of her tension loose. That item about Cullen, that cut-down slug of a story, that's what she had been looking for. Cullen reduced in size, Cullen in his proper place, Cullen on page 8. They sipped their wine in silence.

"You should be celebrating, Annie. You killed the old dragon today."

"I don't want to kill him," she said swiftly. "I, I just want his shadow off me. *I'm* Mayor now and I'm not going to let anybody forget it." Martin studied her face carefully. She still looked prickly.

"Annie, now that you've announced, now that you're pulling Rafferty and Barone and . . ."

"Who told you that?"

"Just a guess, an educated guess . . ."

"Barone talked to you. That's right, isn't it? Tell me." She was pressing hard.

"Well . . ."

"The truth, Paul, the truth. Did Barone call you? He told you I talked to Rafferty, right? You knew everything before I announced him as campaign manager tonight . . ."

"What if I did?" Martin answered heatedly. "What the hell do you want to do, control everybody? You know goddamn well Barone and I are close. You know very well we made arrangements. You were there, for Crissake, at the apartment . . ."

"I don't want to hear about the apartment . . ."

"Why, because it really happened? What the hell do you think you can do, make the world over every day?" Martin placed his glass on the table and took her hands in his. "Annie, you're not God. And I'm human. You know, somewhere in that Catholic schoolgirl's heart of yours, that you've already agreed to do business with Barone, Rafferty, Wendel, with any of them who will do what you say." His voice grew louder. "Admit it, admit it, for Crissake. You can't have it both ways. You've got to be realistic. We fucked in that apartment. It really happened. There's no taking it back. It didn't disappear when we burned the pictures. And we fucked back in there." He swiveled an arm in the direction of the living room. "And you can't take that back either. You knock Cullen out of his job, you knock him off the front page. Then you tell me you don't want to kill him. Christ, Annie, what the hell do you think you're doing?" He took a breath. Ann Marie stared at him blankly. He was right. Goddamn him, he was right.

"Shut up, Paul, shut up." Ann Marie twisted to free her wrists from his tight grip on them.

"Oh, no. Oh, no." Martin leaned forward, a lock of his black hair falling across his forehead. His brook-clear eyes did not blink. "Annie, there's no going back." He lowered his voice. "You *are* the Mayor. You love it, you love the big car, the bodyguards, the front page. You love it more for that than for anything else. And that's fine. I helped make you. I'm going to help you be Mayor. We're going to get rich together. No more of this el cheapo wine. But you can't be two things at once, you've got to live in the real world . . ."

"What's the real world? *Your* world?" Ann Marie sneered at him. "You and your friends and your nice little deals. You and the way you play ball with the people you're supposed to be reporting on. Don't give me any sermons . . ."

"Annie, my world *is* the real world. Christ, you've got the instincts for it. But either come to terms with it or go back to your Catholic school hypocrisy. Christ, you should know enough about the bankers, about Barnes and his crowd. And your cousin Morgan. Where the hell do you think his silk shirts come from? Who the hell do you think he deals with?"

Ann Marie, for reasons she could not understand, was surprised.

"Barone?" she asked softly.

"Yes, and anybody else he has to. I like him. Son of a bitch is a realist. Thank God, he's around, what with a Cardinal who spends most of his time praying."

"You think you know everything . . ."

"Annie, that's your city, that's what you want to govern. It's no Sunday School class." He relaxed his grip on her wrists. "Annie, you're no virgin, either . . ."

"Shut up!" Ann Marie slapped him sharply. He grabbed the wrist of the striking hand. She lunged forward to free herself and the wineglasses wobbled beneath their twisting arms.

"No, Annie, *you* shut up for a change. *I* understand you."

"You only understand yourself. That's all you see. Yourself reflected in the world around you. You don't seem to think anybody can be decent or honest. You think everything is bent . . ."

"Jesus, Annie, I've been taking lessons from you." He pulled her up away from the table. One of the wineglasses tipped, splashed its contents on the smooth table surface, rolled over the edge and smashed on the floor. Ann Marie pulled back and Martin ground the stem of the glass under his shoe. He pinned her against the wall of the hallway beyond the back stairs.

"Annie, make up your mind. You can't run the city halfway. Swim with the barracudas, let them eat you, or get out of the water. Maybe I'm the only guy in this town who'll tell you the truth. They'll sweet-talk you, they'll lie. You need me around, you need somebody to tell you the truth . . ." He leaned against her, lowering his face close to hers. She twisted her head away. Martin kissed her on the side of the cheek, moving his head in motion with hers, searching out the thin line of her lips. She struggled, ducking away. He twisted down after her. She brought her head up suddenly, butting him expertly in the right eye. He yelped and let her go.

"Jesus, Annie, my eye!" He put his hand to it as she slipped past him and back into the kitchen area. Ann Marie was disheveled, breathless, and she had bitten her lip in the encounter. "Damn you!" She moved to the sink and turned on the cold-water tap. She dampened a cloth and pressed it on her mouth. Martin crowded in next to her, reached his hands under the faucet, and splashed water freely on his face. Ann Marie stepped back and looked at him. The area around his squinting, puffy eye was discolored. The rage drained out of her at the sight of his damaged looks. She had taken the round again. She felt better the way she had after she found the page 8 story about Cullen. She had won. She could afford to be nice to Martin.

"Oh, Paul, here, here, let me fix it." Martin, water-spattered, lifted back from the sink. Ann Marie pressed the damp cloth on his eye. "Sit down, Paul, sit down a minute." She guided him back to the breakfast nook. The glass fragments snapped and crunched as he stepped on them again. He seated himself, leaned his head back, and allowed her to pat his face dry.

"I'll get some ice." Ann Marie avoided the particles of stemware and the puddled wine as she stepped toward the refrigerator. Martin, his eyelid pouched out like a battered fighter's, watched as she scooped some ice from a tray and dropped it in a towel.

"That's what I mean about you, Annie. You fight dirty and think you're Clara Barton at the same time."

Ann Marie smiled as she advanced on him with the improvised ice pack.

"Why is it that, whenever you're here, my house ends up a mess?"

The news could not be kept from Cullen forever. Besides, a number of the more influential committeemen, including Hy Lowenstein and Frank Ryan, told Mark Richler that Tom Cullen had better make a statement of some kind soon. Pressure was building. They had to know where they stood. Was Cullen coming back to the party office? It would only be a question of time before some of the younger committeemen began a movement to elect a new chairman. Richler and Maureen broke the news to Cullen the morning after Ann Marie's press conference. They brought the papers. They were spread out across Cullen's lap as he heard them out. He glanced through his dark-rimmed glasses at the headlines and flipped through the pages of the papers with his right hand. Maureen and Richler talked steadily while he examined the papers. The former Mayor's expression, caught as if by a fishhook at the left side of his mouth, remained unreadable.

"Hy says you ought to say something, Tom. He says the other committeemen need a signal from you."

Cullen looked gravely at Richler while he spoke. He removed his glasses with his good hand and placed them on top of the papers.

"I'm getting in a wheelchair today," Cullen said blandly.

Richler glanced at Maureen. Had he heard what they told him?

"It's great what they can do for you these days, that's what the doctor told me. Rehabilitation, that's the ticket. They learned a lot in the war. Did you know that, Maureen?"

His daughter swallowed hard. "Yes, Daddy, I've heard that."

The papers began to slip off his lap and Cullen clapped his hand over his glasses to steady them. Maureen stood up to straighten them out. "Do you want me to take these, Daddy?"

"No, no. I'd like to look them over. I can read pretty well, thank God."

Richler gazed at the old man intently.

"Tom, what should I tell the committeemen, Lowenstein and Ryan and the others?"

"Mark, do you think you could get Helen Morrison to come over? There's a lot of thank you notes I should get around to."

Maureen and Mark exchanged puzzled glances.

"Helen works for Mrs. O'Brien now," Mark said softly.

"Oh, sure, sure, what could I be thinking? You know being in the hospital, not being able to speak, I thought about a lot of things." Cullen motioned toward his water glass on the bedside table. Maureen handed it to him.

"After all, I was Mayor a long time, I've been head of the party a long time." He sighed. "The doctor would stand there and tell me I'd be fine. I didn't believe him. We Irish know the signs of the fellow trying to make you feel good." Cullen sipped the water. "And my old friend, Les Rudy, the head of the hospital—hell of a nice guy—told me about the rehabilitation. Seemed like a lot of work to me. And what for? I was sure they'd move in the City Council this time. I knew it long before you told me. Knew in my stomach." He shifted himself awkwardly in the bed. "So in my heart I decided that an old wreck of a man like me ought to face the facts." He looked from Maureen to Richler. "It's true, it's true." He gestured with his glasses. "I talked to Maureen here about funeral arrangements. Isn't that so?" He looked at Maureen for a moment.

"The O'Brien woman is young. She's bright. Mark, you used to tell me she lacked political experience." Cullen shook his massive head.

"Anyway, this rehab stuff, this long road ahead. It's really too long for me. That's what I said to myself. And I thought of your mother, Maureen. I thought she must be waiting for me. Time for me to go and join her. This is a wonderful hospital, but I decided I'd had enough of it . . ."

Maureen bit her lip, fighting against tears.

"Now you tell me the whole thing's true. Annie's running the city and Rafferty's going to manage her next campaign." Cullen slipped his glasses on and held up the paper. "Look at that!" He dropped the paper and leaned back on his pillow.

"Funny thing. My mind was all made up. This Ann Marie is a powerful woman." He let the statement hang in the air as if he expected a question.

"What do you mean?" Richler asked.

"She's been able to do what nobody else in the city has been able to do."

"What's that?"

Cullen winked. "She's made me stop feeling sorry for myself. She's made me want to get better . . ." A smile, bent at the left corner, spread across his face and he chuckled. Maureen and Richler smiled and, for the first time in weeks, laughed too. "That, Mark, is what you can tell the committeemen."

32

*A*nn Marie fired Cap Malloy at the end of August. She did not speak to him herself. It was time he retired, time he stopped sticking his withered old head into her office, telling the same old stories. Besides, Cap reminded her of Cullen, who, according to reports, was working on rehabilitation. Sometimes he used a wheelchair, and sometimes he walked a little with a cane. She was the boss now. The voting booths had to be disguised as "Information Kiosks" in the various neighborhoods. But the people could still sign up to support her. "A stroke of populist genius," *Time* said. *Time* only mentioned Cullen in passing. *Newsweek* didn't mention him at all.

The committeemen were still balking at offering her their public support.

"What the hell is the matter with those men? Don't they understand what the people are telling them? Don't they know Cullen is finished?"

"The more you say that, ma'am," Francis Rafferty responded, "the more you make him a factor."

"Look, Francis, if you can't get them to make a statement of support by Labor Day, I'll find somebody who will."

"These men aren't used to the new way that you're doing things. I mean, glory be to God, they don't like publicity, for one thing. They don't like putting all their cards on the table when, according to their experience—old-fashioned as that is, ma'am—it's still early in the game."

"They're still afraid of Cullen. Is that right?"

"Not exactly. However, and may God be my witness, we have to continue to educate them. They find it hard to get used to a new idea."

"I want a pledge of support from them—from a group of them at least —by Labor Day. And I want the union chiefs together that day too. Have you got that lined up?"

"Begging your pardon, they've asked for a meeting with you first."

"What for?"

"They want to make sure they understand your attitudes . . ."

"My attitudes are pretty clear. I'm going to press them to hold the line."

"Yes, ma'am, but that's not the same as establishing good relationships with them. Thomas Cullen used to say—"

"Don't quote Cullen to me. He's the one who played ball with them. He gave them everything they wanted. That game is over."

Ann Marie tapped a letter opener against the surface of her desk blotter. Rafferty searched noisily in his briefcase.

"Madam Mayor, would tomorrow at ten be agreeable for you to meet with the representatives of labor?"

Ann Marie nodded and took the paper he handed across the desk to her.

"That's a list of the men who will be coming."

Ann Marie studied the paper and dropped it back on her desk.

"Now as to the fund-raising dinner. Thanks be to God, the response has been just fine. It's set for the twenty-first, which, ma'am, I believe will be your birthday. The theme will be 'An Irish Birthday Party for the Mayor.' We expect the Vice-President, yes, and the Prime Minister of Ireland is coming. They're going to build an Irish village street, a copy of the one your grandfather came from, as the background for the dinner."

Ann Marie smiled. Now Rafferty was talking.

"And there's one other thing I'd like to talk about with you." Rafferty's tone shifted slightly.

"Yes?"

"Well, we think you'll be pleased. The developers have decided to name the entire area on the northwest side after you and your late husband. We've made real headway with the plans. It will be quite a place. O'Brien City, that's the name they want to use. It *will* be a regular little city. So, the board felt that, inasmuch as you're the Mayor, the entire complex should be a tribute to you and your late, beloved husband, Captain O'Brien."

Ann Marie smiled. "Why, that's very nice . . ." She hesitated. "What's the catch?"

"No catch at all. As a matter of fact, the board wants to vote you a share of the profits. Well, ma'am, it's a small share, a fraction of a fraction. Still, in these times and with your expenses . . ."

"No," she said decisively. "The name's okay. Tell them I'd rather have them contribute to the campaign."

"They've already voted it in a board meeting."

"Change the designation. Get it into the campaign fund."

"I must say, Madam Mayor, I think that's a good decision. In the campaign fund you won't have to pay any taxes on the money. If you do want to use a small amount for a personal expense, you only pay taxes on that portion . . ."

"Yes, yes, I know all about that."

"You learn quickly, ma'am."

"That's what they always said at school."

Captain Vincent would have dropped his interest in Phillips except that Palmer told him that the killer had accomplices. Vincent couldn't go back to the television station. A.M., as the headlines now called her, would hear about that. He had learned as much as he needed from the videotape anyway.

He chanced a call to Barnes's secretary. Yes, she remembered making the arrangements. She could find the name if he could hold on. The River Livery, yes, that was it. Yes, Miss Meuser, it was a bit of a tongue twister. Thanks very much.

Vincent inspected the headquarters of the River Livery from across the white, summer-lighted street. The garage lay on the west lip of the Chicago River next to the tangle of expressways. Vincent walked casually past the building. A caramel-colored Cadillac, its diesel engine rattling, moved across the sidewalk and into the street. Another driver with a moustache. The captain turned and walked into the small office. A dark-haired young man stretched and yawned behind the desk, which seemed to be held together by tabs and scotch-taped notices.

"Help you?"

"Yes, I'm with a business that's interested in buying a small building nearby. Only problem, there's no garage space. Do you people rent out any slots?"

"Not that I know of. You'd have to ask the old man. How much space you need?" The young man scratched his stubbled chin.

"Is he here?"

"Not right now."

"When do you expect him?"

"Hard to say. He's usually at the other office." The stress of answering questions showed on the languid young man. He handed a business card to Vincent without saying a word. The captain nodded, stuffed the card into his side pocket, and walked back into the heat-glazed street. He glanced at the card. "Five Brothers Limousines—Anywhere, Any Time, Anybody." The address was on the West Side.

"Well, Morgan, Cousin Morgan, to what do I owe this visit?" The voice was upper-crust Catholic, familiar with priest relatives, slightly acid.

Monsignor Fitzmaurice smiled tightly. "It seemed time to make a call on my illustrious cousin. I know how busy you've been this summer. The Cardinal asked me to send you his best wishes. He's praying for you, he wants you to know that."

"He likes to pray, doesn't he?"

"Most unusual. A saint, they say. Of course, that makes my work all the heavier."

Fitzie looked good. Trim, well groomed, good black silk suit, a notch of blood red beneath his real linen Roman collar. Not one of those plastic inserts never quite cleaned under the rectory sink faucet. None of that for Fitzie.

"Not much left of our family, Morgan."

"Not here in Chicago anyway."

"With you entering the church, the Fitzmaurice line is coming to an end."

"Odd how that happens with some once-big Irish families, isn't it? All of a sudden they've all gone off or all died out. Like the Mulqueens. Sold them a big plot, never thinking they'd need it, and it's all filled up now. The boys all died young . . ."

"Yes, the boys died young." Ann Marie cleared her throat. "What is it exactly that I can do for you?"

"Well, Ann Marie, I do have some business matters to discuss."

Ann Marie eased back in her chair. "Yes?" she asked blankly.

"As you know, I have had extensive responsibility for affairs of the diocese." He raised his dark eyebrows as though they bore the weight of his duty. "I have been asked, informally of course, by the Apostolic Delegate to inquire about something." He leaned forward. "This is at the highest level of negotiation. The Holy Father is planning a peace tour of the world. This fall in a ten-day period he is going to fly completely around the world, stopping at major cities on all the continents in order to dramatize his new peace proposals. He cannot stop in many places, the way the Pope did some years ago. One city in the biggest of countries, that's the plan." He lowered his voice. "Archbishop Lyne, the Delegate, is from Chicago originally. He would like Chicago, at the center of the country, to be the place for the papal visit in the United States."

This was too good to believe. Fitzmaurice talked on about the arrangements, the need for guaranteed support by the chosen city. Ann Marie was busy with a fantasy of herself standing next to the Pope—what kind of a dress would she wear?—welcoming the sturdy man in white to Chicago.

"It would solve many problems if Chicago could accept. Avoid complications in Washington. Avoid them in New York where the UN is. May I convey your reaction to the Delegate?" That was cousin Morgan, all business.

Ann Marie, the front pages already spreading out in her imagination, nodded. "Of course, of course. You'll have our full cooperation. When will this be? We need some time."

"The end of October." The Monsignor explained that the exact date would be chosen that week. It depended on Chicago's willingness to co-operate.

Cousin Morgan. Not so bad after all. She had never liked him much, not since she heard him explain the advantages of selling advertising space on church envelopes. But he was the bearer of glad tidings. What more could she want in heavily Catholic Chicago than the handsome Pope turning his enigmatic Slavic smile toward her?

"Yes, yes," she said impatiently. "We'll get a committee together right away. But you can tell the Archbishop that, yes, Chicago will be glad to have him."

They concluded the discussion, agreeing to have the special events people work closely with diocesan authorities.

"There is one more matter I'd like to discuss with you . . ."

"Yes?"

Fitzmaurice pulled a folded sheaf of papers out of his briefcase.

"I think you will be interested in this, Ann Marie." He unfolded the clutch of stiff papers and placed them on her desk. It was a set of maps and plans.

"What's all this?"

"Plans for a new cemetery."

"What?" The Pope vanished from the stage of her attention. Ann Marie had seen enough of cemeteries. "This is your business, Morgan, not mine."

"Let me fill you in on the concept before you make up your mind." Fitzmaurice spoke smoothly, confidently. "It's true, isn't it, that the vitality of the big cities of this country depends on people continuing to live in them?"

"Yes," she said hesitantly.

"Exactly. The problem is that people forget the other half of the equation. If you encourage people to live in the city, in a sense, you're also encouraging them to die in the city. The notions are inseparable in theology and in urban planning. That's the genius of this idea."

"What idea?" Ann Marie asked uncomfortably. "What the hell are you talking about?"

"It's all very well to build apartments and condominiums in the city. But you have to support them with services, with shops, and all the rest that goes into maintaining metropolitan life. We have precious little to cover the support services needed for death."

Ann Marie swallowed and pulled back from the display of plans in front of her.

"Die in the city now and you will probably be buried in the suburbs. Families face long trips to visit the graves of their loved ones. Suppose, just suppose that we had a centrally located cemetery. A high-rise mausoleum, tastefully done. The best of materials. A religious symbol, a sacred column in the skyline reminding people of eternity. Think about it. What would make the complete life cycle possible again in the city, the way it was in village life years ago? This is the answer."

Ann Marie held up her right hand, policeman style. "Wait a minute. I can always read your brochure. What is it you want to talk to me about?"

"Location is the key. Easily reachable by public transportation, underground parking a definite possibility. Perhaps even a tie-in with a local subway station. A chapel, a library, offices for counselors. But location is essential. Look." Monsignor Fitzmaurice half-rose from his chair and pointed to a city map. "Here is a very desirable area. It has just about everything we need. There are two other possibilities, but this is really the best location."

Ann Marie cocked her head at her enthusiastic cousin. "What do you want from me?"

Fitzmaurice eased back into his chair. "Well, help with the land, of course. Condemnation proceedings will be necessary. Rezoning. It's very complicated. The city even owns some of the land that would be required for this site. And we would need your support to establish an underground tie-in with a subway station. Not much, escalators, an arcade. It might take years without your help, and a lot more money."

Ann Marie felt numb. Death was not a visitor she wanted to entertain. Now cousin Morgan wanted to build a luxury condominium for it in the city.

"I presume we can count on your support."

"Let me think about it. Yes, yes, I suppose so. Yes." She gestured at the plans on her desk. "Can you take these away?"

"Thank you, Ann Marie. You'll be glad you helped. Can I expect your support for the first site?"

"Well, I think we'll have to have it checked out. I'll put you in touch with Larson in the Planning Department." She did not want to talk about it anymore.

Monsignor Fitzmaurice closed his briefcase. "And how is Matthew?"

Matthew? She hadn't seen Matthew very much in the last several weeks. There had been so many dinners, so many meetings, so many nights when she arrived home only after he was asleep. Monsignor Fitzmaurice talked on about having spoken on the phone to their Aunt Molly the other day. Great old gal.

Matthew. Good God, he's ten years old.

"So I told Molly that I'd come out and see her when I was in your neck of the woods . . ."

Matthew, Matthew . . .

"I appreciate your time, Ann Marie. We'll be seeing a lot of you, what with planning for the Pope and all." Ann Marie stood up and escorted Monsignor Fitzmaurice to the door. She signaled to Helen Morrison to come into her office.

Ann Marie was standing by her desk when Helen, pad in hand, walked in.

"Helen, cancel my appointments for the rest of the day . . ."

"You've got the Foreign Affairs dinner and the reception at the Art Institute just before that . . ."

"Cancel them."

"And Mr. Barone is due in a half hour."

"Cancel him too."

"Everything?"

"Everything."

"Shall I give a reason?"

"My reason is I'm not going. Tell them I want the car ready. And call my aunt. Tell her I'm coming home for dinner."

"Well, it was such short notice. I mean, it was the last thing I expected . . ." Aunt Molly, aproned, mittened for work at the oven, had come from the kitchen to greet Ann Marie. "And I told Matthew he could go to the Cub Scout meeting tonight. He so wants to go . . ."

"He can go next week . . ."

"No, Ann, this is the first meeting, this is all the dear boy's been talking about. He's such a good boy . . ."

"Molly, I've canceled my appointments to spend an evening at home. There's no point to it, I'm wasting my time if Matthew is going to be out."

"You'll break his heart if you make him stay home." Aunt Molly turned abruptly. "The brownies! They'll be black as coal . . ." She hurried toward the kitchen.

Damn it. Now I have to make an appointment to see my own son.

Ann Marie followed Molly through the swinging door into the kitchen.

"There, just in time . . ." Molly held a large square pan of brownies, chocolate lava crust smoking. "Just the same as your mother used to make . . ." The smells, the feel as a little girl of coming into the kitchen after school flashed into Ann Marie's mind.

"You see, Ann, the dear boy has to bring these along. All the other lads are bringing something. It's important for him to feel part of the group, to have friends his own age." Molly placed the tray on the cutting board at the side of the sink.

"He'll be down in a minute. I'm fixing him a hamburger for an early supper." She turned back to the stove. "Would you like me to fix one for you? It's no trouble."

Ann Marie stared at Molly's back. Good scout Molly has taken over as

Matthew's mother. At City Hall everybody wanted something from her, everybody had just a little more business to discuss. In her own home she was being fit in just before a Cub Scout meeting. Ann Marie thought she had been imposing on Aunt Molly all these months. And she was actually having the time of her life raising the son she had never had for herself. Ann Marie seethed, stamped out of the kitchen, shoved the swinging door open, banging it loudly against the wall, and headed for the living room. She picked up the briefcase that the bodyguard had left on the hall table, leaned her weight down on it through the column of her arm, released it, and headed back to the kitchen. She ran the city. By God, she would run her own house.

Matthew had just come down the back stairs into the kitchen as she boomed through the swinging door. He was wearing his blue Cub Scout uniform.

"Hi, Mom, what are you doing here?" Matthew walked over to the cooling tray of brownies, dug a finger into the edge for a sample. "Hot, Aunt Molly! Wow!"

"I came home to see you," Ann Marie said. "I haven't been able to see you much lately."

Matthew slipped into the booth of the breakfast nook. Ann Marie walked over and kissed him.

"It's okay, Mom. I know you're busy being Mayor. The kids think it's neat that you're the Mayor."

Ann Marie did not know what to say. She edged into the breakfast nook across the table from him. Aunt Molly was at the stove, the aroma of panbroiled hamburgers rising from the spitting frying pan in front of her. "Matthew's doing beautiful work in school," she called cheerily, a woman at home, at peace, in charge of her kitchen.

Matthew lowered his head and traced a line with his finger across the tabletop.

"Tell me, Matthew, tell me about your school work." Ann Marie reached across and touched her son's busy hand.

He raised his eyes—pale blue, as clear as dawn—and shrugged his shoulders. "Ohh . . ."

"Tell your mother what Sister Mercy said. Tell her . . ." Molly did not turn away from her sizzling pan.

"Well . . ." Matthew pulled his hand free and squiggled another design on the table surface. "She said that my work was very good . . ."

"Go on, child," Molly called.

"And that maybe I could be Mayor someday too . . ."

Ann Marie watched her son, emotion building within her.

"Mom, can I come down and visit your office again someday?"

Ann Marie nodded as Matthew looked up at her.

"Good! Can I bring some of the guys? Maybe Sergeant Berrigan could show us around . . ."

"Sure, Matthew," Ann Marie said, in control again. "I'll have you driven down in a police car."

"No such thing, Ann," Aunt Molly declared, turning from her head-quarter position over the burners. "Matthew's whole class is going on a field trip to a City Council meeting next week. He should ride in the bus, same as the others. You want them making fun of you, Matthew?" She removed the hamburgers from the pan and placed them on split rolls that had just been toasted in another part of the oven. "No such thing. The talk would be all over the place. Isn't Mrs. O'Brien the cute one, using the tax money to ride her son downtown when he's no better than anyone else?" She spread french-fried potatoes, plucked deftly from their warming cove in a lower oven, on each plate. Molly was mistress of the range, mistress of the house. Ann Marie had never seen her this way before. Molly was bounteous, serene, confident of every move.

"Eat, the two of you," Molly called as she turned to check the oven.

"Aren't you going to eat?" Ann Marie asked her as she cut her own hamburger in two.

"No, Ann. I've got a little meeting to go to. The Altar and Rosary Society. We're having a pickup dinner at Katie Murphy's tonight. I'm bringing the salad. Seeing the boy would be at the Cub Scouts, and I haven't been out myself much, I just thought I'd go . . ." Molly wiped her hands on her apron. "And how are things at City Hall? The people are all voting for your program. Peg Foley called me today. Told me how the whole neighborhood where she lives—and you know they're got the Mexicans there in the next block to her now—well, they're all voting for you . . ."

Cub Scouts. The Altar and Rosary Society. Ann Marie knew who must be in charge of that. She had hurried home to a house that would be empty within another twenty minutes.

"Of course, we won't be late. Nine o'clock, the two of us'll be home."

Ann Marie took a bite of her hamburger. "Matthew."

"Yeah?" Between bites, sweetly distracted by thoughts of the Cub Scouts.

"Matthew, do you still wear your cowboy hat?"

"Sometimes. Not all the time. Sometimes, though." He poured ketchup on his pile of french fries and turned toward Aunt Molly. "These don't taste the same as Hamburger House."

"And when, young man, have you been eating at *that* place?" Molly wanted an answer. "*Junk food,* that's what they call it, and that's what it is."

"Oh, a long time ago," Matthew said. "These are good. I mean these are *very* good. They just taste different."

"Matthew, I usually do come home very late."

"It's okay, Mom." Matthew's absolution was too quick, too readily imparted for her. He gulped from his glass of milk.

"Not so much at one try, Matthew," Molly said reprovingly. "It'll make you sick."

"I hope I don't disturb you." Ann Marie looked at large-bosomed Aunt Molly happily mothering her son. "Or you either, Molly."

"I sleep the sleep of the just, Ann," Molly answered. "If you'll excuse me, I'll slip upstairs and change."

Ann Marie and her son were alone. Was there a gulf between them that she could do nothing about?

"Sometimes, Matthew, there are people with me. We have meetings."

"Yeah, I know." His tone was neutral.

"How do you know?"

"Oh, I hear you once in a while." He took another bite of hamburger.

"What do you hear?"

"Oh, just stuff. You know . . ."

"You mean voices? Things like that?"

"I guess so . . ."

"You never get out of bed, you never get scared, and get out of bed though, do you?"

He spoke with a full mouth. "One night I walked down the hall . . ."

Yes? You walked down the hall . . . "What? Was that all you did?"

"I looked out and saw the police car in front . . ."

"Is that all?"

"There you go, Matthew." Molly, wearing a blue dress with large fan-like designs on it, entered the kitchen like a ship under sail. "Time for your meeting."

"Can I have a brownie?"

"At your meeting. With the other scouts. Not a bite before that." Molly sliced the brownies as she spoke. "Here, I'll just put a bit of wax paper on this."

Matthew hopped off his chair, kissed his mother, and, at the sound of a honking horn, took the tray of brownies, kissed Aunt Molly, and pushed swiftly through the swinging door.

"I'll wash these later, Ann," Molly said, as she piled the dishes in the sink. "I'm off now myself." She opened the refrigerator, removed a plastic bowl of salad, lifted the cover to inspect it, and smiled at Ann Marie. "It was good of you to come home early. If we'd only known! But you'll enjoy a quiet few hours. Nice change for you." Molly headed for the door, "See you at nine," and was gone.

Ann Marie rose from the table and stepped across to the sink. She turned on the hot water and let it run on the dinner plates before she placed them in the dishwasher. She looked under the sink for some liquid soap and washed out the frying pan. In a few minutes, she had tidied up the kitchen. *Her* kitchen. *Formerly* her kitchen. She turned on the dishwasher and, as it rumbled into its first cycle, she walked back through the dining room.

She was alone. She had nothing to do.

Ann Marie felt tired and sat down on the sofa by the fireplace. What had Matthew ever heard? Probably nothing.

She was trapped in the dark cavity that guilt had clawed out of her day. What comfort she had depended on offhanded reassurances from her ten-year-old son and her sixty-seven-year-old aunt. They had seen nothing, they had heard nothing. God knew they had said nothing. Damn! Ann Marie lived at the center of a turning wheel, shimmying out favors along the spokes to those who rode the rim. Power was the hub of her new existence, dark and empty and of no weight at all. Like Charlie's casket. She picked up the phone and dialed Paul Martin's number.

33

Ann Marie was unable to locate Paul Michael Martin. Richard Barone, upset about his canceled appointment, reached her with a request to see her the next morning. She tried to go over some paper work but found it difficult to concentrate. When Matthew got home, just before nine, he wanted to watch something on television that Aunt Molly had given him permission to see. Molly herself was full of Altar and Rosary Society gossip. Did she know Monsignor Butler, the pastor, had had another gallstone attack? And that Mrs. Custer's son, the Jesuit, had joined a band of revolutionaries off in the jungles somewhere? A regular Marxist, could you believe it? Ann Marie sat up with Matthew watching a science fiction adventure story about the red queen of Mars, then saw him to bed. His cowboy hat lay on the dresser. Maybe he had outgrown it. When she came downstairs, Aunt Molly was doing needlepoint in front of the television set. The news was halfway over.

"Molly?"

Molly looked up over her glasses and smiled. Ann Marie sat down in the chair next to her. The television weatherman blared loudly about continuing warm weather.

"Do you mind if I turn this down?"

"As you please, dear."

Ann Marie lowered the volume and took her seat again.

"I just wanted to thank you for taking care of Matthew all this time."

"He's a darling boy, Ann, a darling boy. A boy, of course, with a little mischief in him. But he wouldn't be a boy otherwise."

"I, I . . ."

"There's no need to say anything. I've enjoyed taking care of him. He's no trouble."

The power in City Hall was Ann Marie's. Here it was all Molly's. Aunt Molly, needlepoint design draped across her lap, grandnephew tucked in bed upstairs, looked the picture of contentment. Contentment. What would it be like? It sounded good, but it might drive Ann Marie crazy. And yet, regarding the plump, barely lined face of Aunt Molly—how she had underestimated Aunt Molly!—she wished for a share of it.

"Ann, have you ever thought of getting married again?" Molly did not raise her eyes from the work of her scuttling fingers.

"Well, sometimes, I guess. Not really . . ." Molly unnerved her. Ann Marie searched the cabinet of her sudden inspiration but it was empty.

"You're still young," Molly said, breaking off a piece of yarn. "Even though you're the Mayor and all, even though you're so busy, you should think about it."

"It's not that easy. You don't just find a man and marry him."

"I know, Annie. Haven't I been looking all these years?" She dug at the design in front of her.

Ann Marie picked up a section of the day's newspaper that lay on the hassock in front of her. The television played on quietly in front of them.

"Ann, why did you ask Matthew about his cowboy hat tonight?" Molly's eyes remained fixed on the developing pattern before her.

"Something to talk about, I guess. I just haven't seen him with it lately. He used to wear it all the time."

"Is that all?" Ann Marie pretended not to hear the question. Molly tugged at a knot and looked up at her niece.

"Ann dear, I want you to be happy. I know how hard your job is." She adjusted the rubbery mat of the needlepoint. Ann Marie pretended to read.

"I think you asked him about the cowboy hat because you found it on the stairs one night." Molly's voice was calm, matter-of-fact, deliberate.

Ann Marie felt panicky. "I don't know what you're talking about . . ."

"It's all right, Ann, you can tell the truth. You're like you were when you were a little girl sometimes. Your mother would ask you whether you had done something and you'd say no. Do you think sometimes that little boys are more truthful than little girls?"

Ann exploded, "Molly, what the hell are you driving at?"

Molly did not look up. "Ann, I put that hat on the stairs. You ought to know that. I did it to warn you, to make you think about what you were getting into. In your own house, with your own darling son asleep upstairs! Laughing and burning things in the fireplace! It was the laughter —then I smelled the smoke—that woke me. And a hot night in June. So naturally I thought I should investigate. I didn't know what to do. I went to make sure Matthew wasn't awake and, in the moonlight, I saw his hat on the bed. I thought, well, if Annie sees this, she'll think twice about what she's getting into. Then not long ago you had the fight in the kitchen one night. Well, Matthew *did* hear that. And I *just* kept him from going downstairs. I made up a story and got him back in bed. And, like the time before, got in my own bed and made a sound so you'd think I was asleep when I heard you stopping by my door to check."

Ann Marie breathed deeply. "Molly, you're wonderful and all, but this is *none* of your business. *None* of your business!" She threw the paper down on the floor.

"It *is* my business, Ann. First off, I'm your godmother. I'm bound to be interested in your spiritual welfare. I swore to it when I held you in my arms when you were christened. Second, I've been taking care of Matthew for almost two years. Oh, I was glad to do it. But I'm *glad* I was around to do it. He's needed a mother, he's needed as normal an up-bringing as I could manage. And you off all the time. Well, I don't begrudge it to you. You've had a lot of sadness, Ann, a lot of sadness. But I've had the lookout for Matthew. That's why I couldn't let you come in this afternoon and disrupt his life. I wouldn't have it, Ann. The boy comes first . . ."

"Then get out of my house, out of my kitchen . . ."

"I knew someday you'd say that. But you'll think it over. You're the one, Ann, that's brought trouble into this house. I swore to God I'd never bring it up to you about that night by the fireplace. But then you had that row in the kitchen, the broken glass and all. What do you think these things would do to Matthew? You'll have to forgive me, Ann, but what I've said is for your own good . . . and his . . ."

Ann Marie stood up, kicked the newspaper, glowered down at Molly. Goddamn her, she was right. Ann Marie stalked across the room, grabbed her purse, and marched out of the house. She left the front door open and clip-clopped swiftly down the cement walk to the police car at the curb. She looked back at the house. Molly was outlined in the pale light of the doorframe.

"Take me to the Bismarck Hotel," Ann Marie said to the startled driver.

In the car Ann Marie had the driver use the radio to locate Captain Vincent and tell him to meet her outside the Bismarck in half an hour. The captain was in bed when the call came in. Mary, reluctant and disapproving, saw him out of the house. He arrived outside the hotel about five minutes after the car that carried Ann Marie. Her eyes snapped brightly as he peered into the back seat.

"Okay, let's go." The captain pulled the door open for Ann Marie. She stepped out of the car and moved swiftly across the sidewalk. Vincent got in step with her just before they reached the revolving door.

"Do you know how to open a hotel room door?"

"It would be better if we got a key."

"Do it. Room 711." Ann Marie walked toward the elevator while Captain Vincent talked briefly with the assistant manager at the desk. He joined her and they rode up in the elevator in bristling silence. She marched ahead of Vincent down the hallway and stood in front of the suite retained by *Eyes*.

Vincent unlocked the door, pushed it quickly open, and reached in to snap on the light switch.

"What the fuck is going on?" It was Paul Martin's voice coming from the bedroom area.

Ann Marie stepped over the threshold and toward the sound of her lover's voice. Martin was sitting up in bed, holding a protecting arm across a startled-looking young blond woman with wide, stricken eyes.

"Annie, what the hell are you doing here?"

"I don't have to ask you that question. I can see what you're doing."

Ann Marie advanced to the foot of the bed. Captain Vincent closed the door of the sitting room and joined her. Ann Marie gave him an order without looking at him.

"Get this whore out of here."

"Wait a minute . . ." Martin said, fairly calmly considering the circumstances.

"Get *her out* of here!" Ann Marie tore at the sheet that covered Martin's girl friend. She curled her well-tanned body defensively.

"Get out, get out, get out!" Ann Marie shrieked, clawing the rest of the sheet away from Martin.

"Annie, for Crissake . . ." Ann Marie slashed at Martin with her purse. It shuddered against his uplifted arm, popped open, and showered a glitter of lipsticks, compacts, and pens across the bed. The naked young woman hopped onto the floor and cowered in the corner, attempting to shield herself with her hands. Martin swung himself off the bed and lurched forward to grab Ann Marie by the arms.

"Get Miss Modesty out of here," Ann Marie shouted, pushing against Martin, forcing him backward. Vincent beckoned to the girl, who wiggled along the side of the bed and into the sitting room. "Get dressed and get the hell out of here," Vincent said hoarsely. The terrified girl scooped up her clothes and, made awkward by fear, began to put them on. Vincent moved toward the Mayor, who had, in her fury, knocked Martin onto the bed. Martin had folded his strong arms around her and squeezed her into squirming immobility on top of him.

"Let me go, you bastard!" Ann Marie huffed, out of breath.

"You stop trying to kill me, I'll let you go," Martin gasped.

"Come on you two," Vincent said, pulling them apart like a referee at a wrestling match. "Come on, before somebody else calls the police." Vincent did not know what to do, other than try to get them to neutral corners. "Come on, easy now, easy now . . ." He separated them. Martin pulled himself up and, without covering his nakedness, leaned, breathing heavily, against the headboard. Ann Marie, her face almost as red as her tumbled hair, stood at the foot of the bed. Jesus, they *might* kill each other.

"Wait outside, Captain." She kept her eyes on Martin.

"Are you sure . . . ?"

"Outside. Wait outside." She took a deep breath. "I won't need any help with him."

After Vincent left the room, Ann Marie and Paul Martin looked sullenly at each other.

"Annie, what the hell did you come here for?"

"It's your lucky number. 711. I don't know why it took me so long to figure out where you would be when I couldn't find you. It came to me tonight. A lot of things came to me tonight . . ." Ann Marie picked up the articles that were scattered on the bed and replaced them in her purse. "Who was this one, the young reporter? She must be twenty-two. A little old for your tastes . . ."

"Annie, Annie . . ."

"I've heard a lot about your habits. I thought maybe you'd get over them . . ."

"Annie, that girl doesn't mean anything to me."

Ann Marie's eyes flashed. "That's the trouble, Paul. Nothing means anything to you. You use charm on everybody. You don't care what it means to them." She paused, drawing on her deepest reserves of hostility and frustration. "Knock 'em down, knock 'em up. Score another one for P. M. Martin. Well, I'm finished with this sort of thing. Do you understand? *Finished.* You can take yourself and your friend Barone and your deals and your plans to become rich, take them and drop them in Lake Michigan. I'm getting off the train . . ."

"Wait a minute, Annie, wait a minute." Martin was genuinely alarmed. He could tolerate a knock-down, drag-'em-out fight with Ann Marie, he could handle that, but he couldn't stand for the dismantling of his dreams of wealth and glory.

"You want me to get killed? Come on, Annie . . ." He throttled down his irritation and began to purr. "It was a dumb mistake about that girl. I'm sorry . . ."

"Are you? Are you *really?*"

"You know me, Annie, I've never tried to kid you about myself. I can't break all my old habits at once." He smiled and ran his fingers through his thick hair.

Was he honest the way little boys were? Was he trying to grow up? Ann Marie couldn't let him go, not completely, not tonight.

"What do you mean?" she asked, less tensely.

"I mean, the main reason I was seeing that girl was to tell her good-bye. You can ask her yourself. You could have, if you hadn't chased her out of here. I was breaking up. Telling her I couldn't see her anymore. You can't do these things with a phone call . . ."

"You don't have to go to bed to do them, either."

Martin eased off the bed and took a step toward Ann Marie.

"You're right." He said it so cleanly, so undefensively, that Ann Marie was taken aback. She had expected many things from Martin, but hardly a confession, an admission of wrong on his part. That had always seemed beyond him, beyond his concern or his attention.

"Annie, I was giving her up for you." His eyes held hers.

She would like to believe him. Maybe she had to believe him. He tried to embrace her but Ann Marie pulled back and stepped into the sitting room.

Martin picked up his shorts and slipped into them. "Honest, Annie, I know I did this the wrong way. I wish to God I had done it some other way. But I . . ." He pulled on his suit pants and walked barechested into the sitting room. Ann Marie watched him carefully, watched the rise and fall of his deep chest, watched his eyes . . .

"Annie, I want you to marry me . . ."

"You don't mean that. Tell me the truth." Her voice was hard decking above the shifting emotional cargo beneath it.

"I *do* mean it."

"You don't want me. You want the Mayor's office in your pocket . . ." She turned away from him. He took another step toward her.

"Yeah, that's partly true too. I admit it. We're involved, Annie. There's no getting out of the deals you've okayed. You can't make a speech and tell the people about those. You going to tell them all about O'Brien City and how it grew? Have you heard, they've shifted the old people out of there all together? New plan." Martin smiled. "They'll be relocated nearby . . ."

"What?"

"O'Brien City. Great place—if you're young and have disposable income. What the hell did you think Rafferty was telling you about the other day?"

Ann Marie swallowed hard. "He didn't mention that."

"It was in a footnote in the report that was on your desk for a week. Too bad you get bored by these things . . ."

Ann Marie stared numbly at Martin.

"You've got your weaknesses too. Don't forget it. You know damned well you have to deal with these people. We've been all through this. They don't really care about you. I told you I was the only one you could count on for the truth. Hell, Annie . . ." He moved toward her, embraced her, held her against his chest. "Annie, I'm not perfect. But you can rely on me for the truth."

Ann did not fight him off. "What's this deal Barone wants tomorrow?"

"Big stuff. A sports complex. Stadium, racetrack, possible Olympic site . . ." He leaned down and kissed her on the forehead. "It's a good idea. The city could use it. Of course, he'll make a lot of money." He pressed her close. "So will I. I admit it, Annie. I'll make a pile out of this too. And you'll make a great name. All you have to do is make sure the condemnations go off, the tax breaks are given. It's simple. It isn't even really dishonest."

Ann Marie relaxed in the grip of his strong arms. She couldn't be completely mad at him. He was, in his own way, honest with her. He never pretended to be any different than he was.

"Are you serious about marriage?"

"I never have been before." He laughed.

Ann Marie could not help herself. She laughed too. "But this time?"

"This time, yeah, this time I mean it."

Ann Marie nuzzled closer to him. She didn't understand it but she felt better, better than she had all day.

34

*T*he Gray Panthers rallied in front of the entrance to City Hall the next morning. Their signs protested their removal from the new plans for O'Brien City. "Lady Mayor—Unfair!!" read one, "We Lose—Builders Win," read another. Ann Marie had been warned about the demonstration on her car telephone as she rode downtown. She told her driver to take her to a side entrance. She arrived in her office without making contact with the Gray Panthers. They were going to get new housing. It was just in a different area. Hadn't they ever heard of progress?

Ann Marie had not returned home until 4 A.M. Martin had firmly agreed to marry her and they had made love and sat up talking while Captain Vincent waited outside in the hallway. She liked having a strong man on guard. She even enjoyed Vincent's discomfort at carrying out this duty. What story would he give his wife? Ann Marie, bright-eyed and vivacious, despite only a few hours of sleep, felt good as she entered her office. She was at the center of everyone's attention. She bubbled with energy that came with excitement.

The labor leaders filed in and took their places in the men's club chairs that had been moved into her office for the meeting. These men were almost as old as the Gray Panthers. They were bionic marvels, replated and refitted like old battleships with new hips, joints, and pacemakers. Michael O'Flaherty, head of the Building Trades Council, was eighty and the senior of the group. His skin was stretched like a bison's on a tanner's rack but life flashed in the diamonds of his eyes. O'Flaherty greeted the Mayor on behalf of the other union leaders. "We look forward to the good relationships we have always had with the City of Chicago." He descended slowly to his chair and the room grew silent.

Ann Marie studied the veined and spotted faces of these labor chiefs. Composed, tough, uncompromising, they did not want their profitable relationships with Chicago disturbed.

"I come from a family in which there were many laboring men," Ann Marie began, "and the Democratic Party has always been the friend of the union movement." Invigorated by the peculiar journeys of the night before, Ann Marie was eager to succeed here as she had, almost effortlessly, with the cable television franchises, her work as alderwoman, her accession to the Mayor's office.

"I want personally to guarantee to each of you and to your membership the continued support of my administration for your work." The faces of the union heads remained impassive. "We will continue, therefore, to do everything we can to see that fair and equitable contracts are negotiated between the city and those unions you represent." They were old judges who had sat through opening statements many times before.

Ann Marie stood up and pushed aside the paper from which she had been reading. She swept the moonscape faces with her eyes.

"Gentlemen, we really don't need these opening remarks. I want to get to the point and you do too." A stir of interest in the room. "We are living in new times, difficult times. These are 'give back' times for unions. You know it and I do too. It's very simple. You want work for your members. We want to give it to them." She paused and moved to the front of her desk. "But there have to be compromises. And there have to be changes. You want straight talk. Here it is. The city cannot afford the luxuries of the boom years. Face it. There can be no negotiations without the surrender of some of the advantages that were given to you in previous years. So you won't have to wonder what I'm talking about, I expect a reduction in sick leave days and other optional days off." Grumbles rose from the now restless labor leaders. Ann Marie raised her right hand. She was running the meeting as if she were a teacher facing down a class of street-wise eighth-graders. "The teamsters are the first union up for contract renegotiation. I'd like Mr. Fairfield to pledge himself to these small reductions in a joint statement with me at the conclusion of this meeting . . ."

"In a pig's ass," Fairfield shouted angrily. Ann Marie did not break her rhythm. "How would you like to lose that extra crewman on the garbage trucks? I could ask for that too. The people would back me up. If you don't think so, check the results at the information kiosks in your neighborhoods." Fairfield was on his feet. His comrades, anger flaring in their spotted cheeks, shifted unhappily in their chairs. Fairfield, wattles stringy with tension, gestured with his hands. "Mister Mayor . . ."

"Madam Mayor," Ann Marie corrected him.

"Whatever the hell you want. If you think I'm going to make a statement with you, you'll wait a long time. The union movement is not something to push around. Everybody wants the ordinary worker to give something back. We're not going to do that. We worked too long to get what we have. I think everybody here feels the same way." The Greek chorus of his peers growled encouragement to him.

"Mr. Fairfield, unless you make some concessions, there will be less work for your people. It's as simple as that. The people of this city want a new beginning. They're supporting me. *You* don't represent ordinary people. Maybe you did once. But you're wearing a diamond ring and a five-hundred-dollar suit. Times *have* changed. *I* represent the ordinary people. If you don't believe me, go ask them yourselves." She surveyed the raging men before her. Two others had stood up to protest. They were all talking at the same time. Ann Marie smiled. She liked storms. It was wonderful. She circled behind her desk and sat down.

"Mrs. O'Brien . . ." O'Flaherty had waved the others into silence. His voice was thin and worn, silverware that had been in the family a long time. "Mrs. O'Brien. The tradition in Chicago is negotiation. It is the tradition of the union movement. It was the tradition of your predecessor, labor's great friend, Thomas—"

"I'm Mayor now," Ann Marie fired. "Go ahead."

"It's the principle we've always followed. I don't think you can expect us to depart from that without betraying the trust of our members . . ." O'Flaherty sat down as the other men shouted endorsements of his position. Ann Marie studied them coldly. The people would be on her side in this. These men were out of date.

"Suit yourself," she said and sat down complacently as the union bosses rose one by one to express their disagreement with her stance. She listened without a word as each man spoke. When the last one finished she folded her arms and leaned back in her chair. The room was tensely quiet, a battlefield after a heavy shelling. Fairfield stood up again. "Mrs. O'Brien, what do you have to say?"

"I've had my say. I haven't asked for much. I'll have to tell the people that you're unwilling to give just a little in order to help the city. I have nothing more to say. Good day, gentlemen."

The stunned and angry men marched out mumbling to each other, staring at the new Mayor as if she were a murderess in the dock. Fairfield stayed behind while the others collected their coats in the outer office.

"What is it you want, Mrs. O'Brien?" he asked softly. "What is it you really want? Contributions to your dinner? You want to have us put pressure on the committeemen about the party chairmanship? Is that it?"

Ann Marie looked stonily at him.

"In private, we can talk. We can reach some understanding. You want our support, that's it, isn't it? You want us to help you move Cullen out altogether. That's it, isn't it?"

"You figure it out, Mr. Fairfield. I've told you what I want."

He looked at her uncertainly. Was it really safe to put his hand in the cage? He compressed his lips and shrugged his shoulders. Ann Marie watched him cross the office and go through the door without turning around.

"Mrs. O'Brien has thrown down the gauntlet to the fat cat labor leaders of Chicago. For the first time in the city's memory, a Mayor has challenged the unions which have profited so mightily over the years to make a sacrifice for the good of the whole city. They should remember, as they reflect on their position in our society, that Mrs. O'Brien has unparalleled public support. Her sure feel for the pulse of the ordinary citizen has given her enormous strength. When she speaks, the people speak. I hope union leaders are listening. Sincerely, Paul Michael Martin."

Martin looked up toward the control room. The technician held up a circled thumb and forefinger. The commentator rose from the desk at which he had made the tape for his evening program and hurried out of the studio. Barone was waiting for him. Paul wanted to find out how his meeting, which followed that of the labor leaders, had gone with Ann Marie. She had, of course, produced another bombshell with her forthright stand on the union give-backs. She would also overwhelm the Gray Panthers, pushing them off the news altogether. The media would support her tough-labor stance down the line on those issues. They had been editorializing about them for years.

Five minutes after completing his tape, Paul Martin entered the quiet, dark lounge of a Michigan Avenue hotel. Barone sat in a corner drinking a cup of coffee.

"How did it go?" Martin asked, taking the seat opposite the investor. Barone puffed on his cigarette, watching Martin closely as the journalist settled himself at the table.

"No problem, Paul. You must have talked to her. She seemed ready for the concept." He dropped his cigarette into the ashtray. "I must say my partners were impressed." Barone chuckled. "They heard she was tough. Christ, she was fine, just fine. You know this project is the biggest thing that's come along in years."

"You didn't just think it up," Martin said as he signaled for a waitress.

"No, no. We've been working on this for years. The time was never right. Cullen was a little shy of these things the last few years. I couldn't even bring the idea up to him." He gave a pirate captain smile. "This woman has come nicely into line. Sam and Alex promised to organize the Council voting for her. We're all finally in business together."

Martin ordered a gin and tonic. "Don't underestimate her. She's very sharp. Doesn't like details but she doesn't miss anything big, either."

"I hope you're right. This is a complex deal. The tax breaks are essential. These and getting hold of the land."

"Christ, Rich, don't tell me you haven't got all the parcels in one package yet!"

"These things take time, Paul. Rafferty's been assembling these blocks for years. And we've had a contact at HUD for some seed money. Redevelopment funds. But we're going to break up an old Polish neighborhood. Don't worry. We'll have it altogether."

"Can Annie help you with that?"

"If she tells the right things to the right people. Like the alderman for the ward. Hell, he just needs the right persuasion."

"You mean the right amount of money?"

"No, not in this case. This guy's not on the take. We've got to please him to keep him from getting too nosy. He'll need her backing with the people and jobs for the people whose shops and businesses are closed. Things she can give him that will make up for the dislocation. There's plenty for her to do."

"No problem," Martin answered, pulling back slightly as the waitress placed his drink before him. "Annie'll cooperate. She's got everything to gain." He paused for effect. "I told her I'd marry her."

"*What?*" Barone asked, taken off guard, unable to process the news immediately. "You're getting married? Jesus, Paul, *you!* And *Annie!* Jesus Christ."

"Quiet, Rich, we don't want this out yet . . ."

"There's nobody here. Jesus Christ." He waved toward the waitress. "Hey, honey, bring me a Scotch." He shook his head. "I gotta drink to this."

"Rich, there's a price on all this. You know that."

Barone ignored him as he reached for the drink brought by the waitress. He raised it before him. "Paul, here's to you and the Mayor! What a partnership!" He tossed half the drink down and placed it on the table. He held it in position with his hands, lifting and lowering it a quarter of an inch as he continued to absorb the news.

"Rich, the price. The price is going up. I'm delivering the Mayor for you. That puts me in a different league."

"What do you mean?" Barone's grin snapped in the middle and collapsed.

"Well, before, I could put in a good word, threaten her maybe, cajole her. That'll all be different now. I'm not just a friend, not just an outsider."

Barone studied Martin's face. Who the hell did he think he was, anyway?

"I've been a senior flunkie for you, Rich. I've done things for too little for too long. Fixing little things, killing stories for you, providing information. You've been generous, I'll admit that."

Barone frowned and closed his hands on his drink.

"Now, Rich, let's restructure our arrangement. Let's think of ourselves as, oh, say, partners . . ." Martin raised his own glass in a mock toast to Barone.

"Partners? What the hell do you mean, partners?"

"I won't break you. I want twenty-five percent. In cash."

"I can't get you that much cash . . ."

"Come, come . . ."

"Ten percent, take it or leave it."

"Twenty."

"Ten."

"Shall we settle for fifteen?"

Barone scowled, hurt-looking.

"Come on, Rich, you'll just take it away from somebody else. Don't forget who'll say the last words at night to the Mayor. And the first ones in the morning. You think there aren't other people ready to make a deal with me?"

"Christ, Paul, fifteen percent?" He sighed. "Okay. But you'd better deliver."

"Sincerely yours"—the commentator raised his glass—"Paul Michael Martin."

At the same hour on the West Side a sleepy Captain Paul Vincent had just parked his own private car on a crowded street and climbed out. The largely Italian neighborhood had shrunk steadily over the years but, even though it was only six or seven blocks square, remained a vigorous enclave. Black-shawled women sat on the front steps of many of the row houses while children played ball in the strip of street that ran between the cars at either curb. He turned onto a broad boulevard. The Five Brothers Limousine Service was located in a one-story yellow-brick building across the street. He waited for the light to change and walked diagonally across to the office entrance. An unshaven man of about fifty wearing greasy overalls sat behind a cluttered counter. He did not look up as Captain Vincent entered. A wall of glass brick distorted the view of the garage area beyond the office.

"I'd like to get some information about renting some parking stalls."

"We don't have any," the man said, his head still lowered.

"I don't mean here. I'm looking for some near your other place, the one on the river."

"River Livery?"

"Yeah, that's the one."

The man looked at Vincent cautiously. He picked up the phone and pressed a buzzer. "Frankie? Guy here wants to rent some parking stalls over near the river? Wadda you say?" He held the phone while he continued to appraise Vincent. He replaced it and held his glinting eyes on the captain for a moment. "Frankie'll be with you in a minute."

The phone buzzed and the man at the desk grunted. "Frankie's in the back office. Go right through there." He waved vaguely. The captain opened the door in the glass-brick siding and stepped into a cavernous room. Dankness mingled with the odors of gasoline and engine exhaust. He edged through the rows of sleek, silent limousines toward an office that had been partitioned off in a far corner. He knocked on the hollow door and entered. Frankie turned out to be Valentino as he might have looked in his forties: slick hair, dark suit, sloe eyes. He was studying the racing section of the morning paper. A row of clipboards thick with papers hung on pegs along the wall behind him. Above them was a calendar of the month of September featuring a naked woman posed against a blaze of autumn trees.

"I'm Frankie Williams, one of the five brothers." He pointed to a wooden chair by the side of the desk. "I hear you want to rent some parking stalls."

Vincent shook the man's hand and sat down. "That's right. Near the river."

"What kind of business you in?"

"Sales. Distribution. We need space near our new offices. We need access to the expressways."

"Oh, yeah?" Frankie straightened up. He pushed the paper aside. Vincent felt the pressure of expert appraisal.

"Where's your new office? What's the address?"

"We're still negotiating for property. We'll need extra parking though."

"Oh, yeah?" Frankie's favorite phrase indicated disbelief, surprise, the puzzlement of a man talking to someone from a completely different world. "Wadda you sell?"

"We distribute mainly. Jobbers." Vincent decided to take a shot in the dark. "We do a lot in the medical field. Drugs, things like that, for clinics . . ." He let his voice trail off.

"Oh, yeah?" There was more life in Frankie's mix of question and exclamation point. Drugs. Of course Frankie might be interested. Frankie did more than run a limousine service.

"That's very interesting business. Wadda you have, a lot of interstate travel? Indiana, Michigan?"

"Some. Do you have any stalls to rent?"

A young man in a driver's outfit walked into the room without knocking and handed Frankie a piece of paper. He studied it, nodded at the man, and looked back at Captain Vincent. "Naw, we don't have anything, Mister . . . Mister . . . ?"

"Well, it doesn't matter then, does it?" Vincent was being kissed off. He decided to try once more. "I thought you might be interested in drugs. Maybe you'd have people who wanted to drive for us."

Frankie's eyes were clear and hard. "Naw, not in our line, Mister. Good luck." Both men watched Vincent as he rose and walked out of the office. The captain was sure that other eyes were also studying him as he passed through the submarine pen of limousines and headed for fresh air and daylight.

35

*S*ummer sat sullenly on Chicago through the first weeks of September. The union leaders, grudgingly and for appearance's sake, showed up at Ann Marie's side for the Labor Day rally. The people were behind her even though the union rank and file were not. Louis Fairfield talked of a possible garbage strike but continued to negotiate with the city. Monsignor Fitzmaurice had brought additional plans and requests to his cousin's office. So had Anthony Barone and his associates. There would be plenty for Ann Marie to point to as her accomplishments as the time for the slating for the Mayoral primary approached.

The Pope was coming too. Ann Marie in a burst of inspiration at a news conference ignored a question about the Gray Panthers and announced that she and Paul Michael Martin would be married at the Mass for peace which His Holiness would offer in Grant Park in the last week of October. Monsignor Fitzmaurice protested that such a thing was impossible. "Then so is your high-rise mausoleum," Ann Marie snapped. "We'll see what the Cardinal can arrange," Morgan answered.

Captain Vincent had been appointed coordinator of security for the papal trip to the city. It had eaten up almost all of his time since his visit to the Five Brothers Limousine Service on the first day of the month. Ann Marie was at the center of everything. Was there any doubt that, despite the backing and filling of the committeemen, she would gain the nomination? September was a roller-coaster ride, just the kind of month she loved.

Thomas H. Cullen worked every day at the rehabilitation exercises. The former Mayor had moved in with his daughter when he left the hospital in August. He declined all interviews and refused to have himself photographed walking with a cane. He kept his numb left arm in a sling. Cullen finally agreed to accept an invitation from his old friend, industrialist Patrick B. Kinsella, to take a day's cruise on his yacht, *The Irish Wake*. With Maureen and her family, Cap Malloy and Mark Richler, Cullen was driven down to Burnham Harbor early on a Sunday morning and, with a little help from Kinsella's crew members, he boarded the ship and settled comfortably on the aft deck. In a few moments they

were on the green, light-filled waters looking back at the verdant spread
of the parks and the jumbled masts of the harbors that lay on the
twenty-mile-long shelf of Chicago's lakefront.

"Beautiful, Patty. I'm glad I came." Cullen waved his good arm in a
showing-with-pride gesture. "None of your breweries along the lakefront. Just places for the people. Even Toronto, that they write about so
much, Toronto has breweries on the lakefront. I often wonder why people from other parts of the country never appreciate what a beautiful
city Chicago is . . ."

The fingering wind pried at Richler's sun hat and he clapped it down
on his head.

"People don't want to hear good things about Chicago. You ought to
know that."

Maureen joined them. "Larry and Cap are with the kids. They're fascinated by the captain and the way he navigates or steers, or whatever
he does . . ."

"Maureen," Cullen said as he adjusted his dark glasses, "I was just saying to Pat and Mark here, I was just saying how beautiful the city looks
from here."

"You think there'll be much left when she gets through?" his host Kinsella asked.

"She certainly knows how to stay in the headlines," Cullen answered.
"She has a positive genius for it." He shook his head and watched the
city as though it were a stand of patriotic flags on the horizon. "Say, Pat,
are you going to her birthday party? The twenty-first, it is, I believe."

Kinsella pushed a hand through his white, wavy hair. "No, Tom, but
she'll make quite a bundle with it. Of course, she's got the Irish of the
city divided. Half of them for you, half for her. They'll be real snippy
with each other that night. With any luck, it could turn into a real free-
for-all." Kinsella studied the skyline through a pair of binoculars. "Well,
Tom, she doesn't seem to have sent a destroyer out after us.

"Tom, would you like a drink?" Kinsella asked. "Shall it be Bloody
Marys for everyone?" He signaled to a crewman standing under a
canopied bar. In a few moments he served drinks all around. Cullen
gazed at the receding purple outline of the city's buildings, raised his
glass to it, and sipped the drink.

"Tom, a lot of us in business wish you'd make yourself a candidate
again."

Cullen continued to look at the horizon.

"It's almost fall, Tom. You're up and around. You're obviously in good
enough shape to run again."

Cullen shook his head slowly. "I wonder what will become of her."

"What do you mean?" Maureen asked, cupping her eyes against the
sun.

"She's playing with some funny customers. Barone and his crowd. And she's going to marry Paul Martin! They're using her. She's using them. Dangerous with that crowd . . ." Cullen sipped his Bloody Mary.

"What about it, Tom? Have you made up your mind?" Kinsella inched forward in his chair. "You'll have a lot of support if you decide to make a comeback."

Chicago had become a smudge of miniature turrets in the distance. Boils of water rose behind the powerful vessel as it plowed farther out into the lake.

"I'll tell you, Pat, I've given it some thought. Mark knows that." He held his glance on his old associate. "Mark, you've been through a lot with me. I'm sorry some things happened that shouldn't have." He paused. It was the closest thing to an apology that Richler had ever heard. Maureen held her breath. Was her father going to break down? He shouldn't be talking about all this. Cullen cleared his throat. He was glad that his eyes were hidden by sunglasses.

"I've had lots of time to think." The crack was gone from his voice. "And I've learned a lot. Illness does that, they say. But it wasn't the illness that taught me. It was the getting better. I've had time to look at the world. I must say there's a lot I've been missing . . ." He was in control again.

"It's like the evening news. I never really had time to watch it before, except, of course, the part I was on." He laughed and the others joined in. "You see, you think illness is terrible, that weakness is awful. But the television taught me a thing or two. Not the news exactly. More, the ads. If you watch them, they're not geared to health or success at all. They're geared to failure. There's none of us perfect, that's what the ads told me. First, the insurance companies. The whole thing is based on death, accident, or loss, on failure of some kind or other. I never realized it before. You get quite a few messages about that when you watch the television regularly. Then the next batch of ads are for false teeth adhesive, pills for constipation, and the trials of the hemorrhoid sufferer. And I'm not mentioning the heartbreak of psoriasis . . ."

Maureen giggled and the Mayor's old companions smiled. Cullen was enjoying himself, Cullen was in charge of the entertainment. Seated comfortably, his white hair a banner in the wind, he was indeed his old self.

"Then the weatherman. Until you watch the weatherman, you have a different idea about the weather. There was a kind of a mystery to it, a pleasant kind of mystery. And you could take each day at a time. Now they show you pictures of things blowing up in the Pacific that may get here in a week or so. The weather, like everything else, is made in Japan. It may not get here at all. Takes the mystery out of it. And it gives you something to worry about that you wouldn't have without these satellites flashing pictures of the Far East into your home."

He shifted his bulk in the deck chair.

"Things change, that's what I've found out. Like the day Maureen took me down to her local bank. I had opened a small account there years ago. Remember the day you took me, Maureen? And a dandy black fellow took care of me. Three-piece suit and the big smile. I wanted to transfer the money to Maureen's account for the kids' education. I signed the slip right in front of him. Well, he took and checked it at some machine and came back and told me it wasn't my signature. Remarkable. It didn't match the specimen they had on hand. Nothing he could do. A great lad he was. Came from Jamaica. He didn't know who I was, or who I had been. Makes a man think." He chuckled.

Kinsella motioned for another round of drinks.

"So I've decided the whole damned world is either falling apart or about to have bad weather." Cullen accepted the second drink. "So I thought to myself, I'm half a man on a cane now but I'm getting around. I don't have false teeth, hemorrhoids, or psoriasis. I'll be damned if I'm going to let any insurance company collect on me. I like the weather to be a mystery, I like to think God sends it . . ."

"Yes?" Kinsella asked expectantly.

"And before I can't cash a check in any bank, maybe I'd better get back into public life. Seriously, seriously, though," Cullen said, his Bloody Mary sloshing as he wiped his eyes with the edge of his sleeve, "there's something else, yes." He looked at Kinsella and then at Richler and his daughter. "I have a feeling inside. It's like Ann Marie—oh, I know her very well—it's like she's trying to provoke me. The things she does and says . . ."

"To make you mad?" Kinsella asked.

"Well, that's clear enough, Patty. No, it's another feeling. I don't know . . ." He jabbed at the air with his glass, a professor searching for the right word. "I get the feeling she wants it all and she'll fight to the death for it. And at the same time she doesn't want it. It's the funniest damn thing . . ."

"When will you make your announcement?" Kinsella asked. Richler watched Cullen carefully. Maureen held her breath.

"I'll make it myself, sir!" Cap said, snapping to attention and giving a salute. "Give me the word, sir!"

"Now, now"—Cullen surveyed the eager circle around him—"who said anything about an announcement?" He sipped his drink and looked across the silver cloak that spread back to the diminished skyline. "I'm not going to lie down and die, I'm sure of that. I'm just not really sure what Ann Marie is up to . . ." He broke his reverie. "Say, P.B., when the hell are you going to serve some lunch?"

The next morning Ann Marie raged silently as she rode downtown in her limousine. The morning editions were jumbled on the seat next to her. Enterprising photographers for both newspapers had managed to get telephoto pictures of Cullen and his party sitting on the deck of Kinsella's yacht as it pulled away from Burnham Harbor the morning before. "Cullen Planning Return?" the caption teased beneath the grainy full-page picture of the expansively gesturing former Mayor. Stories in both papers speculated on whether the outing with the famed P. B. Kinsella was the first indication of a comeback in the works. Was Cullen getting ready to submit his name to the committeemen once again? No wonder they had been so slow to get in line. They had been waiting for just such a signal . . .

Ann Marie stormed out of her car at the LaSalle Street entrance to City Hall. She did not try to dodge the waiting Gray Panthers. She charged past them before their openmouthed elder, Mr. Solokowski, could get his question out. She marched straight to the waiting elevator, ignoring shouted questions from reporters about Cullen's outing with Kinsella. Ann Marie stalked into her own office and signaled for Helen Morrison to come in. The veteran secretary, smelling gunpowder in the air, moved swiftly, her large bosom shifting the way it did when she hurried for a bus.

"I want Mr. Martin and Mr. Barone here as soon as possible. Get Alderman Noto too. And Wendel."

"What about this morning's appointments? Mr. Schroeder is here . . ."

"Have him come back later. Tomorrow, next week . . ."

"The Korchows are scheduled to deliver a portrait of you . . ."

"What? Who put *them* on the appointment list?"

"Mr. Ohland, your press secretary . . ."

"Tell him to get rid of them. And tell him he'll be a former press secretary if he makes a mistake like that again."

"There's a reporter for *Paris-Match* scheduled at eleven."

"Postpone him. Make it tomorrow . . ."

"But tomorrow . . ."

"Make it tomorrow!" Ann Marie pronounced the words with exaggerated emphasis.

"And you have a luncheon with Mother Francis at twelve-thirty . . ."

Ann Marie frowned. She had already postponed that twice. She couldn't do that again. "That's all . . ." Helen retreated as quietly and quickly as she could. Ann Marie opened a folder that had been placed on the top of her desk. It contained a progress report on the $250-a-plate birthday dinner fund-raiser that was scheduled to be held for her later in the week. She would be thirty-nine. Good God, thirty-nine. Her fortieth year beginning. $670,000 worth of tickets had already been sold. Measure that against projected costs of $150,000. The campaign fund was growing nicely. She searched the list for the name of Patrick B. Kinsella. Or Kinsella Industries. Nothing. Who the hell did he think he was, courting Cullen and ignoring her?

The buzzer on her desk sounded. Mr. Barone and Mr. Noto were in the outer office. The blood brothers entered. Ann Marie got right down to business as soon as they were seated.

"I want you to produce a group of the Democratic committeemen. Today. By this afternoon. I want them to support me in public at a news conference this afternoon . . ."

"But, Annie . . ." Barone began.

"Don't 'Annie' me. I want this *done*. The papers are full of Cullen and a possible return to politics. Let the committeemen see that and we'll never get them in line. Don't you understand that?" Her mood was clean and fierce, a jungle cat rippling muscles down the length of its body.

Noto watched her through half-closed eyes. He was not going to cross her, he wasn't going to soft-soap her, not this morning. Barone clenched his teeth, controlling himself, waiting for the outburst to pass.

"What's the matter, Richard?" she asked angrily. "Can't you deliver this?"

"Yes, yes, of course we can. I just don't think it's, well, I don't think it's necessary." He licked his lips, moved in his chair. "Have you read the dinner report? That's the best showing any Mayor ever got. We'll hit a million by tomorrow. We've got committeemen coming to that. We've got the most important businessmen in the city. You'll have a big war chest. You're winning, you've practically won already . . ."

"Have you read today's paper?"

Paul Martin, smiling broadly, entered as she asked the question.

"Annie, you should know better than to believe the papers." He walked across the room, brought a single yellow rose from behind his back and handed it to Ann Marie. He kissed her on the forehead. "There, my bride-to-be, something for your bud vase . . ." Sam Noto shrugged, raised his eyes to the ceiling, then glanced at Barone. Martin fixed the rose in the crystal vase and looked at Barone and Noto. "Gentlemen, why so serious? Everything is going fine . . ." He pulled a chair away from the wall and sat next to Ann Marie's desk. She seemed slightly softened by Martin's approach.

"They're overconfident, Paul," she said flatly, gesturing toward Barone and Noto. "They think we can't lose."

"They're right," Martin said airily. "The birthday party is going fine, we've got a lock on the City Council, your popularity's at an all-time high . . ."

"I don't like stories like these . . ." She pointed to the morning papers.

Martin grinned. "Cullen only looks good in pictures sitting down. Don't worry. Don't give him attention by reacting to him . . ."

"That's right, that's right . . ." Barone chimed in.

Ann Marie looked around at the men who had become her inner circle, the men who got things done for her. "Has Richler been coaching you? I want those committeemen delivered by this afternoon. I don't care what you have to do to get them here. I want at least twenty of them here for the news conference. I don't want any arguments . . ."

"We may have to make some promises . . ." Barone said.

"I don't care what you promise them. Just get them here. Is that understood?" Noto and Barone nodded. Wendel entered the room and sat down next to Noto. Ann Marie paused. "You too, Alex, you get in on this. They'll explain what I want . . ."

"Annie," Martin said carefully, "don't give away too much, don't promise too much to get these men here today."

Ann Marie handed him a morning paper.

"In a few days you'll laugh about this," Martin said, tossing the newspaper back onto her desk. The other men rose to leave.

"And by the way," Ann Marie's voice held them like children playing statues, "in your big plans, make sure Kinsella doesn't get any contracts."

Barone opened his mouth, thought better of it, and turned to follow a frowning Sam Noto out of the office.

"I'm just delighted that you could find some time for me." Mother Francis raised her glass of bourbon on the rocks. Ann Marie smiled edgily as she bobbed her white wine in the nun's direction. "And to meet here at Candles again. Do you remember the last time we lunched here?" Ann Marie nodded. It was almost two years ago. The beginning of public service. She had been thirty-seven. Matthew had been eight.

"You have lots on your mind, I can see that."

"You started it all." Ann Marie flashed an automatic smile. "Right here."

Ann Marie tried to focus on her old adviser. Women were not much fun as social companions. "You want to tell me something?"

"As it happens, I do. I was going to ask you to be honorary chairperson of our fund drive . . ."

Is that all she wants? "Sure," Ann Marie answered brightly.

"But there's something else, too."

Oh, Jesus.

"Ann Marie, I've known you a long time. I have great affection for you . . ."

"What is it you want to talk about?"

"Somebody has to tell you about the talk that's going around. It's probably in advance of this big birthday party. There's a big split in the Irish about this . . ."

"That's their problem."

"Well, I'm sure that's true and all." Mother Francis hesitated. She lowered her eyes. "Ann, you've got to hear some of the criticisms of you. *I* know you. There are *others* who don't, others who misinterpret you, misunderstand you. They don't appreciate the way you do things . . ."

"I'm listening . . ."

"There have been harsh criticisms of the people around you. You might as well hear this from me. It will come out in the campaign. And I'm your old Poli Sci teacher. And your friend." She grew tentative again. "You know I'm only interested in you . . ."

"Yes, yes," Ann Marie said impatiently, wondering where the waiter was.

"The people like Barone . . . Richard Barone. I've heard some very unpleasant things about him and his connections. And some of those men on the City Council. People like Sam Noto and Alex Wendel, people like Rafferty who tried to hurt you once . . ."

"Where did you hear all this?" What right did Mother Francis have to put her nose into her business?

"Well, I'd rather not mention names . . ."

"Then I can't pay any attention to it." Ann Marie searched the room for someone to take their order. "Busboy," she called, "will you tell our waiter we'd like to order?"

Big white teeth smiled out of a young brown face. "*No hablo inglés.*" Silence fell between them.

"Ann, I know you're annoyed. But listen to me. I've been told that a lot of people see you as strong but naïve. They're using you. And they'll go on using you until they want to get rid of you. The talk is that they're making millions on the deals you've okayed . . ."

"Stop it, *stop* it," Ann Marie said harshly. "I don't want any lectures. You taught me politics. Yes, that's right. All theory. Well, I'm responsible for real politics, the everyday kind. I've had to learn them by myself. You're here criticizing people for making money off me and in the same breath you want me to head your fund drive. You've let these same people subsidize your not very uncomfortable life for years . . ."

"Ann Marie"—Mother Francis retreated—"I'm sorry, I'm sorry. It's none of my business . . ." It was too late.

A red-coated waiter smiled above the tense atmosphere of the table. "I'd like to tell you about our specials . . ."

"We're not ready," Ann Marie said curtly. The surprised waiter backed away.

Mother Francis, stunned by their exchange, searched Ann Marie's face. The girl she had known for twenty years must still be there somewhere.

"Annie, Annie," she said in a conciliatory voice, "I never *meant* . . ."

"That's what everyone says. I didn't expect it from you." Mother Francis was just like the rest of them. She wanted something too. And she wanted to run her life, she wanted her to be the perfect young lady that Our Lady of Peace would be proud of. Aunt Molly, Mother Francis, she had people wanting to run her life everywhere . . .

"You're upset, Ann, but it may be because I've told you the truth . . ."

"If there's nothing else, Mother, I have to get back to my office." Ann Marie rose and unsmilingly walked away from the wreckage of the lunch.

"Dammit, Victor, I don't understand it." Captain Vincent chewed on a wad of paper as he talked to Police Officer Victor Hackman, whose transfer to City Hall had finally gone through. "I knew I was on to something. This Five Brothers operation. Christ Almighty, it's a cover if I ever smelled one. So I went to Judge Land's chambers for a search warrant. He issues it and by the time I drive out to the garage it's stripped empty. Not a car in the place, nobody around. Just a sign. 'Closed Temporarily.' Same thing at the other livery service. I drove past on my way back. It's the damndest thing."

"Somebody blow it on you?"

"Hell, no. I've been very quiet about this. Nobody knew but the judge and he's an honest man. I've known him for years. I've had to play this very quietly. The Mayor would have a fit if she knew . . ." Vincent tossed the wad of paper into his wastebasket. "Christ, Mary's after me to transfer. I promised I'd do it. Then I got this job to take care of the Pope. So I'm stuck here for at least a month . . ."

"And nobody else knew? Just you and the judge?"

"That's right. Just me and the judge and his clerk . . ."

Urban Mulvihill. The big picture.

"The clerk! Of course! The clerk."

"What are you talking about?"

Captain Vincent pushed his chair back. "Come on, Victor, we've got work to do."

36

Honest to God, Tom," Hy Lowenstein said through teeth that anchored a dead cigar at the corner of his mouth, "they're putting terrific pressure on everyone. Frank Ryan told me that Wendel called him and threatened to cancel every insurance contract he had with the city if he didn't show up this afternoon. And Stan Grabyzc, they pulled the same stuff on him. Said his family painting business would lose its city contracts. This is a lot of pressure . . ."

Cullen did not answer. He had already had similar calls from Teddy Mellon and Yes Yes Miller. To mount a show of committeemen strength that afternoon, Ann Marie was shooting the works, attacking in full force.

"Well, I'm glad you called, Hy . . ."

"Tom, you have to talk to some of these men . . ."

"Oh, I think they'll do what they think is right."

"Tom, for Crissake, you want to crown her at the next slating? Is that what you want?"

"Well, I'm sure that's what *she* wants." Cullen laughed. "Hy, you just do what you think is best . . ."

Lowenstein looked at the telephone in his hand in disbelief. Tom Cullen was letting this happen without a fight. Hell, he had enough on these committeemen, on most of them anyway, to keep them in line. Maybe it was the stroke, yes, maybe that was it. It had taken the fight out of him . . .

"Hy? Are you there?"

"Yes, Tom. What do you want me to do?"

"Whatever you think you have to. Let me know how it comes out . . ."

"Jesus Christ, Tom, you're leaving it up to me? You're leaving this up to everybody to make their own decisions? You're not going to fight her?"

"Let me know how it comes out," Cullen said and hung up his phone. He turned to Mark Richler, who was sitting next to the old Mayor in the den of Maureen Coleman's house.

"That's the fifth committeeman you've said that to today," Richler observed.

Cullen smiled absently at him. "That's what we'll tell everybody. Of course, the word must have gotten around by now."

"She'll get support this afternoon. You wait and see."

"Yes," Cullen said benignly, "let's wait and see."

"What the hell do you mean, you've only got eleven committeemen lined up so far?"

"Glory be to God, Mrs. O'Brien, these men have a certain independence to them. They're from the whole area of Cook County, not just from the city itself. Some of them have other engagements . . ."

"Look, Rafferty, I don't want any excuses. What the hell has happened? Has Cullen been putting pressure on them to stay away? Is that it?"

"Not so far as I can tell. Apparently he isn't talking to any of them . . ."

"Come off it, Francis. He won't be able to resist this. We're attacking his base of power. He's got to respond."

"Oh, ma'am, I wouldn't be sure of that."

"Have you called him yourself? Tell him what we're doing, tell him how the committeemen are coming over to my side . . ."

"Oh, Mrs. O'Brien, I'm not sure that's a good idea. You sound, ma'am, if you'll excuse me, like you want him to attack you, that you want him to come out in public against you . . ."

"Call him, Francis. Call him and tell him about the deserters . . ."

"He won't say anything. I know the man. When he won't talk, he won't talk."

"Are you working for him or for me? You still want the sports complex to go through, don't you? You want me to force you to put the senior citizens back in O'Brien City?"

"Mrs. O'Brien, we're talking about separate issues here . . ."

"They're all connected as far as I'm concerned."

"Mrs. O'Brien . . ."

"Call him. And let me know right away what he says to you."

Rafferty sighed as he hung up his phone. "Glory be to God, she's a bitch . . ."

"How long have you been working for Judge Land, Mr. Lynn?"

The clerk, dark-haired, thirtyish, soft-spoken, had the over-cared-for look that came from still living at home with his mother.

"Just eight months, Captain," he said, stamping court documents, carrying on his work while Vincent and Hackman asked him questions. "I really have a lot of work to finish . . ."

"Yes, I can see that." Vincent moved away from the edge of the clerk's desk as the young man reached there for a pile of folders. "That's what Frankie Williams told me." A shot in the dark.

"I don't know any Frankie Williams." Smooth, but a flutter in his eyes when the captain mentioned the name.

"That's funny, he seemed to know you well." Hackman added. The clerk stamped another document, *ker-chunk*.

"You wouldn't want us to tell your mother anything about this, would you?" Vincent pressed his hands down like broom heads on the cleared side of the desk and leaned closer to the clerk.

A more pronounced flutter in Lynn's eyes, dustiness in his voice. "There's really nothing for you to tell." He opened a folder, removed some papers and looked coldly up at Vincent. "You're blocking my light . . ."

The Captain did not budge.

"We've done a little checking on you, Mr. Lynn," Hackman said, flipping open a notebook.

"You have no business doing that." The clerk spoke evenly, as though the police officers were a bothersome but not very important distraction in his day's work.

"What business do you have at the Lowdown? Spend a lot of time there, I understand. Great gay bar. What do you like, the fistfucking, is that it?"

"Really, Captain, *that* is melodramatic of you." He stamped another document.

"You can tell us, Mr. Lynn, we already know about the contest you won there. Best impersonation of Marlene Dietrich, that was it, wasn't it, at their 'July Frolic'?"

Lynn held the stamping device in midair. He looked unpleasantly up at the policeman. "There is nothing illegal in any of the things you're talking about. I am entitled to a private life." He lowered the stamp resoundingly on an official-looking set of papers. "You don't frighten me. And, if you want to, go tell my mother. She will find it amusing, since she made the costume for me." Bang! He lowered his head and stamped another set of papers. Sticks and stones will break my bones . . .

Captain Vincent looked across at his companion. Lynn was tough. Ruffled, full of tics, but in control. The bastard was actually enjoying it . . .

"Well, let's just go over this again," Hackman said slowly. "We certainly want to be sure that we have your story straight."

The clerk looked up as he dropped a file into his "out" basket. "May I assume that you will then go and let me get my work done?"

Hackman grunted and began to review the notes he had made earlier. Vincent backed away from the desk and walked to a chair next to the door. He stretched and sat down. Lynn had tipped off the Five Brothers Limousine Service, he was sure of that.

Let Hackman have another go at him. Good man, Hackman. Vincent studied the back of the earnest young policeman. He could see half of Lynn's face over his shoulder. No flutter in the eye now. Lynn knew the cops were running out their string for the day . . .

Because Captain Vincent was seated at the side of the door, the man who knocked lightly could not see him when he opened it before Lynn could give an answer. Vincent, however, was looking directly at Lynn as the stranger entered. Lynn's face went white, the eye fluttered.

"Chevy?" the stranger asked as he stepped into the room. Hackman pulled around to look up at him as he advanced toward Lynn's desk with an envelope in his hand. Lynn looked panicky.

"Chevy?" the man asked again. Where had Vincent heard that voice before? He could only see his back as the stranger moved toward the desk, cutting off half of Lynn's face again. One terrified eye was fixed on the man as he dropped the envelope on the desk and turned quickly to go. Vincent pushed the door shut and stood up to block the startled stranger's path.

"Well, well," the captain said, "you've shaved and changed your clothes . . ."

Lynn was on his feet, waving the envelope at the man's back. "There's some mistake, this isn't for me . . ."

The messenger was the man in greasy overalls Vincent had met in the outer office at the Five Brothers garage. He tried to bolt past Captain Vincent, who grabbed him by the arms and pushed him back against the desk. Hackman rose as Lynn, his calmness shattered, sat immobile, holding the envelope.

"What's your name?" Vincent asked, holding the visitor tightly in his grasp.

"Fuck you!" the man shouted, struggling to free himself.

"Settle down, settle down," Vincent said, forcing the man away from the desk and facing him against the wall. "Okay, hands above your head. Let's go. Search him, officer, while I call for assistance." Vincent reached for the phone and grabbed the envelope. He completed his call for assistance and hung up the telephone as Officer Hackman removed a snubnosed revolver from inside the stranger's coat and placed it on the edge of the desk.

Vincent inspected the plain envelope, opened it carefully, and removed a folded piece of stationery. In it were five crisp one-hundred-dollar bills.

"Oh, Jesus," Lynn wailed.

"For Crissake, shut up," the stranger said. "Why didn't you warn me you had cops here?" Lynn looked despairingly, as if across an unbridgeable universe, at the crude man by the wall. He put his hands on the sides of his head. "Oh, Jesus . . ."

"You were in a hurry with this payoff," Vincent said as he studied the stationery. He looked at Lynn. "So you're 'Chevy.' This is addressed to you. 'Thanks.' That's all it says. No signature." He smiled broadly. He held the paper by the edge so that Lynn could see. "They should never use business stationery." A familiar title ran across the top of the page. "Five Brothers Limousines. Anywhere, Any Time, Anybody."

"Mrs. O'Brien, I'm only saying that you're pushing too hard." Rafferty had a squeezed look.

"It's two o'clock in the afternoon and you're telling me *I'm* pushing too hard?" Ann Marie clutched the arms of her chair. "You've had plenty of time to work on this and three committeemen who agreed to come have backed off? And *I'm* supposed to take the blame!" She curled and uncurled her fingers. Rafferty stood his ground, Benjamin Franklin reeling his kite up to the lightning.

"We'll have the news conference anyway . . ."

"Begging your pardon, Mrs. O'Brien, but you can't show up with only eight of the committeemen. Can't you see that it will reveal your weakness, that you piped to them and they did not dance?"

Ann Marie's breathing was audible to Rafferty.

"What did Cullen do, just what the hell did he do?"

"I don't think Cullen did anything at all. He wouldn't talk to them, wouldn't tell them anything."

Goddammit, Ann Marie thought, silence from the bear, silence when she wanted him to come out and fight with her . . .

"You see, ma'am, they don't know what Cullen thinks or what he's going to do. That, if I may say, is a classic Cullen move. Or a classic piece of Richler strategy. Perhaps a little of both . . ."

"What the hell do you mean?"

"Well, when Cullen won't say anything, then he plays on all the fears and uncertainties of the committeemen. He could have any of a number of strategies in mind. And he's still the chairman of the party . . ."

"But *I'm* the Mayor . . ."

"They know that very well. Would you let me speak frankly? They will not do anything, certainly not commit themselves to you, before Cullen makes his position clear. They don't know what he's going to do so they are very wary of him. He has plenty on them. And, for all they know and for all we know, he may decide to run again . . ."

"That's ridiculous. The people are behind me . . ."

"The people, ma'am, are fickle. You may not like it, but they could switch away from you very quickly."

"I don't believe that . . ."

"The fact of it doesn't depend on whether you believe it or not."

"I can talk right to them, I can speak directly to them."

"That is your genius, Mrs. O'Brien. I, least of all, would dispute that. We face here, and may God grant us a favorable outcome, a difficult situation. The more you have pitted yourself against the committeemen, the more they have drawn back. You can't threaten them as though they were galley slaves, ma'am."

Ann Marie bit her lower lip. She wanted the committeemen. She wanted their support before her fund-raising. And Cullen—she could not even summon up his features—Cullen was a silent mass, Mont Blanc hidden in the mist. Cullen was keeping them in line by not saying a thing. She took a deep breath. She had told the committeemen to come, she had threatened them . . . Who the hell did they think they were?

"Mrs. O'Brien, there's plenty of time to cancel this news conference. Let's just let the whole thing pass for a while. There's nothing to be gained from it. And your dinner is coming up. Surely, that's enough . . ."

"I'm not canceling it," she snapped.

"Surely, you can see . . ."

Ann Marie looked directly into Rafferty's eyes. "Who the hell are you working for, me or 'Tom' Cullen, as you like to call him? Listen, I want plans, diagrams, whatever you people have got, for the new sports complex . . ."

"But . . ."

"I don't want to hear any more about what I *can't* do, do you understand that? I'm going to announce the sports complex this afternoon. It's the biggest development ever undertaken here. And the people know we've needed it. Get the presidents of the sports teams here, the architects . . ."

"Mrs. O'Brien, there are many arrangements that have not been made . . ."

"They will be. I'll see to that. You just get Barone and his partners down here." She was enthusiastic, bubbling, in the lead car as the roller coaster cranked upward. "Do you hear me? We'll give the people something to think about . . ."

"Yes, ma'am," Rafferty said gravely, rising from his chair. He looked at her carefully. She was radiant again, ready with a new plan, an unflappable hostess setting out cold cuts after the roast has burned. Remarkable. He wondered as he crossed the carpet if he could quietly resign as her campaign manager. No, she would never allow that. And it could never be done quietly. They were all in this—he, Barone, Wendel, Carey, Noto, and even Paul Michael Martin—they were all in it for good now.

"Mary, if I knew, I'd tell you."

Mary Vincent hugged her husband again. She had cried at first, but now her only concern was to comfort her husband. She would scratch Ann Marie's eyes out someday.

Captain Vincent, still numb from being abruptly reassigned late that afternoon, shook his head. He had to repeat what had happened, replay the tape to make sure he hadn't missed something.

"She had this news conference. Big stuff. All about new sports stadiums. Plans for a permanent Olympic site in Chicago. A racetrack . . ." He pulled away from Mary and paced across their bedroom. "I had a call. We'd collared these two in the act of passing and accepting a payoff. I thought maybe I was going to get a commendation. Get to City Hall, that's all I heard. The news conference was a big thing. She knows how to put on a show, let me tell you . . ." He embraced his wife again. "After the news conference, all she said was that I should come in her office a minute. Then she raised hell with me. Told me she had given me orders I was to stop looking into the Phillips thing. She said I was finished at City Hall, that the Superintendent would have someone replace me on the security detail for the Pope's visit. Then she said, 'Goodbye,' just like that. That was it. When I walked out, the policeman at the desk handed me a letter from the Superintendent. I'm to take a thirty-day vacation and then report back for reassignment . . ." He shook his head again. "Hackman's been reassigned to the Wood Street District. I got hold of Hanlon. He just said it was a 'routine reassignment,' that's what he said." Paul Vincent did not know what to think. "And, Mary, they've dropped charges on Lynn and the other guy . . ."

"Oh, Paul, Paul, I was afraid something like this would happen. I told you she was dangerous." Mary held her husband close to her.

"I don't think it was her, Mary, I really don't. Someday I'd like to ask her. I really would . . ."

"Yes, Mark, I saw it on television. Yes, she's good at pulling rabbits out of a hat." Cullen winked at his seven-year-old grandson, Kevin, who had been talking to him when the phone rang. Cullen was frustrated that he could not use his left hand to fondle him while his right hand held the phone. "What's that, Mark? No, I expected they'd back off. As my mother used to tell me, your power expands when you keep your mouth shut. But they owe her something now. They'll be looking for ways to get back with her." Kevin climbed onto his grandfather's lap. "Mark, I've made up my mind on something. I'll need your best plan on how to handle it. Why don't you come over tomorrow? Ten o'clock. Fine, fine. Good night now . . ."

A red-gowned Ann Marie, escorted by Paul Michael Martin, had just entered the Presidential Suite at the top of the Hilton Hotel for the cocktail party that preceded the Israel Awards Dinner. She was to receive a plaque for her previous work with the Missing in Action. She was still angry at the committeemen who had been missing in action that afternoon. Many had called her to apologize, to assure her of their good will. Maybe she hadn't lost so much after all. The things that didn't happen in politics were sometimes as powerful as those that did. The news conference had been a smash hit. She had dominated the evening news with it. Martin told her that there would be big headlines and favorable editorials in the morning papers. She had done herself more good, Martin had said, than if all the committeemen had shown up. The people didn't understand old politicians, he had said, his ferocious lusty smile breaking, they understood circuses. Circuses like the big development she had announced. Circuses—he had grinned—that entertained and educated them. Then he had kissed her so hard that she had to redo her makeup before they left for the evening.

"Mrs. O'Brien, I'd like to talk to you." It was Richard Barone, croupier-looking in a velvet tuxedo.

"What is it?" Ann Marie asked, nodding at a passing justice of the State Supreme Court. The slick and the powerful of the city filled the room. They all wanted to say hello to the beautiful Mayor.

"You did a great job at the news conference," Barone said with no carbonation in his voice.

"I thought so. You don't sound so happy. What's the matter, didn't I mention you enough?"

"No, it's not that. It's not that. Is there somewhere we can talk?"

"If it's important, talk here." Ann Marie shook hands with an elderly financier. Barone nodded distractedly at him as he stepped away.

"We'll talk before we go down to the dinner."

Barone said, "I'll arrange for a room."

"What's this all about?"

"I'll let you know where we'll meet. I'll tell Paul."

Ann Marie circulated through the cocktail party for half an hour, smiling and greeting the distinguished guests who would be seated on the dais with her. They all wanted to talk to her, they wanted to congratulate her on her new leaf for the city, on the wonderful new plans for the sports complex. Oh, yes, they'd be supporting her in the campaign. Oh, yes . . .

She had not liked leaving early in order to gather on the floor below in a suite that the hotel manager had made available to Barone. She was surprised when she and Martin entered to find Rafferty, Wendel, and Monsignor Fitzmaurice already there. She was impatient to get back to the crowd, to hear the rustle of silk and the sound of praise, to feel the approving smiles of the city's high and mighty.

"We have a little problem," Barone said uneasily.

"Morgan, what are you doing here?" Ann Marie asked her cousin.

"Mr. Barone will explain," Fitzmaurice said in his churchy voice.

Nobody looked at ease in the huge room. "What's the matter with all of you? I gave your project a great kickoff this afternoon." She stepped toward Rafferty and pinched his seamed cheek playfully. "I told you I'd show those committeemen . . ." Rafferty did not alter his long-suffering expression.

"Mrs. O'Brien, you may have announced the project too soon," Barone said flatly.

Ann Marie half-listened as she looked around the elaborate suite. "What are you talking about?"

"The deal was far from set. You've drawn attention to it in a way that may jeopardize its completion."

Ann Marie glanced at Paul Martin. "What's your friend so upset about?" she asked, the queen not taking the court too seriously.

"I mean this, Mrs. O'Brien. There are a lot of pieces to a deal like this. We've been working through the HUD secretary's office for improvement money. Well, that comes to over three million dollars. Our Washington contact heard about your announcement and is backing out. He only called me an hour ago. Says the money can only go to rehabilitate housing for lower-income people. Says he can't let it through to us with all this publicity."

"Get it somewhere else, Mr. Barone. You've always told me how important you are."

"Listen, this involves more than that. We've got applications in at HUD, sworn statements, records and projections, all kinds of stuff. This undersecretary is backing out, he's threatening to turn this material over to the Attorney General's office . . ."

Ann Marie studied the uncomfortable-looking men standing in a jagged circle around her. They were staring into a possible federal investigation. That's why they wanted to talk to her. They needed her to save them.

"Mrs. O'Brien," Barone continued, deadly serious, "this is a dangerous situation. This man in Washington was a partner, a secret partner. He's scared now, scared that his role in setting up and okaying these funds will become known. He's threatening to turn us in, take the credit for it, say he was just playing along . . ."

"He'll save himself and let you all explain yourselves in court?" Ann Marie asked. These men—she never had really liked any of them, except Paul. They had tried to ruin her, tried to boss her. Now they were on their knees to her.

"Mrs. O'Brien"—how humble Barone sounded—"the Vice-President is coming to your fund-raiser. We want you to speak to him. He'll understand, he can put this straight for us . . ."

She regarded them coldly. "You got yourselves into this . . ."

"Annie," Paul Martin said anxiously, "Annie, I'm in this too."

"You?" she drew back a pace. "Why didn't you tell me?"

"I thought you knew. You knew I did a lot of business with Rich here."

"I didn't know anything about fraud on the government." She turned around slowly, looking from face to face, tasting and relishing her dominance. "And you, Morgan, are you here to give absolution?"

"Ann Marie, I, I, well, the church is involved too. I didn't think anything like this would come up. And, in the long run, it would all have worked out for the good of the city and the good of souls . . ." His voice, unconvincing in tone, trailed off.

Ann Marie turned away from Fitzmaurice. The room was quiet in an unhealthy way. The suite hadn't been used in weeks and stale air had been the medium for sour revelation.

"Mrs. O'Brien, you can think what you want of us . . ." Rafferty began.

"Don't worry. There's nothing I haven't already thought about all of you. But you, Paul, how the hell could you involve yourself?"

Paul generated the ghost of a charming smile. "I thought you understood. I thought you encouraged me. I didn't know about Washington . . ."

"And you, Morgan, with your pious talk about burying the dead . . ." She turned away before he could answer.

"Mrs. O'Brien," Rafferty said, coughing lightly, "every deal that makes for progress is complicated. Nothing would get done without certain understandings and arrangements. It's not illegal. Personally, I think this fellow's trying to scare us. This deal is not sinful. It's for the good of the city. More importantly, we have to get this back in perspective for your own political good. If this comes out—and it would only be a misunderstanding—the media who love you would destroy you overnight. You understand that, don't you?"

"Why didn't you tell me the danger this afternoon?"

"I had no idea that we had such a weak sister in Washington. I tried to discourage you from having a news conference at all. Surely you remember that."

"It isn't just this one thing with HUD," Barone said. "It's this whole thing. Start pulling off one edge of it and the whole thing comes to pieces. A lot of things that aren't bad could be made to look like they were. For example, that Monsignor Fitzmaurice and I have exchanged some properties in planning this. That could be misunderstood too."

"Especially when it isn't Monsignor Fitzmaurice's property, especially when it's been tax-exempt for years . . ." Ann Marie shook her head. "And you want me to talk to the Vice-President?"

"He'll cooperate. There's a national election next fall. He'll want to keep you happy."

Ann Marie studied the men around her again. "You make me sick," she said, and marched toward the door.

Ann Marie insisted on returning home immediately after the awards dinner. No drinks at Crickets as they had previously planned. She and Paul Martin were settled into the plush upholstery in the back of the Mayor's official limousine. She pushed a button and the glass partition rose behind the two bodyguards in the front seat. Ann Marie had pulled herself into a corner so that there was space enough for another large passenger between her and Martin.

"I know you're sore, Annie, but I didn't know about this Washington business . . ."

Ann Marie stared out the window at the lights, tracer bullets in the night.

"Now, Annie, we're going to be married pretty soon. We can't let a little misunderstanding come between us." His store of charm was low, his zest depleted. Even the sardonic Paul Martin had been severely shocked by the prospect of a federal investigation. They rode in silence for another mile. Ann Marie did not turn her head toward him when she began to speak.

"The first thing I'm going to do in the morning is drop Rafferty as my campaign manager . . ."

"What?"

"He can be named an adviser. The press of other business, some story like that. I'm going to ask Schroeder or Cutler to take over."

"You're going to ask *who?*" Martin was astounded. Ann Marie was always trumping herself.

"You heard me. Schroeder or Cutler. They've wanted more say in the Council. Well, I'll give it to them. And they're the biggest reformers in town." She turned her head toward Martin. "Nobody will ever connect *them* with any fraud."

What the hell was she going to do, dismantle the team? Once she got an idea, there was no way to stop her. What else could she be thinking of?

"Paul," she asked imperiously, coldly. The distance between them on the seat seemed to grow greater. "Paul, I want to know exactly how much you understood about this Washington business."

Bars of light and dark from the expressway lamps flicked rhythmically across his face. He looked straight ahead, contemplating how to tell the truth. And how much.

"Annie, I didn't know anything about this until you did. Honest to God." He signed a gesture remembered from his boyhood on the ruffled shirt above his heart. "I knew about the plans in general. I knew there were contacts in Washington. There had to be. With a project that size, there are thousands of connections with other interested parties, with a dozen governmental bureaucracies. Barone's been in this business a long time. He has to deal with these people every day. He couldn't get anything built otherwise. And nothing would ever be built if somebody didn't make these connections. That's how O'Brien City got built. You ought to know that." He sounded honest, his head cleared by the prospect of hanging.

"What kind of business arrangements do you have with Barone? I want the whole truth now. No holding back. If there's anything that might involve me in—"

He interrupted before she could come to the conclusion that he dreaded. She would call off the marriage if there were any prospect of his being involved in lawbreaking with Barone. Who the hell knew what she would do? Jesus, his best bet was to go through with the marriage. The safest place he could find if anything went wrong was by the side of the Mayor of Chicago.

"Annie, I know I play a lot of things very casually. But I'm not fooling you now. I've helped Barone in a lot of ways. Kind of public relations work. He's paid me. I'll admit that. He's had me on his payroll. But it's all been strictly legitimate. If I gave a project of his a favorable mention it was only after I had satisfied myself that the whole thing was worthwhile, that it was good for the city."

"What did he pay you?"

"A retainer. Two thousand dollars a month. I paid taxes on it, I swear. I'll show you the returns." Martin was fighting for his life.

"Yes, that would be a good idea." She paused. "Anything else?"

"Well, a couple of 'finder's fees.' All legitimate."

"What about that apartment?"

"Hell, nothing wrong with that, nothing wrong with that. Just a friendly gesture. That's all."

"Paul, for the first time since I've known you, you sound scared."

"No, no. Upset, that's it. Upset. I'm as upset as you about this. But I think it will work out. I honestly do." Should he say it or not? Would she rage at him, drop him out of the car, break their engagement? "Annie, this is just a misunderstanding. It'll be all cleared up when you speak to the Vice-President . . ." The suggestion floated in the air-conditioned

darkness, absorbed by the coffin-like cushions, honed by the whirring wheels.

"Paul, how much is Monsignor Fitzmaurice involved in this?"

"Not much. He was just trying to get his project off the ground—er, above the ground . . ." Ann Marie laughed. Paul felt better. "He's a big man in town. He didn't know anything about these details. He's caught in a misunderstanding too. You sure don't want the church embarrassed. That's political dynamite in this city. You remember when . . . ?"

"Cardinal Williams? I certainly do . . ."

The limousine turned off the expressway. In a few minutes they would be at Ann Marie's house. She seemed to have softened during the ride. The tightness in her voice had loosened. She had stopped checking off items on a master list. Now if she would only talk to the Vice-President . . .

"And that's all, that's all you know?"

"That's it." He held his breath. He couldn't tell her about his demands for a percentage of Barone's deals. That was off the books stuff anyway.

"Well, Paul, I feel better about this. You realize I have to know everything?"

"Sure, sure." Martin hunched across the seat to embrace her. She did not push him away.

"You're wonderful, Annie. I'm lucky to be the man to marry you . . ." He kissed her on the cheek, then on the eyes and the mouth . . .

The limousine stopped in front the old steamboat of a house. Paul Martin helped Ann Marie out of the car. They walked up the steps to the porch.

"I won't come in, Annie." He kissed her lightly again. The bodyguard opened the front door ahead of them. Ann Marie stepped across the threshold, then hesitated. Weak light from the lamp that Aunt Molly left on in the living room illumined half her face.

"By the way, Paul. Just one more question."

Martin pumped a charming grin up from the depths of his uncertainty. "Yes, Annie? You want to know whether I've brushed up on my catechism lessons?"

"No." She could not help but smile at him. He did look like a little boy filled with good resolutions. "It's nothing, really. I just wondered how you found out about Captain Vincent . . ."

"Just one of those newsroom accidents. But I knew you'd want to know he was playing Junior G-Man on the Phillips thing . . ."

"Yes, I did want to know. I don't want anything to do with that. Anyway, Vincent's on leave now. I kind of liked him. I wish he had stayed out of that . . ."

Rafferty had not protested his new status as special adviser to the
Mayor's campaign. The newspapers applauded her selection of Louis
Schroeder as the replacement for the leathery old alderman. "In step
with the times . . ." one editorial had said. "Represents the kind of integrity that the job needs . . ." said the other. The mistress of improvi-
sation had triumphed again, winning applause and headlines with her
move. Ann Marie felt better about everything. She would take Cullen
on, even if he remained silent, even if he would not fight directly with
her. She was burying all the troublesome ghosts, she was laying them all
away. Charlie, Cullen, Rafferty, Captain Vincent and his silly escapades.
Barone had new respect for her. So did Paul Martin.

And Mother Francis had called to congratulate her on the appointment of Schroeder. She was so sorry she had spoken so clumsily at their
lunch. Maybe they could try it again. She would certainly be at the
fund-raiser. Yes, and Ann Marie, would Ann Marie still consider heading
the drive for Our Lady of Peace? Wonderful, it would be like old
times . . .

Even Aunt Molly was warmer toward her. Molly liked the idea of Ann
Marie's getting married. That righted a great many wrongs, as far as her
conservative Catholic conscience was concerned. Perhaps Molly would
grant her visiting rights with Matthew.

Matthew. She had to get him out of Molly's grasp before it was too
late. That would be much easier once she was married to Paul Martin.
There would be less strain, less stress, less wondering . . . Matthew,
Matthew. Right now he was doing fine. She could let Aunt Molly enjoy
him for a little while yet. But after the wedding and after she had won
the Mayor's office on her own, she would reclaim her son.

But now she was riding to McCormack Place, the smoky slab exhibi-
tion hall on the lakefront just south of the Loop, for the combination
birthday party and fund-raising dinner. Over $1.2 million, after expenses,
in her campaign fund made the beginning of her fortieth year bearable.
The limousine entered the ramp to the hall. It would be a wonderful
night, a happy birthday after all. Suppose the Vice-President had made
a courtesy call on Cullen at his daughter's home that day. So what? That
couldn't spoil the night that belonged to her. Paul Martin waited at a
special entrance door to greet her and to accompany her, inside a circle
of bodyguards, to the room that had been set aside for her private meeting with the Vice-President.

"Annie, we were in luck," Martin whispered in her ear as they swept
along a wide airless hallway. "We didn't have to ask to set up the meeting. The Vice-President asked for a meeting with you on his own."

Ann Marie looked uncertainly at her escort without breaking her
stride. "What's that all about?"

"Probably to make sure of your support in next year's election. You're important to the President, you know."

They passed through double fire doors and up an escalator. The music from the great hall where the dinner was to be held sounded faintly through the walls. They stepped into a short hallway. Paul touched her on the arm.

"Wait, Annie. I should have given you this before." He pulled a small box from his pocket and flipped it open. The diamond, even in the dull hallway, was a collision of lights.

"Paul!" Ann Marie was genuinely surprised. She had never given up wearing Charlie's ring, she had not thought of this. But it was right, it was part of finishing the long patchy prologue of her life. She embraced Martin and he kissed her until a Secret Service man halfway down the hallway coughed. Ann Marie allowed Martin to slip the ring on her hand, made a quick repair of her makeup under Martin's reacting eye, and moved to the room in which the Vice-President awaited her. Paul Martin smiled. "You won't forget what you want to talk about?" She gave him an exasperated look and passed through the door that the government agent opened for her.

The Vice-President, a kingfisher in evening clothes, moved swiftly toward her, his hand darting out to take hers. A party stalwart, twice a senator, he had accepted the Vice-Presidency when it was clear that no higher office called him. Squat, graying hair ruffed like a bird's, he moved busily around her, escorting her to a chair in the corner of the lounge-like room.

"Mrs. O'Brien, would you like a drink?"

She shook her head and he nodded toward one of his gray-suited protectors who promptly left the room.

"The President sends you his best, Mrs. O'Brien. Yes, he said to me just before I left, you tell Mrs. O'Brien that she's the greatest Democrat in the greatest Democratic city in the country. By gosh, he did." The Vice-President circled around, shaking off energy, and lighted in the chair next to hers.

"Now I'm glad we have a few minutes to talk. And I'm sure you know how sorry the President was that he couldn't come. Yes, sir. I mean, yes, ma'am." He cocked his head and smiled. "Now, Mrs. O'Brien, I hardly need to tell you how important Chicago is in the national picture. By gosh, in the national picture it's just about the key. The saying is that you can win Chicago and lose but that you can't lose Chicago and win."

Ann Marie stared at the kinetic figure beside her. What was he driving at?

"It's no secret, Mrs. O'Brien, that the President has had a long and very close relationship with this city. And, I might say, with your predecessor, Mayor Cullen. Uh, former Mayor Cullen . . ." He fidgeted on the leather chair. "Now the President knows, as we all do, that you're now the Mayor. And we're proud to have you on the team. But, and let's get down to cases, Mrs. O'Brien, let's get down to cases . . ."

"Yes," Ann Marie answered, irritated, anxious to get to her party, "let's do."

"The thing is, the President respects Thomas Cullen. And Thomas Cullen is still head of the party in this county. And very important with other party leaders. Always has been . . ."

"Yes?"

"Well, we have to think of party unity. I saw Mayor, former Mayor Cullen this afternoon and I told him the President's feelings, same as I'm telling you. The President, Mrs. O'Brien, would like you to tone down your criticism of Cullen and see if you couldn't work out some arrangement, some rapprochement, as they like to say over at State, some way of getting along. We've heard from a lot of people, congressmen and, I might add, senators, who say that you've got the committeemen caught in the middle. The feeling is, Mrs. O'Brien, that you, being younger, could do a lot to ease the tension. By gosh, that's it . . ."

So this was Cullen's response to her! He still hadn't spoken directly. But she could feel his power, she could feel the pressure of his big hands being conveyed through this jumping-jack ninny of a Vice-President.

"It's not all my fault, Mr. Vice-President. Does the President know that?"

"Don't misunderstand us. The President is grateful to you for many things. Right now, though, he wants very much to have you emphasize party unity. The election's only a year off . . ."

"Are you telling me that Cullen plans to remain as head of the party?"

"That seems to be his disposition."

"Why doesn't he make it public?"

"He is a veteran, Mrs. O'Brien. You must appreciate that. He would never say it for fear people would think he didn't mean it. He just *presumes* that you understand . . ."

"Are you giving me a message from the President or the former Mayor?"

"You must remember Tom Cullen is still a very important man in Democratic politics. Not that you aren't, not for one minute, by gosh, that you aren't . . ."

Ann Marie was furious. She wanted to push this silly rocking teapot of a man out of his chair and bolt out of the room. She couldn't do that. She still had a favor she couldn't miss getting. Goddammit, she was trapped. For the moment anyway.

"Is Cullen going to run for Mayor again? Do you know that?"

"Well, we don't know. We hope, the President hopes, that Cullen will remain as party chief and that you will stay on as Mayor. If all goes well, that is . . ."

"Did Cullen agree to that?"

"Well, I can't speak for him. He knows how the President feels."

Damn Cullen, damn him and his roundabout ways, damn him and his silence and his pushing back from the dark. Was he going to go along with the President's deal or not? Was he actually going to let her have the nomination on these terms? He still had time, a couple of months, in which to make up his own mind.

"How can I be sure Cullen will go along with this?"

"Well, all we want from you is a period of truce. That's all. A truce, a period of calm, so this can all settle down. If you can provide that, then I'm sure this will work out."

So that was the deal. Silence from her and she might have a clear shot at the nomination. But Cullen, the old power hustler, hadn't said a thing. He still didn't have to. It left him free. But not her. The Cullens never give anything away, who had told her that?

"That leaves the burden on me, doesn't it? What do I get out of this?"

"Well," and the shrewdness of this nervous bird of a man became clearer in the more settled tone of his voice, "it's no small thing to have the Vice-President of the United States at your fund-raiser, is it? And, with your wedding coming up, and everything else, you'll have plenty to keep you busy for the next several weeks. You'll have a million dollars' worth of publicity. What more, Mrs. O'Brien, could you want?"

She studied him. His movements had coalesced into one piercing gaze at her.

"Let me add something else." He lowered his voice. "You won't have any trouble from HUD."

Ann Marie was startled. How was this information passed? How many people knew about this anyway? Was politics nothing but deal upon deal, wink and handclasp, and we're all pals together? Was that what she had to battle with? She would show them.

"You realize my popularity in this city?"

"We do indeed." He was jolly again, shifting, shooting his cuffs, throwing her off balance with his repertoire of anxious tricks. "And we'll give you all the help you need." He smiled and rose from his chair. "May I be the first to wish you a happy birthday?"

Ann Marie managed a smile. She was the Mayor. The people loved her. The less she said the better. She had learned a thing about power, about getting and keeping it.

"By gosh," the Vice-President said as though they had been discussing nothing more consequential than his grandchildren, "I think I'm the lucky man who gets to escort you downstairs tonight . . ."

38

W ell, Tom, she's been pretty quiet."

"Yes, she has, she really has. Of course, Mark, she's got the wedding this week and the Pope himself splashing the holy water at a special altar in Grant Park. That'll put her at the top of the news all around the world."

"She seems to need a big splash now and then, no matter what the issue." Richler lighted a cigarette.

"When are you going to drop the other shoe?"

"No hurry, Mark. Let's just let this string play out."

"Are you still going ahead with it the way you told me?"

Cullen fingered the jade-headed cane that was propped between his legs. He wrinkled his brow and arched his mouth in mock inner debate with himself. "I figure there's plenty of time. Maybe we should let a rumor float. Just to get it in the wind . . ."

Richler smiled, as one does at a complex and intricate machine shoveled out of the earthquake debris and found to be scarred and dusty but in perfect working order. "It'll be a hell of a campaign. One hell of a campaign."

"A tough one, believe me . . ."

"When did you finally decide about this?"

"Oh, I've had it in mind for a long time. Of course, I never expected that the things that happened this year, the stroke and all, would happen. That's the trouble with politics, the damned unpredictability . . ." Cullen shook his head, picked up the thread of his answer. "I really decided one day after I got home here. The grandkids would come and read their lessons to me. And Kevin read something from his nature book. I ought to look it up again. The gist of it was that queen bees can only be killed by other queens . . ." Cullen grinned and stamped the floor with his cane. "That's when I decided that Maureen should run in my place . . ."

"I don't want to hear any more about Cullen!" Ann Marie shouted at Martin in her office after a budget meeting had broken up.

"Let me tell you something, Annie, you've done more to keep him alive than anybody in this town. Do you realize that?" Martin was snappish, pushing her hard.

She looked sullenly at the man who would soon be her husband.

"I'm serious, Annie, I really am. If you hadn't been so scared that he might show up in your office ahead of you some morning, he'd be pretty much a forgotten man in this city by now."

"You don't know what you're talking about." Ann Marie glared at him. Who the hell did he think he was?

"Yes, I do. Ever since the Vice-President shut you out before the fund-raiser, I've been thinking about this. And lots of people have talked about it, people on your side. You've got to stop fighting with Cullen. Honest to God, Annie, I love you or I wouldn't say this. Ask Lou Schroeder, just ask him. He'll tell you the same thing. Even when you don't mention Cullen, you give the idea that you're thinking about him."

"Stop it, Paul, that's *enough*." Ann Marie picked up her phone. Martin reached over and depressed the connection.

"*Listen* to me, will you? Annie, after this wedding you'll be a cinch to win the nomination. The town'll take you to its heart. The committeemen will be wise enough to know that you represent the future. They know who's going to butter their bread." Ann Marie hung up the phone and sat back, resisting Martin, rigid with the anger that welled up when she thought of the trap Cullen had sprung on her through the Vice-President.

"You've got a meeting with Schroeder later. Listen to his advice. He's calm and he underplays things but he's the best connection you've got with the undecided voters and with the independents who are leaning towards you. He'll tell you just what I've said. *Forget* Cullen. Stop running against him. Honest to God, Annie, there have been times when I think you want him to win, that you *want* him to come back . . ."

"Why are you bringing this up now? I've heard you. You can only say these things so many times. I've *heard* you. That's enough . . ." Ann Marie picked up a folder and jabbed the air angrily with it. "You should be busy making sure *your* friends don't make any more mistakes on this sports project. They're *my* biggest problem. Wendel was in here yesterday. You know what he wants? Oh, he puts it very nicely now. He's a gentleman to me and all that. He just wants to get support for reconsideration of that cable television franchise he was so interested in two years ago . . ." She slapped the folder back onto the surface of her desk and reached for the small ashtray. Martin leaned close to her, staring down her pouty gaze.

"Where do you think you would be without the help of these men in the City Council? You wouldn't get a damned thing done."

Ann Marie closed her fingers on the ashtray, lifting it off the desk. Martin grabbed her wrist and held it firm.

"The reason I'm discussing this is that you've put the ball back in Cullen's court. You've got everybody looking in his direction to see what he'll do next. With the wedding you've got a chance to get undivided attention back on yourself . . ." He released his hand and the ashtray rang dully as it dropped onto the desk.

Martin backed away from the desk. "Cool off," he said, "and remember, don't react to questions about Cullen. Don't mention him. And . . ."

"And *what?*" Ann Marie asked impatiently.

"Don't react when somebody asks you if you've heard the rumor."

"What rumor? What are you talking about?"

"That Cullen is going to run Maureen against you for the nomination."

Ann Marie held her tongue when reporters fired questions about Maureen Cullen Coleman's potential candidacy. So it would be Maureen. Fine. This was inevitable. It had been for a long time, ever since they had first joined forces to thwart the takeover attempt against Cullen, ever since they had competed, sweetly uneasy with each other, for his affection. Maureen. Out in the open at last. Fine, that would be just fine.

Today, however, was a day in which Maureen would play no part. Neither she nor her father had been invited to the wedding. Ann Marie would, as Paul Martin said, have the stage of public attention all to herself. The people loved her. A million of them were already assembled for the Pope's Mass at which, through the kind intercession of Cardinal Meehan, she was going to marry Paul Michael Martin, with the Pope himself as the Church's witness. A million people, and she would be the one they cared about, the one they wished well for. Everybody loved weddings . . .

She was in the member's lounge above the Columbus Drive entrance of the Art Institute. Because of the unusual security surrounding the papal visit, everyone associated with the wedding had been gathered in the new wing of the museum. On the east wall of the restaurant, great windows opened on the park, where the crowd seemed to hold still and move constantly at the same time. Bright sun flooded the area that spread from the museum toward the Drive and the silvered lake beyond. A few clots of autumn color hung like air plants in the sentinel lines of trees that bordered the park. Ann Marie inhaled as she looked at the view. It was her day. She would take care of Maureen later.

Her father sat in a wheelchair looking vaguely up at Aunt Molly, who was giving a dumb show explanation of something or other to him. Matthew stood by the window talking earnestly to his old friend, Sergeant Berrigan. A handsome boy. He wouldn't be a boy much longer. Ann Marie, wearing a simple red dress, surveyed the milling crowd that filled the restaurant off the lounge. A muffled din, the tinkle of glasses, the proper music of a string quartet. It might have been a wedding reception instead of a pre-nuptial gathering.

The good spirit of the crowd and the hum of excitement that rose from the anticipated events of the day combined to make Ann Marie feel that she could not possibly lose, not today, not in the election. Not anymore. Still, as she looked around the room, she could not completely overcome certain reactions that she associated with aldermen like Wendel who stood in laughing conversation with Raymond Carney.

She felt used, passed around like an Indian pipe in their daily brokerage of power. Rafferty and Ramirez clinked glasses halfway across the room. These men did what they had to do every day. That was all. That was power. Nothing glamorous. It was a commodity like coal and the traders were indifferent to moral considerations. The market and its needs determined its price and its distribution. Mark the sack and throw it on the truck. Pay today's price. Forget yesterday's. Don't worry about tomorrow's. Business was conducted today, only today. She saw Ramirez talking to Larry Johnson. It didn't make any difference what their background was. Politicians were all more alike than they were different.

She shuddered mildly. The same cast, including Barone and Noto, who were with Paul Martin on the floor below in the rebuilt Chicago Stock Exchange Trading Room, had been present a hundred weeks before when she had made her first visit to the City Council Chamber. There had been political upheaval in the city since then, a revolution accomplished, a new era begun. Everything had been shaken up and yet, two years later, the same people were in place. Everything had changed and nothing had changed. Even Cullen was still around, making a last stand with this silly plan to nominate his daughter. How did Cullen survive? Was he different than these men? Was he here in some way, even though uninvited? Power wasn't a sack of coal for Cullen. It was like his lungs or heart, a part of him. Cullen doesn't think about it, Richler had once told her, he doesn't have to think about it, it's natural to him. Damn Richler . . .

Chicago resembled what she had learned in her Thomistic philosophy class. It was all prime matter. Its basic material never changed, and it never would. There was Franklin Barnes chatting with George Harding. They were part of it. The great prime matter of the city was invested with new forms, with new shapes from time to time. But it remained always the same. The players were always the same. The bankers, the politicians. Cousin Morgan elbowed through the crowd. And the priests. She had to remember that, she would remember that. They hadn't seen anything yet.

"Paul, there's some writer on the phone. He wants to interview you . . ."

"If it's that same guy who used to be a cop in L.A., tell him no . . ."

"He's in town, he says. He wants to stop by . . ."

Vincent groaned to himself. These weeks of inactivity had been very hard. He had repaired everything that needed fixing in the house. He did not want to talk about his experiences, but Mary was in love with the idea of famous people coming to interview him. She gabbled on at the downstairs phone while Vincent changed his shirt in their bedroom. She was just hanging up when, pulling a tie under his collar, he descended the stairs.

"He's coming by later . . ." she said timidly.

"Oh, Christ, Mary, you know I don't want to talk . . ."

"Where are you going, Paul?"

"To see the Pope, to get drunk, to miss this high-style writer . . ."

"Paul!" Mary shook her head. "Maybe you should get out. You haven't been any fun to live with lately."

"Mary"—Vincent turned as he put his hand on the door—"I'm sorry. You understand, don't you? I know I've been hard to live with. That's why I'm going out. Time off for you and time off for me too. You talk to him . . ."

Mary accepted his check-out kiss and watched him as he hurried out the door and down the front steps. Poor Paul. That woman, it was that woman who caused all the trouble and he didn't even want to admit it.

Paul Vincent glanced at his watch. As he remembered the preliminary schedule, the Mayor would just be leaving for the Art Institute and the Pope would be having lunch at Cardinal Meehan's old North Side mansion. With so many people heading for the lakefront for the peace Mass and the wedding it was the ideal time to make the trip he had in mind. He waited by the curb looking back at the bungalow in which he and Mary had lived for twenty years. What the hell had he done wrong to deserve the streak of luck he had experienced lately? A horn sounded. Victor Hackman stopped his car and Captain Vincent climbed in.

"Sure they won't miss you?" Vincent asked as he settled into the front seat.

"Hell, they've sent so many extra men to Grant Park they don't know where anybody is. This is just a long lunch hour."

They headed down into the city, cutting off the expressway at Western Avenue to follow the wide old street as it made its deep cut through factories, storefronts, and brick apartment buildings toward the West Side of Chicago.

"If I'm right, all the limousines will be out today. Hell, it should be one of the busiest days they've ever had . . ."

Hackman nodded. He too was anxious to find out what had happened after they had caught the judge's clerk who, under the alias "Chevy," had warned the Five Brothers that a search warrant had been issued for their garage. He remembered that afternoon very well and its champagne-like taste of triumph. It had lasted all of two hours before they had both been transferred and the charges against the clerk and the garage worker had been dropped. Maybe this afternoon they would find out what had happened.

They parked two blocks from the garage operated by the Williams brothers. The streets were as quiet as they were just before dawn. The old Italian pastor had chartered buses to bring his parishoners down to see the Pope that afternoon. It was mild for late October and braids of tattered yellow leaves still fluttered in the tree limbs that arched across the side streets. Traffic on the broad avenue was also light and the Five Brothers garage looked forlorn and harmless, like an old watchdog abandoned in the countryside. Vincent nodded at Hackman and they crossed the street as casually as they could. The captain had a reputation for remaining cool in emergencies. But he was close to something and could feel his heart pounding as they approached the door to the small office at the front of the building. They looked through the smeared window. There was nobody inside. The captain pulled at the door and it opened. The policemen stepped into the small office where the man in greasy overalls had greeted Vincent almost two months before.

Neither man spoke. Vincent signaled for Hackman to check out the area below the counter while he eased through the door in the grimy glass-brick wall and entered the garage proper. Emptied of sleek automobiles, the place looked larger and dirtier. The smells of a thousand lube jobs lifted off the rack. They mixed with bad coffee, stale doughnuts, and the pungent sourness of the uncleaned men's room. The whole family was driving again today. But they had left their odors behind. A rat that had been finishing the crumbs of a long-past coffee break piped among the hand tools on a shelf along the wall.

Vincent listened at the door of the office that had been partitioned off in the corner, fingered the gun at his belt, and pushed the door open. Nothing. He stepped into the dingy room. The clutter, the clipboards along the wall were as he remembered them. Miss October, holding a pumpkin in front of her loins, gazed dumbly from the calendar on the wall. Vincent moved behind the desk and shuffled through the order sheets loosely piled on its top. Grant Park, almost all of them. Almost. He pulled a paper loose and studied it more carefully.

The office at the front of the garage was quiet and summertime-stuffy. Hackman had gone through the papers and ledgers beneath the counter. Old stuff. Lots of weddings. Even more funerals. Jesus, they must have a funeral or two a day, sometimes three. That's what comes in these neighborhoods filled with old people, great-grandmothers and great-grandfathers who went back almost as far as Garibaldi. He did not hear anybody come into the office. So he did not expect the blow behind his ear

that sent him sprawling in a shower of old order forms onto the splintery
floor.

Captain Vincent slipped several sheets of paper into his side pocket
and opened the desk drawer. Rubber bands, paper clips, pencils. He
picked out a soiled card and looked carefully at it. 2R–3L–1R. Where
the hell was the safe? He looked around the walls. The goddamn thing
had to be here somewhere. Miss October and her pumpkin. Of course.
He ripped the calendar off the wall and tossed it aside—just enough
noise to obscure the sound of Hackman's slumping to the floor in the
dingy street office. The captain opened the safe quickly and pulled at
the contents.

Jesus Christ, they were leather bags, thonged leather bags, larger ver-
sions of the one that he had seen played out like a spider below Phillips's wrist. Jesus Christ. He loosened one of them and dumped the contents, a jumble of plastic bags swollen with a white substance, onto the
desk. Cocaine. Jesus Christ. Vincent studied the bulging packets. How
the hell much was it worth? He shook his head. It was time to stop
fooling around. He'd better get the stuff back in the safe and get a
proper warrant or some judge would throw the whole thing out anyway.
He shoved everything back, flipped the wall safe closed, retrieved the
calendar and rehung it.

He looked around the office once more and stepped through the door.
The knife slashed along the length of his right arm as the man jumped at
him, toppling him over, crashing with him onto the sticky floor.
Vincent had no clear impression of his attacker, just flashes of darkness,
of grunts, of a tumbling, rolling struggle, of cans tipping and rolling
crazily around them, of an animal that had been so coiled to strike him
that he had been hit blind, splaylegged, unprepared, unable to organize
his own response. A face grazed his as they crashed like barrels off a
truck against the wall of the garage. A face full of bristles, an animal all
right, snarling and clawing and trying to kill him. Vincent's arm stung
with pain. Was he half-killed already? They tipped forward, gripped together like trapeze artists, and then fell heavily against the wall. The
shelf shook, the wrenches and drills danced crazily above them, and
twenty years of grit shivered down on them. Vincent heaved against his
assailant and the man went loose, his knife flashing out of his hand and
into the air, hitting the floor and skittering away.

The man crashed down on the captain again. Jesus, I can't go this
way, not with this fucker. I can't let him take me. His assailant spewed
saliva on his face. Not this son of a bitch, this son of a bitch has caused
me enough trouble already. Vincent threw himself against the bristly
man whose leg flailed up, catching the electric drill cord that was hanging off the shelf. The drill tumbled down as he straightened out his leg.

Now or never. Vincent clawed at it, grasped it, dropped it. They seesawed again. Vincent's head scraped against the cinder block wall. Vincent thought of Mary. A terrified face as she opened the door when the policeman came with the news. He butted his assailant, reached for the drill, clawed it halfway into his hand, and cracked it against the side of his attacker's head. He went limp and rolled, sack-like, blood welling in his hair, off the captain and onto the floor. Vincent kicked himself free, and struggled to catch his breath. He grasped the shelf with his left hand and pulled himself up. He looked down at the strong young man who had tried to kill him. The captain's right arm was bleeding but he could still use it. He reached for his gun, probing the stirring man sprawled in front of him with his foot. He was still dangerous, the son of a bitch, he might not even be hurt much. Maybe I should kill the son of a bitch now, maybe I should. Vincent stepped away from the man, away from his feet, out of his range. Where the hell had the knife gone?

"Captain"—he turned to see Hackman's outline against the bright blurred opening of the outer office door—"what's happened?"

"Come in here," Vincent said between deep breaths. "Come in here and take a look at George Phillips."

Hackman moved across the floor, touching the back of his head, feeling a radiation of pain with each step.

"George Phillips? He's dead, isn't he?"

The man on the floor groaned. "Ask him," Vincent said, "just ask the son of a bitch if he isn't George Phillips . . ."

The black-sweatered man on the floor moaned and tried to lift himself on his right elbow. Captain Vincent kicked at his forearm and he collapsed with a shriek of pain.

"Search him, Victor. Be careful." Vincent leaned against the shelf, battling to regulate his breathing. Hackman frisked the man on the floor. He found a knife strapped just above his right ankle.

"Shall I call for help?" he asked, straightening up carefully and moving back a few paces from the squirming man on the floor.

"No, I want to talk to him first. Get up, get up, you son of a bitch." Vincent kicked the bottoms of the man's booted feet. "And do it very carefully."

The man, streaks of blood over his ear and down the side of his neck, struggled to a sitting-up position. He looked up at Vincent, hard eyes riding in his grease-smeared face.

"That's enough," Vincent said. "Now, you are George Phillips, aren't you?"

"Fuck you," the man muttered, touching the injured side of his head with his right hand.

"Just put your hands on the floor, palms down. That's a good boy, Georgie."

Captain Vincent glanced at his own bleeding arm. It would keep.

"We've been waiting to meet a long time, Georgie. You remember me, don't you? You knew we'd meet some day, didn't you?"

"Go fuck yourself," the man growled.

"That's not the way to talk now. I could shoot you, Georgie. Who the hell would know? I might get a medal . . ."

"Captain!" Hackman cut in.

"Don't worry, I have a better idea. Listen carefully, Georgie." He felt gingerly with his right hand in his jacket pocket for the papers he had picked up in the office. "Now, I'll tell you my plan. What I want you to do, Georgie, is get up and go to your car. It's got to be right outside. Then I want you to drive to Angelo Barone's funeral parlor." He shook the papers at him. "The address is right here. We must have come just when you were making a transfer. Otherwise you wouldn't have left any-thing from the funeral parlor here. You wouldn't have left the door open. And you wouldn't have left that shit in the safe. I'll bet it's never in there more than an hour. Thought it would be quiet today, right? Was that the plan?" Vincent circled to the side of the man who had attacked him. "Come on, look up. That's better. Now you go to the funeral home. They're waiting for you there anyway, aren't they? Angie and his two kids, your two playmates. They expect you back with the bags any min-ute. So you go in and tell them what happened. I'm serious. You tell them you've lost the stuff, tell them I kicked the shit out of you, and you need their help . . ."

The man's anger turned to fear. This police captain just might make him do this. "Jesus!" he moaned. "Come on, you're not serious . . ."

"Why not? What do you think they'd do to you? How long would it take them? You've seen them kill men before. You know what it's like. That was your big jack-off thrill, you and your pals. They'd kill you quick, isn't that right, and you'd be gone in one of their caskets, right? Underneath some old paisano, right? That's the way you did it, isn't it?"

"Captain, for Crissake . . ."

"Oh, you do recognize me, you do. We've got to hurry, Georgie. Your pals will be impatient. They've got a coffin lying open to put the pouches in. They'll wonder what happened if you're not back soon. I think it would be better that way in the long run. Why put the state to the trou-ble of trying you, why go through all that?"

"Captain, cut it out . . ." Phillips's voice was choked with dread.

"Why? You always killed on your own timetable. You tricked them, played with them, killed them, and then numbered them, you son of a bitch . . ." Vincent kicked Phillips in the side. "Now, I want you to talk, I want to know all about this. Or, so help me, I'll feed you to your friends . . ."

Phillips did not speak. His eyes said yes for him.

"Get up, get up before I change my mind. I wouldn't mind killing you, do you know that?" Phillips rose unsteadily and Vincent prodded him with his gun into the rear office. "Call for assistance, Vic. We're going to need a Tac Team and we're going to need a warrant to search the Barone Funeral Home." He pointed to the chair behind the desk and Phillips, still terrified, still uncertain about what Captain Vincent would do, sat down carefully. Hackman picked up the phone to make his call.

"You know why I knew you were alive? Because you wrote the number fourteen on that poor bastard's forehead, the guy you killed to make it look like you were dead. I knew it was easy to switch dental records, and it wasn't easy to fix fingerprints. Where'd you get the guy? Probably from around here. One of the drivers, right? So it was easy for the Barones, who deal with bodies and bones all the time, to switch dental records. Right? They knew who it was. Somebody from the neighborhood, some poor bastard who thought you'd fixed him up with something good at that fleabag. Is that right?"

Phillips nodded, wide-eyed.

"You had the nerve to take a ride the night of the prayer service. Christ, with your dark clothes and your moustaches, you all look alike, right? Who the hell would be looking for you? Then you saw me and you knew goddamn well that I saw you. You must have seen me searching the streets. Where the hell did you go? Tell me, you son of a bitch . . ." Vincent poked his revolver in Phillips's chest.

"In the rectory. It was easy, you just walk in. It says it on the door . . ." Phillips's voice sounded tired, worn down.

"So you decided to fake your death. Shouldn't be too hard to find out who the poor bastard was. You couldn't resist the number though, could you? I knew goddamn well nobody else would have bothered to do it for you . . ."

Squad cars had pulled up on the street and the garage was filling with policemen.

"You killed Noto's nephew too, didn't you? Why? Because he found out about you? He was straight and he found out about the queer killings you and the Barone boys thought was fun. That was it, wasn't it?"

Phillips nodded as a police sergeant entered the office.

"And he found out about the drugs you were smuggling, right? Using the bottoms of caskets? Bodies being flown in from all over, old people who wanted to be buried in the neighborhood. Who the hell would notice? Christ, the limousine business for deliveries and pickups. Always picking up the bereaved, always taking them to the airport . . ." Vincent lowered his voice and glanced at the young sergeant standing openmouthed next to him. He poked the barrel of his revolver under Phillips's chin. "One more thing, Georgie, what about that judge's clerk?

Chevy, the one who blew the whistle on our search warrant. Williams pay him?"

Phillips, his head jutted back under the pressure of the gun, nodded with his eyes. Vincent pulled back. "Williams," Phillips said in a croaking voice, "Williams and the other guys who wanted his services . . ."

"He wasn't part of this?"

Phillips shook his head.

"Then who put the finger on us, who blew us in? Williams have connections in the Police Department? How'd that happen?" He waved his gun close to Phillips's face again. "Come on, Georgie, who got us pulled off the case? Who got the charges dropped?"

Phillips hesitated. Vincent pressed the gun against his cheek.

"Barone's brother. Richie Barone . . ."

Vincent turned to the police officer next to him. "Okay, Sergeant, read him his rights. We're going to visit the funeral home . . ."

Vincent glanced at his wristwatch. It was smeared with blood. Christ Almighty, the Mayor's wedding party would be lining up any minute now . . .

39

*C*aptain Vincent assumed command of the team of police who had assembled in the Five Brothers garage. He winced as he replaced his gun in its holster and, for the first time, inspected his slashed coat sleeve and his bleeding arm. He tugged his tie loose and ordered a young patrolman to improvise a sling for him. He was covered with grease and dirt. It didn't make any difference. He had come this far, he wasn't going to stop now. Hackman, his head pounding, came back from his phone call. "Okay on the search." The captain looked around at the members of the tactical team that had responded to his call for assistance. "Okay, let's get 'em."

The seizure of the funeral parlor did not take long. The Barones were busy emptying drug packages that had been shipped in the night before from Miami in a shallow tray that had been inserted beneath the body of a vagrant who had been christened Pietro Sarconi and flown back to what was supposed to be his old neighborhood. The body, resting on a steel table in the embalming room, was scheduled for another flight late that night, under another name, to Montreal. Barone's parlors, a snapshot of remembered nineteen-thirty stucco, was the homely center of a huge drug-smuggling operation. The Barones, evidence spread about them, were stunned. They protested, they wailed, and they were taken away and the building was sealed and a police guard set up within half an hour. Another team of police fanned out to pick up the Williams brothers. Vincent had already left for the Art Institute.

Richard Barone was not alarmed at first. He was often interrupted with important messages at public gatherings. What could his driver want? He took the call outside the trading room.

"Mr. Barone, I just got a call on the radio. The police hit Angie's. A whole squad of them. Took them away, sealed the place off . . ." He went on to describe what little he had been able to learn about the affair. "Yeah, they raided Five Brothers too . . ."

Barone stroked his chin nervously. He could hear the din of the crowd as it reluctantly shaped itself into a processional line in the great hall of the reconstructed trading room. "We'll have to take our places now . . ."

Monsignor Fitzmaurice was speaking. "The Holy Father is about to enter the grounds of the park. Let's all line up now . . ."

"What do we do?" his driver asked nervously.

"Get around in front of the Art Institute. I'll be coming out the Michigan Avenue entrance. Ten minutes." He hung up the phone and drew a breath. Everything was blown now. He would have to move fast to survive this. The cheers from the throng in Grant Park reached through the glass and concrete, causing even Monsignor Fitzmaurice to pause in his monotonous let's-get-in-line spiel. "There, you can hear the crowds now," Fitzmaurice said as though he had hatched the papal egg. "We'll have to march out in ten minutes or so . . ."

Barone adjusted his tie and looked into the trading room at the assembling crowd. A policeman was talking to Sam Noto, a frowning, uncomprehending Sam Noto. Barone stepped back and took the stairway that led to the lounge where Mayor O'Brien was waiting. He pushed past the bodyguard at the door. Ann Marie was alone with Paul Martin.

"I've got to talk to you," Barone said anxiously, closing the door behind him.

"Not now," Ann Marie shot back. "Not now. We've got to leave in a few minutes." The sounds of the crowd cheering the Pope could be heard beyond the silence of Barone's awkward, panicked stare.

"Never mind that shit. Listen, you've got to call off the cops. You're the only one can do it . . ." He grabbed Ann Marie by the arm. She pulled back and Martin stepped between them. "What the hell is going on, Richie?"

Barone eyed Martin wildly. "It may be your ass too. Look, they're trying to frame me, they're trying to hang something on me . . ."

Ann Marie frowned. She had never seen Barone like this, out of control, flustered by his own evil spirit, grasping, desperate, as dangerous as she had ever seen him.

"Listen, you don't know what's happened. That fathead cop friend of yours, Vincent, he's put heat on my brother and his kids. Accusing them of drug dealing, of being mixed up with this Phillips guy . . ."

"Rich, get hold of yourself," Martin said, holding the thrashing Barone by the arms. "What the hell are you talking about?"

"They want to connect me. Don't you see? Get them, get me. It's the old frame. I warned you about Vincent . . ."

"And I took care of him . . ."

Ann Marie stared at Martin. What did he mean, *he* had taken care of him?

"Never mind that shit now. Call off these fucking cops, Annie, for Crissake, you can do it . . ."

"I haven't got anything to do with what you're talking about," she said coldly.

"Like hell you don't," Barone barked, snapping his head toward the door. A swell of cheers rose from the park. "Listen, if I go, you all go . . ."

"I don't have anything to do with you, Mr. Barone." Ann Marie's voice was steady. She was the queen disowning a pretender to the throne. "If you're in the drug business, that's your affair."

"Look, if I go down, I know plenty. I know plenty about this guy you're marrying. I've paid him a long time, I know a lot about him." He waved toward Martin. "You don't know half what I know. You want your husband in jail?"

Ann Marie looked sharply at Martin. The little boy had vanished from his perspiring face. "Well, Paul, what about this? You know anything about drugs? Anything about Phillips? You're the one who told me about Vincent. You didn't tell me you were doing a favor for your friend here . . ."

"I admit I passed the word on that cop. Richie asked me to. Said he was harassing people. That's all I knew. Honest to God."

"What about the drugs?" Ann Marie felt cold and isolated, out of real contact with these two men.

"No, I didn't know about that . . ." Martin looked stunned.

"But you took money from me, you son of a bitch. Put the arm on me for fifteen percent, said you could deliver the Mayor. Pillow talk and all that shit. How'll that sound?"

"You're lying." Martin sounded almost convincing.

"You bastard, you bastard!" Barone looked toward the door again. "I swear to God. I go down, you go down. You go down, *she* goes down . . ."

Ann Marie felt surprisingly calm. She was at the eye of the cyclone again, at the core of the vilest storm she had known. Safe there, if she didn't move, if she just held still. She looked at Paul Martin. He probably had made that promise. It sounded just like him. Paul, so wonderful, so weak.

"And, Mrs. O'Brien, you and your big wedding with the Pope, how would you like it if those pictures of you two hit the papers? Hell, you didn't think I wouldn't keep a set, did you? They're my aces and I'm playing them right now."

The pictures again. Of course. How could she have imagined that she would ever be free of them? Why would anybody be surprised at a revelation of evil in Chicago? Why would she ever expect anything better? She stared into Barone's eyes. He had played his cards. She would play hers.

"Print them. Go ahead."

"Annie, you don't mean that," Martin interjected, "you *can't* mean that."

"Print them, you bastard. The people will forgive me, they'll never forgive you . . ." A hymn swelled up from the park to salute the Pope. "*Viva il Papa . . .*" Its muffled power against the windows accented the silence in the room.

"You'll see, you'll see. You better think again because I'll print them. You'll see. And you better think about marrying this bum. He's fucked everybody." Barone turned and opened the door. Sam Noto snorted, "You son of a bitch . . ." Barone swung a short hard punch to Noto's jaw and the alderman toppled back. The bodyguard rushed to help him as Barone ran down the stairs to the main floor. He pushed past Monsignor Fitzmaurice who, prim and worried, was climbing up to get the bridal couple into the procession.

Ann Marie stared blankly for a moment after the scrambling Barone. Everything evil came together at last. It was not a new thought. Original sin was bedrock for Catholics. Original sin. Apocalypse. The mystery of evil. She had felt its weight when she came up against the stone-faced Oriental ambassadors as she made her case for the MIA's. Men slipped away, men slipping away. Her life was filled with them. Noto struggled to his feet, pushed the bodyguard aside, and stumbled down the staircase. She raised her hand against the bodyguard who stepped toward her to shield her. There was no way to hide from evil. It couldn't be kept out, it couldn't be kept away. It all came together at last, every stream and rivulet of it. No matter their origins, they worked toward each other, cutting new paths, running in fouled streams underground, seeking, always seeking each other. Ann Marie started down the stairs.

"Mrs. O'Brien . . ." This, frantically, from her bodyguard.

"Annie! Annie!" Paul Martin grabbed her arm. A howl echoed out of the gallery that led away from the bottom of the stairs. Ann Marie pulled free of Martin. "What's the matter, Paul, they're *your* friends . . ."

Captain Vincent, looking tarred but not feathered, his bloodied right arm jouncing in its ragged tie sling as he ran, pounded past Ann Marie from the passageway that led from the south entrance of the museum. Two other policemen hurried behind him. Ann Marie started to run after them. A shrieking curse rang back above the clattering of heels from the darkened gallery of Primitive Art.

Barone leaned, sucking for breath, against the wall at the far end of the hall. He could see the blurred, lit-from-behind outlines of his pursuers. Noto, a crazed and dumpy figure, a cartoon of history's every pursuer, stumped along in the lead, shrieking one word, "You . . . You." Its power had hushed the crowd back in the trading room where men and women with frightened eyes looked at each other uneasily. Barone was still a long way from the main entrance. He gulped air and forced himself forward as Noto slammed into a display case, rocking its artifacts and knocking the wind out of himself. He breathed deeply and reached inside his coat. The silver snub-nosed gun flashed in the dim light as he jerked it free.

"Chicago Police!" Vincent roared from twenty paces to the rear, "Chicago Police!" Ann Marie was right behind the officers, drawn into the dark tunnel of the gallery, not caring about anything else—her dress, her flung-away purse—sensing that evil, evil she had danced and flirted with, evil that had pressed upon her with the weight of the sea, was rushing just ahead of her, and that she had to follow it, she had to witness the shape of the violence not yet done that radiated through the air.

Barone had rounded the corner of the gallery. He was on the platform in front of Chagall's "America Windows." He took a deep breath, stumbled against the railing at the side, and sprawled down the step in front of the display. As he picked himself up, Sam Noto, holding the gun firmly in front of him in both hands, heaved around the corner, the sounds of the trailing police clinging to him, discharging a jumbled deadly static from his lumpish figure. Barone stumbled to his feet, reaching his arms out, "Sam, let me explain . . ." He took a deep breath. "Look, Sam, whatever you want. You want money? Anything. For Crissake, Sam, give me a break . . ."

"You know any prayers, say 'em, you son of a bitch."

"I'll give you money . . ."

"You give me my nephew back? Can you do that, you bastard . . ."

Barone stepped back as Noto circled around in front of him. With his wild eyes, his hair flown into points, his dark jacket cowled up behind his neck, Barone was Mephistopheles before the spectacular spread of stained glass, a prince of darkness pleading his case before the bank of subtle and peaceful blues and golds. Captain Vincent, his men, and Ann Marie turned the corner and stopped. "Let's have the gun . . ." Vincent called. The captain held his left arm in front of Ann Marie.

Noto did not hear him. His fierce concentration was on the figure of Barone. "You and your cocksucking brother, and his cocksucking kids . . ."

Captain Vincent took one step toward the alderman.

"I know all about it, Richie. You covered for them. You lied for them. You let them kill the kid and you wept with me . . ."

Vincent was just a pace away.

"Sam, Sam, I didn't know it till afterwards . . ."

Vincent reached for the gun just as the alderman fired it. Barone plunged backward. Noto fired again and Barone crashed through the rich tapestry of glass, exploding it into shards and bits that danced wildly around him as he fell crazily onto the narrow bed of lights behind the display, short-circuiting them as he twisted and squirmed and died in the darkness.

Ann Marie walked quietly back through the long gallery between the bodyguards who had arrived just after the shooting. She took her purse from a policeman who had retrieved it and, ignoring the wedding guests, the officials and celebrities buzzing and calling to her, climbed with an expressionless face up the stairs to the lounge. Mother Francis tried to catch her eye but Ann Marie stared straight ahead. An evil man was dead, but evil wasn't. It was just another battle concluded. Like the one into whose smoke Charlie had disappeared. What did Cullen know about evil? Had he mastered it, balancing his power against its strength? Had he let it be a silent partner, keeping it tame with scraps from his table? Did he ever think about it? Or was his great quiet the sign that he had thought about it, that he knew its secrets, that he knew how to live with it? Did evil pursue Ann Marie? Did it visit wherever she traveled?

Paul Martin was standing with Monsignor Fitzmaurice in the lounge. Fitzmaurice was impatient. Had he heard that a man had just died?

"They could use you down there," Ann Marie said to her cousin. She did not look at Martin.

"We've sent a priest," Fitzmaurice said flatly, dismissing the matter, calling them back to the moment. "We have to get on with the wedding . . ."

"Life as usual, right, Morgan?" Ann Marie asked sarcastically. She walked past Martin to the windows. The chanted prayers of the great crowd pounded on the glass. "Leave us alone, Morgan," she said without turning around.

"But, Ann Marie, the Holy Father . . ."

"Leave us alone." Ann Marie bit out the words. She did not turn around until she heard the door close behind Fitzmaurice.

Paul Martin tried to smile, struggled to summon up charm. He dipped his right shoulder, spread his hands parenthetically, a merchant explaining the raveled cloth, the short change, the hardness of the times . . .

"Annie," he said feebly, "I didn't know any of this. Swear to God. The drugs, the stuff about Phillips. I didn't know a thing. I would never—"

She made a gesture of dismissal. "Paul, you've been trying to explain yourself ever since I've known you. You didn't know this, you didn't know that, you could talk your way out of everything. Including room 711 at the Bismarck . . ."

"Annie, that's all in the past . . ."

"Is it?" She turned away to look back across the park. The Pope was a small white figure by the side of the distant iceberg altar. "Paul, have you ever told me the whole truth about anything?"

"I guess so, I suppose so. Sure, plenty of times." The magic smoothness had gone out of his voice.

"You always thought you could play me off. That's right, isn't it? I want the truth."

"In a way . . ."

"The *truth*, Paul . . ."

"I always cared about your good . . ."

"You took big money from Barone? More than you told me?"

Martin hesitated. "I guess so, sometimes. Annie . . ."

"You promised to deliver me because you'd sleep every night with me?"

"You know men. Big promises. Keeping Barone on the string. He was doing a lot for you . . ."

"All just business?"

"Just business."

"Anything in writing?"

"You know me, Annie . . ."

She turned to look at Martin. "And you don't care that he's dead. It really doesn't make any difference to you . . ."

"Annie, I can't afford to be connected with him. Neither can you." Martin's confidence surged. He waved toward the Grant Park crowds. "They're waiting for us, Annie. Once we're married, and all this is behind us, we'll . . ."

"We'll what?" Ann Marie stepped closer to Martin. "Don't you realize that you and your friends may have destroyed me? That we may not recover from what's happened today?"

"Annie, the people love you. They'll know you didn't have anything to do with this. They'll love us too . . ."

The door opened and Monsignor Fitzmaurice stepped in. Ann Marie glanced icily at him but did not dismiss him.

"Paul, the crowd is there for *me*. You don't have any part of it. It's between me and Maureen now . . ."

"You and Maureen?" Martin managed a sneering laugh. "That's right, you and Maureen. You don't know it, you can't admit it, but something in you has wanted that all the time."

"Don't give me that line again . . ."

"It's true, Annie." He laughed out loud. "It's absolutely true. That thing the shrinks call the unconscious, you can't get away from it. Something in yours has been trying to get Cullen back in office. You've done your damndest, baby. Maureen is pretty close . . ." Ann Marie slapped him hard. He grabbed her hand and pulled her face close to his. "You forget, Annie, we're about to get married."

"Not today!" she said, spitting out poison.

"Ann Marie, the Pope is waiting for us . . ."

She waved him into silence.

"Paul, I loved you, I really think I did. But love doesn't count in the decision I'm making today." She wrenched free of his grasp.

"Annie, Annie, for Crissake . . ."

"I'm not marrying you today." She smiled. "Strictly business. You remember? That's what you taught me . . ."

"But, Annie, what will happen, how will I explain? Suppose they start investigating me . . ."

"You're on television, Paul. Have you forgotten? You can explain for yourself."

"Ann Marie, this is ridiculous," Monsignor Fitzmaurice interjected. "There're a million people out there. The Cardinal, the Pope. We can't call this off now . . ."

"*Can't* we?" Ann Marie picked up her purse. "Morgan, you're such a big shot. You go out and explain it. Tell them what you want. They'll be disappointed in you, of course. But you don't care for worldly honors. You only care for—"

"Ann Marie!" Fitzmaurice shouted. "You can't do this, you can't do this . . ."

She took a lipstick out of her bag and inspected herself in her compact mirror. "I'm probably the *only* one who can do this. Now, get out there and tell them I'll be right along. Alone." Fitzmaurice, shaking his head angrily, left the room.

Ann Marie snapped her compact shut and dropped it in her bag.

"I'll miss you, Paul. I really think I will . . ."

"Annie! Please . . ."

Ann Marie walked to the door, put her hand on the knob.

"What are you going to say?" Martin asked desperately.

"Oh, I'll think of something." She opened the door. "That's how I got here. Remember?" She pulled the door shut.

Ann Marie, flanked by her bodyguards, descended the stairs and marched calmly away from the building. It was like walking away from the carcass of a great whale that had tried to swallow her. Reporters and cameramen danced backward across the sidewalk in front of her. Applause and cheers rose from the edge of the crowded park as she stepped into Columbus Drive. The beast that lay behind her had devoured the past. And Barone and Paul Michael Martin with it. They were ghosts now, as weightless as poor old Charlie's bones. She did not look back.

Ann Marie smiled as she entered the mass of shouting people. She could see the altar halfway across the park where the Pope stood, gesturing with his hands to increase the salutation. The crowd was exploding with noise all around her. They were cheering her. That's what counted. She could trust the crowd, she could always trust the crowd. And she would think of something. She always had . . .